"LET ME GO."

His arms tightened until Charity felt the pounding of his heart against her spine. Slowly and without loosening their hold, those strong arms turned her against her will—or did she willingly turn to his strength? Ah, Luke. Her Luke.

Like creatures possessed, her arms twined around his neck, reaching, clinging. His hands swept the length of her back and submerged in her hair, clenching fistfuls. A salty musk wafted beneath her nose and danced on her tongue as she pressed her face to his.

Shutting her eyes, she tasted him through parted lips, dragged his essence to her very core. She realized they were stumbling toward the house, felt her back come up against the stones, sharp and biting through her dress. Luke's work-roughened hands cupped her cheeks as though he might plunge from a precipice if he let go. His lips, moist, heated, urgent, roamed her hair, her brow, her face.

"God," he said, his voice breaking.

As though God were listening, the wind gathered and hammered the house, flattening them against it. Luke grabbed her closer. His head came down, filling her vision as the crush of his arms became the entirety of her world. His mouth took hers with a rapacious hunger, savage and bruising. Glorious.

Triumph thundered through her. "You remember."

<u>BOOK YOUR PLACE ON OUR WEBSITE</u>
<u>AND MAKE THE</u>
<u>READING CONNECTION!</u>

We've created a customized website just for our very special readers, where you can get the inside scoop on everything that's going on with Zebra, Pinnacle and Kensington books.

When you come online, you'll have the exciting opportunity to:

- View covers of upcoming books
- Read sample chapters
- Learn about our future publishing schedule (listed by publication month *and author*)
- Find out when your favorite authors will be visiting a city near you
- Search for and order backlist books from our online catalog
- Check out author bios and background information
- Send e-mail to your favorite authors
- Meet the Kensington staff online
- Join us in weekly chats with authors, readers and other guests
- Get writing guidelines
- AND MUCH MORE!

Visit our website at
http://www.kensingtonbooks.com

MOSTLY MARRIED

Lisa Manuel

ZEBRA BOOKS
KENSINGTON PUBLISHING CORP.
http://www.kensingtonbooks.com

Chapter One

St. Abbs, Scotland
June 1823

Lucas Holbrook, Duke of Wakefield, pressed his face to his pillow and endeavored to ignore the persistent and vaguely troubling hiss of ocean waves. The sound didn't belong, somehow, in the current scheme of his life. Yet there it was, surging beneath his dreams like the growing swell of a storm.

Still, he might have drifted back into those perplexing dreams if the quarrelsome squawking of gulls hadn't yanked him further from slumber. A salty breeze tumbled through a nearby window, a sweet hint of lavender riding its edges. From just beyond the sill a bird, a lark perhaps, shook its wings and called, "Tseep, tseep."

Lucas hefted an eyelid. The window and its undulating curtains framed a scene of lush rolling meadows and flawless sky. He acknowledged there could not be a more perfect day in all of God's creation.

And, heaven help him, if he had a gun handy he'd stick it in his mouth and pull the trigger.

That's how bad the hangover was.

His shaking fingers dragged the coverlet over his head. Blessing the return to darkness, he groped for images of the night before but could find none within the pounding thunder that occupied the interior of his skull. Trying to remember only magnified the pain as beveled glass magnifies the heat of a summer noon. He felt like a bug about to shrivel . . .

"Good morning, darlin'."

The words pierced like serrated daggers. His brain clenched. He tried to cover his ears with the pillow but discovered he hadn't the strength.

"Feeling any better, m'love?"

Devil take you, no. But even in the aftermath of such a thorough brandy-soaking, the voice puzzled him. It was low but distinctly feminine, and under normal circumstances probably not at all like daggers. It wasn't an English voice either, but emblazoned with a brisk Gaelic brogue.

Not his mother or grandmother. Certainly not Helena. No, his dear Helena would never, ever, under any stretch of the imagination, have set foot in his bedchamber, especially while he was sleeping.

Whoever it was tugged at the bedclothes in an attempt to uncover him.

Oh, you had better tread carefully. He had no desire to hurt this woman, but his battered brain simply could not withstand another onslaught of sunlight and singing birds for the next several hours at least.

"Let me sleep." His protest emerged as a whimper; his swollen lips cracked from the movement. A chorus of pangs, spasms and throbbing aches shrieked from damn near every muscle in his body.

What the devil?

Before he could react, the blankets were whisked from his grasp. Searing light assaulted him amid a sharp-tongued cacophony as potentially lethal as a dozen dagger-points. It took some moments before the woman's admonishments formed themselves into words his pulp of a mind could decipher.

"Serves you right, as I told Father last night. Drinking and fighting like a godless brigand. What were you thinking, Luke Martin? Sometimes you men behave no better than schoolboys."

He slit his eyes to peer at her, making out only a wild blur of coppery curls. The blur and the room around it began to spin, and he shut his eyes again.

"Water," he croaked. "Please, if you've any mercy at all."

He heard the creak of straining bed supports as his companion shifted her weight, followed by the clink of porcelain and the gentle trickle of water.

"Never a thought for anyone else," she scolded as she supported his head and held a cup to his lips. "Why, you might have been killed. And then where would I be, Luke Martin, I ask you that."

He had no answer, a circumstance he thoroughly regretted, for he had the unhappy feeling she wouldn't let the matter drop. Between blessed sips of cool water, he wanted to ask her to slow down and explain. But counteracting her reproaches, a hand descended with a whisper's touch on his brow, followed by something smoother, more malleable, so sweetly moist it absorbed some of his pain.

She kissed him once, twice, reverently, as though he were a sacred object. His flesh smarted beneath her lips but somehow the dull pain comforted with the promise of healing.

He braved opening his eyes once more, gritting his

teeth through the dizziness until his vision cleared. As it did, he met the gaze of eyes so green they would have aroused envy in the loveliest of sea goddesses. A pair of beautiful lips smiled down at him; luscious lips, wide, full, and of a shade of rose that reminded him of his mother's exquisite garden at home.

He didn't know exactly where the request originated, but there it was, springing from his mouth. "Kiss me again."

"I shouldn't even be speaking to you." But her fiery flaxen hair blanketed his face—like a magic balm on the raw places—as she leaned to accommodate his wishes, not on the brow this time but full on the lips.

Flames licked where their mouths met, then bounded to a blaze. Beneath the covers, what might well have been the one unbruised part of him rose to full, curious, rapt attention.

Who *was* this tantalizing angel who had the power to make him forget—albeit temporarily—the worst morning-after of his life?

"Ah, but I suppose it isn't all your fault," she murmured. "That Seamus MacAllister's been goading you for months. Lord forgive me, but it's glad I am you left him in little better condition, though I'd be a good deal happier if it were him with a bottle cracked across the skull."

"Bottle? Seamus Mac . . . who?"

"Seamus MacAllister, silly." She stroked his forehead, her cool, smooth fingertips mindful of the tender flesh.

It was then he noticed his angel didn't sit perched on the side of the bed as a good nurse should. No, she lay beside him *in* the bed, the blanket having slipped to her waist to reveal . . .

She was as naked as a freshly hatched sparrow.

Dear lord. Had they . . . ? Of course they must have, but for the life of him he couldn't remember.

But at least now things began to make sense. His brother, Wesley, would be carrion the minute Lucas found him. Yes, left on the side of the road for the vultures. Obviously, the damned whelp had taken Lucas out, gotten him foxed beyond recognition, then left him in a Drury Lane brothel. Must have thought it uproariously funny. Probably still doubled over laughing.

Well, not for much longer.

"I—I need . . ." Nausea rolled inside him. He swallowed, sucked in drafts of air, clenched his teeth. "I need to send a note to my family."

"Your family?" The wondrous, soothing hand swept wisps of hair from his clammy forehead.

"Yes. They'll be worried." But where were they? And where was he?

Ocean waves. He'd been hearing them since before he awakened, but only now did their significance sink in. He could not be in London. Nor at home in landlocked Wakefield.

Images flashed in his mind. Ships. Many of them, huddled together along a series of docks, whole fleets bumping and rubbing against the pilings with the rolling tide, their many lines squeaking from the strain.

And beyond the shipyards, wide-open fields of rush and sedge grass flattened by the ocean winds. He could almost smell the brine—in fact, he could indeed taste the salt tang of the sea. But which sea? Or was it the Channel?

Blast Wesley for landing him in this none-too-dignified predicament. Except . . . Wesley couldn't have. As far as Lucas knew, his brother was in Ireland with his regiment.

Craning his neck, he surveyed a room that proved tidy and clean, its various appointments of sturdy if plain oak. The bedstead bore the gleam of well-polished brass. Crisp, colorful curtains stirred with the breeze.

Not the typical brothel, he must admit. Not that he had much experience. He didn't usually conduct this sort of business. How ridiculous for the Duke of Wakefield to pay for intimate services when he might have his pick of London's most alluring mistresses if he wished. Of course, he didn't wish, because he had Helena . . .

Helena. She'd wither like a sun-starved flower if she found out. Thank all the powers of the universe that he was . . . wherever he was and not London, where news such as this would make the round of clubs, shops and soirees faster than a man could tie his neckcloth.

"Luke?"

His attention swerved back to the . . . uh . . . young lady with the delectable lips. Not to mention exquisite, honey-tipped, ever-so-inviting breasts hovering inches from his face. His lips pursed.

Without a trace of self-consciousness, she returned his gaze with an odd mixture of concern and—no, surely not adoration. Not after a night of what was, for her, business as usual.

"Forget the note," he said. "Would you kindly have someone hail a hackney while I dress? I must be on my way."

"A hackney." She nodded, though her lovely green eyes held anything but understanding. "It's early yet. You need sleep."

"No, I—" He attempted to push up onto his elbows, but the knife someone had apparently shoved into his head gave a vicious twist. The air rushed from his lungs. He fell back limp, surrendering his helplessness to the embrace of the down mattress.

"Perhaps you are right," he conceded. Bright points of light danced before his eyes, then faded to a blackness that swallowed him.

* * *

"Sweet mercy, he's dying," Charity Fergusson Martin exclaimed, though there was no one to hear. Not even Luke. Especially not Luke.

Springing from the bed, she grabbed her dressing gown from the room's only chair and swung it round her shoulders. She started toward the door just as the clattering of tiny but urgent footsteps echoed from the kitchen. An instant later Skiff and Schooner, twin West Highland terriers, rounded the bedroom doorway. As every morning at the first stirrings of their master and mistress, the Westies barked their greetings and bounded onto the foot of the bed.

"Schooner, Skiff, down."

The shaggy-faced pair regarded Charity with amusement, certain the odd commandment must surely be a joke. Trotting Luke's length, Schooner deposited several wet kisses along his jaw. Luke uttered a fitful moan. Skiff, meanwhile, curled into a comfortable ball on his master's stomach and nuzzled his tiny chin on Luke's hip.

Charity wagged a finger at them. "I said down and I mean it. Can't you see he's unwell?"

The Westies exchanged sullen glances. Reluctantly, they thudded to the hooked rug beside the bed.

"Now, watch him for me and if anything changes, bark."

Barefoot, she padded through the parlor and into the kitchen, in her haste nearly slipping on the braided oval mat as she swung open the kitchen door. Where was her brother? He should have arrived by now.

Luke seemed worse than ever, she fretted as she shaded her eyes to scan the barnyard. The doctor had examined him last night and pronounced cold compresses, a dose of laudanum and a good night's sleep the only medicine necessary.

But her confidence in the good doctor took a sharp tumble, what with Luke carrying on about notes and hackneys. Hackneys? In the village of St. Abbs? Next he'd be asking for the baker to deliver fresh pies right to their doorstep, as they did in the fine cities of Berwick or Edinburgh.

And what were those names he mumbled? Wesley. Helena. Who in the world? And acting as if he'd never heard of Seamus MacAllister.

A gnawing fear gripped her heart . . .

"Dylan, are you here?" she called. Only the chickens replied, their clucking muffled within the hen house walls. In the holding pen beyond the yard, a lamb bleated.

No sign of Dylan, though he'd promised to come by early to help with the morning chores. They had all known last night that Luke would be of little use this morning.

Picking her way across the yard, she squinted into the open barn doors. Within the dusty shadows stood Patches, the brown and white Guernsey milk cow, and several sheep waiting to have their hooves trimmed. An oath of frustration escaped her lips. Then, with a dull thunk of her halter bell, Patches raised her head and leveled a placid gaze at Charity. She realized the cow had been milked.

"Dylan? I need you. Now."

"Mornin', Charity." A plaid-shirted figure stepped out from behind the partition wall in the rear corner of the barn. Tossing a bale of hay to the floor, he swatted at wisps floating near his face. "Devil's nipping at your heels rather early."

Impatience made her want to shake him. "It's Luke.

I think he's taken a turn for the worse. I need you to fetch the doctor. Quickly!"

"Easy, lass, I'm on my way." Thumbs hooked into his waistband, he ambled to the doorway.

"Don't you dare dawdle." Tightening her dressing gown around her, Charity retreated to the house. An afterthought sent her doubling back to the well, where she drew a fresh bucket of water. Luke would need more cold compresses.

He stirred when she entered the bedroom, his lashes fluttering. That seemed a good sign, she thought; it meant he was asleep rather than in a faint. Dampening a linen towel in the bucket, she draped it across his forehead, careful of the raw lump at the hairline.

Skiff and Schooner tapped across the floorboards to sit at her feet. Their moist jet eyes conveyed myriad questions.

"He'll be all right, lads," she said more bravely than she felt. "Don't worry your precious little heads. If you promise to be quiet and keep still, I'll let you sit at the foot of the bed."

She could almost see them nod their promises. Bending, she lifted each fluffy bundle onto the mattress. "Don't you be forgetting to behave now."

After pulling on a dress of sturdy russet broadcloth, stockings and flat-heeled boots, she twisted her unruly curls into a bun at her nape. Leaning over Luke, she pressed a hand to his cheek.

Devil take that Seamus MacAllister. Why, she had a good mind to . . .

She caught herself. For all he deserved it, cursing Seamus would serve no one and nothing. Her husband needed her attention and her nursing skills, not her temper.

Yet even pale, bruised, and unconscious, he stoked a

fire within her. Her gaze traced the broad lines of his
shoulders above the coverlet, the sinewy column of his
neck. She couldn't help reaching out to trail a fingertip
across the seam of his lips, so strong above the square
set of his jaw, yet always so quick to curve in a smile.

Breathing deep, she filled her lungs with the scent of
him, his own masculine essence mixed with traces of last
night's ale and wood smoke. The combination sparked
anger even as it elicited a murmur of passion inside her.
She had every right to be furious with him, but her earlier effort to upbraid him had hardly proved sincere.
She loved him far too much for anger.

Headstrong, the men of St. Abbs had always termed
her; too stubborn, too outspoken, too independent to
ever make a contented wife. The bachelors of the village had always seemed, well, a little afraid of her.

Not Luke. From the beginning, he'd delighted in chal-
lenging her, getting her dander up. Other men might
have infuriated her, but not Luke. No, she'd caught that
gleam in his eye, the wicked bent of his smile. She knew
he understood and even appreciated the mettle that
drove so many others away.

From the day God tossed him out of the sea and into
her arms, she'd held on tight and not let go. Except
once. Only once did she send him away, but he had returned soon enough.

Voices wafted from the kitchen, several talking at
once. Had Dylan brought half the village?

Skiff and Schooner lifted their heads from the mattress, their ears alert and twitching. Looking none too
hurried, Dylan sauntered into the bedroom, followed by
the doctor and the village rector, Mr. Douglas.

"Thank you for coming," Charity said as the two
older men flanked the bed. "The rector?" she questioned
her brother out of the side of her mouth.

"Just a precaution." He shrugged. "You said Luke looked worse."

"Should I expect the undertaker next?"

"No. Time enough for that later."

She resisted the temptation to box his ears. "Sweet mercy, can you never be serious?"

"Never." Leaning, he delivered a loud kiss to her cheek. "You worry too much. It was just a fight. Luke's strong as an ox and twice as stubborn. He'll mend."

Oh, how she wanted to believe him. She took in Luke's pallid features, the damp cheeks shadowed by dark lashes, the usually grinning mouth pinched and colorless. Sweet mercy, her husband was no brawler, not usually. Why now of all times?

This should have been the happiest day of their marriage. She'd held off mentioning her secret until she was certain, and now she was. But if she told Luke about their baby today, he'd likely pass out and forget, and then she'd have to explain all over again tomorrow.

Doctor Campbell bent over him, fingering the inflammation above the brow, raising each eyelid with his thumb. "Pupils are a bit dilated, but the swelling's down some since last night." He rummaged through his bag of medicines and pulled out a small flask. "Here's more laudanum. Mix four drops in a strong cup of tea twice a day. Elevate his head. He'll live."

A torrent of relief swept away a large portion of Charity's fears, though not all. "Are you sure, Doctor? You didn't hear him raving but an hour ago, going on about all manner of nonsense."

"You'd be raving too, lass, with a bump the size of the Stone of Scone on your brow. 'Twill pass in a day or two."

"But won't the laudanum dull his wits? We want him lucid, don't we?" She didn't add that the villagers often whispered about the good doctor's fondness for laudanum, for his own as well as his patients' maladies.

"It's only enough to ease the pain." He adjusted his coat and started for the door, pausing to scratch the dogs' heads. "To ease your mind, I'll stop by again this evening."

A groan from the bed sputtered into a cough. Charity grasped Luke's hand.

"Helena?" he slurred. "Th-that you, my darling?"

She looked up at her visitors in alarm. "You see? He's at it again."

"Might be he's remembering something." The doctor exchanged a pointed glance with the rector.

"We don't know a Helena."

"He might." Doctor Campbell returned to the bedside, his brows merging above his prominent nose. "We don't know who he knew before Seamus fished him out of the sea."

"Now, there's a good bit of irony," her brother said in a decidedly too-bright voice. "It was Seamus that saved Luke from drowning, and now it's Seamus that damn near killed him." Looking sheepish, he ducked his head. "Sorry, Rector."

Charity whirled on him. "Don't you have chores to do?"

"Wouldn't mind a spot of breakfast first."

"Aye, I'll give you breakfast, Dylan Fergusson." She shook her fist. "I'll be serving up empty plates if you don't get out to the hen house and collect the eggs."

She sent him scampering with the sternest look she could muster, at the same time infinitely glad of his presence. Of course, she'd never let him know that, not in so many words, because the impudent scamp would think he had an advantage over her. That was something she had never allowed her younger brother in all his nineteen years on this earth.

"We'll see you again tonight, then," she said to the doctor as he took his leave.

"Got to fence the east pasture . . ."

She spun back toward the bed at the sound of Luke's murmuring.

"There now." The rector smiled encouragement at her. "That sounds like sensible talk."

"We haven't got an east pasture, Mr. Douglas, just the bluffs and the sea."

"Perhaps I should stay awhile longer."

"Please. I'll go brew the tea."

In the kitchen, she needed to stop and remember what to do. A pan. Water. Stoke the fire. Will Luke truly be all right? Cups. Saucers. Dear God, how she loved him. So much it almost frightened her. Spoons. Napkins. Little Jamie MacKenna died after a blow to the head, but of course that had been from a falling timber during a barn fire.

She went into the larder and reached for the biscuits she'd baked yesterday afternoon. Oh, and a plate of leftover mutton for Skiff and Schooner.

After pouring the tea, she lost count of how many drops of laudanum she'd poured in Luke's cup, tossed the contents into the dirt in the yard and started over.

A call from the bedroom sent her scurrying.

"What is it, Rector? Is he—" She slid to a halt just inside the doorway, heart galloping. Luke was sitting up in bed.

She rushed to his side. With a grateful cry and all but forgetting the presence of the minister, she threw her arms around her husband's neck. He stiffened in her embrace, then slowly raised an arm around her back.

"He seems to be experiencing a bit of forgetfulness." Mr. Douglas caught her eye. Silently he mouthed, *He doesn't know me.*

"Dearest, are you feeling any better? You do know who I am, don't you?" She searched for signs of recognition in Luke's deep mahogany eyes.

They crinkled with amusement. "Of course. You're my angel of mercy, the one with the luscious lips."

"Perhaps I should wait in the other room." Mr. Douglas eased toward the door.

With a twinge of embarrassment Charity watched him go, though her relief far outweighed her embarrassment.

"Skiff, Schooner, time for breakfast," she announced. The Westies eagerly vaulted from the bed, their small feet sliding on the hardwood floor as they streamed from the room.

Charity tightened her arms around Luke. "You scared me half out of my wits."

"Hold up, no need to fret. I don't believe I'm going to expire here in your bed. Wouldn't be good for business, would it?"

She pulled back. "Good for business?"

His knowing look made her uneasy; he was obviously privy to something that eluded her.

"Is your head spinning again, Luke?"

"No. At least not like before. A bit woozy, but no cause for concern." He ran a curious gaze over the furnishings and beamed ceiling. "By the by, the name's Lucas, Lucas Holbrook. No one has called me Luke since I was a child. And not that I mean to stand on ceremony, mind you, especially as your nursing probably saved my life. But I'm compelled to point out that upon first acquaintance, most people address me as 'your grace.'"

"First acquaintance?" Renewed fear began as a tremor at the tips of her fingers and quickly threatened to consume her.

"Yes, of course." He flashed a tolerant smile. "And you are?"

Chapter Two

"Sweet mercy."

Ah, of course. It was just the sort of name a doxy would assume, much as an actress might. But why did she suddenly look as though she might faint dead away? Then on second thought, no, her senses seemed in little danger of failing her, especially when her sumptuous mouth opened as if to let out one devil of a scream. Lucas braced for the agony the sound would produce. What the blazes had upset her so? His suggestion that she call him "your grace"?

She neither fainted nor screamed. Hands snapping to hips, Sweet Mercy jerked her chin at him. "Luke Martin, for that kind of jesting I should let Seamus have another go at you."

"Seamus . . ." The name set off an alarm. "Is that the fiend who accosted me? Did he steal my father's pocket watch? Deuced rotten if he did—that watch has been in the family for generations. It should have been in my waistcoat pocket. Do you remember seeing it?"

"You're not jesting, are you?" She sank to the edge

of the bed. Her stare took on the intensity of green fire.

"My dear Mercy, I have been attacked and robbed." His hand went to his forehead. He winced when his fingers came down on a knot the size of a walnut. "I fail to see anything worth jesting in that. Of course, I'll feel infinitely relieved if you tell me this Seamus character has been apprehended. My solicitor, Jacob Dolan, will see to it the unprincipled rogue gets his comeuppance." A thought occurred to him. "Hold up now, I hope this bloke isn't your uh . . . oh, how does one term it politely? Your partner in . . . you know."

She shook her head slowly.

"Your panderer."

"My what?"

He tossed up his hands. "Your fancy man, your bawd cock."

A gasp rattled in her throat. "Luke Martin, if you weren't already black and blue I'd slap you silly!"

"But aren't you a lady of the . . ."

Sparks hot enough to singe shot from her impossibly green eyes.

"No," he said quickly, "I don't suppose you are. Forgive me. It's just that the way you kissed me led me to believe you were . . ."

"Luke Martin, I always kiss you this way."

"Lucas. And why do you keep adding my father's name to mine?"

"Look at me." She took his face between her hands. "Do you not know me? Can you not recognize your own wife?"

Surely he'd heard wrong. The breeze became the only sound in the room. Lucas explored the unfamiliar features while he inhaled an enticing mixture of lavender soap, wild heather, crisp ocean spice. As her hands cradled his cheeks, he had to admit that except for a minor sore spot on the left side of his face, her wondrous touch could make him lose sight of right and wrong and even the existence of a fiancée.

"Luke?" The hands shook him, not ungently but enough to seize his attention.

His mind had wandered. What had they been discussing? Oh yes, that she was his . . .

Wife?

"Wesley *is* in on this, isn't he?" His fist hit the mattress. "He's home on leave, yes? And last night he dragged me the round of those taverns he's so fond of. I'm in Brighton, aren't I? Tell me, where is the little weasel?"

"There is no one here named Wesley." She stretched each word with exaggerated patience. "There is no Helena either."

"Ah ha! The fact that you know about my Helena proves Wesley is the perpetrator of this prank. Talk about bad taste. Just wait till I have at him."

"Luke . . ."

"My name isn't Luke," he snapped, then felt immediately contrite. Hearing his name bandied about so casually by a stranger irked him; but it was the ache in his head and the fact that he couldn't remember how he came by it that fueled his anger. He shouldn't take out his frustrations on her. "I'm sorry, Mercy."

"My name isn't Mercy."

"You told me it was."

"I most certainly didn't." She grasped his hands. "I'm Charity Fergusson. At least I was until the day we said 'I do'. Then I became Charity Martin. Your wife."

"Impossible."

"Sweet Mer . . . I mean, Mother of God. Wait here."

He caught the sheen of tears as she released his hands and hastened from the room.

By God, this was no jest. A horrible misunderstanding perhaps, or a case of mistaken identity. Yet even that seemed implausible. Surely a wife would recognize her own husband. Could the bruises that made even blinking painful have distorted his features into those resembling another man's?

That must be it. As soon as the dear woman returned, he'd explain her perfectly understandable mistake.

Minutes passed in silence broken only by the constant wind, which tossed whiffs of ocean and lavender through the window. Lucas's thoughts drifted, his mind curling around memories that seemed far more distant than they should have. His mother and grandmother, the expansive old house in Wakefield—he felt as if he'd not laid eyes upon them in months. How could that be?

Concentrating, he conjured Helena as he'd seen her last, poised on Longfield Park's front drive beside the fountain with its water-spouting porpoises. She was smiling and waving, bidding him a safe trip.

The memory spread a sense of well-being through him. His friends and acquaintances all agreed that lovely Helena Livingston would make the perfect wife for him. Having lived these past eight years in the guest house with her invalid father, she was already as much a part of Longfield Park, the family seat, as he was.

Equally important, she embodied all the qualities the future Duchess of Wakefield must have: charm, intelligence and, oh yes, beauty, of the classic English kind. Golden hair, ivory skin, azure eyes.

It could only have been days since he'd seen her. Yet that, too, seemed ages removed. He could barely remember the feel of her in his arms, the scent of her hair, the pleasant timbre of her voice. As his eyes drifted shut, the image of his fiancée blurred, only to reemerge as a halo of golden fire, eyes like verdant gems, fresh, freckled cheeks and a voice that washed over him in Gaelic melody.

Her name was Mercy . . . no, Charity. But her charity had rendered him sweet mercy . . . He groaned at his own bad joke and wondered where she had gone, when she'd be back. Whether she would kiss him again.

"Luke?"

He opened his eyes. "Yes, Sweet Mercy?"

"Not that again. My name is Charity."

"Charity," he repeated, hoping to placate. For some odd reason, he very much wanted to see her smile again. "I won't forget."

Yet there was so much he had forgotten. Images and sensations slipped in and out of his mind, wrapped in pain and confusion. Where had he been going when Helena bid him farewell? He pictured the back of a coach, a post-chaise, and himself on horseback following at a hasty canter.

Why? Who rode in that coach?

Damn. Each time he felt on the verge of conquering the chaos, it shattered into a thousand pieces more baffling than before.

One thing he did remember with absolute clarity: just prior to Charity darting from the room, she had told him they were man and wife.

Ah, but he'd already deduced the explanation for that.

"If you'd be so kind as to supply me with pen and paper," he said, "I'd like to dash a note off to my solicitor in London."

A shuffling behind her drew his attention to a figure

in the doorway. He tried to peer around Charity but could make out little beyond a beard and a black suit. His senses leaped to alertness. "Who's that?"

"Our rector." Charity motioned to the man, who took several quiet steps into the room. "Mr. Douglas was sitting with you but a few minutes ago. I brought him back to speak with you."

"Am I in that bad condition?"

"No." She lay a hand, cool and calming, against his cheek. "You're going to be fine. I merely thought Mr. Douglas might help prod your memory."

She moved away and the elderly, decidedly dour-looking rector took her place, leaning over the bed until Lucas stared up at the curling ends of a peppered beard. "I understand you have many questions, Luke. I may be able to answer some of them."

"Tell him about us," Charity prompted. The rector shot a frown over his shoulder, and a silent debate leaped back and forth between them.

"I assure you," Lucas said with a chuckle, "if my throbbing head hasn't killed me yet, neither will anything either of you have to say."

Mr. Douglas nodded and, dragging a chair from the corner, set it beside the bed. With slow deliberation the man adjusted his somber coattails beneath him as he sat. Lucas watched his movements with impatience, wishing only to be alone once more with his sweet angel of mercy.

His conscience nudged. He should be thinking of Helena—only Helena. If she knew of his plight she'd be frantic with worry. Of course, his family could have no idea he'd been attacked. He should be considering how to tell them, how to explain his bruises without sending his poor mother into an apoplectic fit.

"Son?"

"Yes?" He realized the rector had been speaking but he hadn't heard a word. "I'm listening."

"You didn't flinch just now when I told you I presided over your wedding to Charity. Might you be remembering it?"

"Ah, that. I'm not that man."

"Indeed you are."

"I'm afraid you're mistaken. You see, I'm Lucas Holbrook, seventh Duke of Wakefield."

Charity let out a gasp.

"Yes, well, I'm also the Earl of Lynhurst and the Viscount Beckford." Lucas chafed his palm against his morning growth of beard. "I'm rather embarrassed to admit this, but I'm having a devil of a time remembering my present circumstances. I believe my brother can shed some light. If this is indeed Brighton, you might find him at the Langford Hotel or possibly the Brunswick. To give him the benefit of the doubt, he probably has no idea I was waylaid by that rogue, Seamus whatever."

The rector cleared his throat. "My good man, you are nowhere near Brighton or any other English town for that matter, but in the village of St. Abbs, Scotland. The man who attacked you was the very same who found you drifting senseless on a broken timber in the North Sea nigh over a year ago. And as God is my witness, you are indeed the man who vowed before our entire congregation to honor and cherish Charity Fergusson as long as you live."

Luke went as white as the bed linens. "Did you say . . . dear God . . . over a year ago?"

With a sudden lurch he heaved his legs over the side of the bed. The counterpane slid aside as his feet sought the floor, and Charity caught a flash of the muscled thighs she knew so well. She'd stripped his clothes after Dylan and her father settled him in last night. Now she scurried to his side, grasping the coverlet and holding it across his hips while trying to ease him back onto the pillows. He resisted with a strength that surprised her considering his condition.

"Luke, please, you're not yet well." Her voice dropped to a whisper. "And you're not decent."

Unfazed, he tried to push her away. The bedclothes slipped again, but Charity snatched them back in place. Luke swayed precariously. "You don't understand. I don't know where I am, how I came to be here or who you are." He stumbled against her side and wrapped an arm about her waist for support.

"I can answer all your questions, but you must trust me."

His dark eyes held her, searching, suspicious. Even so, his solid weight aroused an all too familiar yearning inside her, warm, heavy, delicious. She might have laughed—or wept—at the absurdity of her reaction, except that it had been so between them since the first days of their marriage; a year had done little to cool their passions.

"Perhaps you should leave us, Mr. Douglas," she said, fighting the urge to wrap her arms around her husband's neck and fall with him into the cozy nest of the mattress.

With a self-conscious nod, the rector backed out of the room.

No longer resistant, Luke sank heavily onto the edge of the bed, drawing Charity down beside him. The mattress still radiated the heat of him, still held the impression of his prone and naked body. How natural it would have been to give him a little shove into that snug space and dive in after him.

Natural yesterday, but bizarrely, appallingly, not today.

And yet, she discovered their close contact affected him whether he will or no, for the telltale bed linen tented with the evidence of his desire. Almost comically, Luke stared into his lap and gawked in surprise, then released her and quickly gathered the quilted counterpane around his waist.

"So sorry," he murmured, turning away.

A forlorn chill replaced the glow of his touch. She suppressed a shudder. "Never mind."

Luke nodded and turned back, staring into her face as if some missing clue might magically appear. "Have you ever had a word or name on the tip of your tongue, but couldn't quite grasp it? That's how I feel each time I look upon your face." He shook his head. "I believe I should know you but . . ."

His made a fist. "The last thing I remember is being at home, in Wakefield. Why, I can even remember having salmon in capers and white wine for supper. Seems like only a night or two ago, but it couldn't have been, could it?"

"Salmon, perhaps, but capers? I'm afraid not from my kitchen."

"Still, how can I remember that, yet draw a blank at your lovely face?"

"You took quite a knock on the head," she said, experiencing a tiny thrill that even in his agitation, he found her lovely. He had thought so over a year ago, too, after fighting his way back from near death and discovering her watching over him.

Brooding furrows creased his brow; the line of his jaw hardened. "Am I being held here against my will?"

"Of course not," she exclaimed, appalled not only by the notion, but by the realization that this alarming development might end the most glorious year of her life.

"You're a free man, Luke Martin. No one orders you about. You take your guidance from the good sense God gave you."

His face tightened at the sound of his name—or, at least, the name he been known by these many months. But he made no comment except to ask, in a voice gone bewildered and boyishly vulnerable, "Then, how did I come to be here?"

"As Mr. Douglas explained, Seamus MacAllister found you drifting at sea. We believe there'd been a shipwreck. Perhaps you'd been out fishing and were caught in a squall. We don't know for sure."

As she spoke the last word, Luke winced. His hands flew to cradle his head.

"What is it?" Her arms went around him. "Lie down."

"No, I'm all right." He straightened, squaring his shoulders, putting space between them. She let her arms slide away to her sides. "I had . . . it was like a vision in my head. Thunder, flashing light. A boat."

"Go on."

"I'm not sure." He knitted his brows, glaring at the far wall. "Darkness. Walls of water."

"Seamus found you floating on a timber. It might have been a piece of mast. You were half-drowned when he hauled you into his skiff and brought you to shore."

She shivered at the memory of the lifeless face, the colorless lips, the broad chest so motionless it could not possibly have drawn breath in or out. When first she'd beheld the nameless man plucked from the sea, she had uttered a prayer for his departed soul.

"Mother and I nursed you for days. When you finally awoke you hadn't the faintest idea what had happened. You couldn't tell us where you hailed from or who your people were. You didn't know your own name. Your clothes were in tatters. Only your manner of speech gave any clue that you were an Englishman and not a Scot."

"Why do you call me Luke Martin?"

"We pored over the family Bible for two whole days, you and I, starting with Adam and working our way along." The memory produced a wistful tightening in her chest. "I thought it was as good a source as any for finding a name. When I came to the Gospel According to Luke, you stopped me. Several days later, you settled on Martin as a surname."

"Martin was my father's name."

Apprehension slithered up her spine. Were Wesley and Helena family members as well? In his earlier rantings, Luke hadn't spoken of Helena in brotherly terms. Could he be . . . married?

Aye, married—to her—and high time he remembered. She stood. "Rest today, and regain your strength. Tomorrow, I'll show you how you've spent the past year of your life."

Chapter Three

That evening, Luke emerged from the bedroom with a determined if not quite steady stride, proclaiming himself well enough to join Charity for supper in the kitchen. She studied the angry purple wound above his brow with no small amount of skepticism, but sighed. Once Luke Martin made up his mind, nothing short of tying him up could deter him.

The meal was interminable. He continually thanked her, for the food, for all she'd done for him, as if she were some charitable boardinghouse proprietress. Later, he asked for a blanket and the location of the nearest settee. After so many nights of vast and varied pleasure, his sudden decorum struck her as a droll jest. But she detected no humor in his somber expression, nor in his formal nod of appreciation when she handed him a blanket and pillow.

She tried sleeping, even succeeded for an hour or two. But she found the bed a cold and dismal place without him, and the night crawled like an injured seal across the beach. Stiff, bleary-eyed but grateful for the dawn, she rose and dressed hurriedly, ate a slice of yesterday's bread and slipped quietly outside to do the morning chores.

She was backing out of the hen house when the kitchen door thwacked. Luke stood on the stoop, back arched, arms stretched over his head. One hand reached to massage the opposite shoulder.

He waved when he saw her. She set down her basket of eggs and wondered what to do. Go to him? Wait where she was? How should she behave with this virtual stranger? She neither wished to seem aloof nor appear too eager. She abhorred their cordial politeness, loathed having to temper her love for fear of driving the man off.

In the end, she watched him make his careful way toward her over the uneven ground, his brow creased with the concentration of keeping his balance. He wore the loose wool trousers she'd made him just last week. A perfect fit, they skimmed his narrow hips and tapered lightly over sturdy thighs. A linen shirt rippled from his broad shoulders, the thin fabric revealing the contoured lines of a chest made powerful by the past year's labors. But his shirtsleeves, usually shoved to the elbows, were fastened at the wrists, veiling the forearm muscles that had burgeoned as well these many months.

Despite his injury, she saw it now as plain as day: the assurance of his posture, the determined set of his chin. How could she ever have believed him anything less than a nobleman?

Duke of Wakefield. How horrifying. Not to mention, oh, what were his other titles? Earl of Lynhurst and Viscount . . . something or other. How could she, simple, Scottish farm girl, be the wife of a peer of England?

The breeze, stiff with brine, whipped spirals of hair from her bun. With a dismayed sigh she stole a glance at her faded work dress, her muddied boots. What had she been thinking? Why hadn't she worn one of her finer muslins, or even the silk frock purchased in Berwick last summer?

What would his Helena have worn? A homespun dress without so much as a length of ribbon or tier of lace? Never, even if the wool *was* some of the finest in all the British Isles.

And did his Helena possess a tangle of brassy curls that flitted loose at the first breath of wind? Did freckles march a wide path across her nose, or calluses mar the milky plane of her palms? The answers were obvious. Charity groaned, wishing she could hide rather than face Luke now.

Too late for that.

"Good morning," he hailed, and as she called a reply a frenzied yelping drowned out her words. From across the yard Skiff and Schooner bounded, like two scuttling storm clouds.

Luke saw them and braced, just in time. The Westies leapt, assaulting his legs and springing to nip at his hands. He bore the attack well, but looked so astounded and sweet that despite everything, laughter bubbled inside Charity.

Then he teetered, and she started toward him. "Skiff, Schooner, down lads, this instant."

"I'm all right." Luke held up his arms to steady himself, holding his fingertips from the leaping dogs' mouths. "That's quite enough now, you two. Go play. Test someone else's patience."

Charity slowed to a halt, resisting the urge to run to him, to throw her arms around him. That would have been the act of a wife, but was she that now?

With an outward calm she didn't feel, she strolled to the low stone wall that separated the barnyard from the holding pen. As Luke approached, his shadow cloaked her, and even that intangible contact quickened her pulse. Her body tensed with eager desire, as if her heart and all that was female inside her had yet to recognize the sudden change in their relationship.

As he sat beside her, their thighs rubbed. Her belly fisted with an ache of both yearning and misgiving. She bit down and wished for the day before yesterday.

"Good morning," he said at the very same time she asked, "How do you feel?"

They laughed and fell silent. Luke shifted uneasily, brushing his fingertips across a sunny spray of scotch roses sprouting beside the wall. Charity leaned forward to pet one of the dogs. Luke flashed a crooked smile.

"I'm better, thank you."

"I'm glad."

More silence, heavy and awkward. Charity frowned. This was not how they were together. They were familiar, comfortable. Openly affectionate.

He held his arms out before him. "I found these clothes in the chest of drawers in the bedroom. I hope it's all right that I put them on."

"They're your clothes, Luke," she managed through a throat gone pinched and dry.

"Ah, yes, of course they are. How foolish of me."

Skiff hopped up to the wall and stepped into Luke's lap. His little pink tongue hung from the side of his mouth, a glistening appeal to be petted.

"Are they always so boisterous?"

"They adore you." How could he not know that? How could he not see how much *she* adored him? "They follow you everywhere, as constant as twin shadows."

He mopped a hand across Skiff's shaggy head. "How in the world do you tell them apart?"

Surely you remember what happened, she wanted to shout. *You were there. You saw it happen.*

"We always could," she said with feigned patience. She lifted Schooner in her arms and pointed to his left ear. "This made it even easier. See the missing tip? The little devils cornered a weasel in the barn one morning, and Schooner had nearly half his ear bitten off in the process."

"Ouch. A harsh lesson learned."

"Hardly. They're entirely fearless and haven't the least notion of their size." The Westy wriggled in her arms. Her elbow nudged Luke's and he flinched away. Pretending not to notice, she swallowed an urge to sob.

He inhaled a long breath, fine nostrils flaring slightly. "What is this place?"

She wanted to cry, scream. These were the questions of a stranger. Nothing more than offhand curiosity.

"Our home, North Headland Farm." She gazed at the stone and timber house she was so proud of, trying to see it through a stranger's eyes. Would a duke find it squalid, beneath his dignity? "It's at the northern end of my family's land. Five hundred acres in all. My dower portion."

His eyebrows arched in appreciation. "And you raise . . . ?"

"*We* raise sheep, of course."

"For mutton or wool?"

"Wool, mostly. Some of Britain's finest, if you don't mind my saying so."

"Wakefield is sheep country, too. But my family owns the land. We don't work it."

A realization struck her. "Do you mean Wakefield in the west of Yorkshire?"

"I don't know of any other."

"Sweet mercy, no wonder you took to sheep farming as though you were born to it. You were." Finally, this glimpse into Luke's past explained how a privileged English duke succeeded where he should have floundered. "Wakefield produces more wool in a year than we could hope to in three. Sheep farming is in your blood."

"Preposterous." He chuckled deep in his throat, sweetly sinister and so familiar goose bumps erupted on her arms. "I couldn't tell you the difference between a ewe and a ram."

"You're as wrong as can be. You've a gift for it, a knack for understanding the patterns of the seasons, the needs of the flocks. We started this farm with only a wee bit of help from my family." Pride nudged her chin higher. "Our yield of wool wasn't much this year, but the next promises to be a bountiful one." *If you stay*, she added silently. *If you don't abandon all our hard work.*

He looked unconvinced as he surveyed the barnyard and the holding pen behind it. The sun, well up now, illuminated the ends of his hair to burnished chestnut, with midnight shadows beneath. He needed a haircut. She wanted to run her fingers through the thick waves.

From there her hand would slide lower to massage his neck and shoulders, while she leaned against his broad back, nestling her breasts between his shoulder blades.

Stop this! But even as she issued the admonition, her nipples beaded against her bodice, aching for the feel of him.

She sucked in a breath. "You built our house."

His astonishment made her smile.

"Not on your own, mind you. Most of the men of St. Abbs helped. And there was already the main room standing. You added the kitchen, larder and bedroom."

He studied the farmhouse with nary a spark of recognition. "Gathering the stones would have taken the better part of a year."

"The stones were already here. English families gather linens and silverware for their daughters' hope chests. We Fergussons gather stones. They're much more useful, especially in sheep country."

"How could I have worked so hard, and have no memory of any of it?"

"Look at your hands." She touched the back of his wrist.

He raised his palms and gaped. "My God, they're ruined."

"Not ruined, Luke, strengthened." Emboldened that he hadn't winced at her touch, she trailed her fingers over calluses grown thick in the past year. His hand closed suddenly around hers. The strength of it made her shiver; made her want to toss pride away and bury herself in his arms. She dared not breathe, even as she dared to hope.

Skiff whimpered, and Luke's hand opened and fell away. "You know I can't stay here." The quiet words fell with damning force. "I have a family, responsibilities, people who depend on me. I've gone missing a long time."

"I am your family, Luke Martin. I depend on you. The success of this farm depends on you."

"Charity . . ." His tongue tripped smoothly over the *r* in her name, in the soft tone he used when they lay together in bed. "I must make arrangements. I am needed."

"By Helena?" Resentment of a faceless woman rose like an illness inside her.

"And the rest of my family."

"Is she . . . is Helena . . . your wife?" The last word nearly choked her.

"No."

Relief surged, only to drown in despair as he continued, "We are to be married in a few weeks' time." He shook his head. "*Were* to be married. She probably gave up on me months ago."

"Then perhaps there's no reason for you to rush off." How eager she sounded, how pitiful. She hugged Schooner to her cheek, seeking comfort in the downy fur.

Luke took a long breath, let it out slowly. "Charity, my dear, I'm so very sorry about all of this. Forgive me for leading you to believe I could be your husband when in fact I had no right to make such a promise. The truth is I'm not Luke Martin but Lucas Holbrook, and I must return to my family and my duties in England."

No, she wanted to roar, *you're Luke, my Luke.* But the gaze of a stranger met hers. Bewildered, regretful, yes, but distant, almost . . . aloof.

Her defensive instincts rallied. If he'd once shown a moment of discontent, of wanting more than the life they'd shared, she would believe him now and wish him well.

There had been no such moment. He'd thrived on hard work, on learning new skills and pushing his abilities to new limits. He'd taken enormous pride in the results.

But more than that, so much more, was how deeply and unabashedly he had loved her. Surely such powerful feelings could not be swept away with a single swipe of a bottle.

She could make him stay. She had that power, as she had learned so recently. At the very least, the life growing inside her would force him to reconsider his obligations. But obligation was a poor substitute for love; would wear thin, no matter how compelling at the outset.

No, she would appeal instead to his heart, woman to man, lover to lover.

"Will you do something for me?" she asked.

"If it is within my power."

"Come with me."

* * *

They tramped beyond the house, out across the headland that heaved and pitched to a jagged line against
the sea. Lucas felt small beneath a broad, porcelain tureen
of sky, eye-tearingly blue and studded with bright, brisk
clouds. The dogs trotted along beside them, as ebul-
lient as the swirling sea foam a hundred feet below.

Glancing over his shoulder, Lucas regarded the house
where it sprawled in a slight dip in the land, its slate
roof pitched low to accommodate the ocean winds. Beyond, sheep dotted the rugged countryside, ablaze with
golden spring gorse. Here and there, a lone ash or
stand of silver birch thrust toward the sky.

Like a fairy tale, he thought. As they came closer to
the promontory, he wondered where his lovely fairy
might lead him. Yet he was oddly content to wait and
see. He experienced not the slightest inkling of distrust,
though for all he knew she might be about to push him
to a rocky death.

Dear God, he almost wouldn't care; would almost willingly, happily, leap from the precipice at her command.
Ah, he was losing his wits sure enough, with thoughts of
ending his life for a woman he couldn't remember beyond yesterday.

Helena. He repeated her name for the hundredth
time like a mantra. No, like a dousing of frigid water to
cool his ardor for Charity. He couldn't deny finding this
Scotswoman enticing in an infinite number of ways, but
he had no right to explore any of them. Not when he
had already pledged his troth to Helena, had been but
a few weeks from marrying her when his life took its
bizarre turn.

"This way." To their right, the bluffs eased to a more
gradual though still precarious slope. At the top of a

path that angled down to the beach, she paused. "Skiff, Schooner, stay here."

Lucas could almost see the wind rush out from under them. Their jowls hung, displaying pointy bottom teeth in a fair approximation of a pout. He understood their disappointment.

"Don't sulk," their mistress chided.

She led the way to a rock-strewn beach. A line of shells and dried seaweed revealed the high tide mark; the beach would cease to exist then, the waves engulfing all but a scattering of boulders. Pebbles crunched beneath their feet as she led him to the largest boulder, flat and wide at the water's edge, its sides encrusted with tiny barnacles. She sat and beckoned him beside her.

"Well?" she said with an expectancy that reached inside him and aroused a fervent desire to please her.

"It's, uh, quite beautiful here."

"No, no." She pushed out a breath. "Do you remember where we are? Why this place is important to us?"

Gulls streaked overhead, bellies flashing in the sun. White-flecked waves crested some twenty feet from shore, then surged to the beach to slap thousands upon thousands of crushed pebbles. The sound reminded Lucas of clapping hands.

It might have been an inlet anywhere along the North Sea coast. He shook his head. "I'm sorry."

"Oh." With a sigh she swept wind-whipped tendrils from her face. "I thought if anything would prod your memory, this would. You asked me to marry you here, the last time."

"The last time? You mean I—"

"Pursued me like a man possessed." A note of mischief entered her voice. "The first time you proposed, you were lying on a cot in my parents' home. I had come in to check on you and straighten the bedclothes. I thought you were sleeping when all of a sudden you grabbed my hand and insisted we belonged together and where might the nearest preacher be found."

He gave a rueful chuckle. "What was your answer?"

"I slapped you and left the room."

"Slapped me?"

"On the wrist. You deserved it."

She pulled her feet up and hugged her knees, revealing the outlines of long, slender legs beneath her skirts. His hands itched to discover just how long and slender. As she chatted on about that first encounter, an inviting warmth emanated from her clothing, a heady blend of body heat and afternoon sunshine. The clean, heather-fresh scent of her hair blended with the sharp salt of the sea. The sweet and tangy mixture fueled an urge to pull her into his arms and taste her, and savor the feel of those endless legs wrapped about his waist.

Helena, he repeated, and tried to conjure sunny blond hair and eyes as blue as the morning sky. All else was madness, the vestiges of not one head injury, but probably several.

"Luke?"

"I'm sorry, what?"

Her brows converged. "Maybe we shouldn't have come down here. You should be resting."

"No. I'm fine. Honest." He touched his forehead, suppressing a shudder when pain bolted through the still-swollen flesh. "See? Good as new. Please go on."

"Well . . ." A moue of doubt smoothed as she apparently decided to humor him. "The second time you asked me came nigh on a month later. It was shearing time and you'd spent the past several days helping Dylan and my father. You were so happy then, like a child with a fistful of sweets.

"Father said he'd never seen a man so satisfied by a hard day's work. And Mother thrilled at the way you attacked her evening meals like they were royal feasts. Dylan said perhaps you'd been in prison, for you seemed a man deprived of both decent food and freedom. No one believed that, though, not even Dylan."

Lucas laughed, offering polite amusement at a memory he simply could not recall. Charity didn't return his laughter, but studied him with a level gaze, stark and assessing. It made him uneasy. People didn't typically stare at the Duke of Wakefield. They looked with respect, deference, more often than not averting their eyes until he addressed them first.

But this woman—this inconsequential, common-born farm woman—dared look him full in the face as if he hadn't a single thought or secret, nay, not even the deepest desire she hadn't already examined from top to bottom.

Not to mention other, more substantial aspects of his person. His mouth went dry.

She watched him silently, observing as he swallowed what seemed a ball of dough with an audible gulp. Then her eyes skewed away and her lids dropped, veiling the speculation beneath. "When the shearing ended there was a social at church. That night you whisked me to a quiet corner and again asked me to marry you."

"Yes, well, a shilling says you didn't accept me then either," he murmured.

"Oh, I wanted to. But I sent you away. I said you must find your past. Before marrying me or anyone, you needed to discover who you were, or at least try."

"Afraid I might have been an escaped prisoner after all?"

"Not even for an instant. I feared exactly what has happened." Her voice faltered, turned husky. "That your past would suddenly reclaim you and steal you away from me."

He felt like the worst of scoundrels. "How long was I gone?"

"Three days." A wistful smile bloomed. "You got as far as Berwick-upon-Tweed, actually made arrangements to take the post-chaise south, but at the last minute raced back to St. Abbs. You dragged me into Father's skiff, downright kidnapped me, and brought me to this beach. You claimed you would as soon throw yourself back into the sea than live without me."

At this her voice cut short. Arms wrapped around her middle, she ducked her chin. Panic gripped him. Was she going to cry? What would he do? Hold her? Smooth her hair and kiss her brow? By God, he'd want to, and didn't for a moment trust himself to.

"You said no one and nothing could ever make you as happy as you'd been here in St. Abbs," she said from the depths of the huddle she'd become. "And you gave me this."

She thrust her trembling left hand in front of his face. On the fourth finger, a star sapphire winked in the sunlight. He recoiled.

"My grandfather's ring." He had thought he lost the heirloom given him by his maternal grandmother, that it had slipped off at sea. Frowning, he studied the plain gold band holding the stone. "Or is it? It's been altered."

"Aye. You had it reset for me." With both hands she reached for his, her grip tight, urgent. A desperation he didn't understand knocked his heart against his breastbone.

The tide lapped closer. Shivers rippled through him as a jolting energy coursed through their linked fingers, a connection that traveled leagues beyond mere flesh.

He couldn't name it, couldn't define it. Yet it felt as vital as the thrash of his pulse, the rasp of his lungs.

"Trust me with your heart," he whispered, the unbidden words bursting from some locked place within.

"Sweet mercy, yes." A tear spilled down her cheek. "That's what you said when you returned."

"And you did. You agreed to be my wife." Agreed to his heartfelt request, his urgent plea. He didn't remember, but he knew it was so.

"Aye. I loved you. I wanted to believe." Her breath quivered around a repressed sob. "I leapt and you caught me. But what happens now?"

Chapter Four

Trust me with your heart.
I wanted to believe.

Lucas couldn't have felt more miserable or more blameworthy. He'd taken both her trust and her heart, twisted them, wrung them out and handed them back. That he hadn't meant to seemed the most hollow of excuses.

They returned to the house in strained silence, arms stiff at their sides, gazes trained on the path ahead. How dare the day be so beautiful; how could the sun be so brazen as to shine upon such a despondent pair as he and Charity?

She opened the gate at the kitchen garden. The Westies barreled through but when Lucas hesitated, Charity questioned him with a look.

He couldn't go back inside. Not now. Not into that house, where he'd lived as this woman's husband for so many months. He feared he'd strangle on the guilt of it.

"Aren't you—"

"No," he said, terse, clipped. He didn't mean to be

ill-mannered; he was simply too overwhelmed to master his voice.

Her face tightened. *Please, no more tears*, he inwardly pleaded. *Not just now.* She had shed just one on the beach before tucking her emotions under control. He'd looked on with a shameful burst of gratitude, his own emotions too raw, too exposed, for him to offer any kind of solace.

"I need . . . time," he said. "To think. I'd like to walk awhile longer. Alone, if you wouldn't mind."

"I understand." Sadness settled across her features.

It seemed he could do little else but hurt her. He hated that. Luke Martin had loved her, of that he was convinced. But he was not Luke Martin and no amount of wishing could transform the Duke of Wakefield into a Scottish farmer.

Yet, something *had* caused that transformation. A blow to the head, or something more? Had life here spoken to some craving, some deep instinct he hadn't known existed?

He might never know. Thinking about it only renewed the dizziness. He stumbled as he started away, and grasped the garden fence for balance.

Charity caught him around the waist, taking his weight against her side. The spell passed in a second or two. He straightened, but it was an effort not to lean further into her inviting warmth and snug curves.

"You're feeling unwell again." Her gaze probed him from head to toe. "You should rest."

An image flashed of the two of them snuggled deep into the heat of their feather bed. "No. I'm fine."

"You don't look fine."

He believed she would know.

She gave a little shrug. "Just remember, as you walk, that all you see is the result of our labor."

He nodded and set off, his sense of relief growing with each step. Being near her tangled his senses until he felt immersed in the heady warmth of heather and the lavender oil she made from the plants bordering the house.

Only when he couldn't see her, hear her, smell her, could he focus his thoughts. He had so much to do in so short a time. Contact his family, for one. He couldn't simply arrive home after being thought dead for more than a year. They needed gentle warning.

Charity's dogs caught up to him in the barnyard, barking their excitement at the prospect of another outing. He acknowledged them briefly but kept walking; perhaps they'd lose interest and return to Charity. To his annoyance, they trailed him like two ducklings following their mother.

His solicitor, also, must be contacted as soon as possible. More than a legal advisor, Jacob Dolan had been a family friend and personal confidant since Lucas's university years. He could only hope his brother, Wesley, had sought Jacob's advice in running the estate. Wes had proved a first-rate army officer but he'd never trained to handle the family fortune. Without help . . . Lucas shuddered to imagine what financial shambles might await him.

Reaching the stone wall bordering the barnyard, he sat, swung his legs over to the other side and stood to resume his walk. He froze. A few yards away stood the largest ram he'd ever seen, with great curling horns that tapered to lethally sharp points.

Beside him, Skiff and Schooner growled deep in their throats. The ram puffed a breath through his nostrils. Rearing his great, shaggy head, he regarded them with either boredom or enmity, Lucas couldn't decide which.

Ewes were gentle; he remembered that much from the tenant farms at home. But why would a ram be called a ram if it didn't tend to partake of that particular activity?

Would it charge if provoked?

To test it, Lucas ventured a cautious step forward. The ram's head came up. It glared, the golden irises shrinking behind its vacuous, vertical pupils. One of the dogs barked. The other yipped. Lucas shushed them.

A surly creature, he thought. *And most definitely annoyed.*

"Old Samson's hoping you'll hand him a carrot," a laughing male voice called from behind him.

The dogs spun around and sprang back over the wall. Lucas whirled to discover a young man standing just outside the barn. He smiled broadly, a gesture Lucas didn't return. Scanning the affable face, auburn hair and light hazel eyes, he felt a vague prickle of recognition. Uncertainty raised his guard.

"Who are you?" he demanded, perhaps more sharply than he should have. "You wouldn't be Seamus MacAllen, would you?"

"Ah, now that's a good one." The youth laughed again. He cocked his head. "But I think you mean Seamus *MacAllister*, don't you?"

"Are you him?"

"I'd say that bottle rattled your brain loose." With the dogs scampering at his heels, the stranger strode to the stone wall and cleared it with a nimble leap. The ram finally settled Lucas's suspicions by retreating several paces into the field.

"I surely didn't expect to see you up and about so soon," the young man said. "I'm wondering if it's wise, though. Calling me Seamus MacAllister, acting like you're afraid of the sheep. Has Charity been giving you the doctor's laudanum? See now, there's your problem. A good nip of scotch is all you need. Set you right and grow hair on your chest." His hand came down on Lucas's forearm. "Let's go into the village and—"

Lucas pulled free. Memory grazed his consciousness. The face before him bore a striking resemblance to the woman in the house. "You must be Charity's brother. Tell me your name."

"You're beginning to frighten me, Luke."

He clenched his teeth. "Humor me."

"Dylan," the youth replied, hooking his thumbs on his trouser braces.

Lucas repeated it, measuring the feel of the consonants and vowels on his tongue. It was not altogether foreign, but not immediate either.

"By St. George's ear," Dylan murmured, "you've gone back to being who you were before you were Luke Martin, haven't you?"

"I never was Luke Martin." Lucas started to turn away but Dylan grabbed his shoulder.

"If you're not Luke Martin, who the devil are you and what do you intend to do about my sister?"

Lucas went rigid. He slanted a look at the hand restraining him. "I'm Lucas Holbrook and I suggest, boy, that you remove your paw."

The grip tightened. "I'm no boy."

"Could have fooled me." His hands fisted.

"I want answers."

"So do I."

Head to head, they glared at one another while the air about them tensed and snapped. Sensing it, the dogs watched motionless but for the quivering ends of their fur.

Dylan pushed out a breath. His fingers eased from Lucas's shoulder. "We're friends, you and I."

"Are we?" In a burst of frustration Lucas kicked the stone wall, hard. A bolt of pain shot through his foot.

"Ouch," Dylan commented.

"Deuced bloody right." Lucas took deep breaths, struggling with a sense of powerlessness, of having no control over his own fate. He scowled at the wall. "Perhaps you should knock me cold with one of these stones. I might wake up happy to be Luke Martin again, and then I needn't make decisions that will hurt people."

"Do you think you've stopped being Luke Martin?" Irony curled Dylan's mouth. "You might call yourself something different, but you're the same man."

"No, I am not." He shook his head sadly. "I'm as different from Luke Martin as it's possible to be."

"Ah, Luke." Dylan shook his head in a *what shall we do with you* kind of way. "You've got the soul of a farmer. And of a Scot, even if you do speak in that peculiar manner of yours."

Part of him actually wished it were true. He sensed something peaceful, simple and enormously fulfilling about life at North Headland Farm. A corner of his heart yearned for it, and for the woman he guessed was anything but peaceful or simple. Their brief encounters had revealed a fire in Charity Fergusson that could heat the iciest winter night.

But the Duke of Wakefield could not hide away indefinitely on a farm in a remote corner of Scotland. He would be naïve to think it—as naïve as young Dylan here. What's more, he'd be a villain to ignore the existence of his family and responsibilities. Yet a villain he must be in either case, for in order to return to his family in England, he must turn his back on this one in Scotland.

* * *

After watching Luke's tall figure recede for several wistful moments, Charity entered the house with a growing sense of hopelessness.

Inside, the first oddity to strike her was the cleared kitchen table. The few breakfast dishes had been washed, dried and stacked away, the chairs straightened. A pair of pewter candlesticks had been moved from the sideboard and placed at the center of the table. Ah, but most telling of all, the curtains above the sink had been shaken out and rearranged into the perfectly symmetrical pleats only one person on earth was capable of making.

Sweet mercy. Not now.

Too late did she remember to paste on a pleased expression. An all-too-familiar figure appeared in the parlor doorway. Still slender despite her years and childbirth, still flame-haired despite the dulling influence of gray, Lara Fergusson angled her chin in a gesture Charity had inherited but did her best to avoid.

"Charity Alice Fergusson Martin, I'm not liking that look on your face one bit." A washrag fluttered like a captured flag from a deceptively fragile-looking hand.

"Mother. What are you doing here?"

"A fine greeting, that. And the question is not what I'm doing, but what are you doing? Eh, girl? Just what are you going to do?"

"You saw the rector."

"Aye. And such a tale he told me. Good grief, your husband going on about being an English duke. Of all the nonsense, I told him. My Charity will never stand for that, said I."

Weariness made Charity want to sink into a chair and lay her head on the table. "He is a duke, mother. And outrageous though it may sound, he is returning to England as soon as possible and there's precious little I can do to stop him."

"Ah." Lara Fergusson moved into the kitchen and tossed her rag to the table. "So you're going to stand aside and let him walk off into the sunset? Are you mad? He's your husband. He belongs here. He loves you."

"Did love me. Now . . . he doesn't even know me." Turning her back, Charity went to the window and gazed out. High up on the ridge that separated the north and west pastures, she spied Luke trudging along with Dylan at his side. Skiff and Schooner pranced behind them.

Her stomach sank. Luke had said he wanted to be alone to think. What he had wanted, obviously, was to be away from her.

"Sweet mercy, how could this have happened?" Her hand thwacked the windowsill, rattling the glass panes. She whirled, wishing to confront whatever power had played this horrible trick. There was only her mother, small and slight but fearless and ready to take her side. "Wasn't I careful? Didn't I send Luke in search of his past before I agreed to be his wife? Yet this—*this!*—is the sorry result of my pains."

Her mother's face blurred behind a sheen of tears. A moment later work-worn hands closed over her shoulders with gentle but firm shakes. "Charity Alice, you must get hold of yourself. Where's your strength, girl?"

"What will become of the farm? We've worked so hard this year, and now . . ." What of the child who needed its father, she wanted to add. Yet that she kept to herself. No one yet knew about the babe and thank goodness. If Lara Fergusson so much as guessed the truth, she'd truss Luke to a pole and toss him into the root cellar.

"It's well-nigh summer," her mother said calmly. "Time for the flocks to roam. Your father and Dylan and I can handle the two farms for a while."

The air cooled Charity's tears as she lifted her face. "What are you getting at?"

"Daughter, you might not be able to prevent Luke from leaving, but you can sure enough keep him from forgetting you when he does. Come with me."

She led Charity into the bedroom, where together they rummaged through the oak wardrobe and cedar clothes press. They conferred for the better part of an hour, until a half dozen dresses lay strewn across the bed, others tossed over the chair. Then Lara Fergusson left for home.

After tidying the room, Charity closed the wardrobe doors, running her hand over the smooth wood. A bittersweet memory flooded her. The piece had been a wedding present from Luke, but before he had proudly presented it to her, she had stumbled upon its hiding place at the back of her parents' barn. She knew she should have walked away, but some curious imp had compelled her to peek inside. One of the doors had nearly fallen off its hinges. Later that evening, her father made the necessary repairs in secret, with Luke none the wiser.

Of course the Duke of Wakefield would have had no experience in carpentry. Even so, he had mastered the skills soon enough and with deep satisfaction.

Charity turned back to the room. One of his work shirts lay folded on the top of the dresser—a soft woolen plaid she had made from their first yield of wool. She held it up to her cheek and sank to the bed.

If Luke left her, what reason would she have to rise in the morning? To find joy on the simple routine of her day? This farm, this house, her heart—all of it empty, shriveled, lifeless without him.

Duke of Wakefield. Sweet mercy. What was his Helena like? Beautiful? No doubt. Fashionable? Of course. Freckled? Never.

And the rest of his family? She considered his offhand comment that while they owned the land, they had never worked it. No, the Holbrooks would never have experienced a single day's labor nor the pleasure of creating something where nothing existed before, nor the pride of earning their wealth.

They would of course be elegant and refined, removed from ordinary people and everyday life. They would not know of the world's sorrows, its unexpected tragedies. They would sit snug in their various mansions, enjoying the comforts provided by the toil of others.

Her fingers curled tighter around Luke's shirt. Her mother was right. She couldn't simply allow her husband to march off to a useless existence—a life Luke Martin would scoff at. It would be akin to letting him lose his soul.

If nothing else, she'd provide him a choice by proving the value of a life beyond titles, beyond inheritances and fashion. He had fallen in love with her once and with very little provocation on her part. Why not again?

She returned to the kitchen to wait for him, sitting at the table with folded hands, straight back, firm resolve. Maybe he wouldn't go. Maybe he'd stay. Maybe he'd remember how much he loved her.

As the afternoon light deepened to amber and her shadow elongated against the wall, she heard his footsteps. She clutched her hands to still them. The kitchen door opened and he entered alone, his intentions evident in the somber cast of his eyes. Her last hope, already so threadbare, unraveled.

"You'll be leaving soon," she whispered.

For a moment he looked as though he'd contradict her. Then he said quietly, "That would be best."

Her chin came up. She knew what she must do.

* * *

"Confound it." Shifting onto his side, Lucas groped and contorted in the hope of achieving the smallest semblance of comfort. The instrument of torture to which he'd confined himself for the night—the parlor sofa—offered none. Hardly meant for sitting much less sleeping, the thing was too short, too narrow, too stuffed with horsehair. His feet hung off, his neck cramped and his shoulders would not be accommodated.

He tried counting sheep, but the swirls of plaster on the ceiling above his head failed to take on the slightest characteristic of those fluffy animals. Rather, they only served to remind him of a certain person's spiraling, lustrous locks of hair.

He tugged at the coverlet Charity had tossed him as she bid him good night. The wool, patterned into a plaid of blues, greens and yellows, had come of this spring's yield, she'd informed him. And a fine yield it was, he must admit. He rubbed a corner against his face. Rich and soft, it smelled of heather and warm summer wind and . . . Charity herself.

Bloody hell. He might have been stretched to his full length on a vast down mattress seeped in the warmth of the angel beside him. But no. He had awakened yesterday no longer the earthy farmer allowed to indulge his passion for the tantalizing Charity Fergusson. He had awakened a nobleman. A gentleman. And that meant one thing as far as she was concerned.

Hands off. If he could no longer fulfill his role as husband, to have her otherwise would dishonor him and make a trollop of her.

Ah, if only she were a trollop.

No, he certainly wouldn't want her then.

Well, perhaps . . .

With an angry lurch he flung the blanket to the floor, suppressing groans as he straightened his aching limbs. Once he'd managed a near approximation of his natural posture, he glowered down at the rumpled tartan. The manners ingrained since early childhood dictated that he pick it up and place it back on the sofa. Even fold it.

Deuced hell, why must being a gentleman cause such inconvenience in his life? Why be denied the pleasure of a woman who made him throb—and who took few pains to conceal her own longings—all in the dismal name of propriety? Well, not only propriety. There was Helena, of course, although for the most part he'd kept his hands off her, too, for the same damned reason.

Because he'd been born a gentleman.

His bare foot delivered a kick to the heaped coverlet, a gesture as futile as it was childish. With a rueful shrug he plucked it from the floor and draped it over the sofa back.

A sleepy whimper reminded him the Westies were slumbering in the nearby kitchen. Lucas froze, hoping the sound indicated nothing more than an enthralling dream. The yapping beasts hadn't allowed him a moment's peace all afternoon or evening; instead they'd vied for his attention like spoiled children. He tiptoed to the front door. Breath suspended, he pushed down on the door latch and shouldered his way outside, into the salt-kissed night.

And walked straight into Charity.

He struck her from behind, her ivory-draped form so straight and still he hadn't seen her. She stumbled but he caught her in his arms, her weight soft and pliant against his chest. The intoxicating essence of lavender melted through him.

Her gasp of surprise took flight like a nightingale on the evening breeze. She turned in his embrace, a slow circle that caused her breasts to skim his forearm, his shirtfront. Another tiny wobble brought her snugly against him.

If he had thought everything at North Headland Farm made of wool, her night rail proved the assumption entirely wrong. Her breasts, round and high, peeked from within fabric as ethereal as a summer mist. Through it, her dark nipples brushed his chest with the sweet caress of ripe plums and nearly brought him to his knees.

She tipped her head back, quirking honey-smooth lips in a self-conscious smile. He felt her pulling away, and realized that was his cue to release her.

"I'm sorry," he said, and like a dimwit added, "I didn't see you there."

"What're you doing up at this hour?" She hugged her sides and gazed up at the sky.

Following her line of vision, he watched as delicate clouds scuttled the mighty Orion. "I could ask you the same."

"I've grown accustomed to having you beside me." She shrugged, grazing him with a glance, her green eyes as dark as the ocean's abyss. Her voice was low, husky, weighted with the burden he'd placed upon her. "To you I've become a stranger. To me, you're the same man who's warmed my bed each night for a year. That bed's a cold and empty place without you, Luke."

"It isn't for lack of my wanting to be there." He only just kept from cringing. Such a stupid thing to say. So useless. He should bid her good night, turn, reenter the house. A gentleman would.

"And not for lack of sanction either." She tugged her sleeves lower over her wrists. "God's or man's, since we are married."

"It would be wrong for us to lie as man and wife when . . ."

She turned away before he completed the thought.

Her squared shoulders declared her disinclination to hear his reasons again.

"Do you know what you love to do?" she asked suddenly, some of the sadness gone from her voice.

Wrap your naked body in my arms and make fervent love to you all night long? It was only a guess, but more than likely on the mark.

"No," he said aloud. "What do I love to do?"

"Walk the farm at night, beneath the stars." A breath of wind fluttered her shift around shapely ankles and pressed it flat against her torso. "I think you enjoy that more than anything else."

"Is that so?" *More than trailing kisses over your body, beginning with those lovely breasts I'm having a devil of a time trying not to stare at?*

"Well, more than almost anything," she amended. The moonlight cast teasing glints in her coppery hair and paled her complexion to alabaster. Her sweet scent drifted on the ocean breeze in intoxicating wisps that stole his judgment and left him dizzy, as adrift as a year ago.

She raised a hand, palm open and inviting, the long, straight fingers extended toward him. A reflection shimmered in his mind—more sensation than cognition—of those exquisite hands skimming over him, caressing, soothing, arousing him in ways his body remembered down to the most shattering detail despite his amnesia.

Hers were not flawless hands. Not at all like Helena's, smooth as milky satin. Even by moonlight he saw the faint calluses marring her palm, and a scratch across her middle finger where she had removed a thistle from a sheep's coat. Yet those imperfections drew him all the more acutely, for they revealed a woman unafraid to touch, to feel, to grasp life.

Irresistible.

His hand rose to meet hers. Despite his certainty that

their future could not be shared, his resolution to remain honorable faded beneath the shadow of Charity's open palm.

Her fingers closed around his and the words *I want you* filled his heart and inflamed his loins. Her essence surrounded him as she stepped closer. Desire twisted inside him, stabbing, burning. He bent for her kiss, his tormented body crying *yes* and ignoring all else.

She kissed him, on the cheek, and said, "Will you walk with me, Luke? For an hour at least, if you can promise no more."

Her candor spread a thousand fissures through his heart. He felt whole pieces of it chip away and fall to the ground at his feet, where they would remain long after his departure from North Headland Farm.

Perhaps he could not be faulted for creating this debacle, but he would despise himself for the rest of his life for having hurt this ingenuous Scottish beauty. It pained him physically to return her pensive smile, to draw breath without blurting inane assertions about wishing things could be different.

Wisely keeping his mouth closed, he gave her hand a reassuring squeeze before following her through the moon-washed fields. They tread softly and talked quietly so as not to disturb the herd. She told him about all the details he'd forgotten: last year's seeding, the summer fertilizing, the autumn breeding, then the spring lambing and finally, the fruit of their labor, the shearing.

It was all very ordinary, one might even say mundane. Just a married couple picking their way across their farm, assessing as they went. But to Luke, roaming the high, rolling landscape dotted with cloud-like sheep felt akin to traveling the darkened heavens, with a radiant angel to lead the way and catch him should he begin to fall.

Chapter Five

"I don't know why you're getting your petticoats in such a knot," Dylan said as he hefted an iron file from the box of tools beside him. "There's no way in sweet heaven or fiery hell Luke's going to leave you."

"Oh, he's leaving all right," she replied, squinting as the sun's first rays angled into the barnyard. In the pasture just beyond, Skiff and Schooner raised a ruckus of barking. An instant later, a frightened grouse scrambled away, flapping its wings and hurtling into flight. "Luke has made that more than clear."

"Then he'll be back, mark me. Now, hold that lassie good and still."

Charity wrapped her arms securely around the first of the sheep to have its hooves trimmed, a creamy tan moorit with a roan face. Her new summer fleece tickled Charity's forearms, while the mixed fragrance of earth and damp wool tingled in her nose. The ewe gave a few half-hearted squirms to express her impatience with the procedure, but soon relaxed in Charity's familiar hold.

It was that very familiarity that won the creature's trust. If only it could be as easy with Luke.

"Why should he come back?" Charity addressed the hopeless question to her brother and the sheep both, not expecting either to produce an answer. She plucked bits of leaves and sticks from the ewe's coat.

"He loves you," Dylan said simply. Kneeling on one knee, he secured a forelimb between his arm and thigh.

"Loves me?" She pushed a breath between her lips. "Dylan, you're a good brother but a dreamer. Just look at me. What is there here for an English duke to love? My calluses? My freckles and wild hair? Or would it be my fine sense of fashion?"

Dylan slanted a glance over his shoulder as he filed the hoof. "It's not like you to wallow. There's plenty to keep Luke here. I can surely see it, even if you are my scrawny little sister."

"Little? Need I remind you I'm older."

"Aye, but I stand a head taller. And in this matter, at least, I seem to be the wiser."

"Is that so?"

"Aye. Where will Luke find a lass as hardy as you among all those fragile English damsels?"

"Humph. Fragile, perhaps, but to be sure their inheritances are anything but." Contemplating the estate Helena would likely bring to her marriage produced a hollow feeling in the pit of Charity's stomach.

"Have you bothered to remind him of all he'd be leaving behind? Does he remember about our warehouse in Berwick? The exports? The investments?"

"Dylan Fergusson, your head is stuffed with haggis if you think I'll try to buy Luke's affection. Besides, he's a duke. Our measly investments will look like pocket coins to him." With an indignant smirk, she adjusted her arms around the ewe. It bleated, and she stroked its warm flank.

Dylan shrugged. "That may be so, but you shouldn't give up on your husband without a good fight."

"For your information, I don't intend to give up. But neither am I going to hold him here against his will. What good to beg or cajole? He'd only grow to resent us."

Contemplating the curling tufts between her fingers, she didn't immediately notice that Dylan had stopped filing. Then she felt his curious gaze.

"What are you gawking at?"

His eyebrow rose. "Who's us? Surely you don't mean me or Mother or Father. What should it matter what Luke thinks of anyone but you?"

"It doesn't matter. I misspoke, is all." She scowled. Her brother was treading perilously close to a subject she had no wish to discuss. "Kindly quit your staring."

"Who's 'us,' Charity?" His voice carried that all-too-familiar note of persistence that meant he wouldn't let it go. His hand covered hers. The sheep stole that moment to spring out of her arms and dart to a corner of the barnyard.

"See what you've done," she snapped. She started to push to her feet but Dylan held her fast.

"Never mind. Look at me."

She glared at her lap until Dylan lifted her chin. With a sigh she braced for the inevitable.

"Charity," he whispered, "are you . . . I mean . . ." His astonished gaze dropped to her belly.

"Dylan Fergusson," she hissed, "if you tell a soul I'll have your tongue out with red-hot tongs." For emphasis she lashed out with one hand, almost but not quite grazing the side of his head.

He ducked out of reach. Humph. He might be bigger nowadays but she could still make him flinch. Unfortunately, she didn't seem able to stop his tongue.

"By St. George's ear, girl, you've got to tell Luke."

"I don't have to tell Luke a thing and neither do you." She met his gaping disbelief with a glared warning that went unheeded.

"A man has a right to know about his own child. It'd be just the thing to make him stay."

"Which is exactly why he isn't to know. Not just yet. Dylan, don't you see?" She grasped a handful of his shirtfront. "If Luke stays because of the babe, he'll feel trapped. He'll regret the day he ever set eyes on me."

"You don't know that." Dylan's voice softened to the tone he always used to sway her to his side of an argument; the tone which, when they were little, had worked more often than not. "You have to give him a chance."

"I plan to give him a choice, a real choice, between his old life and me."

Since yesterday, she'd debated the wisdom of this matter countless times in her mind. This was the first occasion she'd spoken it aloud. It sounded right. It seemed the only rational course. "If Luke continues to be my husband, I want it to be because he loves me. Not because he feels an obligation."

"What if he goes—not that I believe he will—but what if? Will he never know about his child? Can you do that to him?"

"What about what he's doing to me?" Clutching her hands together, she traced the gold and sapphire ring Luke had placed on her finger as a token of his love. A love he no longer acknowledged. "He doesn't even consider us married, Dylan. What if he looks on this child as nothing more than an inconvenient by-blow?"

"Luke would never treat a child that way."

"How can I be certain? I love Luke Martin, sure enough. But what do I know of Lucas Holbrook? He's a duke—a man used to getting what he wants. What if he decides he wants to raise this child in England without me? He's a nobleman, a peer. He'd have the law on his side. Who would defend the claims of a Scottish commoner?"

Dylan placed a firm hand on her shoulder. "Luke wouldn't—"

"No, Luke wouldn't. But Lucas Holbrook might." The barely contained panic threatened to take control. She couldn't allow that, not with so much at stake. With a hard swallow she summoned her last shreds of logic. "He's the Duke of Wakefield, and we can't claim to know the first thing about him."

"I can. He might have forgotten *who* he is, but a man doesn't ever forget *what* he is, nor what he's made of." Dylan's voice grew firm and sure. "There's honor at Luke's core. He'll prove it to you if you give him the chance."

"What use is his honor if it's given without his heart?"

Dylan heaved a groan. "You're a stubborn old she-goat and that's the God's honest truth."

"Aye. Will you hold your tongue?"

"Better that than you rip it out of my mouth."

Relief whooshed from her lungs. "I knew I could count on you."

"For now. I'll bide my time and see what comes. But I reserve the right to change my mind."

Elbows propped on the edge of the kitchen counter, Lucas peered out the window at Charity and her brother. They were tending to a sheep in the barnyard, working together as . . . as he and Charity must have done innumerable times over the past year.

He felt an immediate stab of . . . no, not jealousy exactly, but something quite sharp and equally disarming.

Envy, bone-deep and undeniable. Watching the familiarity between brother and sister made him almost sick with it. The two of them looked so at ease with one another and with their surroundings.

Lucas yearned for that in his life again—then on second thought wondered if he'd ever had it to begin with.

Moving to the kitchen table, he sat and reread the two letters he'd drafted upon awakening a short while ago. In the first, he'd tried as gently as possible to alert his family to his continued existence and his imminent arrival home. The second, addressed to his solicitor, Jacob Dolan, had been essentially the same, minus the endearments.

He frowned. Something was missing, something vital but forgotten. A memory danced and dangled, teetered and swayed. It began with the rapid *clip-clop* of hooves on a cobbled road. Himself on horseback. Tired. Pushing on. Up ahead, always, was the back of a post-chaise jostling toward the sea. The plaintive warnings of a buoy bell echoed in his mind. He all but smelled the foul mists swirling with the odors of fish and mudflats.

He hesitated outside a ramshackle town house . . . then . . .

Gone. The image vanished like a snuffed flame. Trying to force the memories only renewed the ache in his head. Better not to try, to let it come of its own accord.

Gathering the pages of his letters, he went into the parlor, to the secretaire where he had first found paper, pen and ink. Now he searched the drawers for sealing wax, which he found in a brass box carved with Charity's initials.

He stopped, studying the container's intricate etchings. Must have been costly. In fact, the little writing desk, of polished walnut inlaid with satinwood flowers, far surpassed anything he'd expect to find in a farmhouse. His mother might have placed just such a secretaire in her own sitting room.

So where had sheep farmers of obviously modest means come by such a costly piece? And what of the collection of books in the glass-paned case beside the desk? He might have expected a few tomes on farming practices, but poetry, historical works, novels? Not to mention a dictionary and a law book.

Had he introduced the volumes into the household, perhaps unconsciously remembering shades of his former life? Perhaps, but that didn't explain how so much money could have been spared for such frivolities. The very notion raised his gall—until he remembered it was Charity's concern and none of his business.

He sealed his letters and then went outside, intending to inquire about the next post. The barnyard was now empty of humans. A few sheep grazed near the stone wall. The cow ambled before the barn, her bell clanking softly as she chewed her cud.

"Charity?" he called, then regretted it.

The Westies charged out of nowhere, short legs stretched to a gallop. Piercing barks rent the air, frightening the sheep and sending them bleating to the farthest corners of the yard.

Luke anchored his feet. Schooner with the bitten ear reached him first, lunging. He hit Luke's thigh and bounced, landing miraculously on his feet. His twin, delighting in his brother's stunt, rose up on hind legs and yipped louder still.

"Enough, gentlemen." Meaning to calm them, Lucas crouched and massaged their necks. Skiff jumped, his lolling tongue making soggy contact with Lucas's thankfully closed mouth.

"Deuced hell!" He dragged his sleeve across his lips. "Don't you dare do that again. Do you hear me, sir?"

Determined to ignore the troublesome duo, he pushed to his feet and headed for the open barn doors. Prancing along behind and clearly unwilling to take a hint, they nearly tripped him in their eagerness to keep up. He paid them only enough heed to ensure he didn't tread on them.

He heard Charity before he saw her, humming in the deep shadows that swathed the interior of the barn. Seconds later, the metallic gleam of a lethal set of prongs appeared but a few feet in front of him.

He sidestepped just in time. Pitchfork in hand, Charity rounded the corner of the nearest stall and surely would have skewered him.

She saw him and yelped, then swung the prong end of the fork downward. "I'm so sorry!"

"That was a close one."

Her free hand clutched her throat. "Sweet mercy, I could have killed you."

"I suppose I shouldn't have sneaked up on you."

"I know better than to hold a pitchfork like that. But I'm not accustomed to anyone being in the yard this time of day. Usually you've gone out to the pastures by now. Do forgive me." Her bosom rose and fell heavily. Lucas couldn't help smiling that his near demise had so unnerved her.

And then he inwardly berated his selfishness. Better that Charity didn't give a fig what became of him.

"No harm done," he assured her. "Is Dylan still here?"

"Aye, back at the mulch heap. We've got to start loading it into the wagon so we can spread it in the fields. It's something you had planned to do today."

"May I help?"

Stepping out into the sunlight, she assessed him as if pondering an extravagant purchase. "How's your head?"

"Much better."

"Sounds like a lie to me." With all the familiarity of a wife, she combed the hair from his brow with her fingers, leaving traces of coolness on his skin. He watched her luscious lips purse as she studied him. His groin tightened in anticipation of something irresistibly sweet, profoundly sensual.

She smiled. "You've got a full rainbow of colors there. Black and blue, yellow, red, a bit of purple."

"I'm fine." He felt anything but fine, but his discomfort had little to do with his injury. "I'd like to help."

She hesitated, her expression turning from wistful to deflated. He realized how wretchedly inadequate his offer was. How she must long to hear him declare his readiness to be her husband, to love her as she deserved to be loved. But no, he'd pledged a day's work, such a flimsy and lackluster proposal he should have been ashamed.

He was.

"Perhaps you shouldn't," she said. Her chin gave a little jerk that said she'd made up her mind. "You'll need your rest if you're to make the journey south."

The tiniest bit of resentment tinged her tone, though he sensed she hadn't intended it, had only meant to state a simple fact. But he'd put her and everyone one else in an impossible position and no one, least of all he, could conceive of a solution that would leave them all content.

"Charity . . ."

"Never mind." Stabbing the ground with the pitchfork, she brushed by him. The dogs scampered along behind her.

Lucas trotted several steps to match Charity's pace, but she only walked faster. "Help if you wish," she said curtly. Then she slowed and gave herself a little shake. "We'd be grateful for your help. But you mustn't overtax."

If I do, he wanted to say, *will you run those soothing fingers through my hair and kiss my forehead till I'm better?*

"Fair enough," he said aloud. "So what's the mulch for?"

"I know you've forgotten the past year." She delivered a second forceful stab to the ground. "But did you learn nothing about sheep farming in all your years in Wakefield?"

"I never needed—"

"The mulch makes the grass grow thicker and greener. And that makes for hardier sheep."

"Ah."

They walked several paces in silence, and then a thought occurred to Lucas. "Why did that man hit me?"

"Seamus? Because you're English, of course." Another stab. "And because he was quite foxed at the time. Ordinarily, he's not such a bad fellow. He's been known to do us a good turn now and again. He even helped build our house."

"You're joking."

"Not a bit. His loathing comes and goes as the mood suits him. Usually it's too much ale that brings his ire on. It's a fortunate thing he never learned just how English you are. Dylan and Father might not have been able to drag him off you as easily as they did."

"If he knew I was the Duke of Wakefield?"

"Aye. Seamus can stomach an Englishman if he must,

but not an English nobleman. The Duke of York drove the MacAllisters off their land in the north a hundred years ago."

"A hundred years ago?" He chuckled. "And he hasn't gotten over it?"

Charity tensed. "The wounds run deep here in Scotland. A man in your position should know that."

Yes, he did know it. And he knew the wounds would continue to run deep both in the nation of Scotland and right here at North Headland Farm. He stood duly chastised, wishing he could open his mouth once without shoving his foot into it.

Charity saved him from yet another blunder by turning briskly and continuing on to the rear of the barnyard. They came upon Dylan standing at the top of a large mulch heap, tossing shovelfuls into a nearby wagon. Skiff and Schooner trotted the length of the heap, their black button noses working furiously at the sudden bombardment of fascinating odors. They disappeared round the back of it.

"Ah, good evening, Luke," Dylan called with considerable sarcasm.

"Dylan Fergusson, behave yourself. Good evening indeed." Charity angled the pitchfork into the heap. "Luke's good enough to lend us a hand."

"Is he now?" The young man stood the shovel on end and contemplated Lucas from his high perch. "I'd be more impressed if you weren't planning to leave my sister."

"Dylan!"

He ignored Charity's protest. "The mulching is one thing. She and I can get that done. But have you considered the future of this farm once you've gone?"

Dylan set his shovel down. With a lurch he propelled himself down the unstable slope, hitting the ground with a loud thump. "This was her dower portion, meant for her and her *husband*." Dylan took a menacing stride closer and Lucas's defensive instincts braced for a fight. "She can't work the place alone and I'm needed at home. Unlike you English blue bloods, we Fergussons don't hire others to work our land. We could if we—"

"That's enough!" Charity's hand shot up, not especially close to her brother's head, but he twitched and stepped away.

"What point is there in a single woman running a farm?" Dylan persisted despite Charity's warning. He thrust a finger in Lucas's direction. "It's a waste of effort, without a family to provide for. We'll end up having to sell the herd before next spring."

"Over my buzzard-pecked bones," Charity murmured.

"Then why mulch the fields?" Lucas's chin came up. Dylan's forefinger irked him as it waggled closer and closer to his face.

"You tell me. Are we working for nothing?" The menacing forefinger made thudding contact with Lucas's sternum.

He stiffened. "Best not touch me again, boy."

"Or what?"

With a groan, Charity stepped between the two men. Placing a hand on each of their chests, she shoved them apart with more force than Lucas thought those slender arms could wield. "Grow up, both of you."

"He can answer my question," Dylan insisted.

"It's none of your business," she told him.

"Yes, it is." Lucas's anger eddied away as quickly as it had come. The Fergussons deserved answers. "It is his business. It's your parents' business. Hell, perhaps it's even Seamus MacAllen's business."

"MacAllister," brother and sister chimed in unison.

"Whatever. The point is, a year ago I made promises.

I took vows. At least, as Luke Martin I did. You all came to depend on me and now . . ."

"Yes, Luke?" Charity's green gaze glittered with the intensity of her desires and prayers. Lucas felt himself drowning in his inadequacy to grant them.

"Well?" Dylan demanded.

"I have no answers. No solutions." He held out his arms. Charity stared at them, so plaintive he thought she might run into them. But no, she didn't move. He dropped his arms to his sides. "Forgive me."

"Why should she?" Dylan asked and turned back to the heap.

Her back to the house, Charity squinted out over the wind-whipped sea beyond the ragged edges of the headland. Her eyes watered in the glistening brightness, yet it wasn't the glare that repeatedly caused her to wipe confounded tears away on the back of her sleeve.

Four days had passed since Luke awakened a different man. Today, Lucas Holbrook, Duke of Wakefield, would leave North Headland Farm, perhaps forever. Charity refused to help him go; she simply would not see him to the door with a smile and an encouraging word. No, if he insisted on saying goodbye, he'd have to seek her out and probably do all the talking besides. She didn't trust what might come out of her mouth.

"Charity."

Ah, right on cue, he rounded the corner of the house. Her name rumbled again from his throat, a low and husky seduction that licked at her female places even as it wrung her heart dry.

"All is ready. I'll be off soon."

Steady gusts blew off the water, whistling against the bluffs. Luke's voice rose to a shout in his effort to be heard. Charity didn't need to hear his words. Their essence engulfed her like a weed-choked tide.

"Won't you speak to me?" He came up beside her and reached for her hand. "I know you think I'm abandoning you."

"What else would you call it?" She hated herself for asking, having vowed not to argue or cajole when he left. She had certainly not meant to whimper.

He studied the tufted grass at his feet. "I must let my family know I'm alive."

"You've already done that in your letter," she said, and cursed the demon that persisted in making her say pointless things.

"The letter should arrive a day or two ahead of me. It will help soften the shock, I hope. I can only imagine what it would do to my mother and grandmother if I simply showed up at the door. They surely believe me dead by now."

"I'd never have given you up for dead. I'd have scoured the globe until I found you." She cringed to hear those words pour from her mouth. Had she no shred of control? Of pride? But her heart refused to believe Luke's English family could love him as she did, yet not have combed all of Britain for him.

"I'm so sorry to have hurt you," he said, and she shrank beneath his pity. "In all of this," he went on relentlessly, "you are the last person who deserves to suffer. I owe you so much."

He raised her hand, and she felt the warmth of his lips for the briefest instant before she yanked away.

"You owe me nothing. Nothing at all."

Reeling, she stomped blindly toward the bluffs, trying to put distance between them. She couldn't bear his well-bred remorse; couldn't stomach his well-meant concern. The brisk wind buffeted her body, whipping her hair and plucking at her skirts with the same persistence Luke's courtesy chiseled away at her heart.

Aching, angry, she fought the wind then fought the hand that clasped her shoulder. She shook Luke off with a sob that met the wind and became part of it, a high, crooning note quickly whisked away.

His arms snared her from behind, locking beneath her breasts. He pulled her to a halt then simply stood immobile while she struggled for freedom, arms flailing, head bent like a charging bull.

"Let me go."

His arms tightened until she felt the pounding of his heart against her spine. Slowly and without loosening their hold, those strong arms turned her against her will—or did she willingly turn to his strength? Ah, Luke. Her Luke.

Like creatures possessed, her arms twined around his neck, reaching, clinging. His hands swept the length of her back and submerged in her hair, clenching fistfuls. A salty musk wafted beneath her nose and danced on her tongue as she pressed her face to his.

Shutting her eyes, she tasted him through parted lips, dragged his essence to her very core. She realized they were stumbling toward the house, felt her back come up against the stones, sharp and biting through her dress. Luke's work-roughened hands cupped her cheeks as though he might plunge from a precipice if he let go. His lips, moist, heated, urgent, roamed her hair, her brow, her face.

"God," he said, his voice breaking.

As though God were listening, the wind gathered and hammered the house, flattening them against it. Luke grabbed her closer. His head came down, filling her vision as the crush of his arms became the entirety of her world. His mouth took hers with a rapacious hunger, savage and bruising. Glorious.

Triumph thundered through her. "You remember."

"No," he rumbled against her lips. "Maybe. I don't know."

Raising on her toes, she cradled her hips against his, finding in an instant the proof she sought. "You want me."

"Yes." The word was a heated vibration imparted through frenzied kisses. He drew her lips into his mouth, captured her tongue with fevered strokes. His hands slid low, molding to the curve of her bottom. Straining the pliant wool of his trousers, his arousal urged completion.

Charity's leg came up around his in an embrace of thigh and knee and calf. She wanted only to wrap herself around him, take him deep inside her, absorb him so he could never leave. Awareness fled. There was only Luke and his fiery kisses, the crushing strength of his body, her trembling reply, the lashing of the wind.

"It's impossible." The declaration tore from his throat; his arms came up and he thrust away from her.

Teetering from the sudden release, Charity clutched at the protruding stones behind her. The chill wind dried her lips, slapping away the feel and scent and heat of Luke. She stared at him in disbelief, in horror.

"I am a duke," he said, as if that explained all, and indeed, perhaps it did. His hand rose toward her face, then hovered, fingertips quivering. "And you . . . are a farmer's daughter."

"A farmer's *wife*." Bitter anger rose, not aimed at Luke but at the fate that had cast them in such different worlds. At the apparent hopelessness of their situation. At Seamus's damned bottle.

"Don't you understand?" His fist clenched until the veins in his wrist stood out in harsh relief. "I am not a farmer. That was not me."

"It was." She moved toward him but stopped when he stiffened as if she posed a threat. "It was you, Luke, without the trappings of nobility. Without the restrictions of your class. Without the title that dictated your life."

Bold, presumptuous words. But she believed them with the entirety of her heart. They had lived and loved and worked side by side for more than a year. She had witnessed his struggles, his triumphs, his greatest joy. In the intimacy of their bed, she had seen his heart, heard the murmuring of his soul. In the core of her being she knew Luke Martin had found what most men search for their whole life long: happiness.

"The fact remains that I cannot stay," he whispered.

"And neither can I be your duchess." It was part statement, part question. In either case, a waste of breath. She knew the answer.

He raised his face to a draft, stealing a ragged breath. "To step into such a role without a lifetime of training would be . . ."

"Aye, I know. Impossible."

"Yes."

She glared until his gaze faltered. "Is this what it is to be noble, Luke? To believe that all things are impossible?"

"It is responsibility." His gaze flicked back to her, a brave scowl that didn't quite conceal his plea for understanding. "It is setting the people in one's care above one's own needs. It is—"

"Turning your back on love." When he didn't deny it, she shoved away from the wall. "Goodbye, Luke. Godspeed on your journey."

"Charity, wait."

She stopped. Only the most Herculean effort held her tears in check. "Aye?"

"I'll . . ." He crossed some of the distance she had put between them but halted just beyond arm's reach. "I intend to fulfill my responsibilities to you."

"How so?" Only part of her cared. Mostly she longed for the privacy of her pillow, where she might let loose the sobs that pinched her throat beyond endurance.

"I intend to provide—"

"Money?"

"Yes. You'll want for nothing."

She grabbed fistfuls of skirt to keep from slapping him. "Listen well, my lord Duke of Wakefield. I neither need nor want a penny of your fortune. Remember that. Remember it well when the annulment papers free you—"

"Charity, don't—"

"When the annulment papers free you to remarry. And when you take a new, noble bride, remember that Charity Fergusson loved and wanted only the man. Not the title. Not the inheritance. Not the connections. Only the man."

She could stand it not another moment. Stumbling through her tears, she groped her way around the house to the kitchen door. There she came to a halt. On the stoop, the rucksack he'd packed for the journey blurred in her vision. Yanking off his sapphire ring and skinning her knuckle in the process, she set it beside the pack.

The kitchen door slammed behind her. Skiff and Schooner lifted their heads from their blanket in the corner, a silent rebuff gleaming from two pairs of obsidian eyes. They resented having been confined to the house this morning, but Charity knew they would have followed Luke all the way to England.

In her weakness, in her pathetic eagerness to hope, she listened for his footsteps. Nothing. No, he would come quietly to the stoop, retrieve his rucksack and trudge down the twisting lane that led to the village road.

Impossible, he'd termed their relationship. She found herself beginning to believe him, felt her resolve crumbling beneath her doubts. Yesterday she had known what she must do. Today she felt helpless to do more than weep into her pillow.

So be it. Today her sorrow might billow and bluster like the ocean winds. Tomorrow, she would dry her eyes and set about restoring destiny to its proper course.

Chapter Six

Holding her skirts to prevent their rustling, Helena Livingston pushed open Longfield Park's front door—solid oak and twice as tall as a man—and tiptoed into the cavernous Grand Hall. The faint hum of voices sent her glance skittering past the open doorways of the salon, study and formal dining hall. A second furtive glimpse crept up the Grand Staircase.

No one in sight.

Like an errant breeze she crossed to the master's study—once Lucas's, now Wesley's. Or was it?

She pressed her ear to the door. Not a sound. Turning the knob slowly, she pushed inward and put her eye to the gap. Beneath the arched mullioned windows, the desk stood unoccupied in broad shafts of morning sunshine. She slipped inside.

The familiar smells of worn leather and stale pipe tobacco helped calm her racing heart. She might not be a Holbrook—yet—but this house and the people in it were part of her, of who she felt herself to be. Ever since her father had taken ill years ago, the two of them had lived in the estate guest house, dependent on the Holbrooks' largesse but never made to feel indebted.

For as long as she could remember, she'd prepared to be the Duchess of Wakefield. Not so very long ago, it had meant a home and security for her, well-deserved peace of mind for her ailing father.

Yet how very much more it had come to mean. Infinitely more. Her heart, her very life, seemed transfixed within these walls. Yet in one terrifying moment she'd gone from future Duchess of Wakefield to just another guest in this house, albeit a well-loved one.

That was yesterday, and all the yesterdays for more than a year. But what of tomorrow?

Filled with an odd mixture of dread and determination, she strode to the desk. Her breath hitched. There it was. The thing she sought lay in plain view atop Wesley's account ledger.

With tremulous fingers she reached for the letter that had arrived yesterday. She brought it to her face, shutting her eyes and experiencing the texture of the parchment on her fingertips and across her cheek. Inhaling deeply, she drew the essence of the paper into her nose and mouth and lungs, hoping for some tangible hint of the writer imparted by the flesh of his hand as he dragged his pen across the page.

She moved beneath the window and held the letter to the sun's rays. Studying each line and curve of the handwriting, she scanned the words until they swam before her eyes.

The details didn't matter. Chills surged up her back. Slipping two cold fingers into the neckline of her morning gown, she withdrew from her bodice another note, written by Lucas just before he'd gone away. She held it

beside the recent one and compared them, something
no one yesterday, in all their distress, had thought to
do.

The cry she only just managed to swallow would surely
have brought the servants and family running. Her teeth
clamped the insides of her cheeks. The pain became her
focus, much safer than either of those letters. Carefully,
she replaced the recent one atop the account ledger. Her
fingers cramped around the other, reducing it to a crum-
ple.

Standing at the foot of Longfield Park's manicured
lawns, Lucas gazed into the moon-cast shadows of the
rambling manor he knew so well. He lingered beneath
the wide canopy of a wych elm amidst a bombardment
of emotions—relief, anxiety, regret—clinging for some
reason that eluded him to this last remaining distance
between him and the life of an aristocrat.

His family would be overjoyed to see him. Relieved,
as he most certainly was. Tearful, probably. Delighted,
without a doubt.

Still, he hesitated. He'd been gone so long. Was he
ready for another drastic change in his life? Had his decision to travel by coach, rather than cutting days from
his journey by sailing the coast, arisen from a disinclination to challenge fate, or something more? A nagging
doubt, perhaps, about the difficulty of stepping back into
the role he'd quitted more than a year ago?

Scotland, and the lovely Charity Fergusson, would always occupy a substantial corner of his thoughts, his
heart. And that was something he could never share with
his family.

*You without the trappings of nobility . . . without the title
that dictated your life.* Her words washed over him, so dis-

tinct it might have been her whisper instead of the cheep-
ing of crickets, the scuffing of small animals, the distant
fountain bubbling in the circular drive.

He could almost feel her arms closing around him,
gently but resolutely pressing his head to a welcoming
bosom. Meltingly warm. Deeply arousing. He couldn't
think what Helena's arms felt like, much less the sensation of laying his cheek against her naked breast.

Good God, the very idea. Helena was an innocent.
Their courtship had been chaste, civilized. Correct.

His mind returned to the other. His wife. Ah, Charity.
He was so sorry. . . .

Lurking in the shadows of his ancestral home, he felt
the tug of that other place, that other life. At his sides,
his hands felt empty, his arms purposeless. They itched
to build, dig, produce. Embrace. Love.

A groan tore from his throat; his hands flew to his
temples as if to crush the traitorous thoughts. Luke Martin
was an aberration. A mistake at best, a disease at worst.
He, Lucas Holbrook, was the Duke of Wakefield. Why
the devil did he skulk alone in a darkened wood?

Yet his next step took him not toward the house, but
further into the forest. Following a path he'd trampled
countless times as a boy, he circled the property, circum-
venting stables, sheds and gardens. Instinct guided him
through timberland to a treeless rise, stark and eerily
still in the moonlight.

The place once held a Celtic hill fort, though most evidence of the wooden stronghold had vanished centuries
ago. With a running start he scrambled up the steep
bank to the raised plateau. Dragging his ankles through
clover, harebell and tufts of betony, he plowed a path to
its center. There he halted, bathed in ripples of light
and shadow as clouds teased the moon.

Stretching out on his back on a pillow of crushed grass,

he listened in vain for the sounds of the sea, for the wisdom cast ashore by foam-flecked waves, sometimes in whispers and sometimes in roars.

Who was he? Lucas Holbrook? Luke Martin? Both? Neither? Arms crossed beneath his head, he searched the inky sky and considered his questions as vast and varied as the stars, his doubts and regrets more so.

Deep breaths laden with the scents of grass and loam soon lulled him into the relaxed state between wakefulness and sleep. It was then he felt her, first as a golden warmth, then as searing ripples of flame, so relentless and unquenchable he all but cried out for mercy. His beautiful, passionate, incomparably sweet Mercy, with fiery hair and sea-goddess eyes.

"May I help you?"

John Mortimer, Longfield Park's steward of nearly three decades, glanced down his large and notably hawkish nose as he poked his head out the front door. Upon discovering Lucas standing on the top step with his battered hat in hand and his rucksack hooked over one shoulder, he snorted. "If you're inquiring after work, go round to the kitchen entrance and ask for Mrs. Hale, the housekeeper. She does most of the hiring."

Lucas thrust out an arm to stop the door from slamming in his face. "Mortimer, old man, don't you recognize me?"

Outrage blazed in the steward's pale blue eyes, while his lips thinned in preparation of a thorough dressing-down.

Lucas couldn't blame him. Why, he looked more like a wandering laborer than a duke in his woolen trousers, homespun shirt and work-worn boots. He should have paused on his way home for a new suit of clothes—

clothes befitting his station. He'd continually found excuses not to.

"It's me, Mortimer. Your long-lost employer."

Peppered eyebrows shot up. The steward's gaze lingered an instant longer on the plaid shirt and baggy trousers before settling on, then boring into, Lucas's face.

His mouth quivered. "Your grace?"

The title felt foreign and cumbersome. Lucas subdued a wince and nodded. "Yes, Mortimer, it's me. Didn't anyone tell you I'd be arriving?"

"Yes, of course. I—I didn't recognize you in those . . . I'm so sorry . . ."

"May I come in?"

The man gasped with the magnitude of his blunder. "Of course, your grace. Do forgive me. How utterly inexcusable."

"Never mind." To Mortimer's great astonishment, Lucas grasped his hand and pumped it like a familiar friend. "It's good to see you again. How have you been?"

"Quite well, sir, thank you for inquiring." The steward flinched. "I mean not at all well, your grace. Not after the appalling news of your . . ."

"Demise?"

"Yes, your grace. Such dreadful business. For all of us. Though no more so than for yourself I'm sure, sir."

"I was lucky, Mortimer. Fate led me to some kind and generous people, without whom I might not be standing here now."

And that reminded him of a matter that needed immediate attention. He found no pleasure in it, quite the contrary, but if he were to embrace his role as Duke of Wakefield, this task constituted the very first of his duties.

Reaching into his pack, he extracted the letter he'd

composed on the journey here. It was a second letter to Jacob Dolan, explaining his marriage to Charity and his need for an annulment.

"Mortimer, it is of the utmost importance that this go out in the next post. It's to my solicitor in London, and, well, I'd prefer the family know nothing about it."

"Your grace can count on me for discretion." The steward tucked the letter into his coat pocket.

A knot twisted in Lucas's stomach, a knot that could only be untied by seizing that letter and tearing it to shreds. His hands fisted around the canvas rucksack. The movement caught his steward's attention.

"Shall I . . . ?" With a look of distaste, Mortimer held out his hands, and Lucas realized the man wished to relieve him of both pack and hat.

"Please. Go ahead and burn them." But a vision flashed of Charity's face crumpled in despondency as she had turned and fled from him that last day. He remembered, too, the tiny sprig of lavender at the bottom of his pack, plucked from beside the kitchen door as he'd retrieved his things and left North Headland Farm forever. His suggestion to Mortimer stung in its callousness. "On second thought," he amended, "put them in my bedchamber."

In former days, Mortimer would have bowed, clicked his heels and embarked upon his errand. Now he lingered, clearly uncertain.

"Something amiss, Mortimer?"

"The matter of your grace's bedchamber. Ah . . ."

"It is still where I left it, I presume?"

"Not exactly, sir. When we finally accepted that, er, your grace would not be returning home, Lord Wesley, ah, moved into the master's chambers."

"Oh. I see. Yes, of course." It came as no surprise that

his brother not only assumed the running of the estate, but inherited the title with all its rights, wealth and privileges. But thinking it and confronting the reality were two very different matters. It made Lucas feel, well, like an intruder in his own home. "And my things? I hope they haven't been disposed of."

"Goodness no, your grace. Your lady mother wouldn't hear of it. They were stored in the attic, but since the arrival of your letter we've been unpacking and having your personal effects cleaned and pressed. All is ready in the Blue Guest room. Temporarily, of course."

"Of course." Scrubbing a hand across his face, he vowed not to worry about it until he'd had a bath, a shave and a hearty meal. "Please send Preston to my—to the Blue Room."

"Ah, yes, Preston. Your valet." Again, Mortimer assumed a moue of perplexity.

"What about him?"

"I'm afraid he's no longer with us, sir. When we—"

"Yes, yes, when you thought I was dead, you let him go. Is that it?" Lucas hadn't meant to sound snappish, but he was beginning to feel as though he'd been erased from life at Longfield.

"He left on his own," Mortimer explained, looking unperturbed by Lucas's retort. "To enter into the service of the Earl of Farnsworth. Until your grace can engage a new valet, I'd be most happy to serve in that capacity."

"I see. Yes, thank you, Mortimer. That will do nicely." With a deep breath, Lucas steeled himself to handle myriad other changes that might have occurred in his absence. "Is the family in residence? They haven't tarried in London past Season, have they?"

"No indeed, your grace." Mortimer looked and sounded scandalized. "No one went down to London this year or last, as we were all in mourning. Ah, and that leads me to another matter."

"Yes?"

"The staff, your grace."

"Mortimer, no offense, but this guessing game is growing rather tiresome. Whatever else you have to tell me, out with it. Please."

"Besides Preston, sir, quite a number of the staff are temporarily away. Since we've held no parties nor entertained guests since your . . ."

"Departure?"

"Yes, sir. It seemed rather absurd to have so many servants about. Of course, we've begun notifying them to return as soon as possible."

"Good. Well done. So then, I'd like to settle in and . . ."

Footsteps echoed against the high ceiling as a plump figure swathed in generous folds of deep amber muslin appeared on the staircase. Lucas felt a tightening in his chest as Dahlia Holbrook descended to the first landing. What his mother must have gone through this past year . . . Though not his fault exactly, guilt thundered like stormy surf.

Oblivious to his presence, she paused to study a spot on the glossy banister. She rubbed her sleeve across it and peered again. Then, rounding the bend in the staircase, she caught sight of Lucas and went utterly still. Even from that distance, he saw the color drain from her face. Her knuckles whitened where they gripped the rail. Eyes as dark as his brimmed to overflowing.

"Lucas. Oh, my dear son." What began as a whisper soared to a resounding croon as she hastened down the remaining steps.

Lucas braced, reminded of the loving attacks of Charity's boisterous Westies. The next moments were a jumble of arms, a torrent of tears. He returned his mother's choking embraces somewhat more gently, patting her back, speaking reassures, doing his best to comfort but knowing his efforts would fall short in the face of a mother's yearlong grief.

"Oh, it *is* you, it truly is." She raised a tear-stained face to him.

"Of course it's me, Mother."

Glancing over her head, he discovered his Grandmother Mary grinning down at him as she too, descended the staircase. Tall and broad-shouldered, heavily draped in black crepe since the day her husband died, Grandmother rarely sported anything so effusive as a grin. Lucas swallowed a lump.

She waited silently for her turn to greet him, a look of calm delight in her deep-set blue eyes. "Now, Dolly, do leave off." She tsked and pursed a mouth bracketed by lines that had deepened in the past year. "You'll drown the poor boy in all those tears."

"Oh, Mama, you mustn't say 'drown'! When I think of what he's endured . . . oh, my heavens. My poor, dear Lucas. Oh!" The tears continued in earnest.

"Mother, please, I'd hoped my letter would——"

"It did." Holding her lace-edged handkerchief to her nose, she made an effort to stem her weeping. "Only—only hearing from you and seeing you with my own eyes after all this time is . . . w-well . . ."

Whatever she meant to say was lost in a round of hiccuping sobs.

Grandmother reached for Lucas's hand and gave it a squeeze. "You do look a little worse for wear, if the truth be told."

"It was a long journey, Grandmother." The hand in his, though still firm of grip, felt thinner and trembled slightly. Her wrist bone protruded, frail and vulnerable, from her sleeve. She looked tired, this grandmother who had never seemed anything less than immortal to him. He kissed her cheek. "I'm tired but quite well, I assure you."

She raised her quizzing glass; its gold chain clinked against the jet buttons of her gown. "What on earth are you wearing?"

"Goodness yes, those clothes." His mother lowered the handkerchief. "Good heavens, what have they done to you?"

"Who?"

"Those awful people who found you and kept you for more than a year without so much as a note to let your poor family know you were alive." Compared to Grandmother, Dolly had changed little; still petite and round, still as sentimental as always.

"No one knew who I was, Mother. But if not for the exceedingly kind family who took me in and nursed me back to health, I might not be alive at this moment."

Too late did he realize his colossal error in judgment. His mother collapsed weeping against his chest. Grandmother tossed up her hands.

The front door opened. "Good God, it really is you."

"It *is*, oh, it truly is."

Wesley and Helena stood side by side on the threshold, eyes as round as full moons, complexions equally as pale.

Lucas grinned. "I do wish everyone would stop saying that. I'm beginning to think you were all expecting someone else entirely."

"Oh, Lucas." Helena's voice caught. Beneath a wide, beribboned bonnet that hid most of her face, her bottom lip, perfect as a cupid's, quivered.

With gentle hands Lucas extricated his mother from his shirt front. "It's wonderful to see you both."

Though Helena seemed rooted to the ground beneath her feet, Wesley strode into the hall. It was the first time in several years Lucas had seen his brother out of military dress, yet his posture, his quick, efficient movements, remained that of a disciplined officer. That is until . . .

Wesley thrust out a hand, pulled it back, raised his arms, let them fall; the poor man looked utterly perplexed.

"I know how you hate to be undignified, Wes, but . . ." Grasping his younger brother by the shoulder, Lucas dragged him roughly into an embrace that involved a good deal of mutual backslapping.

"Still trying to beat me up, then?" Letting go a laugh, Wesley plucked Lucas's shirtsleeve. "Interesting apparel."

"I couldn't recall my tailor's address."

"What about me?" Lifting her skirts above dainty velvet slippers, Helena swept into the hall. "Have you no greeting for an old friend?"

"Helena. My dear."

He paused to take her in, comparing the details with those of his memories. With not-quite-steady fingers she untied the silk ribbon beneath her chin and removed her bonnet. Smooth, even, fashioned by the hands of God Himself, hers were still the most flawlessly beautiful features he'd ever seen.

Yet his heart beat steadily on, and as he searched for even the faintest hint of a freckle, the compass tucked in his trousers made no stirring to the north.

He walked to her and opened his arms. She hesitated a noticeable moment, her gaze flickering over the others. Except for his mother, they were not a family used to displaying their affections publicly. The hall grew quiet but for the echoes of Dolly weeping into her hanky.

Then, with a little laugh, she stepped into his embrace.

One soft hand slid to his shoulder as she planted a kiss on his cheek. He closed his arms around her, more aware of the structure of her bodice with its hidden stays than of the figure beneath.

From over her head he saw Grandmother's keen eyes watching. More was expected of him. A kiss. A real one. After all, he and Helena had been engaged just before he went away. He bent to find her mouth, but she shyly turned and he grazed her hair.

A distinctly nervous chuckle bubbled from her lips. Stepping away, she lost her balance and swayed. Lucas slipped an arm around her waist.

"Don't faint on me now."

High cheekbones flushed a pretty shade of pink. "It's the excitement of seeing you again, Lucas, of having you home where you belong." Timid fingertips stroked his shirtfront. "I am so very happy you've come back to us."

"As are we all," Wesley agreed in an oddly formal tone. The erstwhile officer again?

Lucas studied them. "Is something wrong?"

"Of course not." Wesley clapped his shoulder. "Other than suffering quite a shock. It's rather like having someone rise from the grave, you know."

"Yes, but you mustn't waste a single moment's worry on us." Their mother drew a quaking breath. "You are home. Everything shall be simply splendid now."

Wesley and Helena traded looks. Grandmother's mouth quirked. Lucas felt as if he'd wandered onto a stage smack in the middle of a play, without the faintest notion of the script.

Chapter Seven

A hot bath, close shave and much-needed haircut did much to restore Lucas's spirits. Wearing a suit of clothes appropriate for an afternoon at home in the country, he strolled the east corridor on the ground floor to find his family. He felt like a new man. Or rather, like the man he used to be, a long time ago.

He found them in the conservatory, his mother and Helena tending potted roses, Grandmother and Wesley seated at the iron garden table beneath the skylights at the room's center.

His heels clicked on the mosaic floor, announcing his arrival. His mother waved a pair of clipping shears in the air. "There you are," she called, "and looking so rested and handsome."

His earlier attire had quite shocked her. He tugged at his neckcloth, knotted artfully by Mortimer. The linen itched, but no wonder. He was quite certain he hadn't sported such a cravat in over a year. Still, one of the fringe benefits of being thought dead, he'd discovered, was that upon resurrection one found one's entire wardrobe cleaned, starched and pressed to perfection.

Dolly's dark eyes shimmered as she watched him make his way around a blossoming cherry laurel and a row of azaleas. When her chin quivered Lucas feared the worst, but she steadied her jaw with a visible effort. Snipping a crimson rosebud, she held it out to him.

"Thank you, Mother." He tucked it into the notch in his lapel. "Now my transformation to a gentleman is complete."

"You were never lacking." Helena treated him to a wide smile from above the basket of roses balanced in her arms. She looked quite the blossom herself in full-skirted, pale yellow muslin. She blushed and shifted her fragrant burden. "You do look wonderful, Lucas."

"Won't you lend us a hand." Dolly clipped another rose. Gardening was her passion and the conservatory was a veritable jungle. Potted trees abounded, a maze ranging from domestic dwarfed oaks to imported fruit trees and exotic palms. Racks overflowed with seedlings and riotous bursts of blossoms. Tall, expansive windows overlooked the bowling green and the arbor beyond.

"Your mother is determined to fill the entire house with flowers," Helena said.

"And why not?" His mother selected a deep pink rose and clipped it with a long stem. "We have much celebrating to do, and what better way to begin than decorating the house with flowers?"

"Celebrating?" Lucas didn't trust the look on his mother's face, the one that told him she'd been making plans without consulting him. He frowned while hefting the basket from Helena's arms.

"Of course, darling. We must plan a ball. Immediately. The biggest and most elegant assembly the district has ever seen. Even more splendid than when you and Helena announced your engagement."

Lucas's reaction to his mother's suggestion began with a knot in his gut that quickly rose to pinch his throat. Yet his sense of panic baffled him. He stole a glance at Helena. At the same time, a clacking echoed through the tile and glass room; it came from Wesley, rapping his unlit pipe against the edge of the table.

His mother continued clipping flowers and laying them in the basket. "We'll announce your homecoming and re-announce the engagement all at the same time. My fondest wishes are to come true after all," she concluded with an adoring wink at Helena.

"Mother, I think . . ." Lucas hesitated. What he'd been about to say would not only disappoint his mother, but quite likely wound Helena, who must be as eager as Dolly to proceed with the wedding plans.

Wesley's pipe struck the table again.

"Perhaps, Dolly, we shouldn't rush things," Helena said lightly, fingering the topmost stems in the basket Lucas held. "Lucas has only just arrived home, after all. I'm sure he's exhausted and quite overwhelmed by all that's happened."

"You are exactly right, my dear." He took her hand and studied her. Was she sincere, or had she sensed his hesitancy? Hoping the former, he bestowed a reassuring smile. "I'd like to enjoy my homecoming quietly before the celebrations begin."

"Are you sure, dear?" Dolly looked crestfallen. "As a peer of England, it's your duty to announce your return and resume your duties."

Wesley's pipe came down with a particularly loud thwack. Grandmother reached over and snatched it from him.

"Yes, but what harm in waiting a few weeks at least," Lucas said, "until we all regain our bearings."

"So you're saying you don't want to let anyone know you're back? No one at all?" His mother shook her head, clearly mystified.

Mrs. Hale, red-nosed and swollen-eyed from greeting Lucas earlier, entered the room pushing a cart that rattled over the mosaic tiles. Lucas caught the aroma of the honey-glazed pastries he'd loved since boyhood. His mouth watered.

Setting the basket of flowers at his feet, he offered an arm to Helena and one to his mother. "It isn't every day a duke returns from the dead," he said as he escorted them to the table. "The moment word gets out we'll be swamped with well-wishers, not to mention the hangers-on who'll think to gain some advantage in being the first to welcome me home and offer me their oh-so in-dispensable services. I think we'd all benefit from time alone—just the family—before the crush descends." He looked pointedly at Helena. "To reacquaint ourselves."

"Well, since you put it that way." His mother sighed.

"The boy makes sense," Grandmother said as they took their seats. "No announcement, no party. No fuss until the Duke of Wakefield says so."

Wesley coughed. Manning the teapot, Helena began pouring steaming amber liquid, concentrating as though her life depended on not spilling a drop.

Grandmother waved hers away. "None for me. And nothing sticky either. I'll lose my teeth in one of those." She pointed to the platter of cakes Mrs. Hale placed on the table. "All I want is to look at my grandson, thank you. And I do hope everyone has finally left off weep-ing. He's not dead after all, is he?"

Beside him, Helena sat so perfectly straight her spine didn't touch the cushion behind her. As she sipped her tea, one slender, flawless, never-touched-a-thistle hand smoothed her skirt. "We have a new neighbor."

"Do we indeed?" Lucas smiled at her. "That's a rare thing in Wakefield, isn't it? Or have times changed?"

"No," she said with a tinkling laugh, "we're still as remote as ever, and yes, Miss Williams's addition to the neighborhood is an unusual occurrence. She arrived only a few days ago, intending our little village as a stopover on her journey south to London. However, she said she so appreciated the peacefulness and . . . oh, how did she put it?" She looked to Wesley for assistance.

He stirred his spoon around in his cup. "The unadorned charm of country life, I believe were her words."

"Just so. She's decided to stay on for a month at least. Perhaps the rest of the summer." Helena's bright azure eyes gleamed. "Reverend Nichols directed her to the old vicarage. It's remained empty over the past year, so of course the parish is quite happy to have the rent money."

"So it seems you have a new friend, for the summer at least." Lucas bit into a soft, steaming pastry. "I'm glad for it."

Indeed he was. He often wondered if the beautiful Helena Livingston resented living so far from town and polite society. Not that she ever complained. But with her striking looks and impeccable taste, she should have been the belle of every Season since her sixteenth year. Unfortunately, Helena's appearances at London's spring balls and soirees had been far too few. Her father's ailing health prevented her from all but brief visits to the city.

"She's the dearest creature." Helena set down her cup and laid her hand over Lucas's wrist in the confiding manner he remembered. "Such a lamb. I can't wait for you to meet her."

"It's lovely to have another gentlewoman close by," Dolly agreed. "We'll be sure to have her over often."

"She seems a tolerably intelligent girl," was Grandmother's brisk assessment.

"I look forward to meeting her." Lucas stole a peek at the hand covering his wrist, trying to will Helena's touch to arouse in him something other than the comfort of friendship. It did not.

From inside the house, the grandfather clock chimed. They sipped their tea, all except Grandmother Mary, who stared across at him without apology.

"Your ring." Leaning across the table, she peered at him through her quizzing glass. Lucas's hand burned beneath her probing stare. "Have you lost it?"

"I'm afraid I have, Grandmother." Actually, he'd found it glittering beside his pack on Charity's doorstep the day he left St. Abbs. He'd left it there. In spite of everything, he felt it belonged to her. "And the pocket watch, too. I'm very sorry."

"Oh dear, no." His mother reached for his hand, lifting it off the table as if closer observation might render a different conclusion. "Not Father's ring and the pocket watch too. How unfortunate. How calamitous."

"Now, Dolly, it's nothing of the sort." Grandmother relaxed in her chair but continued to contemplate Lucas in a way that made his neck prickle. "We have Lucas back. The rest are merely trinkets, after all."

"Stolen by those horrid Scottish people, I'll wager."

"No, Mother," Lucas said. "They were most likely lost at sea. I drifted for days, you know."

"My goodness, yes." Her eyes brimmed.

Deuced hell, he used to know how to guard his tongue around his mother, but he seemed to have forgotten how to temper his words. Now whenever he opened his mouth, it was with Scottish straightforwardness rather than English discretion.

"Tell me, how did the spring repairs go?" he asked his brother for the sole purpose of changing the subject. He knew very well a thorough ride around the estate and tenant farms, as well as a perusal of the account ledgers, would tell him everything he needed to know.

"Tolerably well." Wesley made brief eye contact. "The usual fences and roofs, for the most part."

"For the most part?"

Wesley sucked in his cheeks. "The river flooded back in April. Took out a barn, some chicken coops, even a house. Nasty business. Clean-up and repairs took some time."

"Costly, I'll wager."

"Not as bad as it might have been. Everyone did their share." His brother pulled up straighter, his chin outthrust. "The estate is solvent, Lucas. Check the books if you don't believe it."

"I never doubted." He tried to smile but guilt made it a stiff effort. He *had* questioned Wesley's ability to run the estate with the degree of competence required. As a second son he hadn't been trained for it. Lucas had expected to walk into, if not a financial nightmare, at least a good headache or two before he sorted things out.

"I suppose Jacob has been a help?"

Wesley hesitated. "I haven't consulted with Jacob much."

"Why on earth not?"

"Didn't feel I needed to." His brother shrugged. "Never did get on well with him either."

"Now see here." Lucas leaned forward, half wanting to grab Wesley's shirtfront and give him a good shake. "You had to take over under the worst of conditions.

Surely you should have set aside personal feelings for the good of the family instead of behaving like an irresponsible schoolboy."

Everyone went still. He'd clearly overreacted and he could not explain why, nor what made his hackles rise as if someone had pressed a pistol to his back. A clawing unease clutched at him, a sense of something terribly wrong that needed to be discussed with Jacob.

Dolly cleared her throat. Grandmother's gaze shifted back and forth. Helena traced the leaf pattern in the damask tablecloth. Wesley seethed. Lucas regretted not waiting for a more private moment with his brother, but too late for that now.

"I told you the estate is solvent." Wesley clenched his teeth. "I've done a hell of a lot more than give the ledgers an occasional glance."

"Wes—"

But Lucas's intended apology was cut short.

"I almost forgot," Dolly said quickly, plucking a second pastry from the tray, "Jane Anderson—you know, the wife of that nice Roger Anderson who runs the mill—gave birth to twins last month. Little boys. Can you imagine, Lucas? Twins? The poor woman has her hands full, to be sure. Especially since her eldest girl ran off last winter."

"Ran off?" Lucas frowned.

"Why, yes," she replied around a mouthful of cake and honey. "Like so many other young people these days, moving to the cities to seek their fortune. Rumor has it there might have been a young man involved." Dolly made a moue of distaste and licked icing from the end of her finger.

Lucas went still. A name hovered on the tip of his tongue. A girl's name. Molly, Margaret? As he tried to remember, he sensed a rank, low-tide fog closing in around him; a mournful buoy bell clanged in his mind.

"Speaking of runaways," Wesley said between swallows of tea, "did you ever find the Blackstone girl?"

Lucas lurched, jarring the table. The teacups clattered in their saucers. "Blackstone? What was her first name?"

His brother eyed him, brows knitted. "Don't you remember?"

"Of course I don't or I wouldn't have asked." The others traded glances. "Look here, if this has anything to do with my disappearance, please tell me."

"We wanted to allow you more time before anyone mentioned the matter." His mother wiped her hands on her napkin and turned to him. "Mavis Blackstone was a young girl who disappeared just before you did. Her family worked a farm about ten miles outside of Wakefield. One day her mother appeared on our doorstep, begging for your help in finding her daughter."

"Mavis." Lucas rubbed his forehead. "Did I know her?"

"I don't believe so," Dolly replied. "The mother said the girl had been talking about seeking employment in London. Someone had been putting ideas in her head, it would seem. But when Mrs. Blackstone began making inquiries, she discovered her daughter had boarded a northeastern bound coach, headed toward the coast. Accompanied by a man." She pursed her lips.

"So I went after her, just like that?" Lucas held out his hands, but no answers fell into his open palms.

"You agreed to help," said Grandmother. "You believed you would be able to trace the girl, being only a day or so behind. We advised you to take someone along, but you said you'd travel swifter alone."

"What about her father?"

"Mrs. Blackstone is a widow, dear."

"Where does she live? I'd like to speak with her."

His mother shook her head. "When so much time passed without word from either you or the daughter, Mrs. Blackstone lost heart. We all did," Dolly added, her eyes moist with regret. "Anyway, Mrs. Blackstone took her remaining children and moved away. We don't know where."

"This solves the mystery as to why I went to the coast, but not what happened once I arrived." Frustrated, Lucas slouched in his chair and watched steam rise from his cup. "How did I end up on a ship, lost in a storm?"

Puzzled looks traveled around the table. "That we couldn't say, I'm afraid," Helena said. She slipped her hand into his. "We didn't know anything about a ship until we received your letter from Scotland. Until then, we'd no idea what had happened to you. We simply . . . accepted that you weren't coming home after several months with no word."

"And you moved on with your lives." He pushed a breath between his teeth, more conscious than ever of the time lost, never to be recovered.

"Moved on with our lives?" Wesley's mouth pulled to a sardonic slant. "Hardly. Some of us pared our lives down to nothing and began again."

Anger brewed in Wesley's eyes, along with a simmering resentment that took Lucas aback. Had being Duke of Wakefield meant so much to Wesley, that he'd rather his own brother had remained in the grave?

"Wesley, don't," Helena pleaded as she chased the younger Holbrook brother down the terrace steps. "Don't do this to yourself."

"Don't do what?" Without breaking his stride, he skirted a box hedge and veered into the rose garden, barely missing Dahlia Holbrook's prized Gallicas. "Don't rant? Don't carry on? Don't wish to strangle someone with my bare hands—"

"Don't say that," she cried. "Do not say what you surely don't mean."

That brought Wesley up short just beyond the marble fountain. Panting, he glared at the placid-faced cherub whose task it was to pour water from a Grecian urn into the basin at his dimpled feet. Wesley looked about to strike a smooth, plump cheek.

Helena slowed to a walk, afraid he might dash out of reach again. But his angry gaze dwindled to a noxious simmer as she reached him.

"I don't mean it," he said to his feet. "I'm happy he's alive, by God I am. I love my brother. But Helena . . ."

She took his hand, hoping to calm him. "I understand your frustration, but none of this is anyone's fault, least of all Lucas's. Don't forget he lost more than a year of his life."

His fingers closed tightly around hers. "I altered my entire life, gave up a damned promising military career to come home and take up duties I knew little of and cared less about."

"You got on remarkably well," she reminded him with an attempted smile.

"Yes. It was no easy task but I learned. I worked hard to keep the estate profitable, the village secure. And along the way I discovered a love for this place, a connection I never experienced as a boy."

"Yes. It's what made you such a good duke. We're all very proud of you."

He tugged his hand free. "Such praise rings hollow when the recipient outlives his usefulness. What is there for me now? No longer Major Wesley Holbrook, no longer Duke of Wakefield, no longer . . ."

"Wesley, don't," she repeated but trailed off, silenced by his scowl.

"Damn it all, perhaps Wesley should." He nodded as though continuing the conversation with someone Helena could neither see nor hear. "Perhaps once and for all, Wesley will."

With a bow that held far more bitterness than deference, he stalked off across the lawns sloping toward the stables. Within moments, she knew, he'd be mounted and speeding through the forest, searching out boulders, fallen limbs, rushing streams, and any other scenario that might result in a broken neck.

Stubborn man. She fretted over his parting words. Exactly what did he think it was time to do? She shivered despite the afternoon warmth. Was his tirade all bluster, or should she warn the family that their son and brother, trained to be a warrior, was fast becoming a keg of gunpowder waiting to explode?

At dawn the next morning, Lucas gratefully abandoned a fruitless effort to sleep. A wan glow seeped through his bedroom windows, outlining the imposing twin wardrobes that held his belongings.

As he opened the first, an eerie sensation took hold. He ran a hand over the glossy oak finish, cupped the brass knob in his palm, tested the resistance of the hinges. Damned fine quality, but nothing extraordinary. Why did it feel so familiar, as if he'd built it, or one like it, with his own hands?

He chuckled. Carpentry hadn't been high on his tutors' lists of subjects. He'd spent his childhood absorbed in much more practical pursuits. Translating Greek into Latin, for instance.

Forgetting the cabinet, he instead contemplated its contents. The quantity took him aback. Good heavens, he owned enough white shirts to clothe an entire village. And the trousers: black, buff, brown, black, buff, brown, black, black, black . . .

He'd never before considered the extent of his wardrobe, never realized the enormous waste that went into dressing a duke. Yet for all that, nothing here suited his purposes this morning.

It was no gentlemen's ride about the estate he intended. His restlessness required a good tramp across fields and farms, through wet grass and muck alike. He knew what Longfield looked like from the safety of his saddle. Today he'd learn the feel of it beneath his own feet. Tossed over a footstool were the work clothes he'd worn on his journey from Scotland. He quickly put them on.

Outside, the morning air slapped his cheeks, yet when he drew it into his lungs, he grimaced at its flatness, its lack of North Sea brine.

As he headed toward the south, where the largest of the tenant farms lay, he searched for rugged headland but found only smooth meadows marked by hedgerows. He listened for gulls amid the chirps of sparrows and warblers. He ached for the sound of one voice in particular. . . .

Helena. He must think of Helena. Beautiful and kind and expecting to be his bride. It had been understood for years, since long before the engagement made it official. They were the perfect couple—everyone said so. With Helena as his duchess, he'd be the envy of England. And surely, after all she'd endured in her life—her mother's early death, her father's illness, the loss of their fortune, Lucas's own disappearance—she deserved her happy ending.

He loved her. Truly he did.

But was he *in* love with her? The thought brought him to a dead halt. He'd never asked himself that before. Had never stopped to consider the difference.

What about the fact that he was already married? Having not been of sound mind when he took those vows, did they count? The law would say no. Even the church would agree. His family . . .

Would be horrified. Just as they had recoiled at the sight of his farmer's clothes yesterday, they'd shrink from Charity, a farmer's daughter.

A farmer's wife.

If he thought coming home would erase her from his mind, he'd been horribly mistaken. Everywhere he went, in everything he did, he saw her, felt her, *tasted* her—like a spice permeating the air he breathed.

His only defense against the lustful memories was to feebly chant the name Helena, a reminder of where his first loyalties lay.

Much later than he'd intended, Lucas slipped back into the house through a mud room off the kitchen. Hoping not to attract the staff's attention, he stole into the service hallway. In the kitchen, Cook presided with a long wooden spoon over a simmering pot, issuing orders in a brisk voice that set a handful of maids into motion. An assortment of covered dishes occupied the counters and spilled onto the oak table in the center of the room.

All for an ordinary lunch? Or were they expecting company?

Blast.

With two long strides he stole past the doorway. Making it to the top of the service staircase without being seen, he was about to shoulder his way through the door that opened onto the main part of the house when voices on the other side stopped him.

"What do you mean, you don't know where he is," said an irritated Wesley.

"I'm very sorry, sir." Mortimer sounded frustrated, beleaguered. "His grace must have left before anyone was up this morning. He left no note as to his whereabouts."

"Oh dear," a female voice fretted, "don't tell me he's disappeared again."

"Don't worry, Mother, I'm certain *his grace* will turn up eventually." There was no mistaking the derision in Wesley's voice. "I'm surprised I didn't spot him on my morning rounds. Though why his steward should have no knowledge of his daily schedule is beyond me."

"I have received no schedule as of yet, my lord."

Not about to let anyone bully his longtime, not to mention faithful, servant, Lucas pushed through the door.

"Looking for me?"

"Ah, Lucas. There you are." His mother's relieved expression quickly dissolved. "What on earth are you doing in those clothes again?"

"Didn't see any sense in ruining a good suit."

"You'd never catch me traipsing about like a woodsman," Wesley said.

Lucas wondered at the hostility that had sprung up between them. There had always existed a rivalry, but their separate pursuits in life had for the most part prevented them from clashing. What the blazes would keep them from clashing now? "No?" he challenged. "Do you ever deign to dismount from your horse when you make your rounds?"

"As a matter of fact, yes. Did you ever?"

"Touché," Lucas replied after a second's hesitation. Wesley interacting with the local population? He'd never have guessed. "I believe I will from now on."

"Come to think of it, I did see you earlier." Wesley studied Lucas's attire. "I remember the plaid shirt now, though at the time it didn't occur to me you might be traveling in disguise again. Weren't you chopping wood at the Whitely place?"

"Oh, my."

He ignored his mother's sigh. "Indeed I was."

Wesley merely shook his head.

"Do you think it seemly, dear, to be seen abroad in such attire?" His mother's tone chided gently, stopping just short of an open admonishment. "You are the duke, after all, and must make an example for those beneath you."

"I don't consider Tom Whitely beneath me, Mother." He meant it, although until this morning he might never have made such a statement, much less thought it. "In fact, Tom didn't recognize me. He thought I was passing through and looking for work, and he talked to me man to man, as an equal. I found it one of the most rewarding conversations I've ever had."

"Tom Whitely," Wesley murmured almost absently. His eyes narrowed. "His is one of the smallest of the tenant farms."

"Indeed, he should consider expanding," Lucas agreed. "I noticed that more of his acreage lay fallow than should. Perhaps now that I'm home . . ." He stopped short of offering his suggestion of a small stipend for Mr. Whitely, noting Wesley's scowl at once more having his competence as duke questioned. "Well, if you'll all excuse me, I'll change into something less offensive."

And far less comfortable.

As he started for the staircase, he pulled out several shillings from his pocket. "Make sure this gets back to Tom," he said to Mortimer, dropping the coins into his steward's hand. "But don't let him know where it came from. Let him think he overpaid his rent or something to that effect."

Mortimer smiled with surprise. "I shall, your grace."

"Oh, Lucas," his mother called after him. He paused on the fourth step. "Do change quickly. Helena's father is eager to see you. And we have a guest from the village. That delightful Miss Williams."

With Mortimer's help, he changed and returned downstairs in twenty minutes looking quite the country gentleman in an emerald green cutaway, matching waistcoat and one of those infernally white shirts. Once again, the neck cloth itched. Coughing, he hooked a forefinger into the restricting cravat and tugged.

Little discomforts aside, he looked forward to seeing Joshua Livingston, who'd been like an uncle to him all his life. Their fathers had been boyhood friends, attended the same college at Oxford and remained inseparable into adulthood.

Several years before Lucas's father passed away, Sir Joshua lost a considerable sum in a risky investment with an American trading company. The proprietors claimed pirates intercepted the ships, but Lucas suspected something far less exotic. Unfortunately, since British law no longer held sway in the New World, Sir Joshua found little recompense. He had sought a speedy way to increase his fortune. Instead he lost most of it and, being a second son, had no family estate to fall back upon.

The shock affected his health; soon afterward Joshua Livingston suffered a seizure from which he never fully recovered. He and his daughter had lived here on the estate ever since.

Entering the drawing room, Lucas saw his mother, brother, Grandmother and Helena grouped near the hearth. Sir Joshua occupied one of the spacious wing chairs. A fifth individual, identified only by the top of a wide-brimmed hat ablaze with tiny silk flowers, perched on the settee with her back to Lucas. Ah, the celebrated Miss Williams.

Sir Joshua let out a faint snore, his heavy-jowled face lolling to one side. The poor man often dozed at gatherings, sometimes right in the middle of a sentence. Lucas decided to allow the man his short nap.

His mother saw him and beamed, all traces of her earlier disapproval gone. She gestured with one hand toward the person on the settee, her smiling lips parted in readiness to make the introductions.

If his mother spoke at all, Lucas didn't hear a word of it. As he rounded the settee, a sweet waft of lavender filled his nose. At the same time, he caught sight of Miss Williams's profile beneath her hat brim: the tip of her nose, the curve of her chin, the blush of a plump, candied morsel of a bottom lip.

Even as his mind denied the possibility, astonishment hurtled like a fist to his abdomen, knocking the breath from his lungs.

Helena appeared at the corner of his vision. "Lucas, do come and greet our dear Miss Williams. She is so looking forward to meeting you."

On the settee, dressed in a voluminous gown of pink and ivory lawn, holding a fluffy West Highland terrier in her lap and drowning Lucas in the depths of her sea-goddess gaze, sat Charity Fergusson Martin.

Chapter Eight

Charity gulped, attempting to swallow a mouthful of panic. As her pulse took off at a wild gallop, her vision narrowed until the room and everything in it blurred to a halo surrounding Luke.

Sweet mercy, he was beautiful. Tall, broad, darkly masculine. And even in that fussy suit, still rugged, still a sleek containment of the restless power that stole her breath. An image of what lay beneath the suit flashed in her mind. Her body thrummed in anticipation of . . . pleasures she might never again know.

Breathe, she thought. *Smile. Return his greeting.*

If he ever made one.

Was that shock stealing the color from his face? Utter joy? Or the most abject fury she'd ever encountered?

A muscle in his cheek twitched. Deep brackets flanked a mouth gone rigid.

No, not joy. Perhaps not fury, but certainly not approval either. Schooner dozed in her lap, and she resisted the urge to hug him tight to shield the life inside from the storm threatening to break.

Instead, she clasped her hands, feeling the bulge of Luke's ring beneath her glove. She tried to glean comfort from it, courage. It meant something, didn't it, that he'd left it behind the day he left St. Abbs?

His lips parted and she heard the beginnings of her name as his tongue grazed the roof of his mouth. "Ch . . ." came out on an exhalation. Her flesh went cold. Was he about to divulge her identity? Expose her as a fraud? Introduce her as his wife?

At that moment, Schooner boosted his shaggy head. Spotting Luke, he let out a piercing yip and hurtled to the floor before Charity could restrain him. An instant later, Skiff, who'd been sniffing at the terrace doors, streaked from behind Sir Joshua's chair. Discovering the source of his brother's excitement, Skiff yelped and bounded toward Luke, his small but sturdy feet barely skimming the rug.

Oh, dear, perhaps it had been a mistake to bring them. Perhaps this entire plan constituted one monumental, disastrous mistake.

"Will you look at that." Luke's mother, the dowager duchess, watched in astonishment as the Westies launched a loving attack upon her son's ankles. "One would think those dogs *knew* Lucas."

Miss Livingston's father awoke with a lurch. With bleary eyes he surveyed the scene. "What's all the racket?"

"Miss Williams's little dogs appear to be instantly enamored of Lucas, Father." Miss Livingston laid her hand on her father's shoulder and enunciated in a loud voice. "You do remember my telling you that Lucas had returned home, don't you, Father? Here he is."

But Sir Joshua's eyelids were already drooping. Miss Livingston cast him a resigned but fond look. As if she weren't dressed in airy muslin of the finest quality, she crouched and opened her arms to Skiff and Schooner.

Charity winced. Surely the Englishwoman would shrink from their messy kisses and coarse white hairs clinging to her costly skirts.

Peals of laughter filled the room when Schooner landed an especially wet lick beneath Miss Livingston's chin. She gathered both Westies to her, heedless of the consequences to her gown. "We insisted Miss Williams bring them today," she said, looking up at Luke, "rather than leave them cooped up at the vicarage. Aren't they the most adorable creatures you've ever seen?"

"Priceless," he murmured through a pinched mouth.

Depositing the dogs gently back to the floor, Miss Livingston rose to her feet. "Lucas, aren't you going to greet our dear Miss Williams?"

Charity would never know how legs as boneless as wet twine supported her as she stood. Nor could she have explained where she found the composure to curtsy, reach out her hand and say in the steady English she'd practiced on her journey there, "Your grace, a pleasure. Your family has told me so much about you."

He flinched at the sound of her voice, angling his head as if trying to hear her better. Each word she spoke acted as a thread tightening his facial muscles.

She flicked a gaze around the room, gauging the re- actions of the others to Luke's strangely mute behavior. Wesley merely raised an eyebrow. Lady Mary watched with a shrewd expression. Charity had quickly learned that the elderly woman, though often reticent, missed little.

"Lucas?" Miss Livingston took hold of his arm.

At the sight of the Englishwoman's familiarity, ratio- nal thought fled. Something hot, as bitter as bile, rose up inside Charity, sickening, strangling. She used every ounce of willpower to stand unflinching before the man she loved while he stood beside the woman *he* loved. At that moment she could have done Helena Livingston harm. Oh, yes, the desire felt as real as anything she'd ever experienced.

The Englishwoman had far exceeded Charity's worst expectations. Poised, polished and protected from the sun since birth. Oh, curse the fate that had bestowed the perfect Miss Livingston with the right to link her arm through Luke Holbrook's with the fondness of a wife while she, common Charity Fergusson of the freckles and unruly hair, must address him as a stranger.

At Miss Livingston's prompting, Luke shook his head as if to dismiss a bad dream. From beneath hooded lids, his eyes glittered darkly. "Miss Williams. I'd welcome you to Longfield, though having only recently returned myself after a lengthy absence, I hardly feel equal to the task."

Miss Livingston barely suppressed a gasp. "Lucas, what an odd thing to say."

The dowager duchess hastened to her son's side. "Odd indeed, Lucas, dear. Longfield Park is your home and always will be."

He gave no sign of acknowledgment, but continued staring unblinking questions and accusations at Charity.

"You mustn't feel strange or out of place here," his mother went on with a note of urgency. She offered Charity a weak smile. "My son has been through a terrible ordeal, Miss Williams. I'm afraid he might not quite be himself yet."

"Do leave the boy alone, Dolly. He's tired." Pushing her tall frame away from the mantle, Lady Mary stepped forward with a rustle of black taffeta. "I'm certain Miss Williams quite understands."

"Yes, please don't apologize." Charity started to add that she didn't need or wish to be treated as a guest, but Luke cut her off.

"Indeed, Mother, you needn't make apologies for me.

I am perfectly capable." He inclined his head toward Charity. "Forgive me, Miss Williams, I misspoke my sentiments. I hope I did not offend."

"Indeed not, your grace." She tried to smile, but nothing in his countenance encouraged her effort.

No, his expression made her want to squirm, bite her nails, burst out crying. She fisted one hand within the folds of her gown and swallowed. Her baby—their baby—needed her to be strong.

"I do look forward to becoming better acquainted," he said, his voice a cold, smooth sickle gliding back and forth across her heart. "I'd be fascinated to learn just how on earth you found your way to our little hamlet. And why."

"Lucas . . ." Clearly mortified, Miss Livingston dug her fingers into his arm.

But what would beautiful Helena Livingston say if she knew the answer to Luke's question? A chill grazed Charity's shoulders.

"Yes, well, we shall all become better acquainted now that Lucas has returned home." Dahlia Holbrook fingered the cameo brooch at her throat. "You know, Miss Williams, Lucas was quite deprived of polite society this past year. Oh, when I think of those horrid Scottish people who practically kidnapped him—"

"Kidnapped him?" Charity's hands started for her hips. This was the first she'd heard of that theory and it rankled, especially after all she'd done to encourage Luke to find his family.

"I wouldn't put it quite that way," Luke replied.

"Oh, I would," said his mother. "Keeping him from us for so long without a single note to let us know he was alive—I never."

"As I've already told you, Mother, they didn't know who I was."

"Bah! Did they ever attempt to find out? I think not. And we needn't wonder why. They'd have to be daft not to recognize an English nobleman when they saw one. They were plotting, those dastardly Scottish—"

"Oh, Dolly, do leave off the dramatics." Lady Mary brushed at imaginary specks on her gown. "Lucas is home. For that we should be grateful and stop questioning how and why. If he says those people didn't know who he was, they didn't know."

The room fell to an uncomfortable silence, broken only by the sounds of the dogs stumbling over one another as they sniffed Lucas's shoes and pawed his ankles.

Lady Mary certainly knew how to intimidate when she wished, Charity thought. Yet she felt no fear of the elderly woman. If anything, she admired the rare combination of sharp wit and frugal tongue. Not one to waste words, Lady Mary could stress a point with an adamant look or a twitch of those wide, straight shoulders.

Strolling to the window, Wesley Holbrook let out a huff that held both exasperation and amusement. A moment later, the man who'd been identified to Charity as Mr. Mortimer, the Holbrooks' steward, appeared in the doorway. "Your grace?"

"Yes," Luke and Wesley said as one. As if controlled by the same set of strings, their faces swerved toward each other and their gazes locked.

Their instant reaction sparked the air like stud rams colliding. The others flinched, but Charity experienced a moment of understanding. Luke had not returned home to find his life exactly as he had left it. Situations had changed, and the people, too. And that might work to her advantage.

Mr. Mortimer fidgeted. "Luncheon is ready."

"Not a moment too soon," Lady Mary said. "I for one am famished. You may all stand here debating pointless matters or you may accompany me to the dining room. Mortimer, escort the hounds into the kitchen. I'm sure Cook can find something to their liking. Helena, dear, wake your father but don't tell him he was snoring. It'll only upset him. Wesley."

At her barked command, Luke's younger brother marched to her side and offered his arm. Prompted by his daughter's gentle shaking, Sir Joshua sputtered and woke with a start.

"Time for luncheon, Father," Miss Livingston said. "Our first meal all together with Lucas. Isn't it wonderful?"

"Lucas?" The elderly man scratched his chin as if hearing of Luke's return for the first time. Bouncing his considerable bulk forward in his chair several times, he managed, with his daughter supporting him, to come to his feet. He noticed Charity and bid her good morning. Then his hazy curiosity drifted to Luke.

"Yes," he concluded, "Lucas it is. Good to have you back, my boy. That shipwreck story turned out to be a load of rubbish, didn't it? Thought so. No one listens to me." Turning to his daughter, he leaned a beefy hand on her shoulder. "Where are we going?"

"To the dining room, Father," she replied, bearing his weight against her but showing no sign of discomfort. "Time for luncheon."

"Come, Joshua." Luke's mother lifted his ivory-inlaid cane from beside his chair. Placing it in his hand, she waited while he established his balance. Then she slid her hand into the crook of his elbow as though it were she and not he that needed to be guided.

Charity's respect for the duchess rose several notches. She would not have thought the frivolous woman capable of such insightful tact.

"You may escort me, if you please, sir," Dahlia Holbrook said.

"A pleasure, madam."

That left Charity with Luke and Miss Livingston. Not intending to wait to be snubbed, she moved to follow the others. Luke stopped her.

"Kindly allow me to escort two lovely ladies to luncheon, Miss Williams."

Miss Livingston beamed with approval. Yes and why not? He played the gallant for her sake. Charity obliged by slipping her hand around his arm, watching out of the corner of her eye as Helena did the same at his other side.

The very feel of him had changed. His posture, his stride, even the slant of his chin all seemed rehearsed as if in front of a mirror. Gone was the cocky humor, the good-natured boldness. Poise had replaced the easy-going appeal that had won him so many friends in St. Abbs.

Though she walked bravely at his side, the beginnings of despair blew a cold breath across her heart. Was it within her power to summon Luke Martin from the depths of this indifferent stranger?

Following supper that evening, Lucas retreated to the privacy of the Blue Guest room. Tucked beneath his arm were the estate diary and account ledgers for the past year and then some. Settling into an overstuffed chair by an open window, he lit a lamp and began poring over the records of the last year's wool and mutton yields. In a relatively short time he concluded that Wesley had done well enough after all. The accounts balanced, the totals revealed profits.

But beyond the basic figures, he deciphered little else as his eyes blurred over the pages. In the back of his mind, a sense of having left something unfinished nagged. What was he forgetting? Part of it, surely, it had to do with his disappearance and its connection to the young Mavis Blackstone.

But other, quite different thoughts occupied his mind at the same time. Confound Charity Fergusson for turning his world on end—again. What game was she playing, showing up in his home with her fancy clothes and aristocratic airs? Even her Scottish brogue had dissipated like so much mist. Had it ever been real? Had anything about her ever been true?

His gut clenched around pinching knots of anger . . . and desire. Because yes, damn it, the very sight of her today had all but obliterated his nobleman's dignity and left him a seething, sizzling mass of lust. He was ashamed to admit it but there it was, a galling, unpalatable reality.

He'd been taken in, pure and simple. At the thought of their last moments together in Scotland, his fingers shook with rage . . . and passion, God help him. Ah, her declarations of love had very nearly brought him to his knees that day; had damned near convinced him he belonged with her and to hell with England and titles and responsibility.

Fool. Insufferable lackwitted fool, to have been so duped. He supposed it only a matter of time before she made her demands, whatever they were, though it didn't take a genius to recognize a fortune hunter.

He slapped the estate records onto the table beside him. Brooding would gain him nothing. Neither would holing up in his room and agonizing over the spurious Charity Fergusson. It would only drive him mad.

He went downstairs, seeking his family. They'd be on the terrace outside the drawing room, where they gathered nightly in fine weather.

His taut nerves settled as he crossed the drawing room. Their voices, so comforting in their familiarity, wafted in snippets through the open doors and windows. Oh, they would probably toss worried looks at him, as they'd been doing since his arrival home. He could endure that now, because if nothing else at least their concerns were sincere. Sincerity had taken on a whole new importance for him today.

An instant before he reached the threshold, however, something coherent took shape from the disembodied fragments of conversation. Much to his chagrin, the discussion centered on him.

He paused to listen, slipping into a shadow beside the doorway.

"Lucas barely spoke two words to her as we walked her back to the vicarage." Helena's voice dipped to a murmur. "I could do nothing to draw him out. He was most perplexing."

"And when he did speak to Miss Williams earlier," his mother said, "it was to utter such inexcusable things."

"Yes, even I found him downright rude." His brother's footsteps echoed against the outer walls. "But his arrogance is no surprise really, is it?"

"Wesley, what an ungenerous thing to say." Lucas saw the flash of satin hems as Helena whirled to scold his brother. "After all Lucas has been through, to disparage his character is not in the least bit fair."

Thank you, my dear.

"Don't blame me for raising the subject."

"We are concerned about him," their mother said defensively.

"As am I." Lucas heard the flare of tinder followed by the pungent fragrance of tobacco smoke. "Perhaps that blow to the head never thoroughly healed."

Why, that whelp. Go on, Helena, my dear, defend me again. Don't let him get away with that.

"Oh, Wesley . . ."

Lucas pricked his ears.

"I fear you may be right."

What?

A firm tug on his lapels helped gather his dignity as he stepped onto the terrace. Helena visibly winced at his unexpected appearance. His mother expressed her surprise with a faint "Oh," and Wesley let loose one of his sardonic chuckles, the sound becoming increasingly odious with each occurrence.

"Good evening, everyone."

They traded swift glances.

"Lovely night. Just look at those stars. Has Grandmother retired already?"

Helena nodded and looked away. His mother became quite concerned with smoothing her sleeves, adjusting her bodice. Wesley pulled several long draws on his pipe.

Lucas walked out among them. "Your concern for me is touching but I assure you, quite unnecessary."

"Lucas, we're sorry to have spoken behind your back. That was wrong of us." His mother touched his arm. "But we are a bit troubled. You haven't been yourself at all."

"Perhaps not. But that doesn't mean I'm one sheep short of a herd."

"Pardon?"

"Never mind." He tugged his collar. The damned neckcloth pressed his throat like a yoke. Swallowing, he worked the knot loose until Mortimer's handiwork dangled on either side of his collar.

Helena watched him, her mouth curling in a perplexed sort of smile. His mother frowned. Only then did he remember that a gentleman, even one enjoying the relatively relaxed atmosphere of his country home, did not remove his cravat in the presence of ladies.

"Sorry. It's been a while since I've worn one of these wretched things."

His mother's mouth pursed, no doubt in unspoken censure of those awful Scottish people who neglected to provide her son with proper attire during the months of his captivity. She and Helena traded glances as if to say, *No, he's not at all himself.* Leaning on the low terrace wall, Wesley watched them through a haze of smoke rings.

"We surely don't mean to criticize," his mother said. "Your clothes and how you wear them are your own affair." Her pained expression declared the opposite. "But, Lucas dear, the way you behaved toward our dear Miss Williams . . ."

Ah, finally, a matter worth discussing. "Yes, 'our dear Miss Williams.' Just what do we know about the young lady?"

"Why, Lucas," Helena said, "you sound as though we have reason to suspect Miss Williams's character."

We most certainly do! It was a bellow inside him, tamped only by the amount of explaining he'd have to do afterward. How could he reveal Charity's deceit without divulging his own?

"Before we take someone into our home and hearts," he said, trying his best to sound rational, "we should know a little something about them. Don't you find it odd, for instance, that our dear Miss Williams seems to have been traveling alone?"

"Ah ha." Helena tossed her hands in the air. "That surely brands her a criminal."

"Would you travel alone?"

"Well, no." She tipped her head to one side. "But my circumstances are quite different."

"How so?"

"I have my father. I have Dolly here and Lady Mary. You and Wesley." She linked her arm through his mother's and raised her eyebrows at him.

"We think Miss Williams must be all alone in the world," his mother confided in an undertone. "No family to speak of, no one to see to her interests, poor dear."

"Quite right." Helena nodded with certainty. "We've seen it before. Remember that adorable Miss Burns who became penniless when her father was forced to leave both title and fortune to a male cousin? It's shameful how the laws of this country so often disinherit those most in need."

"And you believe this has happened to Miss Williams?" Lucas wanted to shake some sense into sweet, trusting Helena.

"Isn't it obvious?"

"No."

"Lucas, use your common sense. She's such a sweet, well-bred young lady." His mother held out her hands, palms down. "Have you noticed how she never removes her gloves, not even to dine? Such genteel manners are becoming quite the rarity nowadays."

"Perhaps she is hiding calluses."

"Lucas, the very idea." Helena tsked and rolled her eyes. "You really are being abominable. Miss Williams is a gracious, gentle, completely harmless soul. You'll soon see how ridiculous you're being. Why, just yesterday you were happy we had a new friend so close by. What on earth happened between then and now to so change your opinion?"

What happened? Why, he learned that gracious, gentle, *harmless* Miss Williams was perpetrating a fraud against his family and making fools of them all. He discovered the woman he left grieving in Scotland, whom he had believed a blameless victim of circumstance, had recovered her composure in record time in order to chase him down and . . . well, he'd learn soon enough what— or how much—she wanted.

Worst of all, he'd learned that, in spite of those particulars, the very sight of her set his lust frothing and seething with volcanic intensity.

He hated that she did that to him.

"You see, Lucas, you can't even devise an answer." Helena shook her head at him, in effect tossing him into the category of hopeless dolt. "Miss Williams's situation is truly lamentable. The poor dear can't even afford a maid."

"It's an outrage," his mother agreed, her expression grave. "And she bears it so bravely."

"Yes, it's an inspiration how cheerful she remains in her adversity."

"We must simply adopt her, that's all. Convince her to remain in Wakefield where we can see to her well-being."

"Oh, Dolly, what a splendid idea." Helena threw her arms around the other woman. "That's just what we'll do. And I've another idea. Why not send Mrs. Hale's daughter, Esther, down to the vicarage each day to see to Miss Williams's needs?"

"Oh, but do you think Miss Williams will accept such a gesture? We wouldn't want to wound the dear child's pride."

"Hmm." Helena tapped a finger against her bottom lip. "Supposing we told her Esther is new at being a maid and very shy, and we thought her training would best be accomplished away from the bustle of the manor."

"I do love the way your mind works." Dolly rubbed her hands together. "You're positively devious when you wish to be."

Lucas swallowed a sigh. They'd made up their minds about Charity and nothing he could say—short of the incriminating truth—would dissuade them. They would only think him hard-hearted. Ungallant. A cad.

He tipped a little bow. "If you'll excuse me, perhaps a short stroll before retiring might help clear the misconceptions from my poor, deluded brain."

He started to turn away then stopped. How could he have forgotten to ask Helena along? Guilt prickled his scalp. It seemed he'd lost his manners along with his memory during his time away.

"Will you join me, my dear?" He held out his hand.

She hesitated before taking it and giving it a squeeze. "No, thank you. I'll keep Dolly company a while longer. Wesley can walk me home. Won't you, Wesley?"

From his perch on the wall, Wesley launched several sweet-scented smoke rings into the air. "At your service."

"If you're certain." A sense of relief made Lucas ashamed.

Helena smiled. "I'll see you tomorrow, won't I?"

"Of course." He raised her hand to his lips. "Good night, then, my dear. Mother. Wesley."

Walking into the shadows beyond the terrace lanterns, he let his feet choose his direction. They took him through the woods to the Celtic hill fort. With a running start he scrambled up the side of the mound.

And there she was, standing at the top.

Chapter Nine

As though she had been waiting for him, her mouth quirked with a notable lack of surprise. A lantern glowed on the ground at her feet, the grass carefully trampled flat beneath and around it. Her hair flowed unbound down her back, its spiraling ends catching the golden light. The pink and ivory gown she'd worn to luncheon had been replaced with a simple green skirt and linen chemise. Exactly what she had worn the day they parted.

He waited, spellbound. She hardly seemed real; more like a specter from another time, another life. Yet even if she had been a ghost he would not have been afraid. Inside him, an energy gone dormant since leaving Scotland sparked to life. Lifting his face to the breeze, he could almost catch the scent of the sea. And in that moment, ah, how he regretted that second letter to his solicitor.

She moved and broke the spell. He flinched, and a whispered oath escaped his lips.

"Have you grown afraid of me, Luke?" The brogue returned as thick as ever. "I wondered when you'd come."

"What made you so sure I would?"

A corner of her mouth lifted. "When I stumbled upon this place my first afternoon in Wakefield, I knew it would be a favorite spot of yours. What is it?"

"It once held a Celtic fort."

She nodded, looking about. The lights from both the manor and the village twinkled beyond the trees. To the north and south, the fields of the tenant farms stretched into the distance like lengths of velvet, beribboned to the west by the silver-flecked Calder River.

"Aye," she whispered. Moonlight put diamonds in her eyes. "My Luke would love just such a place."

"I am not Luke Martin." His earlier anger returned in full measure. Her very presence here stung with betrayal. "Just as you are not Charity Williams."

"Ah, but I am," she said with wink. "I took my father's first name—William—as you did when you became Luke Martin."

"I repeat, I am not—"

"She's very beautiful, your Helena."

"Leave her out of this. Why have you come to Longfield Park? And how the devil did you manage to arrive before me, dogs and all?"

A silent chuckle shook her graceful shoulders. "We sailed the coast, of course. How did you come?"

"Never mind." He scowled. The brazen imp knew quite well he'd come by post-chaise. As if he'd have risked setting foot on a ship. "You haven't answered my first question. What are you doing here?"

"I needed to see your family for myself," she replied matter-of-factly. "I had to know what you'd chosen over me."

"Can't you understand I never had a choice?"

"Oh, Luke." Like jewels tossed in a blaze, her eyes glowed fierce in the lamplight. "There are always choices."

He didn't know about that. Only one thing felt certain. "You must leave here immediately."

"Why?"

"Why?" he parroted. A vein in his temple thrashed. How dare the charlatan question him?

"Yes." Raising her skirt, she drifted closer. The familiar scents of lavender and heather tightened a chord inside him. He knew he should turn and leave, go back to the house, but conviction drowned in her nearness, in the enticing fragrance of her hair.

"Are you thinking I've come after your money?" she asked. "Is that why you're angry?"

"What else am I to think?" he demanded, unable to look away from the rise and fall of her bosom. "You show up here with your fancy threads and phony accent and expect what from me?" A fresh burst of anger thrust him forward. He meant to intimidate her a little, show her he'd take none of her nonsense. But she didn't shrink, not even when his taller, broader frame cast a shadow over hers. "Where did you come by those clothes you wore earlier?"

Her eyes narrowed, yet that cunning smile persisted. "Do you think I stole them?"

"Did you?" The question came out with far less force than he wished, his bluster dissipating in the curve of her throat and the fullness of lips suddenly too, too close.

"You assume that because we Fergussons work our land and bear no title that we're poor and ignorant, that we could never aspire to the polite society you English are so fond of." She made a sound of disgust. "How little you know of us, Luke. How small-minded you are."

"Answer the question."

"The dress is mine. You should remember it. I wore it for our wedding." She started to turn.

"We're not finished yet." He caught her wrist and

swung her around, harder than he meant to. She veered into his chest, her breasts deliciously soft against him.

God help him, his arms closed around her. A groan—of both pleasure and pain—slid from his throat. Charity shivered. Grabbing handfuls of his shirt, she pressed her parted lips to his neck. Their warm vibration nearly buckled his knees.

She grazed him with her tongue, and fire melted through him. His genitals pulsated, the cadence taken up by a voice thundering in his head. Take her. Here. Now.

He shook with wanting from his core outward.

Need, rutting and wild, sent his lips plummeting to hers, hard and wet, demanding. He drew her lips into his mouth until he felt her breath hot in his throat. Through a thin layer of linen he found her breasts and sought the nipples, dark and sweetly ripe.

She moaned, rocking her hips against his in a beguiling rhythm. He took it as permission to tug her neckline. Heedless of ripping threads he exposed a perfect breast. Like the greedy stag he'd become he drew it into his mouth fully intending to devour it. She mewled, a faint kitten sound deep in her throat. Lust spun like a fireball inside him, and his reasons for resisting her scattered like so much ash.

When her thigh rose against his, his hand snaked beneath her hem, skimming her calf and tracing her leg to where the skin became its smoothest, its most tender. Through linen knickers he found the moist flames between her legs.

Ripping the bloomers aside, he sampled her heat with his fingers. Her arms tightened around him and his mind emptied of all thought save that of the sheer pleasure they were about to share.

Then, suddenly and horribly, he felt a change. Charity's

arms slackened. Her pliancy receded, creating small hollows between their trembling bodies. The night air chilled the perspiration on his brow, beneath his shirt. Gentle but resolute hands pushed at his chest, forcing him to step back.

Breathing hard, Charity stared up at him. He saw clear comprehension in her beautiful green gaze; he saw his own image, naked and helpless in the power she wielded over him.

So much for dignity. So much for control. So much for resolve.

"You're so very right, Luke," she whispered. "We're not finished yet."

He shut his eyes against her, trying to block her out while the thunder in his head subsided and his heart stumbled to its natural pace. "Sorceress. You've bewitched me."

When he opened his eyes he realized he had spoken to no one. She had taken her lantern and disappeared down the side of the mound.

He stole out of the house again the next morning, tiptoeing through the corridors lest he disturb his slumbering family. He'd tried to dissuade himself, had adamantly ordered himself to remain in bed until a decent hour. Yet once again, dressed in Luke Martin's clothes, he set out across the estate.

The villagers and tenant farmers didn't recognize him. They greeted him with handshakes, inquired about his business in Wakefield, exchanged anecdotes about their families. They slapped his back and laughed at his jokes, offered him a pint and suggested he settle permanently in the area.

It was the eye contact that most amazed him. Such a

new sensation, as unsettling as it was gratifying. Under normal circumstances, ordinary people paid him little regard. They respected him, of course. They deferred to his opinions and suggestions. But rarely had the local inhabitants so much as met his gaze.

In Luke Martin's clothes, he might tread uninhibited into their world, be one of them, enter into their discussions without causing a deferential silence. His workman's garb transformed the aristocrat into an everyday bloke bearing no resemblance to the blue blood up at the manor.

His family would never understand. Which was why, upon returning home later that morning, he thanked his good fortune the ladies had set out on a carriage ride and Wesley had sped off on his horse.

Of course, that did still leave . . .

"Good heavens, your grace. Far be it for me to dictate what you should and should not wear, but after all the effort that went into readying your grace's wardrobe, well, what can one say?"

Mortimer.

Lucas stopped at the top of the stairs and glanced down at his perplexed steward. He couldn't help noting that the man was beginning to sound distressingly like his mother. "It's not that I don't appreciate it, Mortimer, old man. In fact, I'm off to change right now, if you'll excuse me."

"Your grace has a visitor, waiting in the drawing room."

Charity? His traitorous pulse bucked at the thought. At the sound of footsteps—too heavy for a lady's—he leaned to peer over the banister. A familiar face tilted up at him from the drawing room doorway.

"Dolan!"

The man's sharp blue eyes regarded Lucas with amusement. "A true pleasure to see your grace alive and well, even if your steward here doesn't deem you at all presentable for company."

"What are you . . . why are you . . ." Lucas bit down on his stammering tongue. Never mind that his second letter to Jacob Dolan, explaining his need for an annulment, had apparently reached London with lightning speed. Lucas certainly never expected his solicitor to respond by traveling all the way to Wakefield. He could have handled the matter from his London office.

The man smiled up at him. "We'll talk when you're . . ." He gestured at Lucas's clothing. "When you're ready."

A half an hour later, having traded Luke Martin's woolens for a tailored suit and one of those numerous white dress shirts inhabiting in his wardrobe, Lucas joined Jacob in his study. The change of attire made him feel more capable of discussing business, unexpected though the visit was.

"It's good to see you, Jacob, though you certainly didn't need to come all the way to Wakefield." Lucas poured two brandies and handed one to his solicitor.

"Of course I had to come." Jacob swirled the liquid beneath his nose. "You were, well, dead, for all the world knew. This was one miracle I needed to see for myself."

Lucas grinned, then sobered. "You aren't here about the annulment?"

"Annulment? Good heavens, what annulment?"

"You never received my letter?"

"I did receive a letter from you about a fortnight ago, from Scotland. Was there another?"

Lucas nodded, and Jacob settled into the long leather sofa beneath a portrait of Lucas's parents. "I think your grace had better start at the beginning." He chuckled and sipped his brandy. "And please feel free to include every luscious detail."

Pacing, Lucas began with the morning he'd awakened

to discover the enchanting but thoroughly unfamiliar Charity Fergusson in bed beside him. He ended with their tempestuous farewell on that windy day on the headland. Despite his companion's keen interest, Lucas offered only those details needed to determine the legalities. As for Charity's inexplicable effect on him whenever she came near—he considered that beyond his solicitor's expertise and none of his business.

When he'd finished, a spellbound Jacob leaned back and crossed one ankle over the other. "A bit of an indiscretion while you were away, eh, your grace?"

He ended with a lewd snicker Lucas didn't appreciate in the least. The hairs on his neck prickled. It irked him to hear the man make a sordid joke of his marriage to Charity. But before his anger could assert itself, his solicitor's face turned serious.

"I do hope there isn't a child involved."

Lucas shook his head.

"Your grace is certain?"

Lucas gave a start. "Of course I'm certain. What can you mean by that?" Was Jacob implying that he'd abandon his own flesh and blood—pretend his own child didn't exist—in order to extricate himself from the marriage? "You'd better explain yourself, Jacob," he said with quiet warning.

The other man cocked his head and shrugged. "Are you certain the woman isn't increasing at this moment?"

"Her name is Charity," he retorted. "Miss Fergusson. That is . . . I mean to say . . ." How should he refer to her? He shook his head. At least he knew with confidence the answer to Jacob's question. Otherwise, he would not have left Scotland without her, no matter how infeasible their marriage would have been.

"If my wife were with child, I'm quite sure she would

have told me. She isn't one to mince words. As it happens, she's made no allusions whatsoever to the possibility."

"In that case, not to worry. We'll have the matter cleaned up in a trice, nice and tidy." The solicitor stared into his brandy for a long moment. "Since you've been home, has all been well? Business as usual? Nothing extraordinary?"

"What are you getting at?"

Jacob waved a hand in the air. "Nothing necessarily. It's just bloody bizarre, you vanishing so abruptly. Do you remember anything about what happened?"

"That's strangest of all. You'd think once I regained my memory, I'd remember what led me to Scotland. Not so. It's as if a wet sack were tied around that part of my brain. It's damn suffocating."

"And quite a mystery." Jacob brought his snifter to his lips, watching Lucas from over the rim.

Lucas's thoughts swerved in another direction. "Did you inspect any of the wool shipments to London during the past year?"

"Some, though not all."

"Find anything unusual?"

"No, nothing at all. What should I have been looking for?" He leaned to his left, placing his brandy snifter on a side table.

Lucas's thoughts leaped again. "Does the name Mavis mean anything to you? Mavis Blackstone?"

Jacob hesitated, his expression turning thoughtful. "Yes, it does, actually, but only from what I'd heard from your family at the outset of your disappearance. They said you'd gone in search of the girl as a service to her mother. Did you ever find her?"

"No. Or maybe." Pacing, Lucas shut his eyes, tapping his fingertips against his forehead. "Something has been nagging at me about the matter, hovering at my shoulder." He shook a fist. "*Why* can't I remember?"

"I wish I could be of more help."

"You have been, just by listening to my ranting without eyeing me askance."

Jacob seemed about to say something when hooves and coach wheels crunched along the drive. Feminine voices drifted through the open windows facing the front of the house. Lucas glanced out to see his mother, grandmother and Helena alighting from the carriage.

"Jacob," he said over his shoulder as he waited to see if anyone else stepped down from the coach. He caught himself holding his breath. Had Charity accompanied them? "You must do me an enormous favor."

"Name it."

He gestured toward the ladies shaking out their skirts and retrieving their reticules from the carriage seat. "My family hasn't the slightest notion about my, uh, marriage. Don't let on, not a hint."

"That shouldn't be too difficult, your grace."

Lucas turned back to the room and said grimly, "Yes, but you see, she's here. My wife followed me to Wakefield. And she's become a great favorite of my family, especially Helena. Only, they haven't the foggiest notion who she really is."

The solicitor's peppered eyebrows shot up. "By heavens, your grace does have a predicament." He tsked. "A grave predicament."

The morning heat clung like sodden vines, dragging at Charity's every stride. Yet the breeze cooled her cheeks well enough. She supposed the problem wasn't the weather but the corset, camisole, petticoats, oh, the interminable layers she had always deemed unnecessary at home. But in Wakefield, her masquerade made them essential. Their lack would surely have caused a scandal in the Holbrook household.

On the other hand, the same ungainly feminine trappings didn't hinder Miss Livingston or the dowager duchess in the least. Quite the contrary, walking along on either side of Charity on the road to Longfield Park, the two Englishwomen seemed oblivious to the encumbrances that made her want to drop gasping to the nearest grassy embankment.

"We're so pleased you're joining us for breakfast this morning," the dowager duchess said. "I do hope you forgive us for not collecting you in the coach. But it is such a lovely day for walking."

"Oh, I couldn't agree more," Charity half-lied. It was a bonny morning, true enough, dappled gold and green in the early sunshine. Beyond ancient stands of oak and pine, the last of a fine mist rose from Longfield's rolling pastures. The bordering hedgerows teemed with birds of every sort, chirping and squawking in their morning search for food.

Yes, it was all rather idyllic, in an English sort of way. Ah, but she missed her craggy hills, her cliffs, her sea with its sun-cast diamonds and silver-tipped waves. She missed Luke, his love, their life, and a future unclouded by social rules and beautiful fiancées.

And she missed *not* having corset stays poking through their cotton lining to pinch her just beneath the arm.

Trailing behind, Skiff and Schooner tripped through tangles of violets and primroses at the roadside. With fierce growls they snapped at butterflies and batted at the bumblebees hovering over glowing blossoms of amethyst and topaz.

With little dancing steps Miss Livingston ambled across the road, laughing as she bent to pet the dogs.

She lingered to pluck a handful of wildflowers. With one of her dazzling smiles, she held them out to Charity. "For you, Miss Williams."

"How perfectly beautiful." Charity gathered the bouquet in both hands. She hadn't lied this time, but Miss Livingston's simple gesture puzzled her. She would not have thought such insignificant blossoms worthy of the gentlewoman's notice. Why, they were mere weeds in comparison to the spectacular blooms she'd seen in the Holbrooks' conservatory and the duchess's rose garden.

In Charity's opinion, there existed nothing more delightful than the heather, gorse and bluebell that carpeted the headland each spring and summer; she much preferred nature's efforts to anything coaxed by artifice. Could it be that Miss Livingston, too, preferred the wild varieties to their hothouse cousins?

Untying her wide-brimmed bonnet, the younger Englishwoman plucked it carefully from her neatly dressed hair and turned her face to the sun.

"Careful," Charity warned, "or you'll rival me in freckles."

Miss Livingston's laugh made the slender bridge of her nose crinkle. "I can only hope they'll look as charming on me as on you."

"You're too kind." And, Charity thought, a quite gracious liar. "I'd lose them all, if I could."

"Nonsense." Luke's mother slipped her arm through Charity's. "They are most becoming and don't ever let anyone tell you differently."

Charity accepted the compliment with a little nod. She could never quite decide what to believe about these two ladies. They had befriended her so readily. Too readily, and she didn't understand or quite trust it. They fawned over her incessantly, complimenting her clothes and what little jewelry she wore. It all made her uneasy.

One would think she were a long-lost relative instead of a stranger.

What did they want from her?

Miss Livingston swung her hat back and forth at her side as they walked. "Were you raised in the country, Miss Williams?"

Why, did her glaring lack of style scream of a provincial upbringing?

But she had her story ready. "I am from Berwick-upon-Tweed as you know, but as a girl I spent many summers at our family home in a village just south of the Cheviot Hills. I suppose I ran about without my bonnet more often than I should have."

"What village was that, may I ask?" The dowager duchess swatted at a cloud of gnats swarming near her shoulder.

"Kirkheaton." It wasn't a complete falsehood. She had been to the English village several times with her family to purchase sheep.

"Ah, yes. I thought I noticed the tiniest hint of Border Country in your speaking." The duchess adjusted her hold on Charity's arm. "It's quite captivating."

As she pondered an appropriate response to this latest compliment, they turned onto Longfield Park's broad, sweeping drive.

Charity's gaze wandered to the distant rooftops thrusting above the trees. Extensive and rambling, the house stood as a testament to its own history, which extended as far back as the Middle Ages. Soon after their initial meeting, Miss Livingston had pointed out the original wing of the house with its granite turret that had once been a freestanding tower.

The main portion, accented by mullioned casement windows and diamond-patterned brickwork, had been added during the reign of Henry VII. The colonnaded walkway spanning the west wing was of a design Miss Livingston had termed Palladian. By all rights, the house should have been disjointed and awkward, but some miracle of form blended each addition with a solid yet graceful beauty.

Charity's stomach clenched. What could she possibly offer Luke in exchange? A squat little farmhouse, whose only claim to history was the single year they'd spent loving one another in it. Sweet mercy.

"Miss Williams?"

Charity flinched, suddenly aware that Miss Livingston had spoken her name more than once. She had been so lost in her thoughts the summons had failed to rouse her. Little wonder. Her assumed name, though derived from her father's, was so unfamiliar she constantly needed to remind herself to respond to it. Perhaps it would be better to alleviate the problem before blundering irrevocably.

"I do wish you'd call me Charity."

Miss Livingston's eyes widened in surprise.

Oh, dear. Was that a mistake? Such formal creatures, the English. It no doubt took years for acquaintances to reach a first-name basis. Her naïve suggestion would surely give her away as socially gauche and thoroughly un-English.

She commanded her cheeks not to redden beneath their curious perusal. Yet just when she was sure they'd taken offense, both ladies broke into smiles.

"Nothing would give us greater pleasure, Charity, dearest," Miss Livingston said. "That is, if you'll return the kindness by calling me Helena."

"And I am Dolly to my friends." Lucas's mother leaned to inhale the fragrance of Charity's little bouquet. "Mama has been called Lady Mary all her life, but having been plain Miss Fairgate before I married, I still find titles rather burdensome. Let's have no more of it, shall we?"

"No indeed." Miss Livingston—Helena—carefully side-stepped as Schooner darted perilously close to her hems. "It was so gracious of you, Charity, to break down the wall we all wished gone. Doesn't our English upbringing make gooses of us all?"

"Indeed, I've always found difficulty in addressing my own sons as Wakefield and Holbrook." The dowager duchess—or Dolly now—wrinkled her nose. "I suppose it's at my instigation that, whenever it's just the family, we revert back to the boys' Christian names. So much less stuffy, and one of the many reasons I prefer country life over Town."

"Perhaps in Berwick," Helena ventured, "society need not be so stiff? If such is the case, I should very much like to visit there someday."

"Do you mean that?" Charity regarded both women with unfeigned surprise. Astonishment, really. Dolly preferring her country home over Town, Helena enjoying wildflowers over hothouse roses. Did she honestly value true friendship more than polite society?

"I most certainly do," Helena replied. "I haven't had the opportunity to take many holidays. There was that one summer before Papa's illness when we all went to Brighton. And of course I run down to London occasionally to visit my cousin, Tess. But other than that . . ." Her smile vanished. "Oh, goodness, my manners. Please don't think I'm hinting for an invitation, Charity, dear. I'd never impose."

"After the welcome you've all shown me?" Charity's shoulders slumped beneath a quite unexpected weight of guilt. "How can you speak of imposing? It would be

an honor and a pleasure to welcome you—all of you—
into my home. Someday, when . . ."

"What a lamb you are," Dolly said with a pointed look
at Helena that made the younger woman bite her lip.
"Yes, someday, when it is convenient, we shall visit you
in the north. Such an adventure it shall be, too. But
right now we must make haste to the house, or I fear
the men shall leave us with nothing but a few crumbs of
dry toast and the dregs at the bottom of the teapot."

Sweet mercy, Charity thought as they hurried along,
what on earth prompted her to extend such an invitation? She'd taken temporary leave of her senses, that's
what. Thank goodness Dolly had politely dismissed the
idea, at least for the foreseeable future. But why the
subtle but unmistakable warning between the dowager
duchess and Helena?

Were they hiding something?

Perhaps that slip about calling her by her first name
had aroused their suspicions. Or had Lucas issued warnings about her? But how could he have without revealing his part in the truth? And surely Helena and Dolly
could not be such accomplished actresses as to summon such convincing naiveté at will. Could they?

These and a dozen other questions went unanswered
as they reached the house. This would be the second
time Charity joined the Holbrooks for breakfast. The
first had been a casual affair in the oversized morning
room set back from the house's more formal rooms, ad-
jacent to the butler's pantry. With minimal intervention
of the servants, the family had helped themselves to a
vast array of delicacies: fresh fruits, porridge, eggs prepared in a variety of ways, elaborate breads and pastries.
Enough food to feed an entire village. The Holbrooks'
self-indulgence had both dismayed and offended her.

As the front door closed behind them, Skiff and Schooner streaked the length of the Grand Hall. They disappeared behind a curtain that concealed the swinging door they'd already learned to open. From there, Charity knew they'd totter down a narrow flight of stairs to the servants' domains. This was not their first visit to Longfield Park and the voracious little beasts were no doubt anxious to see what treats Cook had saved for them.

Charity and the ladies proceeded past the study, drawing room and dining hall, heading for the same hidden door. As they stepped through, strained undertones drifted from the morning room.

"Confound it man," Wesley Holbrook hissed, "how is it you never know where he is?"

"Oh, dear," Dolly murmured.

"His grace did not see fit to leave word of his whereabouts, sir." Mr. Mortimer spoke above a steaming heap of oatcakes. He looked as though he'd very much like to set the tray down, but Lucas's brother blocked his path to the sideboard.

At the oval table, Sir Joshua Livingston sat slumped in his chair, dozing lightly over his breakfast plate. Every now and again as Wesley's or Mortimer's words sharpened, the elderly gentleman snorted, jerked upright, then sank back into slumber.

"Do you ever bother asking?" Wesley demanded, his face flushed with the effort of curbing his desire to shout.

"That hardly seems my place, sir." The oatcakes took a treacherous slide toward the edge of the tray.

"Damn it, man, you should be earning your keep somehow."

"Wesley," Dolly chided, stepping into the room. "That will be quite enough. Why on earth are you upbraiding poor Mortimer?"

Wesley turned, his hand a tight fist. "He's gone missing again."

"Who, dear?"

"Lucas, of course. He promised to meet me early this morning. We were to ride out and inspect the estate together."

Dolly and Helena exchanged glances. "Perhaps he rode out alone?" the younger woman suggested.

"None of the horses are gone. Wherever he went, he went on foot."

"I do hope he wasn't dressed like a vagabond again." Dolly tented her hands beneath her chin. "So inappropriate."

"Yes, and once again he's gone off and left our dear Miss Williams without a proper host," Helena said with a perplexed frown.

Gazing at the ceiling, Wesley replied to that charge with something between a cough and a sneer.

"That's quite all right." Charity's attempted smile fizzled as she looked from the ladies to a scowling Wesley. "I'm sure his grace has much more important matters to attend to."

"My dear Miss Williams," a firm voice behind her admonished, though not unkindly, "here at Longfield we believe there *is* nothing as important as welcoming guests and seeing to their comfort."

Lucas's grandmother strode into the room, nudging her way between Helena and Dolly with an imperious flourish. "What's this about the boy having other matters to attend to? Where is he?"

Dolly's eyebrows pulled together. "Ah . . ."

Wesley cleared his throat.

With a graceful sweep, Helena moved to the elderly lady and kissed her cheek. "Good morning, Mary, dear. Did you sleep well?"

"Girl, at my age I'm more concerned with waking than sleeping. Now, I distinctly heard myself ask a question." Lady Mary cut a path to the head of the breakfast table. Mortimer scurried to pull out her chair. "Will anyone venture to answer it?"

Sir Joshua at that moment snorted so loud he woke with a start. "Eh? Answer what?" Blinking, he scrubbed a hand across his flaccid cheek. "Are we having a game of riddles?"

"No, Josh, dear," Mary said loudly, "we're wondering where the devil my grandson's got to this morning."

"Ah. A good boy, Lucas. He'll be back, mark my words. Never was a shipwreck."

"Yes, you were right, Papa." Moving behind his chair, Helena pressed her hands to his shoulders.

"We don't want to upset you, Mama," said Dolly.

"Bah." The elderly lady paused as Mr. Mortimer set a cup of tea at her elbow. "Thank you." She pointed toward the kettle of porridge steaming on the polished walnut buffet. "I'll have some of that, please." She eyed the others. "I'm waiting."

"We can't seem to find him," Dolly said lightly, as though she thought it of little concern.

Lady Mary dismissed this with a wave. "He went for a walk."

"Since dawn?" Wesley leaned against the sideboard, shaking his head.

"Oh dear." Dolly bit her bottom lip. "You all don't think . . ."

"Think what?" Lady Mary spooned sugar onto her porridge.

Dolly gripped the caned back of a dining chair. "Lucas seems to have fully regained his memory, but what if his head injury had lasting effects? Why, he could be wandering about in a daze, lost and confused. Perhaps those awful Scottish people did something to his mind and . . ."

Charity lurched forward. If she heard one more word about those awful Scottish people, she'd scream. "Dolly." She paused to unclench her jaw. "I'm sure you couldn't be more wrong—"

Lady Mary cut her off. "No, perhaps Dolly's right. What time is it?" She made a deliberate show of opening the locket pinned beneath her shawl. Drawing her brows together, she peered to view the time. "Nearly a quarter past nine. By now he'll be halfway to Scotland, won't he? Better send out the dogs."

"Oh, I suppose we'd better have a look about." Wesley plucked a slice of currant bread from a platter and dunked one corner into a pot of preserves. He ate it in three large mouthfuls and shoved away from the sideboard. "Can't have him dottering about or lying face first in a ditch somewhere, now can we?"

"I'll come with you." Helena lifted her skirts and trotted to catch up as Wesley made a swift retreat from the room.

"Yes, you young people go." Lady Mary gulped a good portion of her tea. "Dolly and Joshua and I will wait here in the event he returns. Mortimer, some of those sausages, please."

Charity slipped out to follow Helena, but slid to a halt when she almost collided with a tall man in a tweed suit and plaid waistcoat.

"Well, good morning," he said with a bland smile. Below a thin shock of graying hair, he studied her with a casual air that made her feel as if she should know him, though she had never seen him before in her life. She offered a polite nod and he continued into the morning room.

"Good morning, Jacob," she heard Lady Mary say.

Lingering in the corridor, Charity wondered who he was and when he had arrived. And why he'd looked at her as if he knew a secret about her.

Shrugging, she leaned over the railing of the service staircase and called for the dogs. She was answered by the clicking of their nails on the wooden floors below. Like scudding clouds they scampered up the steps.

Outside on the drive, Helena rushed to her side. "Charity, dearest, I'm very sorry about this. We're all so worried about Lucas. He's been acting rather strange and after all that's happened . . ."

"No need to explain." Charity pressed the other woman's hand. Helena looked so thoroughly distressed Charity found herself very much wanting to reassure her. "I'm certain you and Lord Wesley will find him safe and sound."

"Wesley's going to search the farms on horseback while I take the curricle into the village. I could drop you at home on the way."

"I wouldn't dream of delaying you a single moment. I can see myself to the vicarage."

Helena hesitated. "Are you quite certain you don't mind? I'll be wretched if we've hurt your feelings."

"Not at all. Find his grace and ease poor Dolly's mind. I'm sure it's just as Lady Mary said. He's gone for a walk." Which is exactly what Charity intended to do, as soon as she could extricate herself from Helena's well-meant but inconvenient concern.

Helena kissed her cheek. Returning to Wesley, she swung her sunbonnet up by its bright ribbons and secured it on her head. When the two glanced back over their shoulders, Charity waved them on with a cheerful smile. The moment they disappeared down the path to the carriage house and stables, she grabbed up handfuls of her muslin skirts.

"Come on, lads," she said to the dogs, "we've got to find your father."

A hunch sent her dashing into the woods.

Chapter Ten

On the wide plateau of the hill fort, Lucas straightened his back and lowered the head of his shovel to the ground. Raising an arm, he wiped Luke Martin's shirtsleeve across his brow. He sucked in a moist draft, a remnant of a breeze that barely stirred the surrounding trees.

Why did the confounded wind never blow here? And when it did muster something resembling a gust, why did it bear no hint of life, no semblance of the salt-tanged adventure that filled him with each blast off the North Sea?

Had the North Sea wind filled him with a sense of adventure? What had put that thought in his mind? He couldn't remember anything specific about the wind or his time in St. Abbs, other than his tempestuous parting with Charity.

Why couldn't he remember?

And why couldn't he forget? The woman haunted his every waking hour, then stole into his dreams as well. Seeing her here in Wakefield didn't help. Thanks to his family's zeal for their new friend, she'd become a semi-permanent fixture at Longfield, present for tea, dinner, games of whist in the conservatory. And always looking quite the delectable morsel in her finery.

Yet it wasn't her finery that attracted him. At the snap of his fingers, he might enjoy the company of at least a dozen much more fashionable women. Charity's allure had nothing to do with clothing or style or witty parlor chitchat; no, hers was an untamable vitality that no amount of sashes or lace could subdue. From the edges of her feigned gentility, her spirit, her impudence, her sheer pluck teased with a toss of copper curls and a saucy grin.

Leaning an elbow on the shovel's long handle, he dragged his loose shirt hem across his face. Grit rolled along his sweating skin. Surveying the plot of ground he'd leveled thus far, he nodded approval. Odd how flat the plateau appeared until closer inspection revealed the dips, hillocks and fissures wrought by centuries of weather and settling earth.

He only wished he understood his strange need to smooth ground in the middle of nowhere. With a shake of his head he shrugged, trusting that something would eventually take form.

Repositioning his shovel, he stomped down on it and shoved it deep, grunting as he loosened a solid chunk of earth and tossed it aside. The growing ache between his shoulders became his focus while the steady chop, scrape, swish of his chore muted the sounds of the surrounding forest. A tune came into his head: light, easy notes that tripped like birdsong through his pursed lips. He took it up with enthusiasm as he worked. The name of the song eluded him, but he was pretty damn certain he'd never heard it in any English drawing room or concert hall.

A sudden fierce yipping alerted him to the presence of visitors. Like morning mist, Skiff and Schooner surged over the rim of the plateau. Close behind but moving more slowly, Charity panted as she took the last few strides of the ascent. At the top, she dropped her skirts and pressed her hands to her sides, leaning as she caught her breath. Lucas stood transfixed as her luscious breasts nearly spilled from her neckline's generous scoop.

An image flashed in his mind: his lips on her nape, hands reaching to cup those lovely breasts, Charity arching and purring with pure delight.

A memory? Or a wish?

The shovel fell from his hands with a thud. He folded his arms, trying his utmost not to appear disconcerted. "What are you doing here?"

"I could ask you the same." Her labored breathing continued as she came closer. Lucas pretended indifference while his fascination centered on the tops of her breasts swelling softly above her bodice. "Of course, since this is your property," she added, "my inquiry would be most impertinent."

Leaping through the tall grass, the dogs rushed him, jumping against his legs with delighted yips. He bent to give them each a cursory petting, but his eyes remained fixed on Charity.

Her striking beauty never failed to startle him. With her copper-gold curls, sea-green eyes and freckles, she was a palette of sunny summer colors. Today, she offered the perfect picture of a country-bred gentlewoman, her spiraling locks tucked but hardly tamed beneath a straw-brimmed hat, her hands encased in dainty lace gloves.

Lifting her flowered skirts high, she gingerly side-stepped heaps of turned-up earth. "Skiff, Schooner, down lads. Leave his grace alone."

They dropped to all fours, contenting themselves with blackening their fleecy muzzles in the piles of dirt.

"You can drop the accent," Lucas told her in his sternest voice. She lowered her skirts, but his gaze lingered on her hems; he couldn't help but hope for another glimpse of those pretty ankles. He swallowed. "It'll gain you no advantage over me."

She shrugged, her gaze tarrying over his opened shirt and the view within its gap. Lucas felt a rush of heat. He sucked in a breath, very much aware of how it made his chest swell. He couldn't help but enjoy the resulting flare of her nostrils, the momentary flash of fire in her eyes.

"My mouth could use a rest anyway," she said in the familiar, melodious brogue. Her lips relaxed, resuming their lush fullness that tended to diminish, he'd noticed, with her English pronunciations.

Her mouth needed a rest, eh? He immediately thought of rewarding ways to keep it busy. His own lips pursed as he imagined ravishing hers, opening her mouth to the scorching caress of his tongue.

She watched him, smiling as if reading his thoughts. He scowled. "How do you do that? Turn an English dialect on and off as if by magic?"

"Magic?" Her eyebrows rose. "Are you going to accuse me of bewitching you again, Luke?"

So she *had* heard his charge the last time they'd met here. Perhaps there was some truth in it after all.

He waited for an answer, his face a careful blank or so he hoped.

"This is no magic," she finally replied. "Would you be forgetting I lived a full year with an Englishman, who oft times, if I may say it, enjoyed the sound of his own voice."

"I beg your par—"

"Oh, don't be getting your dander up. It isn't your fault. You obviously inherited the tendency from your mother. You also have her lovely dark eyes. Your good sense, I daresay, comes from your grandmother. But never mind, I, too, loved the sound of your voice. You never once heard me complain, did you now?"

"No."

Her eyebrows shot up again. "Would that be a memory?"

"I . . . don't know." Again he envisioned his hands traveling her body, his lips following. He raked a hand through his hair, sweat spiking it between his fingers.

"Perhaps we should leave it be for now," she said quietly. She looked about. "What is it you're doing here?"

Squaring his shoulders, he steeled himself to give the stupidest answer he'd ever had to utter. "I'm not quite sure."

She chuckled. "It's an awful lot of work for no good reason." Shading her eyes with her hand, she surveyed the plateau. "The place is airy and light, but hardly convenient for a vegetable garden."

"No, not a garden."

"What then?"

He nudged the shovel with the toe of his boot. "I felt like working. Is that a crime?"

"Of course not. You always did enjoy a good day's labor."

Shrugging, he ambled to the base of a hillock and propped one foot on its slope. It was a deliberate attempt to put space between them. The other night had taught him that he could venture just so close to her before taking complete leave of his senses.

"I've realized something since returning home," he said, staring down at Skiff and Schooner. Frantic sniffing indicated they'd found something fascinating. A spider, perhaps, or a beetle. "There's precious little for me to do here on the estate. It would seem my tenants carried on perfectly well without their duke these many months."

"But they did have a duke, didn't they? Your brother, Wesley."

"In name, perhaps. Wesley wasn't raised to inherit a duchy. He trained to be a soldier, not manage estates. He did a good enough job keeping the books, but to be sure, Wakefield owes its success during my absence to its farmers and tradesmen." He ground his heel into the dirt. "I should be happy about that, shouldn't I?"

Charity once more swept her skirts high, providing not only an ample view of her ankles, but a bonus peek at gartered calves. For an irrational moment Lucas envisioned his eager hands in place of those garters, indulging in the delightful task of holding her silk stockings in place. Or not.

She came to stand in front of him, close enough for her sweet fragrance to tickle his nose and tease his brain. "You're needed, Luke, more than you know. More than you're willing to admit."

The inference sent the familiar guilt searing through him, while the presence of his solicitor here in Wakefield acted as hot coal against his conscience. Sooner or later, the annulment process would begin, putting an end to the marriage that never should have been.

He spanned the hillock in a single stride, putting it between him and Charity. "Did you come here for a reason?"

"Aye. Your family is looking for you. They're worried. Apparently you forgot to meet with your brother this morning."

"Damn." He swiped a trickle of sweat from his brow.

"I did forget. So they're all out combing the country-side?"

"Just Helena and Wesley."

"Yet you're the one who knew where to find me."

Her eyes darkened within her lashes. "They don't know you as I do."

No, they do not. "I'd best return to the house," he said, and brushed his hands on his brown wool trousers.

"Indeed." She watched him with a half-smile, and he realized she must have made these trousers for him. "And I should be getting back to the vicarage. No more family scenes for me. Not today."

"I'll walk you partway."

"No need."

"Indulge me."

"Your grace is too kind."

"His grace intends to make certain you don't find any more mischief—at least not today."

Her hands snapped to her hips. "Of what are you accusing me? I've done nothing wrong."

Ignoring his own counsel, he strode to her and grasped her shoulders firmly. "You're pretending to be someone you are not."

"Am I?" Her shoulder muscles bunched beneath his hands, belying her calm façade. Still, her gaze did not waver from his. "Or is my presence here making it more difficult for you?"

The question put him on his guard. He released her. "Making what difficult?"

"Leaving me. And Scotland. And the life you loved."

He felt the old arguments rise up: it had never been his life in the first place; the man she married no longer existed, had never existed; and he, Lucas, Duke of Wake-field, belonged here. He'd said it all before to no avail. He must show her, must convince her that Luke Martin was gone forever. He must make her understand that a duke's life is mapped out years in advance—from birth, really—and cannot be altered by a wish or a whim.

"Come to supper tonight," he said quickly, before he could change his mind. At each of her prior visits, he'd paid her the attention civility required but little beyond. Tonight he'd take pains to emphasize the barriers between them: his role as head of the family, his responsibilities, and both the obligations and constraints of being a duke.

Her gaze sharpened. "Do you mean that?"

"My dear, I assure you Lucas Holbrook never says a thing he doesn't mean."

"Neither does Luke Martin."

He let that pass. "Will you come? I'll need to let Mother know so she can inform Cook."

"Aye," she said slowly, uncertainly. "I suppose your family owes me a meal after this morning's failed breakfast."

"Good. I'll send the coach for you at seven."

"This seems a rather sudden change of heart, Luke. Just the other night you ordered me to leave Wakefield."

"An order you seem determined to ignore. That being the case, perhaps you should stay on a while longer, just to see how very different our worlds are. Then you'll understand my decision." His hand rose and, before he could stop it, grazed her cheek. She drew an audible breath, and his chest tightened. "Perhaps you'll even forgive me for it."

"The gauntlet has been thrown then," she said with amusement.

"Meaning what?"

"You wish to prove a point. Well, I've a point to prove as well." She eyed him from beneath gold-tipped lashes.

"You think you know what you want, where you belong. You think Luke Martin is a ghost. I know different. The question is, when are you going to stop being a hard-headed lout and accept the simple truth?"

Spanning the gap between them, the vixen kissed him soundly on the lips. Before he could respond with anything more than a startled, lustful moan, she twirled and hurried away.

"Come lads," she called to the dogs. "We'll walk ourselves home, thank you, Luke. Better change those vulgar Scottish clothes before your mother sees you. You'll only send her into a fresh tizzy." Gathering her skirts, she disappeared down the side of the hill.

As he stared into vacant air, Lucas's lips burned. He wanted to call her back, if for no other reason than to soothe his smarting lips with more kisses. Of course, there existed a hundred reasons why he should not call her back, and only one that made it a good idea anyway.

Searing, lust-tingling lips. And a compass straining due north.

When Charity judged she'd gone an ample distance from the hill fort, she stumbled to a halt and gripped the nearest low branch. As her other hand cradled her abdomen she doubled over. A cold sweat prickled her forehead. Her mouth watered with a bitter taste.

With tilted heads, Skiff and Schooner studied her curiously.

She groaned. The malady had taken her quite by surprise and with alarming swiftness, necessitating a speedy retreat from Luke. Not once in the past weeks of her pregnancy had she suffered the slightest twinge of illness. But perhaps this resulted from having missed breakfast. Yes, please let it be that.

Releasing the branch, she slowly sank to her knees, trying not to jar her unsteady stomach. Her hands pressed her lips as nausea rose. Skiff tried to climb into her lap but she eased him away.

"Not just now, darling."

Deep breaths helped some. She found the hem of her petticoat and used it to wipe her brow. Shutting her eyes, she tried to conjure the sensation of cool ocean breezes washing her wretchedness away.

Little good it did. A tremor surged through her, running first hot and then frigid. Her stomach rolled toward her throat, stopping just short of disastrous results. With sagging shoulders, she curled until her head rested on her knees. A warm wet tongue licked her temple while a furry body pressed snugly against her side.

She remained so for some minutes, heedless of the earth soiling her dress and beyond caring if someone should see her.

And then, almost imperceptibly at first, the queasiness began to recede. She lifted her head. A humid breeze grazed her face, rejuvenating in comparison to her pitiful condition of moments ago.

Perhaps she might make it back to the cottage. Shifting her weight, she negotiated her feet beneath her with the help of some vines creeping up the trunk of the young aspen beside her.

Her knees trembled but held. The dogs watched as though ready to assist as she ventured a step, and then another. Somehow, her feet conveyed her all the way to the vicar's cottage, where she groped her way to her tiny kitchen. Her mother always insisted an empty stomach brought on the heaves in expectant mothers. After forcing herself to pick at the remains of the meal she'd purchased in the village the evening before, she took to her bed.

With Schooner tucked against her stomach and Skiff curled warmly into the small of her back, she drifted off to sleep, her last thought a prayer that this would not happen again.

Knocking at her front door yanked her from fitful dreams some time later. Shadows slanted across her tiny bedroom. She wondered how long she had slept. With excited barks, the Westies leapt from the bed to investigate.

Much to her annoyance, both the knocking and the barking persisted. After taking a long swig of well water from the cup on her bedside table, she rose and smoothed her rumpled dress as best she could.

The nausea had passed, thank heavens, and she found herself able to walk from the bedroom to the foyer. Through the semi-circle of glass set at eye level in the paneled front door, Helena peered at her and waved. Moistening her lips in preparation of assuming her English accent, Charity slid the bolt free.

"I'm glad you're in," the Englishwoman said brightly. Behind her stood a girl in a starched blue dress and crisp white apron. A frilled linen cap helped restrain riotous auburn curls not unlike Charity's own.

Helena bent to pat the dogs' heads as they capered around her legs. Straightening, she studied Charity. "Are you unwell, dear?"

Charity's hand started toward her stomach but she caught herself in time. She decided on a modified dose of the truth. "I experienced a bit of dizziness earlier. But I'm fit as a fiddle now."

"It's because we all went scurrying after Lucas before you'd eaten, isn't it?" Helena looked both mortified and contrite. "Or was it the walk home? The sun is most relentless today. I should have driven you."

"You mustn't give it another thought. A nap has quite

restored me." She opened the door wider, glancing at her other visitor waiting silently on the path. "Do come in."

"Thank you." Helena gestured for the girl to follow. "This is Esther. She's training to be a maid of all work. Esther, dear, this is Miss Williams."

The girl curtsied. Skiff and Schooner sniffed her hems and turned their round faces up to inspect her.

Though no more than fourteen or fifteen, Esther's plump figure and full bosom made a snug fit inside her maid's uniform. Carrot-bright ringlets threatened to dislodge her prim cap, and a liberal sprinkling of freckles adorned her cheeks and nose, winning Charity's immediate sympathy.

"Welcome. How do you do?" A moment too late Charity realized her cordial tone would have been appropriate between equals, but hardly between gentlewoman and servant. Had Helena noticed? A wash of shame heated her face that her charade now forced her to act the superior with a child who might have been her neighbor at home.

"Esther," Helena said, "why don't you familiarize yourself with the kitchen while I speak with Miss Williams."

Esther curtsied again and walked the short length of the foyer to Charity's tiny kitchen. It wouldn't take her long to learn the room's layout and everything it contained. But the question was, why?

Helena slipped her arm through Charity's and nodded toward the parlor. "May we talk?"

"Of course. Do come and make yourself comfortable."

They sat together on the brocade sofa. Helena patted her knees, a signal the dogs understood well. Hopping up, they prodded and pushed to make ample room in her narrow lap, then settled in for the thorough petting they knew they'd receive.

"Oh, dear," Charity exclaimed, noting Helena's elegant, forest green carriage dress. "They've been nosing about the garden. They're none too clean."

"No matter." Helena continued petting. "The little darlings. Clean or dirty, they're a joy."

Charity felt a warmth of appreciation for the sentiment. It was one she shared, but never expected to hear from a noblewoman's lips. Helena surprised Charity so often by being exactly the opposite of everything she had ever expected of the English.

"They certainly adore you," she said with a laugh.

"And Lucas as well," Helena replied. "Which reminds me, I thought it only right that you knew what feeble-witted sots you've befriended. It turns out Lucas had simply forgotten his plans with Wesley this morning and went on rounds alone."

"His grace is lucky to have such a devoted family." Charity wondered what Helena would think if she knew who had been the first to find him.

"You're a dear to be so understanding." Helena reached for her hand. "Anyone else would have been thoroughly offended."

"Nonsense." Realizing she was not wearing her gloves, Charity started, but managed to conceal it with a cough. Would Helena detect the sorry state of her palm and realize Charity Williams was no gentlewoman?

Oh, she had tried to soak the calluses away; she'd even scoured them with wet sand and a bit of sea sponge washed up on the shore. But nothing could smooth away a lifetime of work, not a moment of which she'd ever regretted until now.

Sliding her hand free, she stood. "May I offer you some refreshment? Tea, perhaps?"

"No thank you, dearest." Helena patted Charity's vacant spot on the sofa. "Do sit with me a while. We've more to discuss. And from now on, I hope you'll allow Esther to prepare your tea and see to all your needs."

"Whatever do you mean?"

"You'd be doing the Holbrooks an enormous favor if you'd allow Esther to train here for a time."

"I don't understand."

"Yes, well, she's quite new at being a maid, and so painfully shy and uncertain that she makes a nervous muddle of nearly any task."

Charity couldn't help noticing that it was Helena who seemed uncertain and nervous, speaking much too rapidly and petting the dogs' backs with restless strokes.

"Not that she's incompetent, mind you," Helena went on, her voice a note higher than usual. She scratched Schooner rather roughly behind his bitten ear, annoying him until he nipped the air near her fingers.

"Oh, so sorry." Her hands gentled. "Anyway, we think Esther needs to gain confidence before she's ready to serve in the busy environment of the manor. Bringing her to you seemed the perfect solution. If you've no objections. You will help us, won't you?"

If you'd first tell me why you're lying.

Charity stroked beneath Skiff's chin to conceal her hesitation. Just why did the Holbrooks wish to provide her with a maid? Had she so roused their suspicions they were sending in a spy? Maids were notorious in that capacity, after all.

But the way Helena put it, how could she refuse? The Holbrooks and Livingstons alike had shown her nothing but kindness thus far. And now that Charity thought of it, a slew of invitations had resulted in her dining far more often at the manor than here in the cottage. Could the Holbrooks' generosity stem not from hospitality alone but genuine concern for her welfare?

Such compassion didn't seem terribly English to her.

"Of course Esther may train here," she said, smiling and emphasizing the word *train*.

Helena blushed, and Charity knew this was all some sort of friendly conspiracy. "Thank you. Dolly will be so pleased." After placing each dog gently on the floor, she came to her feet. "The other reason I stopped by was to ask if you'd like to accompany me into the village. It's rather late in the day for this, but of course our debacle over Lucas threw us off schedule. You see, several times each week after breakfast Dolly or I take the leftovers into the village, to distribute among some of our poorer families."

Charity stared at the other woman, remembering the Holbrooks' overburdened sideboards and her own blazing disapproval of their wastefulness. Sweet mercy, she'd been hasty in her judgment. And very, very wrong. "You say you do this every week?"

Helena fidgeted with the buttons on her carriage jacket. "It's a small gesture, but we do what we can to offer comfort."

Charity had so intended to dislike this Englishwoman, her nemesis and rival for Luke's heart. But Helena Livingston seemed bent on making it a devil of a task.

"I think it's lovely." A tear formed. She quickly blinked it away. "Thank you for asking me. I'll just get my hat."

Chapter Eleven

For what seemed an eternity, in reality only the past several minutes, Lucas had feigned interest in the latest trend in skirt lengths, of all things. They were awaiting supper in the drawing room, and Jacob had just imparted the apparently fascinating news that, in London at least, hems were on the rise again, ostensibly to allow peeks at the intricacies of silken-clocked stockings. Grandmother dismissed the notion with a *humph*, while Helena fired off an eager round of questions.

Lucas yearned to untie his dratted neckcloth, undo his topmost buttons and draw a halfway decent breath. But this, after all, was how a duke spent the better part of his time: trapped in the confines of torturous clothing, debating trifles among a gaggle of one's family and friends.

He was on the verge of mastering the art of yawning without opening his mouth. Matters could be worse, he supposed. Then again, he couldn't help acknowledging that neither hems, cravats, nor any other of life's trivialities were what set him on edge. It was Charity, or rather the lack of her. She was late. He'd sent the coach a full thirty minutes ago.

He stared at the others through glazed eyes until suddenly the sound of his mother's voice, echoing from the Grand Hall, roused him to attention. He pricked his ears.

"Why, Charity, you're a vision of enchantment tonight. "We're so pleased you could join us."

Yes and about time. Lucas mumbled an excuse, quite unnecessary as the others paid him no attention, and moved to the doorway.

Mid-step across the threshold, he went utterly still.

Charity stood with his mother near the mahogany hall table, bathed in the glow of the tiered chandelier above her head. In a gown of pale rose silk and bold black lace she was . . . astounding. Demure and dramatic. Elegant and alluring. A lady in the most aristocratic sense of the word.

Forgetting to breathe, he watched his mother's fingertips rise almost reverently to the frillwork of Charity's shoulder-baring bodice. "Oh my, is this Spanish lace, my dear?"

Great bloody heavens, never mind the lace. What that dress did to her cleavage should have been prohibited by an act of Parliament. Only, he was glad it wasn't. He'd known, from his glimpses of her that first morning in St. Abbs, that her breasts could make a man forsake an entire duchy, but . . . had she always been quite this buxom?

Dolly stepped back to admire the trim at the gown's waist and hem, as well as the matching gloves enveloping Charity's arms to the elbows. "Such divine needlework."

"Thank you. But no, I don't believe the lace is Spanish."

The chandelier sent glints of fire chasing through the labyrinth of curls secured at the crown of her head.

"Well, it's simply stunning," Dolly said.

A gross understatement. Why, even Helena, whose shimmering blue silk gown set off her fair hair and flawless skin to perfection, paled in comparison, seeming somehow too flawless, too tame. Not Charity. Even contained within stays and petticoats and all the trappings of gentility, her feisty spirit mocked him, laughed at him, dared him to . . . to peel those trappings like the leaves of an artichoke.

"You must give me the name of your modiste," his mother continued fawning. "Is she in London?"

"I . . . ah . . ."

Charity's hesitation swept the cobwebs from Lucas's brain. She might appear every inch the lady in her finery, but she'd never manage the challenge of such a question. He doubted she had ever entered a dressmaker's shop, much less engaged the services of one.

He stepped into the hall, fully intending to save her from an embarrassing moment. As to why he felt obliged to dash to her rescue . . . well, he'd deal with his mutinous instincts later.

"This particular clothier is in Berwick-upon-Tweed," she replied, "and now I think of it, I do believe she told me the lace was English-made."

Lucas halted mid-step, the flame of his gallantry fizzling. Humph. Right, then. Charity Fergusson had no need of his knight-errantry. No, her tongue produced falsehoods faster than ordinary mortals could speak their own names.

"Ah, Lucas. There you are." His mother stretched out her hand to him. "Don't stand there gawking, however dazzling our guest is tonight. Do escort Miss Williams into the drawing room while I inquire with Mrs. Hale about supper."

"A modiste in Berwick-upon-Tweed, eh?" he remarked as his mother's high-heeled boots clattered away down the hall. Raising Charity's hand to his lips, he took no pains to conceal his sarcasm. But on the sly he contemplated the slight jiggle of those glorious breasts when she moved. He liked that very much.

"Indeed, your grace, in Berwick." A quick toss of her head sent one of her carefully arranged ringlets tumbling loose. Her hand flew to prevent a full-fledged revolt of the pins and ribbons holding her coif in place. "Believe it or don't. Once again you make assumptions based on your preconceived notions."

An intoxicating sweetness of heather and lavender oil threatened to scramble his senses. "As you say," he whispered, "but tell me, how does a busy farm wife find time to have dresses made all the way in Berwick-upon-Tweed?"

"I did not. This gown belongs to my mother." She jerked her chin. "It surprises me to discover how precious little your grace knows about fashion. This is years out of date. I nipped here and tucked there to make it presentable. Your grace's mother was simply being kind."

"Oh."

"Yes, oh," she mimicked with a haughtiness that irked him no end.

Being off the mark about the dress—and being chastised for it—put him in ill humor. "Don't call me 'your grace'."

"Why on earth not?"

"Because that impertinent thrust of your chin makes a mockery of what should be a term of respect."

"Ah. Well, then, I promise to restrain my impertinent chin if your grace will forego unfair and incorrect judgments."

Humph.

Stiffly, he offered the crook of his arm. "Shall we join the others?"

"Perhaps we'd best or they'll begin to wonder." She slipped her fingers into the bend of his elbow.

Through the ebony web of her glove, his sapphire caught the light and sparked like a mysterious star in the night sky. "I can't believe you're wearing that."

She frowned. "Didn't I just explain . . ." Following the direction of his glance, her forehead smoothed. "Ah, yes, the ring. It's mine, isn't it? I tried to give it back but you wouldn't have it."

"And if someone notices? Won't that expose your little deception?"

"Won't it expose yours?" She flashed that wicked little grin of hers. "Not to worry, it's been reset. Like me, your ring is in disguise. And surely you're not the owner of the only star sapphire in the world."

Peeved that she had got the better of him yet again, he didn't respond. His gaze dipped once more to her marvelous cleavage, a dark abyss inviting exploration. Like the riffling pages of a book, a dozen different means of embarking on that exploration scrolled through his brain. Had he actually done any of them?

He felt a sudden and quite sharp poke to the ribs.

"Ouch."

"Stop ogling my breasts."

"I was doing no such thing."

"Liar." Her mouth quirked. "I know why you're out of sorts. Didn't think I could manage it, did you, Luke?"

"Manage what?"

"You know very well. Fitting in with your kind is not as difficult as one might think. Nothing to it, really."

"We'll see." He stared at her profile, hoping to catch some hint of doubt but hang it, the slant of that chin matched the bravado in her voice. "So where are the terrors tonight?"

"You mean the terriers."

"I said what I meant."

"Pooh." She made a face, but laughed. "I left them home. They pouted, but I stood firm and told them this dinner party was for humans only. They don't seem to grasp the distinction."

"You've spoiled them."

"*I've* spoiled them?" Her fingers bit into his arm. They had neared the drawing room threshold but she tugged him off to the side, out of view.

"*You're* the one who insisted on buying them from that man in Edinburgh," she whispered fiercely. "*You* hand-fed them oatmeal when we realized how undernourished they were, and afterward *you* not only allowed them the run of the farm, but let them follow you everywhere, be it the pastures, the village tavern or to church on Sunday. I spoiled them, indeed!"

"But I don't even like them. Not much anyway."

"Luke Martin, you loved those dogs. Almost as much as you loved me. So while you stand there opened-mouthed and choking on that, I'm going to greet the rest of the family." With a twirl that raised a flounce of petticoat, she disappeared into the drawing room.

Open-mouthed? True. But only partly because her revelation threw him off-balance. Good God, her show of spunk invigorated every nerve ending in his body. He'd wanted nothing so much as to stifle her arguments with hot, wet kisses. It wouldn't have helped matters one bit. But by heaven, he'd have enjoyed it.

That was the damn simple truth. He would have enjoyed it.

* * *

The glow of Charity's small triumph lasted exactly as long as it took her to join the gathering in the drawing room.

Helena swept toward her, smiling, taking her hand, as usual making Charity feel so much a part of the family. The pleasure of that, too, lasted the briefest of moments. From the corner of her eye, she noticed the man she'd met earlier that day, the one named Jacob. She bit her lip as apprehension mushroomed.

"Mr. Dolan," Helena said, "meet our dear Miss Williams, our newest neighbor here in Wakefield."

Dolan. Jacob Dolan—of course. Luke had asked for him upon awakening that fateful morning in St. Abbs. He had mentioned him several times after and sent a letter to him as well. Jacob Dolan was Luke's solicitor, the man who saw to all his legal matters.

Such as . . . annulment.

With a cordial smile he reached for Charity's hand. He spoke some words, a greeting that stung her ears like the buzzing of a wasp. The pressure of his fingers on hers, though light, became unbearable.

"A—a pleasure to meet you, Mr. Dolan." Had she formed the words correctly? Remembered to use her English accent? She didn't know. Couldn't be sure. Her pulse trounced in her temples. She felt queasy, unsteady. When Jacob Dolan raised her hand to his lips, she snatched it back. The insult would have been too much.

It wasn't his fault. But that didn't matter. She loathed him anyway.

"Tell me, dear," Dolly said, rescuing her from an awkward silence, "did Esther suit your needs this afternoon?"

"Esther?" Charity blinked. Jacob Dolan's quizzical gaze held her a few seconds more before he moved away. Flicking the tails of his evening coat, he settled in the wing chair beside the one Lady Mary occupied. Charity regained her ability to breathe. "Oh yes. Esther did splendidly. Thank you so much for—"

"No, no, my dear, thank you. You're such a lamb to take poor Esther on. You're doing us a greater favor than you can guess." Dolly traded a distinctly cunning glance with Helena, then tossed an even shrewder one over her shoulder at her mother. "I'm certain she'll thrive under your capable tutorage."

"Esther?" Wesley Holbrook looked puzzled. "Is there a problem with—"

Lady Mary's pointed black shoe rapped Wesley's heel. He fell silent.

Charity pretended not to notice, more than willing to play along with their little deceit. Anything to avoid having to interact with Jacob Dolan. "She did a first-rate job helping me prepare for tonight," she said. "Indeed, she'll make an excellent lady's maid someday."

"Who'll make an excellent lady's maid?"

Charity hadn't noticed Luke enter the room.

"Esther Hale," she told him. "Your mother has sent her to assist me at the vicarage. She says it's because the girl is shy and would train better in a quiet setting, but I can't help but feel an unfair advantage in the bargain." She turned back to Dolly. "Really, I'd feel infinitely relieved if you'd let me pay her wages."

"Never!" Dolly's eyes popped wide. "You mustn't even think of it, my dear. A favor is a favor. We are most indebted to you."

Charity sighed. "If you insist."

The conversation drifted. Charity spoke little, studying the faces of the others. Could she have been so utterly, profoundly wrong about these people? Could an English aristocrat truly possess a conscience? A heart?

If their kindness didn't let up soon, why, she'd positively like them. And where would *that* leave her and all her plans? Because, Jacob Dolan or no, she had no intention of giving up on Luke. Not by a country mile.

She felt the weight of Luke's scrutiny. Certainly he was attempting to figure how she pulled off mingling with his family without blundering completely. Poor man. He thought her provincial—no, worse, a country bumpkin. His aristocrat's mind equated simple life and hard work with banality. He'd no memory of how hard work had raised the Fergussons to relatively privileged means, nor did he recall the importance of education in their household.

She winked at him, lifting the corner of her mouth in a grin only he could see. He frowned and swept his gaze away.

His brother drew her aside just then, leading her toward a cabinet near the terrace doors where he began explaining the workings of an antique water clock. Abruptly, his description of the Medieval piece trailed off. "Do keep a watchful eye on Esther, Miss Williams," he murmured.

"Oh?" Taken aback, she blinked. "But she seems a good girl to me. Not one to find mischief."

"That's not what I mean." He fingered one of the bronze griffins gracing the clock. "It's for her safety I ask this of you. There have been several girls over the past year or so who have run away from home, quite without warning. I fear someone may have lured them away, perhaps a man with the kind of promises that turn a young girl's head."

"Good heavens, how deplorable."

"Yes. My suspicions may be completely off the mark, mind you, so you needn't discuss it with her. I wouldn't want to create a panic, after all, and inspire parents in the district to keep their daughters under lock and key. But do be aware of the company she keeps."

"I most certainly will, my lord."

A small sigh escaped his lips. "Holbrook will do, Miss Williams."

As they awaited supper, Lucas watched his solicitor watch Charity. His eyes narrowed, and he repeatedly reminded himself to wipe the scowl from his brow. At one point earlier, Jacob had caught his eye and mouthed *your wife?* Lucas had tipped his head in confirmation, then wished he hadn't. Jacob continued his silent perusal in a way that began to infuriate Lucas, as though Charity were some trollop and he next in line to sample her wares.

Her brief conversation with Wesley hadn't elicited nearly the same response, though it raised his curiosity that she and his brother should find anything to talk about at all. At least Wesley didn't leer at her the way Jacob did.

Lucas thought back on his letter to his solicitor, trying to remember if he'd in any way portrayed Charity as less than a lady. Of course, she wasn't a lady by English standards, just a common farm girl. The thought fueled his anger, not so much at Jacob but at a society that judged by all the wrong principles, as if money or title were any substitute for character.

Then again, would he have stopped to consider the difference a year ago? His time in Scotland had changed him, and he had Charity to, well, thank for it.

But that didn't make standing beside her alluring form, tucked, draped and displayed in all the right places, a damned bit easier.

He breathed a sigh of relief when Mortimer an-

nounced supper. Now at least he'd have a solid rosewood barrier between him and this vision of sophisticated
seduction she had become tonight. It didn't help matters, however, that Helena insisted he escort *their dearest
Charity* to the table. Generous, trusting Helena. Believing
herself so secure in Lucas's love, she felt no compunc-
tion about seeing a beautiful and apparently available
woman on his arm.

Sir Joshua had retired early tonight. As they took
their seats around the table, Wesley escorted Helena to
her usual place near the head of the table, to Lucas's right.
Dolly, smiling, drew Charity to the seat nearest her own
at the foot of the long table, about as far from Lucas as
it was possible to be.

And from where he could watch her on the sly. Smiling
and conversing with Wesley and their mother, she appeared at ease despite the formality of the dining hall.
Even so, he caught her quick assessment of the flatware
arranged on either side of her plate, the way she traced
the etched design with the tip of her finger. Would she
be able to maneuver her way through the courses without fumbling over which spoon to use for the soup, and
which for the pudding?

As the servants poured the wine, other questions
crowded his mind. Had her offer to pay Esther's wages
been sincere? Where would Charity Fergusson obtain the
funds for such an expense? No, he concluded, merely a
bluff, one she knew his mother would never call. So why
didn't he? Why continue to aid her deceit when he might
end the farce and get on with the business of his life?

"Lucas, a toast, if you would." His mother raised her
glass and smiled expectantly from across the table.

Charity's fist closed around the stem of her wine gob-
let. When she lifted it from the table, a vision flashed in
Lucas's mind: Charity before a room full of people, her

fist raised, voice loud with conviction. They were arguing about . . . about him. About why she continued to fraternize with the Englishman now that he was well. Why not send him on his way? He didn't belong. Wasn't one of them. But Charity stood firm, defending him to all those indignant villagers.

He's a man the same as you, Seamus MacAllister. And a hard worker like you, Will Callum, and you, Duncan MacMillan. He's one of God's own, as are we all, yet you'd treat him with less regard than you would a cur on the side of the road.

She had stilled their tongues, quelled their anger, made them ashamed.

Helena reached across the table and patted his wrist. "Lucas, dear, is something wrong?"

"No, I . . . was just thinking." He blinked the memory away and stole another glance at Charity. Her eyes were pinned on Helena's hand where it lay atop his.

He felt lower than low, unable to look either woman in the eye. The most hypocritical bastard ever born.

"To good friends, old and new," he managed to say in something resembling a jovial voice, though he heard only hypocrisy. "May they always be with us, in our hearts if not in our home."

"Here, here."

"Yes, a lovely thought."

"I'll drink to that."

Jacob raised his glass and downed half the contents. "To good friends. Old . . ." He looked pointedly at Charity. "And new."

Conversation resumed while the servants uncovered steaming platters and rotated them around the table. Lucas helped himself to Davenport fowl with its savory stuffing, spoonfuls of stewed cucumbers and a generous portion of grilled eel. At least here was one dependable thing in his perplexing life: Cook's copious talents.

He prepared to dig in with relish when he heard an intake of breath across the table. Lips compressed, Charity stared at the platter of eels in the servant's hands beside her. Beads of sweat gleamed across her brow.

His mother noticed as well. "Charity, dear, is something wrong? Is the dish not to your liking?"

"Oh, no. I mean . . ." She pressed trembling fingers to her lips and tried to smile. "It looks wonderful. It's just that the last time I dined on eels, they didn't quite agree with me."

Lucas decided her skin had taken on a distinctly green cast.

"Not to worry." Wesley signaled for the servant to move on. "We won't send you to your room for not eating your eels."

The lingering steam from the platter brought a glaze to her eyes. Her features were pinched, and she held her breath for several moments after the servant moved away. Lucas watched her, speculating. Dear God, was she going to be ill?

She held her own but picked at her supper; little passed her lips but for small bites of bread. It would seem the sight and smell of Spitchcocked eels had destroyed her appetite for the evening.

An odd reaction, he concluded, from someone who had grown up beside the sea.

Not again, Charity lamented as she rushed downstairs to Longfield's kitchen. Darting between two maids, she nearly made one drop a porcelain teapot. Her elbow sent a butcher knife spinning off a countertop. Sweet mercy, where the devil was the sink?

All would have been well during supper had it not been for those horrendous eels. Slimy, pungent things, and so close to her nose. Not that she didn't like eels. She did. Or, she used to. Oh, but now . . . ugh! Only the most colossal effort of self-control had held her stomach in check until supper ended.

Afterward, she'd rushed off with a mumbled excuse about her shoe strap breaking and going in search of a maid who might be able to fix it. No, she had insisted over Helena's and Dolly's anxious protests, they must go out to the terrace to enjoy the evening; she would join them momentarily.

Oh, but perhaps not. With one hand supporting her stomach and the other pressed to her mouth, she skirted several more startled servants as she rushed to the water pump. A few feeble tugs on the handle were all she could manage. Not a drop rewarded her efforts.

"May I be of service, ma'am?" a female and decidedly cockney voice at her shoulder asked.

Charity did not—could not—look up. "Water. Please."

"Surely."

A wide hand with stout fingers worked the pump. Seconds later, cool, clear water flowed from the spigot. Feeling in no condition to observe propriety, Charity dunked her face into the stream.

"Towel please," she croaked after a minute. Head between her shoulders, she leaned her elbows on the drain board. A square of white linen appeared before her trembling hands. "Thank you."

She mopped her brow, cheeks and chin and gradually felt able to straighten. "Ah, much better, thank you."

"Feeling a bit under the weather, ma'am?" From within a broad face, kindly brown eyes regarded her.

"Just a bit." She held the damp towel to her forehead, debating the wisdom of confiding in the Holbrooks' cook. The woman's first loyalty would of course be to her employers, but Charity decided she had little choice but to risk it. "Ah, if you wouldn't mind, I'd rather the family not hear of this."

The woman tipped her head. "As you wish, ma'am."

"I don't want to alarm them, you see."

"No, ma'am."

"It's just a reaction to something I ate. I'm fine now."

"Very good, ma'am." Cook nodded and sidestepped to a counter stacked with newly washed pots and pans. Lifting one in each hand, she hung them on hooks suspended above the counter.

"So then . . ." Charity ventured, "you won't mention it?"

"Mum's the word, ma'am."

Phew.

"Not nearly enough brandy in that cherry custard," Grandmother mumbled as Lucas escorted her out to the terrace. The others filed out behind them, all but Charity, that is.

"I thought it quite tasty," said Helena. "Didn't you think so, Mr. Dolan?"

"Indeed yes, the finest. Not a better to be found in all of London, I daresay."

Wesley reached into his breast pocket as he cleared the threshold, took out his pipe and tapped it against his palm. "I thought the wine was a bit off."

"You're not going to light that thing, are you?" Dolly wrinkled her nose.

"Of course I'm going to light it."

"Over there." Grandmother pointed to the far end of the terrace.

Lucas listened to the others argue about dinner and tobacco smoke, thinking all the while how much he loved this family of his. His cantankerous grandmother, his taciturn brother, his sentimental mother, and beautiful, kind, steady Helena.

Not one of them possessed the slightest inkling of the turmoil spinning inside him.

Yet, standing beside Helena and pretending to study the night sky, his thoughts stole back to Charity. He was worried about her. Had she taken ill?

Helena sighed. He took her hand, thankful that thus far she hadn't guessed the truth; amazed, really, that she couldn't see the bonds connecting him to Charity.

Duty. He owed that to Helena. And he loved her. Of course he did. Who wouldn't? But with Charity . . .

No. It could never work. And it wouldn't be fair, not to either woman. For all Charity's success in fooling his family, tonight revealed sure signs of the strain—to her nerves, her strength, her spirit. What price, then, would a lifetime of pretense exact?

At the same time, Helena would never recover from the pain and humiliation of a broken engagement. Given her remarkable beauty and gracious intelligence, she might, under normal circumstances, find a worthy husband. But Sir Joshua had lost nearly everything in his business ventures. There was no fortune, no dowry. What future could possibly await a woman lacking in income *and* bearing the stigma of having been jilted by a duke?

Jilted. It was about the worst word that could be attached to a lady. So final. So ruinous. And of a certainty to be followed by the equally contemptuous term of spinster. At best, she might land a third or fourth son equally lacking in fortune, certainly without property. Or perhaps a clergyman or a well-to-do merchant.

Helena Livingston, the wife of a merchant?

It wouldn't be so for Charity. She enjoyed the support of a strong and devoted family, a circle of friends, a far more forgiving society. In time she'd find love again. Marry again.

The idea ignited a white-hot urge to pummel his fist through the nearest wall. He clenched it and turned his attention back to Helena.

"It's a lovely evening," he said, feeling like an imbecile for drawing on the weather for conversation. "Just look at that moon."

Together they strolled farther across the terrace, looking up at the sky. The moon could not have been more unspectacular. A little more than half full, it reclined in a sky partially obscured by clouds. A handful of stars winked here and there.

"Dazzling," Helena replied, her face filled with the desire to find it so. But even optimistic Helena could not help being disappointed. Frowning a little, she turned back to Lucas with a wan smile that said, *well, never mind.*

But every moon is brilliant, when you're kissing the person you love beneath it.

The thought startled him. He'd heard it somewhere before. An instant later he realized the voice in his memory bore a distinctly Scottish lilt.

What the devil was happening to him? Why the sudden onslaught of memories? If indeed they were memories and not fabrications of his muddled brain.

He whistled a few notes to cover his sudden loss of composure, then realized it was the same tune he'd whistled at the hill fort. A melody he could only have learned in Scotland. He compressed his lips.

"A perfect night, isn't it," Helena called to Wesley, puffing his pipe near the garden steps.

"About the same as any other, I'd say."

"Such enthusiasm," Lucas mumbled. Leading Helena to the terrace wall, he sat on the edge and patted the place beside him.

She hesitated, head tilted upward. "Oh, look! Was that a shooting star?"

"I doubt it, not from behind those clouds."

"No, I'm sure it was." She extended her arm above her head. "Just there, where the sky is clear. Mary, Dolly, do join us and watch for meteorites. You, too, Mr. Dolan."

"It's been a rather long day." Jacob bowed to the elder ladies and bobbed another at Lucas and Helena. "His grace kept me hard at work poring over the books."

"Oh, such a dastardly taskmaster," Helena scolded with a chuckle.

Jacob smiled. "If you'll excuse me, then, I'll say good night."

"Good night, Jacob."

"See you in the morning, Mr. Dolan."

Helena beckoned again to Wesley. "Join us?"

"I'll beg off, too." He took a long draw on his pipe, sending out rapid smoke rings. "Could use a walk before retiring."

Dolly watched her younger son disappear into the shadows of the colonnaded walkway, one finger tapping her chin thoughtfully. "Wesley's becoming surlier and surlier recently. What on earth has come over him?"

"Me." Lucas crossed one ankle over the other.

"You?" Dolly tsked. "You're his brother. He's overjoyed to have you home."

"I'm afraid it's not so simple, Mother. Wesley sold his commission to become duke, and now he's left with neither. He can't help but feel resentment toward me."

"That's ridiculous," his mother began, but Helena spoke over her.

"That's so insightful of you, Lucas. I'm sure that would explain Wesley's mood of late. Poor dear. He must be feeling terribly superfluous."

"Has he confided in you?"

"Me? No. Why would he?" Her widening eyes reflected the torchlight a few feet away. A bit too innocent, Lucas thought. It made him wonder.

"Oh, bah." Grandmother Mary tugged at the corners of her shawl. "The boy is intelligent and hardly useless. He'll come into his own, whether by returning to the army or entering into some other enterprise. In the meantime, if he's surly, so be it. I'm going to bed."

"I'll help you upstairs, Mama."

Lucas watched them go with a twinge of uneasiness. "Do you think they're conspiring to leave us alone?"

Helena looked surprised. "Perhaps. But maybe we should go in, too. It's grown chilly."

"Are you cold? Forgive me." He removed his suit coat and draped it over her shoulders. "There. Now we can linger."

Like her, his instinct was to end the evening early. But he'd had a goal tonight, one he'd not yet achieved. It had to do with Charity, of course, but where the devil was she?

Helena chewed her lip and looked uncomfortable.

"Is something wrong, my dear?"

"Of course not." She giggled, which was not like her at all. "It's just that . . . perhaps I should go inquire after our guest. She said her slipper broke, but during supper I thought she looked unwell. And just this afternoon, I stopped by the vicarage to find her looking most pale. She worries me."

Her words disturbed Lucas too, for they confirmed his own fears that perhaps Charity had taken ill. "Quite right," he said. "Let's search her out."

"Search who out?" Charity stepped out onto the terrace, eyebrows raised in inquiry.

"Thank goodness." Helena jumped up from the wall. "How are you feeling, dearest? Are you ill?"

"What on earth made you think that?" Charity smiled. Lucas noticed she hadn't answered the question, but deflected it with one of her own.

"Why, during supper . . ." Helena trailed off uncertainly.

"It was the eels." Charity moved closer and cupped a hand over her mouth. Her voice dropped to a whisper. "Please don't tell the cook, but I simply detest them and have since I was a little girl."

"Then why did you disappear for so long?"

"My shoe, silly. But a handy maid set all to rights with needle and thread."

Helena looked as unconvinced as Lucas felt. The pinched look had not completely left Charity's face, and shadows hovered beneath her eyes.

Reaching out, Helena grazed Charity's cheek. "Well, I'm very relieved. Do join us. We're stargazing."

"Ah, a perfect night for it," Charity murmured with a brief glance at the sky. Her gaze found Luke's and changed. A sheen of sadness took him aback. Guilt tapped at his heart. He rose and, before he knew what he was about, started toward her, his palm open and seeking.

"However," she said just as he reached her, "I will leave it to the two of you. That is if you don't mind my borrowing the carriage for the journey home."

"You needn't rush off."

"I'm afraid I must. I shouldn't leave my dogs alone for so long. They've not yet grown accustomed to their surroundings, nor to Esther either. There's no telling what mischief they've fallen to."

"Oh, of course. How horrid of us to have forgotten the poor dears." Helena turned to Lucas. "Do order the carriage brought round, won't you?"

"No, no." Charity held up the flat of her gloved hand. "Stay and enjoy the stars. I'm perfectly capable of asking Mr. Mortimer to order the carriage. I—"

Whatever she was about to add became lost in an odd grinding above their heads. A fleeting glance upward was all Lucas had time for. A bolt of alarm ripped through him.

Instinct took over. His hands shot out, clenching a silken sleeve in one, a lace sash in the other. Using all his weight, he lurched forward, toppling the two women as he shielded their bodies with his.

A crash shook the terrace just beyond his feet. Shards flew, ricocheting against his legs and back, splintering across the stone floor. Startled yelps and breathless cries echoed in his ears.

Lucas trembled deep at his core. This had happened before. Or something like it. He hurtled back in time to . . . a place whose details drifted within a murky haze. Yet the crash evoked sensations so real, so tangible, they could only come from memory. He heard . . . voices, muffled but threatening. He smelled . . . tasted . . . seawater. Burning wood. Gunpowder.

Good God.

Yet quick as lightning the images vanished. It was the slate terrace and not a wooden deck beneath his palms; the gasps of two distressed ladies and not the roar of waves and the groan of timber filling his ears.

"Are you both all right?" Lifting his head, he searched the terrace from over his shoulder, fully expecting to find some evil presence lurking within the shrubbery. Slowly he rose to his knees, eyes narrowed as he scanned the garden perimeters. "Are either of you hurt?"

"I-I'm all right," Helena replied, her voice small and shaking.

"What on earth happened?" Charity sat up, blinking rapidly and wrapping her arms about her middle.

"I'm not sure." He pushed to his feet. A smashed heap of stone occupied the exact spot where he had stood only moments ago. Beyond it stretched the same quiet, vacant shadows as before, as tranquil as if nothing had happened. The trees and bushes barely stirred. The crickets, silenced by the crash, gradually resumed their chirping.

Detecting no immediate danger, Lucas stepped over the stony rubble to where he could view the second story. The windows and small balcony of Wesley's bedroom were directly above. The balcony stood empty. The diamond-paned windows were as black as empty eye sockets.

A light shone further down, from the corner bedroom. The casement opened and Jacob Dolan stuck his head out. "What on earth was that dreadful noise?"

Before Lucas could reply, his mother bustled onto the terrace, hand to throat, eyes wild with alarm. She halted, gaping at the disarray.

Lucas extended his hands to Charity and Helena, helping them to their feet.

"Good gracious," Dolly said between gasps, "what's happened?"

Lucas gestured toward the littered fragments. "Something fell from the balcony. I believe it was the stone owl."

"Oh, how dreadful. Was anyone hurt? Ladies?"

"Perhaps a bruise or two," Helena said more calmly now. "A scraped palm. Nothing worse. Charity?"

"Just the wind knocked out of me." One hand pressed her abdomen and she inhaled a shaky breath.

Helena's lashes narrowed as she studied her friend. "You are feeling ill again, aren't you?"

"No, I'm quite all right, I assure you." Charity's hand fell to her side.

"No bumps on the head?" Lucas asked. "I tossed you both down pretty roughly. I'm sorry for that."

"Thank goodness you did," Dolly exclaimed. "Why, how in the world could the owl have fallen? It's part of the balustrade."

"Decades of rain and wind must have worked it loose," Lucas said. "I blame myself for not having it checked periodically."

Mortimer hurried through the doorway. "I thought I heard a commotion . . . my word." He surveyed the scene. "Is everyone all right?"

"Safe and sound, Mortimer," Helena assured him. "Though a bit shaken, to be sure."

The steward nodded with relief.

Jacob appeared behind him, his tie, coat and collar gone, shirttails loose. Panting as if he'd run across the house and down the stairs, he stared over Mortimer's shoulder. "What the blazes?"

"A bit of a mishap." Helena took Charity's hand. "No one was harmed, though."

The solicitor pushed his way past Mortimer. Clearly taken aback, he walked a slow circle around the rubble. "By heavens, someone could have been killed."

"We were lucky," Lucas told him.

"Did anyone hear anything before it happened?" His gaze darted to the balcony. "See anything?"

"No, nothing," Lucas said. "It just fell."

Furrows formed between Jacob's eyebrows. Squatting, he picked up a palm-sized chunk of the bird's carved body, weighing it in his hand. He turned it over several times. His frown lines deepened.

"I'll have this mess tidied straight away," said Mortimer, turning to go back inside.

"Call a maid to do it." Lucas kicked at the shards with his toe. "I'd like you to accompany me upstairs to check the balustrade, in the event it, too, is loose."

"I'll come with you." Standing, Jacob dropped the fragment; it chipped as it hit the terrace.

"Not necessary." Lucas clapped a hand on the other man's shoulder. "Mortimer and I can see to it."

Jacob hesitated. "I'll check through the house then."

"For what?"

"To see that all's secure, of course."

"Thank you for the concern." Lucas delivered another firm pat to his solicitor's shoulder. Good old Jacob. Never one to emote, but always loyal, always the steady friend. "There's no reason to believe the entire house is going to fall down around our ears."

Jacob sucked in his cheeks, clearly worried. "No, I suppose not." Turning, he went into the house.

Mortimer started to follow.

Lucas called him back. "Miss Williams has had a most trying evening. Please order the carriage brought around immediately."

"Very good, sir."

Lucas reached for Charity's hand, discovering that his fingers were trembling as they closed around hers. When he thought of how close they had all come to being injured . . . a sickening feeling gathered in the pit of his stomach. "Are you certain you're all right? Perhaps someone should accompany you home."

"I'll go," Helena was quick to offer.

With a start he released Charity's hand. How improper for him to have grasped it. Helena seemed unperturbed, but his mother regarded him curiously. A wave of guilt heated his face.

"I wouldn't hear of it," Charity protested. "Not at this hour."

"I can at least ride in the carriage and see you inside," Helena insisted. "Just to be certain you're all right."

"But what about you? You've had just as much of a fright." As Charity uttered the last word, she swayed and her eyelids drooped.

"Oh my," Lucas's mother exclaimed.

Lucas was beside her in an instant, catching her warm weight against his chest. Her head sagged to his shoulder, bringing her face close to his cheek, her fragrant hair beneath his nose, but for once his body didn't react. His heart did. A cold fear raced through him. "Char—Miss Williams, are you all right? Can you hear me?"

"Dear me, I'll get the smelling salts." Dolly trotted into the house.

Within seconds, Charity's eyelids fluttered. One hand went to her forehead, while the other grasped at Lucas's shoulder as she attempted to straighten. He experienced a surge of relief that left his limbs weak.

His mother reappeared, a small phial in hand. "Oh, perhaps this isn't needed after all."

"Forgive me," Charity said, slurring as if just awakening from a deep sleep. The brogue asserted itself. Startled, Lucas shook her gently. She blinked up at him, her gaze sharpening. "I—I don't know what came over me."

"No, forgive me, Miss Williams," he said fervently, for the moment not caring what the others might think of his emotional display. "I fear I must have injured you when I pushed you out of the way." He looked over at his mother. "We must send for the physician at once."

"No, please don't." Charity gently pushed her way out

of his arms. "I assure you there's nothing wrong with me a good night's rest won't cure."

Dare he believe her? There was such a delicate look about her, utterly contrary to the vibrant lass he'd encountered in Scotland. Had he done this to her?

"That may be but I insist you stay the night." Dolly took a decisive step closer. "No arguments, my dear. We'll have Mortimer send someone to bring Esther and the dogs up, along with some of your things."

Steadier now, Charity put several more inches between her and Lucas. "I wouldn't want to impose . . ."

"Impose?" Dolly gave a flick of her hand. "Don't be a goose. I'd never forgive myself if you became ill in the night with only a young girl to look after you. We won't hear of it, will we, Lucas?"

"Most assuredly not," he readily agreed, though part of him felt rather less than certain. Charity spending the night under his roof? Mere paces down the corridor from his own room? Judging by the sudden lurch of his pulse, it hardly seemed a good idea. And yet neither would he risk sending her to the vicarage until he felt assured of her wellbeing.

"Skiff and Schooner are a handful . . ." Charity began.

"Two adorable, delightful little handfuls." Helena smiled her most beautiful, generous, reassuring smile. Lucas had adored it growing up, though now it only evoked fond memories. "Dolly, if she continues to put up a fuss, we'll simply have to restrain her, won't we?"

Either her or me, Lucas thought. But aloud he said, "You might as well give in, Miss Williams. There's no arguing once these two ladies have made up their minds. And besides, we'll all sleep better knowing you're well looked after."

Charity sighed. "Since you put it that way, I will stay, thank you."

His mother and Helena beamed with satisfaction. Lucas wagered that only he had discerned the apprehension in Charity's voice.

Chapter Twelve

With Mortimer close on his heels, Lucas entered the duke's private chambers, his for a full eight years but now inhabited by his brother. Although these rooms remained as familiar as his own face, he was, in fact, trespassing. They had not secured Wesley's permission to enter.

Mortimer held the lantern high as, like a pair of conspiring thieves, they tiptoed across the fine Aubusson rug. Once out on the balcony, they each released a breath of relief. Examining the balustrade didn't seem nearly the invasion of privacy as walking through a man's private rooms. Never mind that they were Lucas's rooms by rights.

Bending, he studied the rail, running his fingers along the jagged ledge that had been the owl's perch for some fifty years. Bits of mortar, weakened by decades of wind and rain, crumbled at his touch. Yet something about the irregular surface spoke of a deliberation surpassing the means of mere nature. "Hold the light closer."

The lantern swung in Mortimer's hand, its glowing

circle careening back and forth against the wall of the house, the tops of the trees, the damaged railing. "Have you discovered something?"

"I'm not certain." Indeed he was not. Suspicion, like the unsteady lantern, tossed a patchwork of light and shadow across his thoughts. Sitting back on his heels, he gazed between the newels to the terrace below.

This was Wesley's room. Wesley, who had clearly been less than content since Lucas's return. Restless, snappish, the younger Holbrook had fallen to brooding, his once affable if irreverent humor silenced by a growing dissatisfaction. Why? What was it that plagued him?

And where was he now? Had anyone seen him since he vacated the terrace?

The others had all been accounted for. All but Wesley.

"Your grace," Mortimer prodded gently, for the second time, Lucas realized.

He jerked his head up. "Find my brother."

"Lord Wesley?" The lantern's circle repeated its frenzied seesaw, throwing a dizzying array of shadows over the two of them. Had Mortimer guessed the direction of Lucas's thoughts? But the dependable features remained smooth and unperturbed. "I'll see to it immediately, sir."

"Wait." Lucas pushed to his feet. How could he even think to accuse his brother of such a base deed? Ill humor did not a murderer make; and besides, Wesley's brooding might have nothing at all to do with Lucas's homecoming.

He pressed a palm to his brow. Why had his suspicions leaped to so hasty a conclusion? It smacked of paranoia, dementia. How ludicrous, to accuse his own brother of . . . the unthinkable.

Still, something or someone had caused the owl to fall.

"I'll speak with my brother," he said to Mortimer with a shake of his head. "I need you to attend to more important matters. First thing tomorrow I want you to begin a thorough inspection of the entire house. Hire men from the village to assist you, for I want every railing, window, door, staircase and balcony of this old edifice examined for damage or wear. I want every lock tested, every hinge oiled. We can't tolerate another incident like tonight's."

"No, indeed, your grace." Mortimer reached out his free hand. It hovered for a moment before settling on Lucas's forearm with the comforting familiarity he recalled from boyhood. "Such a thing will never happen again, your grace. Not on my watch."

"I'll rest easier for that, Mortimer."

But he wouldn't. The more he thought on it, the more convinced he became that this was not the first time his life had been threatened. The crash of the owl had triggered a memory, one of brine and fire and—yes, this too he believed as a certainty—gunpowder.

But who wished him out of the way, and why?

There had always existed a rivalry between the Holbrook brothers. A constant one-upmanship that had prevented them from ever becoming true friends. Which sat a smoother saddle, aimed straighter, ran faster? Who had excelled more at university? And who had won their father's unconditional devotion simply by virtue of being firstborn?

Did it come down to that? Could Wesley covet the title of duke to such a deadly extent? The notion sickened Lucas, and almost made him wish he'd gone down with the ship all those months ago.

* * *

Helena put her ear to the partly open door of her father's bedroom. Even breathing punctuated by occasional snores confirmed a sound and peaceful sleep.

The maid who tended their needs waited patiently in the gloom of the landing. Helena put a finger to her lips and moved away from the door.

"Agatha, dear, I'm terribly sorry to keep you up," she whispered, "but I need to run up to the main house. I . . . forgot something there earlier."

"I'll watch over Sir Joshua as long as you need me to, miss."

"There's a lamb. I shan't be long."

Guided by candle glow, Helena found the graveled path that led, not to the house, but in the opposite direction. Lamplight seeped from beneath the wide plank doors of the stables. Her heart quickened.

The hinges squeaked as she stepped inside. Peering down the row of stalls, she spied a dark head and pair of broad shoulders above a divider. He hadn't heard her enter; at least, he didn't turn. For several moments she held her breath and studied the efficient motions of the man grooming his horse.

In the dusty gloom and from this distance, she could barely tell the Holbrook brothers apart. A match in height and build, they both possessed abundant waves of dark, thick hair. Even their mannerisms were at times mirror-like, though she doubted they realized it. Still, her heart ascertained the differences between them even when her eyes could not.

She lingered, watching, enjoying the flow of his muscled arm as he ran a brush in long, even strokes the length of his bay gelding. Then the brush abruptly stopped, hanging in midair as Wesley went still.

"Who's there?" he demanded and pivoted, squinting in her direction.

She hurried down the aisle. Startled, the horse flicked its tail, stamped a hoof.

"I'm sorry," she said, half-breathless. "I should have spoken when I came in."

Patting the gelding's blond mane, Wesley relaxed and grinned ruefully. "I suppose I needn't be so jumpy. Come here, you." He flicked open the stall gate. Catching her by the wrist, he yanked her almost roughly to his chest. "So, my pretty little phantom, what brings you here? Me, I hope."

"Of course you." She snuggled against him, loving the warm, solid feel of him. "I suspected I'd find you here. When you said you were going to take a walk around the house, I knew that meant a madcap ride through the forest. And in the dead of night no less. Wesley Holbrook, one of these days you're going to—"

He stopped her scolding with a kiss that began hard and hungry, then softened as the initial urgency waned. Heat spread through her like molasses set to boil, and almost made her forget why she had come.

Tipping her chin away, she ended the kiss, though not the embrace. "So then, you did go for a ride?"

"Indeed." He patted the horse's still-damp flank. "I've just finished brushing Caesar down."

"And you weren't anywhere else since you left us earlier? You didn't return to the house?"

"What sort of question is that?" He stepped back, holding her at arm's length. Something in her expression must have given her away, for his features suddenly hardened. "What's happened? Out with it. Is there some trouble brewing concerning Lucas?"

"No, nothing like that," she swiftly replied.

"He's probably peeved that I left earlier. I suppose he

expected me to hang about the terrace and watch him fawn all over you."

"He was doing no such thing."

"I'm sure he's quite disappointed I missed the performance." He released her suddenly, arms swinging to his sides. "One designed to prove he's master here, of you and the estate both."

"Wesley, will you please listen to me?" She meant to take his hand to seize his attention, but he grabbed her up in his arms again.

"I'm sick of pretending everything is 'simply splendid' as my mother would say. And I'm sick to bloody death of pretending you don't mean any more to me than a sister."

"Darling, you're hurting me a little." She gasped, partly for breath but more so because, oh, how she loved it when he pressed her tight. Still, there were matters to be discussed. "Please, we must pretend a little longer, for Lucas's sake."

Wesley eased his hold but his expression remained hard. "If Lucas has a problem, let Lucas handle it. I'm through letting him handle you. Or manhandle, I should say. I won't allow it anymore. Do you understand me? We're going to tell him and everyone else the truth. This very night."

"Wesley, we can't."

"All right, then, first thing in the morning."

"That's not what I mean." Reaching up, she framed his face with her hands. "This isn't only about Lucas, you know. Think of your mother and grandmother. They'd be scandalized. We were in mourning, and it was beastly of us to defile Lucas's memory by carrying on as we did."

"Mourning? For what?" He tossed his hands in the air. "He was never dead."

"We didn't know that. And not knowing, we had no right to fall in love. It was . . ." She groped for words. "Shameful. Dishonorable. Not to mention in very bad taste."

"Perhaps, my darling, but fall in love we did." Looking anything but ashamed, he cradled her chin in the warmth of his palm. "And it's time we stopped worrying about what other people think."

"Oh, Wesley, how can we? Our entire society is based upon worrying about what other people think of us. Who are we to change society?"

"My dear, before I fell in love with you I had no idea how adorably batty you could be." His forefinger tapped her nose. "Now that I do know, I'm more hopelessly besotted than ever. But tell me, why the devil were you interrogating me like a Bow Street Runner when you came in?"

"Oh, yes. That." The reminder startled her back to the disturbing events of the evening. "Something occurred on the terrace after you left. Something that could have ended most tragically."

"Well? Don't make me guess."

"You know the stone owl on the balcony railing outside your chambers?"

He nodded.

"It fell and shattered right where Lucas and Charity and I were standing."

"Good God." His face paled; he snatched her hands. "Are you all right? Darling, were you hurt?"

"No, Lucas pushed us all out of the way and the owl shattered on the terrace floor."

"Thank God." He pressed moist kisses to her palms. Then his head came up. "Your questions . . . you thought I might have had something to do with it, didn't you?"

"No. Of course not." Her hands trembled in his. She tried to take them back but he tightened his grip.

"Yes, you did. How could you?"

"I didn't. Not really. I knew you could never do such a thing." Feeling wretched, she dropped her gaze to the ground. "It's just that you've been acting so strangely ever since Lucas returned. Angry and not at all like yourself."

"I admit I have been angry." His hold gentled a fraction. "It hasn't been easy, slipping back into my big brother's shadow. But I'm certainly not angry enough to hurt him or anyone else. Good God, that owl might have *killed* someone. But for you to suspect me of . . ."

"Wesley, please." She found the courage to raise her face. "I'm sure it was just an accident. The railing is old, and the owl simply worked loose. I'm so terribly sorry for inferring otherwise. Can you forgive me?"

He dragged her close. "You know damned well I can and do."

"And you trust me, as I swear I trust you?"

He paused long enough to kiss her. "With my life."

"Good. Then you won't tell anyone about us for the time being? You'll let me handle it?"

"And how exactly do you intend to do that?"

"I have a plan."

"Oh no." He took a firm stride backward. "The last time you had a plan, I ended up being the straw effigy for Guy Fawkes Day and was nearly burned to death."

"Yes, but the children loved it." She waved the memory away. "This is quite different, and you won't have to do a thing. It involves our dearest Charity. Have you noticed how Lucas looks at her?"

Wesley shook his head.

"So like a man to understand nothing." She drew in a

breath. "Unless I'm greatly mistaken, there's a growing regard there. Lucas simply hasn't realized it yet, because he believes himself still in love with me, of course."

"If he loves her and you love me, why continue to pretend?"

She groaned. "These are delicate matters. They must be coaxed along with the utmost care."

"Bent on playing matchmaker, are you? I see burning effigies all over again, only this time it might be your hide that gets scorched, my love."

"You needn't be so cynical. I've a good feeling about this, and it could very well lead to a happy ending for all concerned."

"I hope you're right."

"So do I," she murmured.

The great clock in the Grand Hall chimed midnight, its sonorous echo riding the stillness through the house. Charity rolled onto her back, staring in perplexity at a ceiling whose carvings puzzled her, until she remembered she was at Longfield Park, a guest in her husband's home.

Her hands smoothed her night rail over her belly, offering comfort to the little one inside. Thank goodness Luke's shove had done little more than alarm her. If anything, her rump would be sore in the morning. But as her mother always said, once a bairn grabbed hold in the womb, it took more than a tumble to shake it free. Her queasiness, too, had abated; she felt thankfully steady.

And decidedly wretched.

She sat up, gazing into the darkness. Across the room, the curtains stirred with the gentle night breeze, punctuated by the faint pops and snaps of insects busily exploring the ivy clinging to the sill.

Beside her, Schooner let off a sleep growl, no doubt dreaming of the weasels and rabbits he longed to conquer. Skiff's shaggy head popped up from the coverlet. As fully awake as Charity, his jet eyes gleamed in the darkness.

"It's all right," she whispered. "Go back to sleep."

He raised his chin and stared back as if recognizing her assertion for the sorry lie it was. Oh, nothing was all right. Far from it. Such a simple plan—come to England and remind Luke of how much he loved her. Why couldn't she make a success of it?

She knew why. Those blasted Holbrooks. They were supposed to be contemptible. Spoiled, conceited, superficial. *Why* weren't they? Why did they make it so difficult to despise them? Why had she begun to despise herself instead for deceiving them?

She buried her face in her hands. What had once seemed rainwater clear now stretched as a hopeless mire between her and her dreams. Yet, if she listened very closely, she could hear her conscience whispering that maybe, just maybe, Luke belonged here among these people who not only loved him, but held more in common with him than she could ever hope to.

Skiff nudged her forearm, his warm nose leaving a damp trace on her skin. She stroked his chin as desolation gathered around her heart. "Do you suppose, little lad, that Luke is right? That the man I loved never existed? Could such an awful thing be true?"

Skiff's ears twitched in a gesture as closely approaching a denial as could be offered by a dog. She tightened her arms around her stomach. "Sweet mercy, you're right. This little life is no more an illusion than the man who helped create it."

Rising, she lit the bedside lamp and went to stand before the dresser mirror. By the midwife's estimate, she was approaching three months. Already, her breasts felt fuller, heavier, though she supposed only she noticed the difference. Then again, Luke had continually stolen peeks at her all evening, leading her to suspect he not only noticed but enjoyed the difference.

Head cocked, Skiff stood poised near the edge of the bed, wagging his tail and watching as she surveyed herself before the mirror. She smoothed her night rail against her torso. Her stomach lay flat, or nearly so. But her hips flared rounder, her waist thicker. Soon she'd develop that odd dark line that divided an expecting mother's belly in half. Her cousin, Emilie, had showed her when she was increasing.

No, the child was certainly no illusion. He or she had been conceived in love and in the commitment of marriage. Did it matter that Luke recalled neither? Or that the news would shock his family and set the tongues of English society wagging?

Of course not—not to the child. He or she would enter this world fully expecting and deserving the love of its mother *and* father. All the excuses in the world would not make up for the loss of either.

She snatched her dressing gown from the foot of the bed, then realized her mistake. Not only had she alerted Skiff to her eminent departure but she'd awakened Schooner as well. In an instant both Westies were pawing at the bedroom door, tails gyrating in their eagerness to go.

Stiff-armed and resolute, she pointed to the bed. "You two stay. Go back to sleep."

Their tails wagged harder, so hard their little bodies shook.

"I said stay."

With blithe disregard, they pushed their button noses

to the gap between the door and floor. Their front paws worked as if to tunnel through.

"Oh, all right. But be *quiet!*"

Thank goodness the hall runner muffled the patter of trotting footsteps. At the end of the corridor, the dogs led the way onto the wide gallery that overlooked the Grand Hall below. The clock downstairs ticked, echoing the rapid beats of her heart. Along the wall beside her, gilt-framed portraits depicting generations of Holbrooks glared down in disapproval as she stole past.

Doing her best to ignore their accusations, she counted off the rooms until she reached the one she knew to be Luke's, opposite the Grand Stairway. In the rose garden a few days before, Helena had pointed out the master's chambers. It was the one from which the owl had fallen.

No light outlined the room's elaborate double doors. She tapped lightly. Waited. Hushed the dogs, whose sniffing and snuffing seemed loud enough to wake the house.

Luke didn't come. With a deep breath, she tried the door handle. Unlocked. She hesitated, staring down at Skiff and Schooner. "Do I dare?"

Skiff barked his encouragement.

Charity's finger flew to her lips. "Shush! Oh, sweet mercy." Quickly, she backed away from the room lest Dolly come hurrying out of hers to see what the commotion was about. How would she ever explain her hand on Luke's doorknob in the middle of the night?

At the top of the stairs, a new idea formed, one that took her outside into the moonlit night.

On the garden path minutes later, she bent to gather a handful of pebbles. Then she climbed the terrace steps and stood beneath Luke's windows, on the very spot littered with shattered stone earlier. Selecting a pebble, she tossed it high.

It pinged against the window. Interested in the sound, Skiff and Schooner cocked their heads as if they, too, expected some response. Charity waited. No movement behind the darkened panes. She tossed another, then another. *Wake up, Luke. Look outside.*

"Care to tell me why you're throwing rocks at my brother's window?"

Stifling a shriek, she spun about. Pebbles showered from her palm and clattered around her bare feet.

The dogs clambered for attention against his legs, but Luke ignored them. He watched her, an eyebrow quirked in amusement.

"Your brother's window?" was all she could think to say. "I thought it was yours."

"Not for the past year or so. But if I'd guessed you'd set about breaking my windows, I'd certainly have pointed out the correct ones."

She laughed in spite of feeling foolish.

"You're looking better." From out of the darkness, his hands appeared on either side of her face. More tenderly than he'd touched her in a very long time, he framed her cheeks in his palms. Her body responded like a blossoming flower, desire curling moist and warm.

"I'm fine now, thank you." But she wasn't, not at all. His touch left her greedy for more, yet she savored what little he offered, scarce daring to breathe.

"I'm glad. You had us worried."

Us, she wanted to challenge him, *not you?* His hands fell away, yet one returned to slide beneath her chin, tipping it upward. He stood close, so close. If she reached her arms around him, would he return the embrace, enfold her in the power of those sturdy arms that made breathing an arduous but exhilarating task?

He studied her, eyes darkened by concern. The aristocratic male scents of starch and hair tonic were underscored by something deeper and fiercely sensual, an earthiness that belonged only to Luke Martin. It made her want to wrap her arms and legs around him and fall to the ground; urged her to press her lips to his and breathe him in, drink him in, surrender her singleness to the joy of being part of him.

"There has been a change in you since Scotland." He leaned closer still and she braced, waiting—praying—for the contact that didn't come. "Something is . . . different."

A warning blared in her mind. She stepped back. The dogs flinched, letting out a yip, a snort.

She pulled her stomach in tight. "I'm the same as ever."

Luke's eyes narrowed with a mixture of doubt and amusement. "I'm still fascinated to know why you were throwing stones at what you believed to be my windows." He angled a glance down the length of his nose. "And while dressed so charmingly, I might add."

"I . . . I wanted . . ." Hugging her dressing gown about her, she stopped. Wanted what? To tell him about the child? Then why had she just tried to conceal its evidence? Ah, she knew the answer: nothing would have changed between them. Even if he embraced the idea of fatherhood, he'd still be the same aristocrat with plans that did not include her. Her heart and yes, her blasted Scottish pride, could not have endured it.

"I wished to speak with you," she said feebly. "Without the others present. Without my having to pretend I'm Charity Williams."

"You put yourself in that position."

"I know," she admitted in a whisper. "But do you remember the night we walked the farm together, when I showed you everything we had accomplished in the past year?"

A faint frown accompanied his nod.

"I didn't plead or try to cajole you into staying, did I?"

He gave a reluctant shake of his head.

"I just thought . . ." Her courage failed her. What *had* she been thinking, running outside like an asylum escapee in her nightgown, still pathetically hoping to find Luke Martin in the sophisticated stranger standing before her?

"Never mind. It doesn't matter." Head bent, she turned away, intending to go back into the house.

He stepped in front of her. "Doesn't it?"

She looked up into those handsome features, sharpened by moonlight. Within harsh planes and deep shadows, his gaze burned with a fierceness of wanting. Of recognition. Of understanding. Her breath caught.

"Luke." The word flowed from the deepest part of her soul. A sound tore from his throat. He lurched and his arms went around her. Her last thought before his mouth seized hers was whether he wanted her of his will, or against it. Then their tongues met and she thought no more.

Desire, so long denied, rose as a fever inside her. Weeks of pretense dropped away, leaving her weak and shivering in Luke's arms. She felt his response in a deep shudder that shook her limbs. His lips vibrated against hers with half-words, moans, and she replied with sighs quickly inhaled. Like youthful lovers they groped one another, artless and eager to penetrate layers of clothing. Dizzy, trembling, they stumbled and caught themselves, never losing the desperate contact of their kisses.

Luke's trousers tented, a hard ember against her belly, and she raised to her toes, easing him between her thighs and closing tight around him.

Not enough, not nearly enough. She wanted more. Wanted him inside her.

As if reading her thoughts, he grabbed her dressing gown and tugged it high. The cool breeze swept her female parts. His warm hand followed.

Ah, yes.

"The rose garden," he whispered, hoarse, winded. "No one will see us."

Yes.

He reclaimed her lips, continuing an endless kiss she'd gladly drown in. She could do little more than cling to his shoulders as they blindly maneuvered toward the garden steps. Certain they'd tumble at any moment—probably trip over the dogs—Charity giggled into his mouth. He answered with Luke Martin's most sinister, sinful laugh, low and deep in his throat.

The dogs' sudden barking startled them to a halt.

"Deuced hell." He whisked his hands out from under her robe, then reached up and dragged her arms from around his neck. His eyes were wide, bright with alarm. "Look."

From the direction of the stables, a figure came running down the graveled path. Flaxen hair streamed out behind, flashing like the tail of a shooting star against the night sky.

"Helena," Charity hissed, and was nearly ill.

"Could she have seen us?" His voice came tight, ragged. He stepped briskly away from her. "Shake out your dressing gown. Smooth your hair."

Harlot. He didn't say it, didn't have to. It spoke from his curt orders, his look of utter horror.

Or was it simply her own guilt, spurred by the night breeze swirling about her bare ankles and the hot traces of Luke's kisses on her swollen lips.

"Straighten your shirtfront," she said, shaking and miserable.

Just yards from the terrace steps, Helena slowed. Charity held her breath. Perhaps the Englishwoman hadn't seen them and would turn where the path forked toward the guesthouse.

She did not. Helena halted, saw them and continued toward them at a slower pace. Charity and Luke waited side by side like criminals before their judge. Raising her skirts, Helena took the steps carefully. When she reached the top, Charity clearly saw discomfiture on her beautiful face.

"Tell her anything you want," she whispered out of the side of her mouth as Helena bent to greet Skiff and Schooner. "Blame me. I won't contradict you."

Did he blame her? His mouth opened and then closed as Helena approached. Charity braced for the worst.

"Good evening. Out for some air?" Helena clutched her hands together. A little smile blossomed, wilted, burgeoned. "Yes, me too. All alone. I've been restless tonight. Must be that scare earlier. Too jittery to sleep. Are you feeling better, Charity?"

"Much." The word rasped like a rusty hinge. She cleared her throat. "Thank you."

"I'm glad to see Lucas escorted you outside." She treated him to a smile of approval. "We wouldn't want our dear Charity wandering alone in the dark, would we."

"Y—yes, I discovered her pacing the halls, so I suggested . . ."

Yawning, Helena pressed her hand to her mouth. "Goodness. I suppose I am tired after all. I do believe I'll turn in now. See you both in the morning."

"Yes, good night."

"Sleep well."

"Mind you don't stay out much longer," she called over her shoulder as she descended the steps. "We mustn't allow our darling Charity to catch a chill."

They stared after her for some moments after she disappeared beneath the trees.

Charity was the first to release a breath. "Sweet mercy. Did she truly suspect nothing?"

"She is the most trusting soul I've ever known." Luke hung his head.

"She's too good to be true."

"Too good for the likes of either of us."

She couldn't refute that. "Just once, though, I'd like to see her pitch a tantrum."

"Never happen."

"I suppose not."

"I'd like to think we'd have come to our senses even if she hadn't come along. I—I'm sorry for . . ." He plowed a hand through his hair. "So damned sorry for the way I lost control."

The last thing Charity wanted was to hurt Helena, but she hated the remorse burning in Luke's eyes.

"You had wished to speak to me." He frowned at his feet.

She wished he would look at her. Reach for her. Kiss her again.

Sweet mercy, *was* she a harlot?

"No. I'm sorry to have bothered you." Her knuckles whitened around fistfuls of her robe. "I promise I won't throw stones again. Not at your windows, nor anyone else's."

As she turned toward the house, the significance of her words struck her. She'd come to England filled with foolish notions. She had judged Luke's family and found them lacking. She had despised Helena Livingston for being beautiful, clever and freckle-free.

That was the most ironic joke of all, for if Luke chose Helena, it wouldn't be for any of those reasons. No, any man alive would pledge his soul to Helena Livingston for the simple fact that she was the better person: kinder, more thoughtful, infinitely more honest. Freckles had nothing at all to do with it.

And then, of course, Charity had made her most colossal mistake of all. She had misinterpreted Luke's lust as something more. For something he obviously didn't feel.

"Charity, wait."

She stopped, hoping against logic for a miracle, ready to accept any compromise that might reunite them as man and wife. His polished pronunciations traveled straight to the part of her that would always be his. Even as Luke Martin, he'd said her name in exactly the same fashion: smooth, even, the tip of his tongue barely skimming the roof of his mouth as he rolled the *r* in his very English, not-at-all Scottish way.

Silent, she waited to learn which man had beckoned.

"It's late and very dark," he said with his proper English concern. "I'll walk you inside."

There. How simple. She accepted his offered arm and called to the dogs. On their way into the house she marveled, in an off-hand sort of way, that the fracturing of her heart could be such a silent, inconspicuous event that even the crickets continued their chirping undisturbed.

Chapter Thirteen

"I suggest a game of bowls after breakfast," Dolly announced as she carried her plate from the sideboard. "I believe it just the thing to take our minds off last evening's unsettling events. What do you say, Lucas?"

He'd all but forgotten the falling owl, after what occurred later on at practically the same spot. In comparison, the owl had become an almost trivial matter.

He could hardly bear to think of it—Charity, Helena, all three of them there together . . . yet he'd thought of little else since.

"Lucas?"

"Eh? Ah, bowling. Certainly, Mother, if everyone's agreeable."

"Mr. Dolan, will you join us?"

"Hm," the solicitor agreed around a mouthful of buttered scone.

"We haven't bowled in quite some time." Helena spread preserves on a slice of soda bread and set it on her father's plate before taking her seat beside him. "Do you play, Charity?"

With both hands wrapped round her coffee cup, she peered over the rim and nodded. "Tolerably well, if I do say so."

"Good, then it's settled."

As the others finished breakfast, Lucas went outside to set up the bowling green. Even in the morning's relative coolness, he found himself tugging at his collar in order to fill his lungs with air. Not surprising. On his instructions, Mortimer had tied his necktie especially tight and the laundress had added extra starch to his collar. His morning coat buttoned over a snug waistcoat while form-fitting breeches tucked securely into boots so buffed his reflection ruminated up at him.

He'd reached an adamant decision after last night's fiasco. No more of Luke Martin's clothes. No more traipsing into the woods to build God only knew what. No more lusting after what he couldn't have. From now on he'd be a duke. Correct. Stiff. Polished. English. This was his armor, to protect himself from . . . himself.

Crossing to each corner of the green, he set the wind indicator flags in their holders. The breeze blew from the north today, slightly cooler than of late but still not brisk or bracing, not salt-tinged. The air dragged with the heaviness of the Yorkshire moors, a brooding, pensive kind of breeze. It made him uneasy.

No, more than that. He stood still, listening. Eyes darting, he scanned the arbor beyond the green. Had he heard a rustling, a whisper, or was it his imagination? An animal, perhaps?

He hesitated, unsure. Perplexed. Feeling as though he were being watched.

Turning, he searched the rooftops, balconies and walkways. Had Mortimer arranged the house inspection so quickly? Lucas saw no one, but the unsettling prickle persisted . . . .

Muffled voices, angry threats. They'd coursed through his mind immediately following the crash of the owl. Why did he think of them again now? Why did he suddenly and for no good reason expect to hear the cries of foghorns and smell the fetid brine of low tide?

"Here we are," his mother hailed from the conservatory door, startling him back to reality. She waved and proceeded toward him.

He returned her greeting and tried to shake off his apprehensions—he was simply jumpy, unnerved by recent events.

The others streamed out behind her. Helena and her father took up the rear, Sir Joshua tottering with the help of his ivory-handled cane. A pair of footmen followed carrying a chair. Skiff and Schooner yapped and darted back and forth among the group, tails arced high like shaggy quarter-moons.

Lucas watched the approach of family and friends. Except for Grandmother who wore her usual black, they were all clad in pale colors and lightweight fabrics. Men and women alike sported efficient little straw hats and looked ready for a morning of amiable competition.

And then there was Charity. In airy, shell-pink cotton and a coif that spilled more copper spirals than it contained, Lucas thought she looked ready for something else entirely.

She looked . . . ready to be taken into his arms, tumbled and fondled until they were both breathless and trembling. Even surrounded by his laughing, oblivious family, his hunger for her didn't abate. Not in the least.

Last night, during the madness that almost made him forget who and what he was, he'd glimpsed an image so vivid he'd very nearly dragged her into the rose garden to have his way with her. He had seen himself loving her in their expansive feather bed, learning, seeking, adoring every inch of her with the words *I do* fresh in his mind—recently spoken, fiercely meant, sincerely promised.

Insanity. He must not let it rule him. He must be prudent. Steadfast. Incorruptible.

Who was he kidding?

Just then he saw Jacob step out of line. When Charity caught up to him he continued at her side and murmured something that made her toss back her head and chuckle. Her reply in turn made Jacob grin.

Lucas's eyes narrowed to slits. He hadn't liked his solicitor's familiarity toward Charity. Yet Jacob's innuendoes had remained much too subtle to warrant intervention on Lucas's part. He regretted ever revealing her identity to the man.

While the footmen placed the chair on level ground and Helena settled her father into it, Lucas considered Jacob's attitude. Was he, in truth, responding to the situation differently than any other educated, well-to-do Englishman would? Why, Lucas remembered his own response a couple of years ago to a friend's affair with a Drury Lane actress. He'd clucked his tongue and eyed the woman with as little respect as Jacob eyed Charity.

Still, it raised his hackles.

"Lucas, you be with Charity."

He flinched. "Excuse me?"

Helena shaded her eyes with her hand and squinted through a shaft of sunshine. "Didn't you hear? We're making up teams. You, Charity and . . . let's see . . . yes, and Mr. Dolan. That leaves Mary, Wesley and me to make up the other. Very good, then."

"Isn't Dolly playing?" Charity asked. Lucas heard the tightness in her voice and saw how she glanced at

Helena only briefly, her cheeks staining. Breakfast had been interminable for them both, and this game would be more so. How they would bear it he didn't know, but somehow they must appear cheerful and normal for the sake of the woman they'd nearly wronged so inexcusably.

"I shall roll the jack and officiate." His mother held up the measuring tape she'd brought from the house. "I always officiate."

"And I shall cheer everyone on," added Sir Joshua. "That's my job."

"And an invaluable one at that, Father," Helena replied with a fond smile.

Charity abruptly pulled away from the group. For one frightening moment Lucas thought he saw tears gathering on her lashes. She stared out onto the green for a long moment, then scooped up a wood from the gaping canvas sack that held them. Her gloved palm ran a pensive trail over the wooden ball, smoothing back and forth across its slightly flattened side. Today her gloves were kidskin, he noticed, a soft and pliable disguise for a farmwife's hands.

"So, then." Helena clapped for attention. The Westies scrambled across the lawn to her, assuming she'd called for them. "Let each team select their woods and decide who shall play lead and who'll be skip."

Grandmother selected the black woods for her team— she always chose the black. Lucas stooped, selected a dark brown and offered Charity a smile. "Would you like me to review the rules?"

"Not necessary. I've played before. Of course, we used stones instead of woods."

Was that a joke? Sarcasm? Hard to tell when she wouldn't meet his gaze. She didn't seem inclined to look at him much at all today. Yes, well, perfectly understandable. He'd found it impossible to meet his own reflection in the mirror that morning.

Jacob elbowed her arm. "Stones, eh? You must hail from quite hardy stock, Miss Williams."

Lucas wanted to shove him away. How dare he touch her?

"Oh, that's nothing. My ancestors bowled using the heads of their enemies." With a wink, she chuckled; yet beneath the gaiety, her tone threatened to splinter.

Jacob's barked laughter echoed into the arbor beyond the green. He patted Charity's shoulder in a gesture of camaraderie that nearly made Lucas leap on him with flying fists.

"We have our own rules," he said loudly, stepping between them. "We tend to be rather unorthodox."

"I'm sure I'll have no trouble catching on." Stepping over to the mat at the edge of the green, she assumed a ready stance, drew her wood back in one hand and thrust it forward with a quick snap of her wrist.

The weighted and biased wood rolled in a swift arc, coming to rest dead center on the green.

Jacob whistled through his teeth. "Miss Livingston, I must thank you for your insightful designation of teams."

"Don't be so sure of yourself, Mr. Dolan," Helena returned. "Are you forgetting that Lady Mary is a former West Yorkshire Grand Doubles champion?"

"Not at all." He offered Grandmother a deferential nod. "But with all due respect, her ladyship might have met her match. My dear Miss Williams, would you care to play lead?"

My dear Miss Williams? Lucas seethed. The fellow was altogether begging for a backhander to the jaw.

Charity shrugged. "If you like."

"I believe you'll bring us luck." Jacob slapped Lucas's shoulder. "Wouldn't your grace agree?"

Humph.

The game began with Dolly rolling the jack but came to an abrupt halt when Skiff and Schooner noticed the small white ball rolling through the grass and capered after it. Despite the laughing admonishments of the players, the dogs nosed the jack out of play.

"Oh, I *am* sorry." Charity rushed onto the green. "Naughty lads, you mustn't do that again."

"Can't fault them for their enthusiasm," Joshua called from his chair. "Bring them here, I'll look after the chaps."

After Dolly rolled the jack a second time, she flipped a coin to determine which team would roll first. Lucas's team won. After a glance over her shoulder to ensure that Skiff and Schooner were happily occupied, Charity took her place on the mat.

Lucas called words of encouragement that were thoroughly ignored. Teeth clamped on her bottom lip, she swung once in practice, assessing the weight of the wood. Sir Joshua complimented her form. She drew back her arm, took a long stride forward into the customary crouch and propelled the ball onto the green.

As the others watched the path of its neat arc, Lucas caught himself studying the strain of her dress across her shoulders, twitch of her bottom as she held her position. The wood hissed smoothly through the grass, stopping less than an arm's length from the jack.

The group released a collective *oooh*.

Charity slowly straightened. With a trace of her old vitality, she pivoted on one foot, grinned and curtsied.

"Beat that," Jacob challenged.

"Nice shot," Lucas told her as she stepped off the mat.

"Thank you." She smiled, though not at him. No, her attention focused on Sir Joshua as he issued directions to Skiff and Schooner, clambering for room on his wide lap.

"See here, young fellows," the old man gently scolded, "stop pushing. Plenty of room. Step up. No need to crowd."

"That was indeed a good shot," Helena called. "But Mary, dearest, you're up. Show them how a champion does it."

Years melted from Grandmother's demeanor as she clutched her crepe skirts in one hand and rolled her wood. The powerful thrust set the chain of her quizzing glass clacking against her buttons and brooch. Her wood knocked Charity's, causing both to scoot at right angles from the jack. Lucas's mother sauntered onto the green with her measuring tape, declaring Grandmother's wood to have settled closest to the jack.

"And that, my darlings, is how it is done," Grandmother said.

"Bravo," said Sir Joshua. "You young people must never underestimate your elders."

The game proceeded. Lucas rolled, then Wesley, Jacob and finally Helena. The points garnered at each end tipped back and forth until Lucas's team gained a substantial lead.

Charity grew weary. Even a bit shaky, in Lucas's estimate. He'd noticed shadows beneath her eyes at breakfast; they had since darkened, making those sea-goddess eyes stand out in contrast like two bright but brittle gems.

He experienced a pang. In Scotland, she'd shown such spirit, such fiery bluster. Today, despite occasional shows of spunk, she seemed to be suffocating, drowning in her own unhappiness.

But what pained him most was how she paled each time Helena spoke to her. How her eyes misted at Helena's good-natured teasing, her offhand kindnesses, as if each one pierced her heart.

He understood. He shrank inside each time Helena glanced his way, though she conveyed not the slightest sign of rebuke. Perhaps she really had seen nothing last night, suspected nothing.

Following the game, they lunched on chestnut soup and cold pheasant in the conservatory. Charity consumed little, spreading her food on her plate the way he remembered doing as a child to fool his nurse.

When tea and cakes arrived, she announced her intentions of returning to the vicar's cottage that very afternoon.

"Oh, must you?" Helena looked crestfallen.

"I think I should."

"Why on earth would you want to do that," Dolly said, fork in midair. "We've plenty of room here."

Grandmother studied Charity from across the table. "You don't look all that well to me. Stay another day at least, until you're quite restored. My daughter is right. We've scads of room. There's no good reason for you to rush off."

"No one ever says no to Grandmother," Wesley leaned to confide.

Charity worried her bottom lip, no doubt perplexed by Grandmother's brusque expression of kindness. "You are all so good to me. I hardly know why I deserve it."

While Helena and Dolly trounced her with protests, Grandmother continued examining Charity closely. Then Lucas discerned the focus of her fascination. Charity had removed her gloves. She rarely did so in company, but she'd soiled them bowling and had set them aside to eat.

In the brightness of the conservatory windows, his star sapphire glittered; the milky center glowed like a tiny flame. Grandmother's gaze adhered to the spot. One delineated silver brow angled pensively.

* * *

Charity awoke the next day determined to convince the Holbrooks of her much restored health. The feat would require no small amount of playacting, for in truth her stomach threatened to rebel even now, in the relative comfort of her bed. Yet it was a bed provided by the Holbrooks, and spending another day under this roof would be torture, pure and simple.

Her life was a shambles and no mistake about it. Luke showed no inclination of breaking his pledge to Helena. If anything, he seemed more steadfast than ever. But hurtful as that was to bear, it didn't come as a surprise. Luke Martin never broke a promise, not to her nor anyone. Except for his promise to be her husband, but then Lucas Holbrook had made no such promise.

What did surprise and dismay her was that the very people she had intended to dislike were now some of the dearest friends she'd ever known. If only she could honor them as true friends and take them into her confidence. How lovely it would be if she, Helena, Dolly and even Lady Mary could discuss the child over tea, sort through names and lay wagers on whether it would be a boy or a girl.

Sweet mercy, a cozy scene, and one that did her no good to imagine. But the idea of admitting her pregnancy to yet another person raised gooseflesh on her arms.

Luke. Dylan had been right, she'd never be able to live with herself if she hid the truth from the child's own father. Her dilemma was when. If the timing were wrong, the news might raise Luke's ire. He might accuse her of trying to trap him in the marriage. He might simply despise her.

But she couldn't lay abed all day agonizing over her plight. Hand gripping her stomach against a rush of queasiness, she made her way to the dressing table and contemplated her reflection in the mirror. Awful. Hideous. Her freckles burst starkly from a blanched background. She looked as though she had two black eyes. Her riotous hair stood on end.

Esther's reflection joined hers in the mirror as the girl strolled in from the dressing room. A white gown embroidered with lively sprays of delicate crimson blossoms hung across her arms. It couldn't have suited Charity's mood less.

"Good morning, miss."

Charity's reply came as a hitch in her throat.

The maid stopped short, regarding her reflection. "Oh, dear."

Quick as a startled rabbit, Esther tossed the dress onto the bed and moved to the washstand. She snatched the pitcher in one hand and the bowl in the other. The next instant brought her to Charity's side and just in time. She thrust the bowl beneath Charity's chin.

It was over in a minute or two. Esther efficiently whisked the bowl out of sight and returned with a handkerchief, which she moistened in the pitcher.

"There you are, miss. Better now?"

"Much, thank you." Charity drew a tremulous breath. Her hands shook as she pressed the cloth to her mouth. "I don't know what came over me." She tried to laugh but it came as more of a groan.

Concern filled Esther's face, along with no small amount of conjecture. This wasn't the first time the child had witnessed one of Charity's bouts.

"I'm really all right now."

"Mum always says there's nothing like ginger tea to ease . . . a dyspeptic stomach." Esther's brow creased as if to ask if the explanation would suit.

"Yes, dyspepsia. It's certainly plagued me in recent days. Perhaps a result of my travels."

"Yes, miss." Moving to the bed, the girl began to arrange the covers.

"Esther . . ." Charity stopped, unsure. Dare she trust the young maid? Servants were notorious gossips. Would the entire Holbrook household know her secret by lunchtime?

"It's not for me to ask questions, miss. Nor to tell tales." Esther faced her, unblinking. "I work for you, for the time being at least."

Charity gulped a breath. "Thank you, Esther."

"I'll go see about that tea, miss."

Somehow, she made it downstairs to the morning room where the Holbrooks, the Livingstons and Mr. Dolan had already congregated. Helena had saved Charity a seat at her side. She managed to nibble some dry toast and, with the strategic use of conversation, gave the appearance of eating a small meal.

"Another glorious day," Helena declared when the servants began clearing the sideboard. Glowering clouds darkened the morning room's windows, but no one bothered to contradict her. "Since Charity seems determined to return to the vicarage—you naughty thing you—I propose that Wesley, Lucas and I accompany her there. It's such a lovely walk. Mr. Dolan, would you care to join us?"

"Terribly sorry, Miss Livingston." Jacob Dolan patted his lips with his napkin and tossed it beside his plate. "His grace has a considerable workload for me today. A veritable slave driver, he is."

Charity wondered what tasks would keep the solicitor too occupied for a walk. Did they include finalizing a set of annulment papers? She tried not to blame him, even tried to be civil to him, but she loathed his presence at Longfield Park all the same.

After breakfast she returned to her room to gather

her shawl and reticule and set her bonnet on her head. Sweet mercy, the humid weather turned her hair to a frizzled cloud. Even so, the mirror offered a much more presentable picture than the bedraggled ragamuffin of earlier.

Esther had gone on ahead, bringing Charity's things to the vicarage in the Holbrooks' carriage. Since rain threatened despite Helena's opinion to the contrary, she'd sent the dogs with Esther as well. They'd been bathed the day before and she didn't need them splashing through puddles. Excited by the prospect of a carriage ride, they'd bounded up the steps and onto the red velvet seat, barking out the open window like two school children setting off on an adventure.

She returned downstairs just in time to hear Wesley Holbrook voicing his excuses to Helena and Luke. "I hope you'll both forgive me if I don't come along. The head groom informs me my horse is showing signs of colic."

"Oh, dear, not colic." Helena's pretty mouth pursed. "That can be dreadfully serious in horses, can't it?"

"If not taken care of in time." Wesley tipped Charity a little bow as she joined them. "Enjoy your walk, all of you. Miss Williams, always a pleasure."

"Well, then," Helena said, dismissing Wesley's departure with a cheerful shrug, "shall we start out?"

She linked her arm through Luke's, lifting an eyebrow until he remembered to offer his other to Charity.

She really didn't suspect, Charity thought in amazement. Helena's heart was not breaking, nor did she find any reason to detest her new friend. Charity was glad for Helena's sake, but it didn't erase the guilt that made her want to hide her face in her shawl.

Luke apparently shared that guilt, evidenced by the look of utter dismay he fruitlessly tried to conceal behind a careful smile. Poor man, trying to look and act normal with his fiancée on one arm, his wife on the other.

As they reached the first turn in the drive, Helena brought them to a halt. "Good gracious," she exclaimed, "how could I be such a goose?"

Luke and Charity traded puzzled looks.

"I'd nearly forgotten. I promised Father I'd write several letters for him. Business in London. The post goes out this afternoon, so I mustn't keep him waiting. Oh, dear, you'll both excuse me, won't you?" She didn't linger to hear their responses, but retraced her steps up the drive. "See you both later."

"Well." Luke watched her go, staring for several moments after she disappeared around the bend. "That leaves the two of us. Rather smacks of a conspiracy, if one didn't know better."

"You needn't come along if you don't want to." Charity released his arm. "I can make my way perfectly well."

His hesitation lacerated her already ragged emotions. Then, to his credit, he shook his head. "No, I'll walk you. I'd like to. If it's all right."

She shrugged and abruptly resumed walking, taking long strides and clasping her hands tightly around her reticule.

"Slow down." He trotted a few steps to catch up.

"Why?" she shot back, using anger to cover the hurt of knowing he was only being polite, correct. "What's the point?"

"The point? Of what?"

"Of you walking with me. Of pretending we're merely cordial acquaintances." Her legs pumped harder beneath her skirts until she was almost running. A chilly burst of wind scattered raindrops across her cheeks.

He caught her by the shoulder and spun her around

to face him. They went still, glaring at each other, breathing hard in the effort to restrain impulses to which neither wished to succumb.

"See here," he said, "can't we be—I don't know— friends?"

"No." *Nooh*. She'd said it the Scottish way, too tired, too damnably worn out, to keep pretending. She tried to pull away but he held her fast.

"Please," he said. "I never meant to be your enemy. Never meant to hurt you." The backs of his fingers grazed her cheek, skimming the rain droplets away. "I don't blame you for anything. I wish we could find some way to resolve our differences and be friends."

"How?" She was making it difficult for him, she knew, but only by standing firm and shielding herself with stubborn anger could she keep the tears from flowing.

"We could start by not resenting one another."

Resentment. Yes. She hadn't thought of it that way, not exactly, but it was true, right on the mark. She resented him for leaving, for choosing his English life over the one he'd shared with her. She resented that he couldn't remember how extraordinarily happy they'd been together. Most of all, she resented that he could look at her, stand beside her, even hold her in his arms, and not realize she carried a child created in their love.

That's what she wanted—for him to guess her secret and be overjoyed. Insist on returning to Scotland as her husband.

"It seems there's no solution that will satisfy us both," she said. "We want different things."

She waited for him to agree. How could he do otherwise? When he didn't, she searched his face. "Am I wrong, Luke?"

"I don't know." He bent his head, studying his feet. Tiny beads of rain misted his dark hair with a silvery sheen. "I don't want you to be unhappy. I'm uncertain about a thousand other things, but I do know that."

She believed him. With the rain gathering on his hair and shoulders, he looked utterly forlorn as he tried to sort out his life. He wanted to fix things between them, make it all better. But how? With words? Impossible.

He raked a hand through his hair and scowled. So confused, so desolate. She knew because she felt the same way. If nothing else, they were joined in their unhappiness.

The instinct to kiss him overcame all the reasons why she shouldn't. She slipped her hand beneath the shank of damp hair across his brow, lifting it, pushing it back. He shut his eyes and let her. She pressed a soft kiss, just a comforting touch of her lips, to his right temple. A shudder passed through him and he sucked in a breath. When he lifted his face, his eyes shimmered.

"Some things I might never remember," he told her. "But others I'll never forget. I know I loved you."

Head bowed, she nodded. She could think of no other response, nothing that hadn't already been said. They simply began walking again, arm in arm, quiet, the silence of unspoken thoughts heavy between them.

I know I loved you. The words filled her heart and spilled through its splintered edges. But she walked on beside him, warm tears and chill rain mingling on her cheeks.

It began raining in earnest when her cottage came into view. Luke took off his coat and draped it across her shoulders, raising the collar to shield her neck. His thumbs brushed the base of her throat, causing her pulse to catch and jump.

"Won't you come in," she asked at the door. "I'm afraid you'll be drenched if you start back now."

Before he could answer, barking blared from inside,

followed by the pattering of tiny racing footsteps and shouts from Esther.

Charity flashed him a crooked smile. Sheltered by the thatched overhang, she shrugged out of his coat and handed it back.

"It doesn't look as though the rain will continue much longer," he said with a glance at the sky.

He tossed the damp coat over his shoulder and turned to go. She should have opened the door and gone inside. Instead she lingered, watching him as he strode to the gate. She had always adored the flow of his long, sturdy limbs, the push and pull of his muscles, the determined set of his posture.

To her puzzlement, he stopped, hand poised on the latch. For several moments he looked out over the narrow meadow flanked by the road on one side and a tract of forest to the south.

He retraced his steps to the door. "Do you suppose Dylan will remember to close off the west valley to the sheep this fall, and open the southern plateau instead?"

Sweet mercy, when had he remembered such particulars as those? She did a double take before finding her tongue. "I couldn't say. Had you mentioned it to him?"

"I don't remember. Perhaps I'd better write to him. Unless you think you should do it."

She thought about that, wondering how Dylan would react to any letter from Luke, let alone one instructing him on how to run the farm in his absence. Probably kick up his ire good and quick. But if Luke suddenly recalled such an intimate detail of farming, who knew what other revelations might strike him in the course of drafting that letter.

"I think it best if you did it," she said, feeling reckless.

Luke nodded. He lingered, brows knit, studying the cottage's simple clapboard façade. She could almost see the uncertainties twisting and turning in his mind, forming themselves into a coherent question. Finally, he said, "We weren't poor, you and I, were we? Your family either."

She shook her head. "No, not poor. Though not wealthy in the way of Longfield Park. Nowhere near so."

"No. But the kind of prosperity achieved through hard work and good sense."

"Yes, like that. We worked hard, and we enjoyed the benefits."

He nodded, making no move yet to leave. After another pause, he asked, "You don't think Helena contrived to leave us on our own today, do you?"

The question took her aback. "Why would she?"

"Why indeed," he said, and started on his way.

Chapter Fourteen

Later that same afternoon, Mortimer organized a team of local men to begin inspecting the house for wear and damage. Tom Whitely, holder of one of the smaller tenant farms, led the crew as they jiggled window latches, replaced aging hinges, and pushed carefully against balcony railings.

Lucas took special interest in the proceedings, not because he didn't think Mortimer and Tom Whitely capable, but because if he didn't occupy his mind with matters other than Charity he'd go insane. Images of her bandied about his brain: Charity smiling, laughing; Charity in his arms; Charity in bed beside him, naked. Memories, or figments of his imagination? Either way, they were starkly vivid.

He worked with the men until supper, after which he let Sir Joshua beat him at chess in the drawing room, then went over several legal matters concerning the estate with Jacob. He ended the evening at Helena's side on the terrace.

"I feel so much safer now that the renovations have

begun," she told him. She looked especially lovely in salmon silk, a color that reflected the soft flush of her perfect cheeks. She truly was beautiful. So why did that beauty affect him so little?

"They have scads more to do," he replied, "but it's mostly a precaution. We have little reason to believe anything else will come crashing down on our heads."

"Amen to that. Oh, there's your brother. Wesley!" Wesley glanced out at them through the drawing room's open doors, stuffed his hands in his pockets and drifted away. Helena sighed. "A shame Charity didn't return for supper."

"Hmm."

"Perhaps she'll be persuaded to join us for luncheon tomorrow."

"Perhaps."

"She's such a dear."

"Yes."

"I'd give anything for her curls. Oh, and those eyes. Simply exquisite. Like emeralds."

"Mm hm."

"She's quite well read. Did you know that?"

Lucas shook his head.

"Oh yes. Milton, Marlowe, Shakespeare, all the classics. Modern writers too, like Byron and Shelley. And I do believe she's read everything by Walter Scott."

"One wouldn't think she had time enough for so much reading," he said absently.

"Why on earth not?" Helena stared at his profile and he realized his mistake.

He couldn't very well explain that the routine of a farmwife left little time for books. Shrugging, he pasted on his most convincing grin. "Attaining such skill at bowls requires a great deal of one's time."

"Ah, how true." She nodded, her smile playful. Lucas

relaxed. "Beautiful, intelligent *and* athletic. Quite a combination."

"Hmm." Sweet Helena, he thought. She adored her new friend and why shouldn't she? She hadn't enjoyed the company of a woman her own age in a very long while. But as she enumerated several more of Charity's finer qualities, Lucas fought to keep from squirming. How the devil was he supposed to agree with his fiancée about his wife's attributes?

His fiancée? Good heavens. The day he proposed— such a long time ago—he'd been utterly confident of doing the right thing. The sensible thing. The expected thing. So expected, in fact, she'd barely blinked an eye before accepting, nor had anyone else when they heard the news.

Everyone knew marriage among their class hinged on matters of fortune and inheritance. He'd felt especially lucky to be able to say truthfully that he loved his bride-to-be. He loved her even now. Like a sister, like a dear friend.

Not like a wife. Or a lover. He'd learned the difference these last few weeks, God help him. Against all his determination to the contrary. He knew what real love felt like, and pretending otherwise was like running uphill at full speed, gasping for breath and desperate for a glimpse of a summit that never appeared.

He'd lost his mind. Yes, that would explain Lucas's behavior that very next morning, when he donned clothes he swore he'd never wear again and set off for the hill fort.

No one at the house would notice his absence, or so he hoped. His mother and grandmother were still abed. Wesley's door had been ajar when Lucas passed it, revealing empty rooms within. Lucas supposed his brother preferred making morning rounds in the cool of dawn. What Wesley failed or refused to realize, however, was that he needn't make morning rounds at all now that Lucas was home.

Upon reaching the mound he set to work. On previous trips he'd dug and leveled an area about ten paces in diameter at the center of the plateau. Today he brought an ax. He needed branches—thick, sturdy ones. And after that, vines, thin and pliant.

At last, he knew what he was building: a small pavilion, the kind found in private gardens. Like stars bursting from the clouds, the knowledge had come to him last night as he'd drifted off to sleep, the answer so clear he felt as if he'd known it all along.

Though, why he elected to build it so far from the house he couldn't say, nor why he'd chosen to accomplish the task himself rather than sensibly hire a carpenter.

Well, that was where the insanity came in.

He shouldn't be here. He shouldn't be dressed in Luke Martin's clothes. He had vowed not to. But like a man habitually in his cups, he seemed enslaved by his own worst inclinations. It brought to mind the Viscount Haversham, an old friend from his university days. One night Lucas had gently suggested that perhaps Haversham should ease up on the brandy. The young man had regarded him sadly over his snifter. *Can't do it, Wakefield old boy,"* he'd said, *"it's who I am."*

Who I am.

Ax in hand, he descended to the forest surrounding the hill, whistling a tune that had become permanently stuck in his brain, one only Luke Martin would have learned.

The melody died on a discordant note as a realization struck him. Building this pavilion was something Luke Martin would do, or perhaps had already done, back in Scotland. Did that mean Luke Martin lived inside him still? The thought unsettled him, for it proved how little control he had reestablished over his life.

It was Charity's fault. For showing up here and working her way into his family's hearts, for the way she looked in her dressing gown—sweet and voluptuous as a ripened peach.

Voluptuous. The word wouldn't have come to mind previously. Slender and lithe, yes. And beautiful, in a fresh, unspoiled way that made her equally desirable in a bed of finest silk or a pile of hay.

The notion made him swing his ax with undue force, throwing off his aim. He hit a rock lodged in the ground, sending jolts up his arms so hard his teeth chattered. Served him right, he supposed.

Voluptuous. Could Charity have filled out that much since Scotland? Or had he simply failed to notice? After all, he hadn't been well. But surely the curve of her breasts had swelled, deepening the shadow between them.

Ax raised, he went perfectly still. He and Charity lived as man and wife for a year, sharing a bed during all that time. Even now, he could hardly keep his hands off her.

Could she be . . .

No. If she were, surely she would have told him, desperate as she was to hold their marriage together. It would have been the easy solution. He never would have walked away under those circumstances.

He tossed down the ax and swept a shirtsleeve across his brow. In the same instant something whizzed by his head. He heard a sharp crack close to his ear, like his ax striking rock again. Even before he decided what the source might be, he flattened face down to the forest floor, mouth and nose pressed to pungent dirt and dry, tickling weeds.

The report echoed through the trees, ricocheting off trunks and dissipating into the foliage. A new sound took its place, a steady thump-thump that could have been the echo of horse hooves or his own thundering heartbeat. An acrid scent drifted, overcoming that of damp earth.

Lucas didn't know how long he lay. One by one the birds resumed their trills and chirps; unseen creatures continued their scampering through wispy ferns and tangled brush.

He listened for footsteps, voices, breathing. Nothing. In fact, all seemed so normal he began to believe he'd imagined the entire episode.

Pushing upright, he peered through the trees, seeking any movement, shape or color not in keeping with forest life. Again, nothing. Perhaps, as he dove for the ground, his unseen assailant had retreated on horseback. Or perhaps his imagination had vilified the mere cracking of a bough.

Using the tree beside him for leverage, he pulled to his feet. And saw it.

A gash in the bark as long as his forefinger, revealing a pale streak of fresh, pulpy wood. Lucas brought his nose close, inhaling the burning tang of gunpowder.

First the owl, now this.

Bullets, and the rhythmic thumping of hooves. Who had access to guns and horses, not to mention the skill to move stealthily through the forest?

Who might want him gone? Who had motive? Suspicion sent a tremor racing up his back. His hands shook.

"Son of a mongrel bitch." He swept the fallen ax from the ground at his feet, and sped off for home.

"Where in bloody hell is my brother?" Lucas shouted as he burst through the kitchen garden door. It slammed behind him, eliciting a clinking from a row of pots hanging on hooks from the ceiling.

Startled, Cook gaped from over a worktable heaped with pans, mixing bowls and colanders of peeled pears. A chopping knife hung suspended in her right hand. By her expression, Lucas suspected she contemplated using the thing on the barking madman who'd just disturbed the peace of her domain.

He wouldn't have blamed her. What a sight he must make, dressed in Luke Martin's work woolens, splattered with dirt, an ax dangling at his side. But in the next moment she recognized him. Her face relaxed and she wedged the knife into the nearest pear, sending out a sweet spray of juice.

"I believe Lord Wesley is above stairs, sir. In his rooms, perhaps."

"Thank you." Regaining a modicum of dignity, he strode rather than sprinted through the kitchen. He stopped to lay his ax on a countertop before reaching the door to the stairwell. He'd recovered that much sanity during his mad dash home. "Sorry to have startled you."

Thus ended his efforts at civility. Traces of gunpowder still burned his nostrils, flaring them with outrage. When the owl had fallen, Wesley had been nowhere to be found. When Lucas crept out of the house earlier, Wesley was already gone.

As he took the stairs two at a time, his breath came in

boarish grunts. Mortimer's voice called up from the foyer. "Your grace, a moment, if you would."

"Not now."

"It concerns the house inspections, sir."

"Later."

"They've been halted for today, sir. Mr. Whitely has not shown up to supervise and—"

"I'll deal with it later, Mortimer."

Achieving the landing, he charged his brother's bedroom door—his own bedroom door, damn it—like a teased bull. He barely turned the knob before setting his shoulder to it and forcing his way through.

It hit the wall and bounced, rebounding back toward his face. He warded off the blow with his palm and kept going, sighting Wesley at the foot of the poster bed, standing in shirtsleeves and stocking feet. A riding crop and hunting jacket lay across a nearby chair. He looked up at Lucas in alarm. "What the blazes?"

"Where were you just now?"

To Lucas's indignation, his brother glanced down at himself and smirked. "Let's see. Attending a royal ball?"

"Answer the bloody question." Lucas clenched his fists. "You've developed a habit of disappearing, of being unavailable at inopportune times. I demand to know why."

"What is this? First Helena, now you. Are the two of you co-founders of the Wesley Holbrook Harassment Society? If so, I suggest you find some other amusement because it's becoming damned tiresome." That infuriating smirk appeared again. Wesley turned away, working at the buttons of his shirt with an air of bored dismissal. Something in Lucas snapped.

He snatched his brother's shirtfront and hauled him against a bedpost. Pulling back his right fist, he took aim. Staring into utterly baffled features, he hesitated, and in the interval Mortimer sprinted into the room. "What's the meaning of this?" the steward demanded, his tone that of a scolding schoolmaster. He gripped Lucas's upper arms and hauled him backward, away from his brother. The force of Mortimer's grip wasn't necessary. Lucas's anger had passed and he no longer felt the inclination to strike his only brother due to circumstantial evidence and a keen sense of sibling rivalry.

"I haven't needed to break the two of you up in at least a half score years." Outrage sparked in the steward's eyes.

"He started it." Wesley pointed an accusing finger. Adjusting his shirtfront, he rotated a shoulder. "Damned near maimed me without so much as a by-your-leave."

"Don't exaggerate," Lucas growled.

"I intend to stand here until I'm certain the two of you can behave like the gentlemen you were born to be." Mortimer's disapproval darted back and forth between them.

Wesley hissed through his teeth. "The problem lies with him. I'd come upstairs to rid myself of the stench of horse when this lunatic burst in and accosted me."

"It's all right, Mortimer, you can go." Lucas folded his arms. "I promise my brother will come to no harm."

The steward looked unconvinced. But brushing his hands together as if washing them clean of the matter, he shrugged. The door closed softly behind him.

"Someone shot at me in the woods just now," Lucas abruptly said.

"Good God." The horror in Wesley's eyes was too raw to be anything but genuine. It was also fleeting. His spine stiffened. "You think I did it."

Lucas shook his head. "I thought, perhaps, but . . ."

"Christ, I've been out riding. I visited the mill and

several of the farms. Ask the Andersons if you don't believe me. I've just come from their place. I talked with both Roger and the wife. Saw the twins as well."

"Were you near the old hill fort?"

"I took a nearby trail. I don't deny it. Certainly doesn't make me an assassin."

"Did you hear a shot? Did you see anyone in the area?"

"A shot? No. Look, at least a half dozen tenants besides Roger can vouch for me." Wesley paused, his Adam's apple twitching. "In fact, I was doing you a favor, not that you deserve one. I've been asking after the girl you went searching for when you disappeared."

"Mavis?" Lucas's nape prickled.

"Blackstone, yes. Her family owned a small farm about ten miles south of Wakefield. She disappeared the same time you did. Makes one wonder, doesn't it," he added with a trace of malice.

Lucas ignored the insinuation. The prickling became cold-tipped needles. "Did you learn anything?"

"Only what we already knew, that the family sold out and moved away."

"Does anyone know where to?"

Wesley shrugged. "They only came into Wakefield occasionally. No one knew them well. But you probably think I'm merely inventing an alibi to cover my guilt."

"I don't think any such thing," Lucas said quietly.

"You thought I pushed the stone owl over as well." Wesley's upper lip curled. "You think I'd knock you off to remain Duke, don't you. You damned arrogant goat. Has it ever occurred to you I never wanted it in the first place? That all I want is . . ."

"Is what?"

"Never mind." Wesley's gaze seared through Lucas to something beyond. "It doesn't matter."

"Yes it does. Wes, I'm sorry. Please . . ."

"It was probably a hunter." Wesley pushed the words through a jaw rigid with anger. "Someone who didn't want you to see him because he shouldn't have strayed so close to the house. Can't have Saint Lucas catching a poor bloke breaking a rule or two in order to feed his family, now can we. It's so like you to blow it out of all proportion."

"First the owl and now a bullet? Wesley, think. Isn't that a bit too much of a coincidence?"

"Why would anyone want you dead?" He said it like an accusation, as if Lucas had made it all up on a lark.

"I can't answer that. But I'm beginning to think it has to do with the shipwreck I supposedly died in."

"You've taken leave of your senses. Stop this, Lucas. Stop it this instant. You're making Mother half-mad with worry. Grandmother hasn't stopped grumbling to herself since your return and poor Helena, well, Helena's never anything but cheerful but even she's beginning to show clear signs of bewilderment. I suggest you wake up, stop dressing in that barbaric manner and behave like the duke you're supposed to be."

Wesley ploughed a path to the door and swung it wide. He stepped into the corridor but did a swift about-face. "And get out so I can finish changing."

Chapter Fifteen

Lucas locked the door of his study and turned to regard his solicitor's puzzled, if not quite wary, expression. If everyone else in the house thought he'd gone batty, why should Jacob feel any different? Still, if he could depend on anyone to help him sort through recent events with a modicum of logic, it was his cool-headed solicitor.

"Jacob, I believe there have been two attempts on my life since I've been back in Wakefield, one when the owl fell and then again today."

"Today?" Jacob leaped up from the sofa. "Good heavens, your grace, what happened?"

"Someone shot at me in the woods not an hour ago."

"God's teeth." The man's complexion paled. "Are you certain about this? I mean certain the shot was intended for you?"

"No," he admitted as Wesley's rationalizations echoed in his brain. "I'm not certain about anything anymore. But to put it in scientific terms, I have a strong hunch."

"Any clue as to who might want to do you in, or why?"

"Not yet." Lucas shook both his head and his fist. "I'm beginning to suspect the attempts began over a year ago. Jacob, I haven't told anyone else this yet, but I believe the ship I was on was deliberately scuttled."

Jacob sank back onto the sofa. "What makes you think so?"

"It's a jumble of vague memories, but they all point to an explosion. Flashing light, a blast, the reek of gunpowder. All I know is whoever went to such great pains to arrange my death must be damned disappointed at my resurrection. I just wish to bloody hell I knew why I'm such a threat." He started pacing back and forth in front of the sofa, skirting Jacob's outstretched legs. "Of course, theft comes to mind, but what besides wool do we have in Wakefield? What could possibly be worth murder?"

Jacob shook his head. "Or worth blowing up a ship? Explosives are nasty business. Risky and expensive."

Lucas came to an abrupt halt. "By God, Jacob, this smells of more than mere theft. It reeks of some kind of plot."

"As in a coup? With spies and pistols and ultimatums?"

The words were like an awakening slap. Lucas's bluster died with a puff. He felt suddenly ridiculous. The shot in the woods very well could have been a hunter's misfire. A horrible coincidence, like the owl.

His shoulders sagged. "You'll have to forgive me, Jacob, old boy. My head injuries have left me . . . a tad out of sorts."

Jacob eyed him uncertainly, his expression somewhere between compassion and pity. "Perhaps there are quite logical explanations for all that's happened."

Lucas nodded.

"Still, one can't be too careful. Perhaps your grace shouldn't be alone until we have some answers."

"Perhaps."

"For instance, your grace might consider not disappearing from the house unaccompanied and without a trace."

"Perhaps you're right, Jacob."

But the next day, he did exactly the opposite.

While the safe course might have been to hole up in the house like some cowering milksop, the idea galled him. This was his home, his land.

In the first glimmer of dawn, he saddled a horse and set out—alone. Not on Saracen, though, as he would have liked. No, he'd learned his favorite horse had been sold off soon after he'd been declared dead. Apparently his mother couldn't bear seeing the once spirited Thoroughbred mope. Today, Lucas had to make do with a young Cleveland Bay newly added to the stable.

As the horse found its stride, Lucas adjusted the pistol tucked in his waistband. If someone shot at him again, damn it, he'd shoot back. If the source of yesterday's bullet turned out to be a poacher, well, he'd handle the matter with somewhat more diplomacy. He had purposely dressed the part of a duke, to lend authority to any action he might take.

Ducking low branches as he entered the forest, he thought back on his journey home, how he had chosen the plodding post-chaise over a much swifter sailing vessel. Coming by sea had seemed too much like tempting fate a second time.

So what the blazes justified his actions this morning? Why *not* stay safely at home, out of harm's way, or at least travel with an escort? Were these the actions of a man whose very existence affected the lives of so many others?

Not in the least.

His old friend's drunken assertion spurred him on: *It's who I am.* So obvious. So simple. Why had he ever fought so hard against it? These were not the actions of a duke but of a man like Luke Martin, who took chances, enjoyed risks and listened to his heart.

And who loved Charity Fergusson. Yes, he could admit it now. Wanted to admit it. Hell, he wanted to shout it to the world. Because, even without specific memories, he knew she had set him free, truly free, for the first time in his life.

He reached a junction in the path and came to a decision. Without breaking his horse's stride, he steered onto the trail that curved out of the forest and onto the main road, leading toward the vicarage.

A risk taker, a cavalier—the notion made him laugh out loud. His horse lurched at the sound. Lucas patted his neck and slowed the pace long enough to shrug out of his riding coat. After a couple of circular swings, he tossed it into the air behind him. Then he loosened the reins and leaned forward to enjoy a brisk stride. A whistle broke from his lips, the song that sprang to mind whenever he thought of Charity.

Alone when he shouldn't be, cantering through the forest with a gun at his hip, racing to the beautiful Scottish lass who held his heart in her hands—Lucas couldn't remember ever experiencing such a thrill at being alive, or feeling so much like . . . himself.

"She's not here?" He hadn't planned on this development. The exuberance that had propelled him to the vicarage deflated by several degrees.

"She went out for an early walk, sir," Esther told him.

"Alone?" He knew Charity hadn't taken the dogs, for

here they were, lunging at his legs until he stooped to greet them properly.

"Yes, sir, all alone."

"Did Miss Williams say where she was going?"

"No, your grace, she didn't. But she wore her sturdy boots, the heavy leather ones with the pull straps."

"Thank you, Esther." That might be the clue he needed, for Charity wouldn't don such footwear for a walk into town nor a visit to Longfield Park. The alternative, a trek through the woods, raised an alarm inside him. Someone had shot at him yesterday. Accident or no, Charity could be in danger.

As he turned to remount his horse, the Westies streaked out the door after him.

Esther followed in swift pursuit, bending in vain to capture Schooner. "Come here, you little . . . Sorry, your grace, they're always getting away from me."

With a quick pounce, she captured Skiff in her arms, then shooed Schooner away from Lucas's feet. He stepped into the stirrup and swung up to the saddle.

"Don't let them wander out of the garden, Esther. And stay out of the woods yourself. Mark me?"

If she responded, he didn't hear. He was already cantering away.

At the center of the hill fort mound, Charity stared in disbelief at Luke's recent labors. He'd leveled the plot, pounded oaken boughs deep into the ground, and gathered piles of vines waiting to be woven into an airy, sun-dappled rooftop.

All her convictions of the past hours burst like ocean waves through a crumbling seawall. How positive she had been, how certain she'd reached the right decision. But now—this! A sob clogged her throat.

She clutched her hands and tried to consider her options. But there weren't any. She couldn't possibly remain in Wakefield, not after that wretched scene the other night, when Helena nearly stumbled onto her midnight tryst with Luke.

A faint rustling caught her attention. As she listened, the sound became louder, more distinct: twigs snapping, branches brushing aside and whipping back into place. A rider, she concluded, and headed this way at a good clip.

Minutes later, Luke ascended the rise. He led a roan horse behind him, its front haunches bunched with the effort of the climb. Charity's lips curled in a bittersweet smile. She should have been taken aback by his arrival, but not so. It was almost as if she had summoned him, and indeed she had, in her heart if in no other way.

He released the reins. The animal wandered a few steps and dropped its head to graze.

Luke went motionless when he saw her, an expression of intense relief passing across his handsome features. "You're all right, then?"

She started toward him slowly, wanting to run into his arms and knowing she hadn't the right. "What an odd question," she said. "Of course I am."

He raked a hand through his dark hair, tousled and glistening with perspiration. "Thank God for that, Sweet Mercy."

The tears came without warning. Just gathered and spilled over, beyond her control. *Sweet Mercy.* He'd called her that upon awakening that first morning back in Scotland, rousing them both from the dream of Luke Martin. What did it mean that he called her that now?

His blurred form ran to her. She couldn't see for the blasted, burning tears but she felt his arms wrap tightly around her; ah, so very tight.

"By God, you shouldn't be here," he said, his voice ragged with unmistakable panic. "It isn't safe. Why are you crying, my dearest? Are you sure nothing's happened?" Lifting her off her feet, he crushed her closer.

She shook her head, gasping in the sheer exhilaration of being held by him, held without the hesitation and guilt that had sullied every impulsive embrace of these past few weeks.

"By God," he repeated. "I rode out this morning in a mood to challenge fate. I never thought you might do the same. I'd never forgive myself if anything happened to you."

"I don't understand." No, not a bit of it. But his arms felt wonderful, breathtaking. For now she didn't care about the rest. Except that he was beginning to hurt her, leading her to believe his mysterious concern stemmed from no small matter.

She thought to ask him what was wrong, then remembered she had something to tell him, nearly forgotten in the pleasure of his arms. It was all right to enjoy this moment, she decided. Not like their last encounter, when Helena almost saw them. This was different, because it would be the last time.

"I'm leaving," she said into his shirtfront, and dared to slip her fingers between his shirt studs and caress his humid skin.

He went utterly still. "What do you mean, leaving?"

"I'm going home to St. Abbs. You were right. I should never have come."

"I wasn't right." His hands moved to her face, bracketing her cheeks in Luke Martin's stubborn strength. "I was wrong, quite wrong."

"You and I will only end up hurting people we both

care about," she said quickly, before her courage waned. "And I do care about your family, in a way I never dreamed possible. I won't go on deceiving them."

"Nor will I."

Her heart skipped a beat, then pounded with the force of a cannon. "What are you saying?"

"I'm saying . . ."

There were no words after that, only kisses, deep and hot as the inner fires of a forge, and hands everywhere with caresses soft as lamb's wool one moment, rough and groping the next like sailors at the rigging in a storm.

Clothing hit the ground in heaps. Luke peeled her underthings away, freeing her breasts and hips and thighs to the cool touch of the morning air, the warm kiss of the sun, the blazing insistence of his hands. She felt liberated, giddy, as insubstantial as mist.

A laugh escaped her as his shirt studs thudded to the ground and fine linen gave way with taut rips. His trousers followed; he kicked them away like wayward mongrels. Something heavy thunked to the ground along with them. Charity wondered briefly about it but decided she didn't care.

Naked, they sank to their knees, breathless and tee-tering in their haste to deepen their kisses, to consume as much of each other as possible. They lost their balance and sprawled into the rushes, creating a snug nest of harebell and betony. The pungent scents of grass and earth mingled with the musk of desire. Charity savored the taste of Luke's kisses, a sweet spice she remembered well from their lovemaking in Scotland. How had she lived all these weeks without the pleasure of him?

"I love you," he told her, a fierce whisper. His tongue traced her ear's outer folds, his lips nuzzled.

Oh, yes, like that, she thought, arching her neck, squirming with ticklish delight. Inside, joy blared a triumphant note.

His next words awed that joy to a profound silence. "I know I love you and I know why I love you." His lips nestled against her cheek, a warm vibration. "You showed me who I am—who I really am without the title and all the rest. Your husband."

"The man I love." She might have said more but words melted to moans as he kissed his way to her breasts, entrapping the nipples between his lips and administering divine torture.

Lust, jagged and piercing, streaked through her. She arched, thrusting her breasts higher, heightening the sensations. When his teeth gently closed on her nipple, a spasm shook her frame and sent the sky spinning above her head.

Control became a forgotten matter as she wrapped her arms and legs around him. With handfuls of his thick hair she pulled his face to hers in a desperate need to feel his mouth against her own. His lips were warm and open, as devouring and unrelenting as she craved. His body weighted hers to the ground beneath her, his chest broad and rough against her breasts, his stomach hard and rippled against her belly. His penis prodded, impatient to be where she very much wanted it.

Perfect happiness filled her, and yet, merciless, a thread of honor tugged her heart.

"Luke, wait," she panted, but that was all. She discovered she couldn't say it, couldn't speak the name that hung between them for fear the very sound would destroy this newly unleashed passion and drive them apart.

"Helena," he said for her, drawing his lips away just long enough to form the syllables. The rest he managed between kisses, between tender and not so tender nips at her neck, her shoulders, her breasts. He positioned himself more firmly between her legs but she felt his restraint, his trembling effort to maintain this last scrap of control. "I love her as my dear sister, but I cannot be her husband. It's time I was honest with her. In truth, I think she already knows."

"Then you and I . . ."

"Oh, yes, my darling." On the last word, he drove into her, a single long sweep that buried him. Charity cried out. Luke began a steady rhythm and she met each thrust, desperate to fill the emptiness of the past weeks. She sensed the same frantic need in him each time he plunged anew, his face rigid with the effort of channeling a ferocious passion pent up for too long.

Their lovemaking beat a wild cadence on the earth beneath them. Each stroke drove her closer to ecstasy and threatened to shatter her soul. Just before she reached the brink, Luke pressed his lips to her hair. "Trust me with your heart."

"I always have," she cried, just as her being splintered into a thousand shimmering embers.

She must have dozed; how long, she didn't know. She shifted her leg, the one not thrown across Luke's waist. The grass felt cool and dewy against her skin, and she realized she'd not slept long at all.

"Did I wake you?" he asked softly, trailing his fingertips up and down her spine.

She purred. At some point, he'd gently lifted her and rolled, positioning her head on his shoulder, her torso across his own. A perfect berth for perfect dreams.

"No, my love, you didn't wake me," she said. "I woke myself to be sure this was no dream."

A breath of a chuckle raised his chest. "It's real enough,

dear wife. As real as our marriage vows. And now that your Luke has finally awakened, he won't drift off again."

She shut her eyes, savoring her happiness. "You never left me, not really. You only pretended to go away. That proves it." Lifting her hand, she pointed to his half-built structure.

"What do you mean?"

"I know what it is—the bower you promised to build for me, once the mulching was done and herd released to the summer pastures."

He pushed up on an elbow, raising her with him as he sat up. His lips parted as he regarded his handiwork, but he said nothing.

She smiled up at him. "You planned to build it out on the headland, overlooking the sea."

His brow creased, smoothed, creased again. "Was there a song about it? Something about a bower on a hillside?"

" 'Tween fields of heather and the great roarin' sea, I'll build a shady bower for my bonnie Annalee.' You used to sing it all the time." She smiled at the memory. "Only instead of Annalee you'd sing 'Chari-tee'."

"That's the song I've been whistling." He shook his head. "It's been driving me to distraction, both the whistling and the building."

"You promised the bower as an anniversary gift. It's rather overdue, wouldn't you say?"

He grinned and kissed her. Drawing back a little, he studied her face with an adoration that turned her insides to drizzling honey. He reached out a hand to stroke her belly.

"Tell me," he said, "since I've missed our anniversary, would it be a fitting gift for a new mother?"

Her breath caught. "How did you . . . ? Oh, Luke. Can

you forgive me? I'm so sorry I didn't tell you. I should have, but—"

"Sh." He placed a finger on her lips. "Why on earth would you confide in a man who'd abandoned you? It's you who must forgive me. Can you?"

Her arms snaked around his neck. "Done. But how on earth did you know?"

"I didn't until just now. I suspected, but holding your delectably naked body in my arms proved it beyond a doubt." Ducking his head, he suckled each breast with warm kisses and lowered her onto the grass. She raised her arms above her head, a long sigh of pleasure escaping her lips. "You were always glorious, my love, but in the past few weeks you've grown the bosom of a goddess."

"You!" She swatted him, laughing. "Isn't that just like an uncouth farmer."

"Aye, lass, and I intend to show you just how uncouth I can be." He pinned her beneath him, his face inches from hers. "I'm going to show you every day, and every night."

His head dipped, and he drew her lips into his mouth, probing, stroking with his tongue. Renewed aches spread through her, and her female parts sizzled in anticipation. But a concern surfaced through her bliss. She pushed him a little away.

"How will we explain to your family? To Helena? How can we avoid hurting them?"

"My darling, when they see how happy we are, and how right it is for us to be together, they'll forgive us and offer their blessings. I'm certain of it."

"Helena, too?" Charity shook her head as misery flooded her heart. "I can't bear the thought of how betrayed she'll feel. And I can't bear losing her friendship. I've come to love her so."

"You won't." He pressed a warm kiss to her forehead. "I believe that in her heart of hearts, Helena has already realized she and I aren't meant to be together. I've agonized over keeping her at a distance, but in truth she's been just as distant."

"But what will she do? I know Sir Joshua is destitute. What future will she have without you?"

"I have no intention of neglecting her future. She's beautiful, intelligent, sweet to a fault, and if she needs a dowry besides, I'll provide her with one that will have England's most eligible bachelors lining up at her door."

"She deserves no less. You've earned your place in heaven and in my heart for giving it to her." To her delight, her praise brought heated color to his face.

"Once Helena's future is happily secured," he went on, becoming more animated, "I'll introduce you to all of England as my duchess. Mother can plan her grand ball, the most extravagant the country has ever seen. We'll spare no expense for the new Duchess of Wakefield."

"Duchess?" She waited for him to grin, laugh, chuck her beneath the chin. He didn't.

"Of course. As my wife, you'll—"

"No. Oh, no."

"No? Why no?"

Feeling suddenly ill, Charity shoved at his shoulders, struggling against his weight to sit up.

"What's wrong? What did I say?" With a baffled expression he drew up far enough for her to roll out from under him.

Her joy fled. Feeling stupid, foolish, swindled by fate, she rummaged through the grass for her clothes. "I'm no duchess, Luke. I never will be. And if you believe otherwise, you're surely not the man I married and this is no dream, it's a nightmare."

Chapter Sixteen

For several bewildered seconds Lucas didn't move; he couldn't, nor could his brain decipher what in God's name just happened. He merely stared as Charity struggled into her petticoat and camisole, yanked ribbons into knots, swore over hard-to-reach hooks and flung her corset aside in frustration.

"Will you please calm down and explain why you're upset."

She held her dress in front of her like a shield. "You truly don't know?"

"How could I?" He tossed up his hands. "One moment we were ecstatically happy, and suddenly—this."

"You . . ." She thrust an accusing finger as if he'd committed some sordid crime. "You aren't Luke Martin. You're Lucas Holbrook."

"Of course I'm Lucas Holbrook. I can't deny that. Surely you didn't expect me to walk away from my birthright."

She smiled without humor, without warmth. "Yet you expect me to walk away from mine. From the farm we worked so hard to build. You wish me to be someone I'm not and live in a world where neither of us belongs." She paused, shaking her head. "What we just did, the things we said . . . I thought you'd finally realized you belong with me, in Scotland."

"What I've realized is that I love you, that I don't wish to live another day without you." Standing, he caught her hand and pulled her closer. She tried to resist him. "Isn't that what you wanted all along? To be my wife?" She angled her chin but he trapped it with his free hand, forcing her to meet his gaze. "Isn't it?"

"Aye, to be the wife of the man I loved. That's all I ever wanted. Nothing more, nothing less." Her eyes filled with moisture that stubbornly refused to spill over.

"Just the man," he whispered, drawing her yet closer with each word. "Not the title, not the wealth."

Her expression softened at the memory of her own assertion. When those honeyed lips parted, he kissed them and eased his tongue into her mouth. Even as he debated the wisdom of doing so, he realized she didn't protest. He pressed his advantage, gathering her hips against his own. The heat of renewed arousal throbbed, cradled tight between them.

"The man is what you have, my darling," he whispered against her mouth. "I was born to be Duke of Wakefield. I wish to share all I have with you. And with our child. If it's a boy, he'll be heir to Wakefield, the future duke."

"Ah." Without warning she shoved away.

"Now what did I say?" His erection met cool air; a shock of disappointment shook his frame. Damn it, when would he learn? He accomplished far more with kissing than speaking.

"Is that how you think of our child?" she demanded.

"Not a sweet babe conceived in love, but a recipient of all the silver you'll collect over your lifetime?"

He kicked at blades of grass, knowing if he dared open his mouth again, even to refute her charges, he'd only dig a deeper hole in which to bury himself.

Still, he had to risk it. Somehow he must make her understand. "Charity, you are my wife. I love you. I love this child—I swear I do. But I was born to certain responsibilities. You must understand."

"No, you must." Her gaze, flinty, resolute, drifted from his face toward the surrounding countryside. The tears that had been threatening held their own, reflecting bright sky above and a dark well of sadness within. "I love and want the man you were born to be, not the position you were born to hold. There is a world of difference between the two. Or so I believed."

Bending, she plucked her dress from where it had fallen during their kiss. She tossed it over her head and worked her arms through the tight sleeves. Twisting and turning, she struggled to fasten the buttons up the back. Lucas knew better than to offer his assistance, not with that look on her face. His gut knotted. He felt shut out, dismissed, and damned if he knew what to do about it.

"That we love each other is not the question," she said. "It's how. And where. If you were no longer here to be Duke of Wakefield, would there be no other to take your place? Are you as indispensable as all that?"

He knew she meant Wesley. "Should I disappear again, pretend to be dead?"

She had turned away, searching for one of her boots. She snapped back around. "Does being duke make you feel alive?"

No. But he didn't admit it aloud.

She let out a sorrowful sigh. "I am sorry for you, Lucas Holbrook. Trapped in a life not of your choosing is one thing. But to be given the gift of choice and refuse to embrace it is saddest of all."

She emphasized the last word by shoving her foot into the retrieved boot. Lucas watched her stomp off, backside swaying with a quick, determined rhythm. Too late did he realize her intention.

"Charity, wait."

"I love you," she said calmly as she gathered his horse's reins in both hands. "You'll know where to find me."

"You're taking my horse and leaving me here?"

"Aye. There's something I must do, something I should have done long ago. And then I'm going home. I want to see my mother. I want to tell her she's going to be a grandmother."

"She doesn't know?"

She shot him a level glance. "If Lara Fergusson knew, it would be her and not me speaking to you now, and be assured she'd be standing at the trigger end of a loaded musket." Leading the horse, she headed toward the slope of the mound.

"You shouldn't be riding in your condition."

"I'll be careful. Besides, taking your horse should give me the head start I need. It's time to stop lying, Luke. We were wrong, both of us, to ever have done so."

"Don't go." He started after her. "It isn't safe."

She showed no indication of hearing, but started down the descent. It was then he realized that, hang it all, he was still naked. Doubling back to his scattered clothing, he thrust his legs into his trousers. He consoled himself with the fact that she couldn't possibly leave Wakefield before he caught up with her. The eastbound coach wasn't due in until day after tomorrow.

There was still time to fix this. He would find her,

talk sense into her. There was the baby to think about, after all.

What if she wouldn't listen to reason? What if the stubborn harpy insisted upon returning to Scotland? After the most painful journey of his life—that of finding his heart—could he lose her now?

No. Never mind reasoning with her. Good God, did he actually speak of inheritances? Responsibilities and duty? No more of that. No more demands. He'd simply tell her how much he loved her. Needed her. Wanted her to stay.

Would she stay? Could someone like Charity, as sensual and unpredictable as the Scottish seaside, find happiness in a landlocked home, a rule-locked society?

He jammed his feet into his shoes. Grabbing his shirt, he cursed his former preference for studs over laces or buttons. How the devil would he ever find them all, scattered through the grass and wildflowers?

To hell with them. He shoved his shirt hem into his trousers. After feeling through the flattened rushes for his pistol, he tucked it securely into his waistband.

He'd head for home first, since that seemed to be the direction she'd taken through the woods. He could only guess she planned to confess the truth to his family and bid them farewell.

Her own strategy might work against her, he realized as he ploughed down the hillside. His family loved her. Truly loved her. They were not a fickle bunch and furthermore, conspiracy was not an unknown concept to the Holbrook-Livingston ladies. He'd lay a hefty wager they'd work out some way to keep her.

He should have known they'd adore her. How could he not have guessed that, when he himself had never stopped adoring her for a single instant, no matter all his claims to the contrary?

The visions filling his mind were so clear he couldn't fathom ever having forgotten in the first place. North Headland Farm, the sheep, the crags, the sea—the freedom. Freedom to be himself and love the woman of his dreams not because she made an appropriate wife for a nobleman, but because, by God, she matched him in wit and lust and sheer, unbridled, exuberant love.

The realization, the remembrance of it all, stunned him like a blow to the head all over again. He understood—suddenly and finally—how infinitely much he had to lose, and how much of his life was determined and defined by his love for this woman, and hers for him.

He had to find her. Of course he'd find her. She couldn't leave on the post-chaise for two days, after all.

What if the little spitfire found some other way?

Though his chest ached to bursting, he pushed on through the forest as if the devil's own stallion ran hard at his heels.

Charity hovered in the narrow hallway outside the Holbrooks' morning room, watching with a kind of dull fascination as the family prepared to break their fast. Lady Mary, Dolly, Wesley, Helena and Sir Joshua were all there. Only Jacob Dolan was missing, which suited Charity perfectly fine.

No one noticed her. She wished they would. Otherwise she might very well stand there all morning, gaping, mute, unable to initiate the very thing she'd come to do.

If she lingered long enough, would Luke arrive? She had taken the woods at barely more than a walk. Despite her grand bravado in rushing off to do the right thing, once in the saddle she'd remembered that anything faster than a modest trot could endanger her child.

So then, where was Luke? Had he discovered it an easy thing, after all, to let her go?

Helena's elegant form swept past the doorway as she moved the length of the table. Her father smiled as she set his plate before him. Charity caught the aromas of oatmeal, eggs and sausages. Lady Mary, in her habitual place at one end of the long oval, held a newspaper to her nose, scanning what must have been week-old information since periodicals didn't come often to Wakefield. Barely taking her eyes from the page, she nodded or shook her head at the various dishes Mortimer carried back and forth from the sideboards.

Dolly hovered near Wesley, asking if everyone had enough to eat and would they care for a drizzle of treacle on their scones. Helena leaned across the table, reaching for sugar and cream for her father's coffee.

Such a pleasant scene. Charity had the odd impression she might observe them all day without their noticing, as if she were invisible, a brief apparition quickly gone and best forgotten.

But then vigilant Mortimer spotted her.

"Ah, Miss Williams. Good morning. I'll set another place." He bustled to one of the room's ponderous china cabinets.

"Oh, Charity, dear." Dolly bustled across the room to her. "How lovely of you to join us."

Helena looked up from her plate. "Why, if I'd known you were coming I'd have met you halfway and walked back with you."

Charity held up a hand to silence the polite greetings. "Please, this shan't take but a moment." She didn't bother to school her tongue, and saw the fact register on their faces. Little frowns of puzzlement formed as they took in the state of her dress, crushed and grass-stained, ill fitting without her corset and half the buttons done up wrong.

Oh, *was* Luke on his way? Would he arrive in time to prevent the irreparable harm she was about to do? Minutes from now, his family would loathe her.

She hesitated, but no footsteps echoed from the Grand Hall, no voice shouted her name from the servants' staircase.

"Mr. Mortimer," she said, allowing her Rs to roll, "you needn't set an extra place. I won't be staying long and I'm not in the least bit hungry."

"You sound different, Charity, dear." Helena smiled uncertainly. "Are you feeling quite all right today?"

"Aye. I—I've come to say goodbye—"

"You're not!"

"Do say it isn't so."

"Where will you go?"

"Is there an emergency?"

"Is somebody ill?"

"Did someone die?"

"Please, if you'll let me explain." Again, she stemmed the flurry of pandemonium with the flat of her palm, feeling cornered by a small army, one quite capable of closing forces against her.

"Yes, do everyone hush and let the girl speak." Scraping back her chair and rising slowly, Lady Mary turned a stern countenance to Charity. "What is this nonsense about saying goodbye? Surely you need not rush off so suddenly. And exactly why *are* you speaking that way?"

"This is the way I speak," she said quietly, "when I'm not pretending otherwise."

"Pretending," Helena repeated with emphasis, a startled look on her face.

Lady Mary hushed her.

With a deep breath Charity prepared to continue, but the words, heavy and bitter, stuck in her throat. Her gaze darted from face to face, each ranging in emotion from curiosity to dismay but all equally expectant.

"I'm not who you think I am." Her voice shook but nonetheless scaled the dark paneled walls to echo against the carved ceiling. She swallowed. "I'm not who I said I was. I'm a fraud, you see. A fake."

Eyes narrowed, brows furrowed, chins angled. She could see they were trying their best to comprehend but not making a great success of it.

"My name is Charity Fergusson," she continued, "not Williams. And as you can plainly see, I'm Scottish, not English. It was my family Luke stayed with while he was . . . away."

Dolly gasped, but Lady Mary silenced her with a scowl. "Go on."

"I . . . oh, how can I say this?" She fisted her hands in her skirts. "I followed Luke—Lucas—here because I . . . fell in love with him and couldn't bear for him to leave me."

Even from behind a thickening mist of tears, she saw Helena's jaw drop. She quickly looked away. Oh, she deserved all the animosity the Englishwoman could muster, but the coward in her couldn't face the end of a friendship that had come to mean so much, so very much.

But perhaps she might still ease some of Helena's pain, her sense of betrayal.

"I was a fool," she said to the beautiful young Englishwoman. "Lucas belongs with you, Helena—Miss Livingston. He always did, he always will. There's nothing for me but to go home where I belong."

"But—"

"Please let me finish before I lose what little courage

I have. I'm so ashamed of deceiving you all and taking advantage of your kindness. But you see, when first I came to Wakefield, I'd no idea how fond I'd grow of this family. And how much I'd despise myself for lying to you."

Her throat closed. Tears obscured those dear faces she'd never forget. She and the Holbrooks were forever linked through her heart and through the life inside her. Her hands drifted to her belly. Oh, she very much wanted this lovely English family for her child: a gift beyond value. But how? Despite all her elegant airs and borrowed dresses, she could never be a duchess. Could never lie her way through life, even with Luke beside her.

Because she'd never be good enough. Never grand enough. Never be what Helena was: a gracious and generous lady. It had nothing to do with freckles or the lack, nor wild brassy hair nor even her common Scottish accent. It had everything to do with integrity, something she'd lost along the way and found where she'd least expected: in the honest faces of these English aristocrats.

Faces she could no longer bear to see. Whirling, she took off running, intent on nothing more than retreating to the solitude of the vicarage, the comfort of her Westies. She heard voices and footsteps behind her but didn't pause, not even when Helena pleaded, "Charity, wait. Please. We must talk."

Helena scurried after Charity but came to an uncertain halt in the doorway.

Oh, dear, what an appalling quagmire. What should she do? Catch up to Charity and blurt the truth, or find

Lucas first and end what should have ended the moment he had arrived home?

Oh, foolish, foolish girl, she berated herself. Lying never accomplished a blessed thing; she should have known that from the start. Now Wesley was angry, Lucas confused, the family dumbfounded, poor Charity guilt-ridden, and all of it—*all* of it—her fault.

She jumped when Dolly tapped her shoulder and said, "Good heavens, what was that all about?"

"Oh, Dolly, I've made a terrible mess of things. Our darling Charity loves Lucas while I . . ."

The bewilderment in Dolly's face deepened.

"Dearest Dolly," Helena continued softly, gently, "I love your younger son. I'm frightfully sorry. Oh, so dreadfully sorry, but that is the simple truth. I—we—didn't mean for it to happen but . . ."

From over Dolly's shoulder, Helena sought Wesley's support. He shoved his untouched plate away and cleared his throat. "We're in love, Mother, and there it is. I, for one, am not in the least bit sorry."

Helena's heart surged. She had dreaded this moment for months, since long before Lucas's return. For even if he had never come home, explaining her utter and complete change of heart would have been an unpleasant and delicate matter. She was supposed to have been in mourning for her fiancé, after all. But now the truth was out. Now it would be dealt with.

Lady Mary's gaze bore into her, one fine silver brow arched to a shrewd slant. Perhaps this news hadn't shocked everyone as much as Helena had expected. Her father, on the other hand, nibbled the end of a sausage and looked baffled as usual.

She turned back to Dolly. "Do you despise me?"

"Despise you? I suppose not. I mean . . . no, of course

not. But my dear, you and Lucas are engaged. Engaged!" Her hand flew to her throat as if she'd choke on the word. She glowered at her younger son. "Wesley Holbrook, how could you?"

"I thought he was dead. We all did."

"Then you should have been mourning him, not seducing his poor, grieving fiancée."

"He didn't do any such thing." Helena caught Dolly's hand. This was not going well. Not at all well. "It wasn't like that. It just . . . happened."

"Just happened," Dolly repeated with no small degree of sarcasm. Then her face softened and she returned the pressure of Helena's grasp. "What are we to do about poor Lucas? He'll be positively crushed."

Helena tried to speak assurances but the words emerged as a stutter.

Wesley pushed to his feet. "I have a certain feeling Lucas's answer just went running from the room."

"Indeed." Lady Mary folded her arms in an authoritative manner. "Helena, are you quite certain you love Wesley and not Lucas?"

"Oh, yes," Helena replied, and marveled that she could feel both relieved and utterly miserable at the same time. "Forgive me, but I'm as certain as can be."

"Good." Lady Mary gave a firm nod. "Because that's Lucas's ring Charity has been wearing. There's a lot more to this tale than she's telling."

"But Mama," said Dolly, "Charity's ring bears no resemblance to the one Lucas lost other than being set with a similar sapphire. Not a common stone, to be sure, but neither is it a complete rarity."

"Cod's wallop." Mary brushed an imaginary stray hair from her face. "I selected that stone for your father and I'd recognize it anywhere, in any setting. But that's not all. Unless I've lost all power of perception, Charity Williams or Fergusson or whoever she may be is with child."

There was a collective gasp.

"Dear heavens." Dolly pressed the back of her hand to her forehead. "I think I shall faint."

"Dolly Holbrook." Her mother shook her finger. "You'll do no such thing."

"But Mama, an illegitimate child? Just think of the scandal, the disgrace."

Lady Mary slapped the tabletop, rattling teacups and silverware. "Good heavens, as if it would be the first. Why, if there's a single wellborn family in all of England without at least one by-blow in its midst, I'll eat my quizzing glass."

"I . . . suppose you're right." Dolly's fingertips tapped an uncertain rhythm on the buttons of her bodice.

"Of course I am. And if this girl is carrying Lucas's child, we're speaking of your grandchild and my great-grandchild. The circumstances of its conception are not nearly as important as the fact of its existence, in my estimate."

"Nor in mine, when you put it that way," Dolly agreed.

"We'll simply arrange for them to marry before the child is born. If they aren't already," Mary added in an undertone that sent a bolt of astonishment through Helena.

A fork clattered onto porcelain, startling them all. Helena ran to her father's side. She retrieved his fork from his plate and replaced it in his hand. "It's all right, Father, nothing to worry about."

"Did I hear correctly? A little one on the way?" Looking up at her with an oddly clear expression, he waved the fork in the air. "Just what the place needs, by God, little ones tramping about, raising a clamor. Should get some dogs to entertain them. A pony, too. Dredge the pond so they can splash about in summer."

"I rather hope it's a girl child," Dolly said in a dreamy voice. "How lovely, to have a little girl to dress and spoil and play tea party with. And really, I've grown quite fond of Charity, albeit she isn't what we originally envisioned for our Lucas. Do you think she'll do, Mama, as his duchess?"

Mary shrugged. "Why not? She fooled all of us into believing her gentle born. She's sharp and clever and what's more, to go to such great lengths she must love Lucas very much indeed."

"But you heard her, she's given up on him." Helena hoisted handfuls of her skirts. "I have to catch her and tell her it's all right, she needn't go."

Dolly caught her arm. "Oh, Helena, all those awful things I said about Scottish people. She must detest me entirely. Do tell her I didn't mean it. Not really. Tell her I was only upset about Lucas."

"I'm sure she knows, but I'll tell her anyway," Helena said, and scampered from the room.

Just before she pushed through the swinging door into the Grand Hall, Wesley called to ask if he should accompany her. The rustle of Mary's black taffeta followed.

"You're not needed," his grandmother told him. "This is between the two women, and the women shall resolve it."

Rather than taking the road, Helena opted for the wooded shortcut to the vicarage. Her dress would suffer but she'd reach Charity that much sooner.

The path took her beyond the bowling green and arbor and past the old mews, where former dukes of Wakefield had once kept prized hunting falcons. The brick structure, built to resemble the Tudor portion of the main house, sat empty and decaying, though Wesley had often spoken of renovating and obtaining some birds.

Through towering oaks and slender birches the sun angled into her eyes. She shielded them with her hand and ducked beneath branches as she rounded the corner of the building.

She became aware of voices, muffled through the foliage at first, but swiftly becoming distinct over the rustling of her feet through old, dead leaves. Angry words took shape the exact moment she realized she should not have heard them, should not have been there.

"His death must look like an accident, you idiot. Not a murder. How could you have been so stupid as to shoot at him?"

"I'm sorry, sir," a second man muttered. A gust of wind swept the branches aside, and Helena recognized a local farmer.

Too late to turn and run. She froze, staring. The other man turned and swore, and Helena's world turned on end.

Jacob Dolan.

For a frantic moment she thought to feign ignorance, to mumble something cordial and slip away. But Jacob's expression went from dismayed to ruthless in a fraction of a second. The farmer sprang, arms snaking out and seizing her around the middle. A hand that reeked of dirt and wood smoke clamped across her mouth, biting against her upper lip.

"Get her inside, quickly," Jacob Dolan said, and Tom Whitely hauled Helena into the dank gloom of the abandoned mews.

Chapter Seventeen

As urgency spurred Lucas past the stables, from the corner of his eye he saw his horse being tended by a groom. Giddy relief surged through him—Charity had arrived safely. Headstrong wench, she might have fallen during the ride, injuring herself and the child.

A hasty inquiry with Mrs. Hale sent him skidding through the house to the morning room. Catching hold of the lintel he slid to a halt, arrested by the scene inside.

Breakfast sat ignored and congealing on the plates. Grandmother loomed beside the table with her arms stiffly folded, glaring down at a pair of poached eggs as though they were offending schoolboys. Mother paced and sighed before the window. At the table, Wesley slouched with head in hand, pensive and brooding. In contrast, Sir Joshua looked delighted and strangely lucid, and rambled odd nonsense about governesses, ponies and dogs.

Charity was nowhere to be seen.

Lucas cleared his throat for attention. "Has Charity been here this morning?"

"Oh, my dear Lucas." His mother circled the table and swept toward him, hands open and reaching. "My poor, dearest boy—" She stopped short, eyes gone wide. "What on earth's happened to you?"

He'd forgotten about his missing shirt studs, his discarded coat, the bits of grass sticking out from his hair. One hand started toward his neckline; his collar, too, had been forgotten at the mound. And the pistol—quickly he positioned his arm to hide the brass-studded butt at his hip. "I haven't time to explain."

"Were you thrown from your horse?" She began a hasty inspection, running her palms over his shirtfront. "Are you hurt? Shall I have Mortimer fetch the surgeon?"

"Now, Dolly," said Grandmother, raising her quizzing glass, "he looks intact enough to me. Don't smother him."

"No, indeed." Wesley lifted his chin from his palm. "It's time to come clean with him." He raised an eyebrow. "And he with us."

Tightening her grip on his hands, Dolly gazed up at Lucas with an irksome mixture of fondness and consternation. "It was quite dastardly of you to keep such a secret from us."

"Oh, don't scold the boy either." Grandmother continued surveying him through her quizzing glass. "I'm sure he had his reasons. I'm equally sure he'll share them with us in due time. Isn't that true, Lucas?"

Eager to have his information and be off, he dismissed the question with a shake of his head. "I've no idea what any of you are talking about. Where is Charity?"

"Why, she returned to the vicarage, of course," his mother said.

"Yes," Wesley added, "and Helena followed to reassure her she needn't rush off to Scotland. Especially under the, uh," he coughed into his hand, "circumstances."

Sir Joshua poked a finger at the air. "Cumber Spaniel—just the thing. Had one myself as a boy. Followed me everywhere."

"What?" Having time for neither his brother's innuendoes nor Joshua's babbling, Lucas turned to go. "Never mind."

Plunging down the servants' stairs two at a time, he reached the garden door as footsteps echoed behind him. Without slowing his pace, he glimpsed Wesley from over his shoulder.

"I'm coming with you," his brother called. His determined expression brooked no debate.

Lucas tried anyway. "No, you are not. I have an urgent matter to discuss with Charity." The last thing he needed was an audience as he bent his knee and begged her for another chance. "It has nothing to do with you."

"Oh, yes it does, brother." Refusing to be put off, Wesley matched his pace shoulder to shoulder, crossing the gardens to the stables. "It has a damned colossal lot to do with me, and with Helena, too, so let's make haste."

"I'm fine, Esther," Charity insisted for the third time since she'd arrived home. "May we please just pack my things and straighten the house."

The girl tarried by the foot of the bed, fingers absently combing the fringe of the shawl Charity had handed her to fold. "You're off on a trip, then, miss? A little visit somewhere? Am I to accompany you?"

"No, dear, not a visit." Charity hovered at the open wardrobe, surveying the dresses. Cousin Emilie would be happy to have her flowered muslin frock and silk evening gown back. "It's time I went home."

The girl's curiosity burned her back. Even the dogs

seemed perplexed, their little eyes darting to track her every move from the comfort of her pillow.

"A sudden decision, miss," the young maid said after a weighty pause. "Have you discussed it with the Holbrooks?"

Charity turned, intending to comment on Esther's uncharacteristic cheekiness. But when her mouth opened, the truth somehow slipped out. "The Holbrooks already know, Esther, and they cannot but agree with my decision."

"Oh, I can't fathom that, miss, truly I can't." She shook her head, making the rusty curls framing her face dance. "Not with the way they go on about you all the day long. You're a great favorite amongst them and they'll not take well to your leaving. Not at all well, miss."

No? Then where was Luke? Where were any of them? Surely they'd had plenty of time to follow her by now.

"You couldn't be more wrong," she said, letting the skirt of Emilie's gown slide from her fingers. She sank onto the edge of the bed and cradled her head in her hands. Schooner vaulted into her lap, while Skiff fell to gnawing his favorite toy, a braided length of fabric scraps. "They'll rejoice at my going, Esther. It will make life simpler for everyone."

"There now, miss, you mustn't fret." The girl sat beside her, a plump arm providing a warm support at Charity's waist. "Is it . . . because of the babe that you're leaving?"

Charity met Esther's gaze full on. "Yes. No. The Holbrooks don't know about that. Not yet. You mustn't tell them. And it isn't what you think."

"Oh, I don't think a thing, miss. Not my place. Except, I don't understand why you're running away from people who love you. Who'll help you if you give them the chance. I know the Holbrooks, miss. They're decent folk, every one of them."

"Yes, yes they are." Charity sighed, having neither the energy nor the heart to explain.

"Seems to me, miss, that if you're running because of the babe and don't want the family to know about it, it must be because a certain one of them is responsible."

Charity froze. Could this youngster truly be but fourteen? "How did you . . . ?"

Esther shrugged. "You and his grace have been dancing on hot coals round each other. And I hear things from the other servants. I know about young girls and noblemen, and such as goes on between them. Only, it's hard to fathom his grace taking advantage of a lady the likes of yourself, miss."

"Oh, Esther, he didn't. You must never think that of his grace. Not ever." Charity grasped the girl's shoulders with a shake that startled them both.

"You're like a she-wolf defending her mate, miss."

A she-wolf, yes. Such instincts are what had driven her to Wakefield in the first place, along with the certainty that she would succeed. Well, she hadn't succeeded, not in the least. Oh, she'd managed to rouse Luke's memories, his heart, his passion—and not any of it enough to outweigh the duties he'd been born to.

Her hands slipped from Esther's shoulders and she apologized with a shake of her head. "It's so very complicated, dear. All I know is, it's time I went home where I belong."

"I shall miss you."

Charity searched the maid's freckled features, momentarily forgetting her own dilemma as she recalled Wesley Holbrook's warning concerning the girl's welfare.

"Esther, you'll return of course to the main house once I've gone, won't you?"

"Where else would I go, miss? Though I'd rather stay here with you."

"Yes, but no one has offered you employment elsewhere, have they?"

Esther screwed up her face in thought. "Well, that nice Mr. Whitely, that works up at the house sometimes, mentioned once how girls can earn a pretty purse working in fine town houses in the city. But Lord Wesley overheard me talking about it with my mum, and he shook his finger at me and said good girls stay home where they belong."

"And so you put Mr. Whitely's suggestions out of your mind?"

"Of course, miss." A wash of scarlet crept up the girl's neck. Charity had a sudden hunch.

"Because Lord Wesley said it?"

The blush deepened, and Esther fell to petting Schooner intently. Charity threw an arm around her and hugged her close. "Lord Wesley is handsome and a good man besides. But take some advice from me. Don't set your sights higher than your station. It'll only break your heart."

"I know that, miss," the maid said quietly. The fire in her cheeks gradually cooled. "And Lord Wesley would never, you know . . . he's too honorable for that. Besides, he's already set his cap for . . ."

"For who?"

"Oh, it's not my place to gossip, miss."

Urgent banging on the front door cut their exchange short. Schooner bounded to the floor and Skiff darted after. Together they scuttled from the room, excited yips filling the cottage.

"Who on earth?"

"I'll go see, miss."

Charity waited in the bedroom, stomach twisting and hands trembling. Could it be Luke? Was he here to convince her to stay in Wakefield? Or was he suddenly willing to return to Scotland with her? Dared she hope?

Or could it be Helena, come to confront her? For an instant she contemplated diving into the wardrobe.

Coward. Helena deserved the opportunity to deliver a scathing reproach. Charity stood, lifting her chin and tugging her bodice, which simply refused to lie smooth without her corset.

The front door thwacked against the wall as it opened. Charity started at the sound. Brisk footsteps echoed from the vestibule.

"Is Miss Williams at home?"

Luke.

Her heart pounded. As she reached the tiny passage connecting her bedroom to the foyer, she heard Wesley Holbrooks's voice as well.

"Is Miss Livingston here?"

Bounding over Esther's feet, Skiff and Schooner trotted circles around their visitors. Esther bent to shoo them away.

"Yes, sir, n-no, sir," she stammered. "I mean, Miss Williams is here, sir, but Miss Livingston is not."

"Charity." Seeing her in the passage, Luke stepped over the dogs and squeezed past Esther. "My darling, you're here. You're all right."

Pulling her into his arms, he kissed her as if he hadn't seen her in weeks. She not only let him, she melted against him and kissed him back with a greediness that belied her earlier resolve to be strong.

He held her at arm's length. "Everything is all right, isn't it?"

"Well, I've been better of course," she said, and felt immediately stupid. But how could everything be all right after what happened at the hill fort?

"Yes, about this morning," he said, echoing her thoughts. "You made your sentiments perfectly clear, but as you once told me, my love, we aren't yet finished."

Stepping back, she suddenly saw him with her eyes instead of her heart. "What in heaven's name happened to you? You look worse than I do."

He fumbled to close his gaping neckline. "Priorities, my darling. I chose you over my usual dapper appearance and shirt studs."

She laughed and reached for him again.

Her hand brushed Wesley's shoulder. He stood right behind Luke in the cramped passage, which hardly accommodated two much less three. "I hate to interrupt this touching scene," he said, "but how long ago did Helena leave?"

"Helena?" Charity cast puzzled glances at the brothers. "She hasn't been here."

"She has to have been. She dashed off to follow you. Lucas and I didn't pass her on the road, so . . ."

"Perhaps she changed her mind and went home," she said, her voice gone small. She studied her feet, hardly able to look the younger Holbrook in the eye. "I wouldn't blame her if she never wished to lay eyes on me again."

"I don't like this." Wesley gripped Luke's shoulder. "Something might have happened to her."

"Sweet mercy." Charity studied the two of them. "Do you think she met with an accident? I'll never forgive myself."

Luke's arms went around her. "Don't worry, my darling, I'm sure she's safe. She probably did return home."

As his embrace tightened, she felt evidence of his arousal against her hip. It took her aback. Now? With all that was happening?

Her hip?

"What is that?" Stepping back, she caught a flash of bright, polished brass protruding from Luke's waistband. He attempted to conceal it with his arm, but she grasped his wrist. "Is that a pistol?"

"Ah, yes, actually."

"Have you lost your wits? What need would you have of such a thing?"

"Lucas believes someone shot at him in the woods the other day," Wesley calmly informed her.

"Dear God."

Luke thwacked his brother's chest with a half-closed fist. "Idiot." He turned back to Charity, raising the same hand to graze her cheek with the backs of his fingers. "Strange things have been happening, beginning with that falling owl. Coincidences, perhaps, but I'm not taking chances."

"Oh, Luke." She threw her arms around his neck as if her fiercest embrace might protect him from harm. Her thoughts took an abrupt turn. "Sweet mercy, Helena might truly be in danger."

"Yes, and I'm going to find her." Wesley pivoted and returned to the front door. "Lucas, are you coming?"

"Stay here, my love," Luke admonished as he turned to follow. "Lock the doors."

"Wait." She snatched his hand. "Where will you search? The two of you can't go running off blindly."

The brothers exchanged glances. "We should split up," Luke suggested. "Wes, you check the guest house. I'll search the village."

Wesley shook his head. "We would have passed her

on the road. With us on horseback, she hadn't had time to out-walk us yet."

"Maybe she didn't take the road." Luke considered. "There are other routes. I think it unlike her, but perhaps one of the woodland trails."

"This could take hours." Stepping out into the front garden, Wesley retrieved his mount from a thoroughly ruined patch of pansies growing beside the path.

"May I make a suggestion?" Charity reached behind Esther and scooped Schooner into her arms.

"If it's a quick one." Luke eyed her quizzically.

"The dogs."

"My darling, we haven't time for them right now."

"No, no. They're terriers."

His expression went blank.

"Terriers are bred to hunt small game. Trained to follow scents."

"By God, yes." Yanking his foot from the stirrup, Wesley did an about-face. "We could take them back to the house and have them sniff something of Helena's. They could track her from there." He frowned at the squirming Westy in her arms. "Do you think they're up to the task?"

"Of course." Charity felt a moment's indignation.

"Let's go." Luke reached for Schooner.

Charity whisked the dog out of his reach. "I'm coming with you."

"Oh, no, you're not," the brothers said as one.

"I most certainly am. They're my dogs, after all."

"Actually, darling, I bought them. It so happens I remember the incident. It cost me a small fortune to prevent their previous owner from drowning them in the Firth of Forth." Luke fell silent, gazing the length of his nose at her. "On second thought, perhaps you'd be safer up at the house."

Her stomach muscles tangled at the thought of facing Dolly and Lady Mary again. "I don't think so. Not after . . ."

"Nonsense." He peered around her into the house. "Esther, your mistress will need her hat and shawl. Yourself as well."

"Luke, please . . ."

"Lucas," Wesley called, his voice tight with impatience. "We have to go."

That settled it. With no time to argue, Charity found herself perched before Luke in his saddle, returning to the very place she had thought never to see again. At least, not this soon.

Chapter Eighteen

As Lucas and his brother trotted to keep pace with Skiff and Schooner on the wooded trail, Wesley extended a hand. "Give me the gun."

"No." Lucas patted the weapon at his hip.

"You'll only shoot your leg off. Besides, if these suspicions of yours prove true, I'm better trained to use it."

"Then you should have brought your own."

"Don't be an ass." Wesley's out-thrust hand rapped Lucas's arm. "Just give me the pistol. Now, Lucas."

"No."

"Damned stubborn goat."

Ahead of them, the Westies snuffled along the leaf-strewn path, dodging here into tangles of weeds, halting there to sniff the wind.

"This seemed a good idea at the outset," Lucas murmured, "but I'm wondering if these dogs don't think they're simply out for a stroll. What was I thinking anyway? Helena on a trail? Through the woods?"

Wesley's lip curled. "Yes, Helena on a trail through the woods. Why not?"

"It isn't her style." Lucas peered through the foliage, searching for signs of human activity.

"How do you know her style hasn't changed since you've been away?"

He ignored both the question and his brother's derisive tone. "Perhaps we should have tried the village."

Wesley snorted, a *what would you know about it* kind of sound. "Helena was determined to speak with Charity," he said. "Nothing would have deterred her unless ... unless something's happened to her."

His voice caught, and this Lucas didn't ignore. Wesley turned away before Lucas met his eye. He contemplated his younger brother's rigid profile.

"Look Wes, I just don't think Helena would have ventured into the forest. She's afraid of dark, damp places and anything that crawls. Even the birds make her jumpy—"

"Birds." Wesley sprinted forward, catching up to the dogs. "I think I know where we're headed. Unless I miss my guess, these two will veer left at the fork up ahead."

"The mews?"

"Yes. I'd forgotten, but the shortest route from the house to the main road is a trail that cuts right by there. The place is falling apart. Helena easily could have injured herself on a piece of rubble. She might have turned her ankle, fallen and hit her head."

As if the Westies heard and understood, they reached the fork and bolted forward, galloping as fast as their short legs allowed.

Charity tiptoed along the Grand Hall and prayed no one would notice her. From the depths of the dining room came the muffled sounds of morning housekeeping—the brushing of the curtains, the dusting of buffets, the polishing of the graceful rosewood table.

How she wished Luke had escorted her inside and smoothed the way with Dolly and Lady Mary, but of course he and Wesley had raced off with the Westies to find Helena. And now even Esther abandoned her, scurrying below stairs to visit with her mother. That left Charity alone to negotiate an uncertain tide, or drown.

Still hoping for a rational—and harmless—explanation for Helena's mysterious disappearance, they had all agreed not to alarm the two elder ladies by mentioning the matter. Dolly would be beside herself with worry. And for all her fierce noise, Mary possessed a softer heart than most people guessed and she was terribly fond of Helena.

Still, it would have given Charity a topic of conversation other than that deplorable scene in the morning room earlier. How to explain her sudden reappearance? As she passed Luke's study, she considered ducking inside and hiding under the desk until his return. She might have, except that just then Dolly stepped out from the drawing room.

"Charity." Her hand went to her bosom. "You've returned."

She sucked in a breath and braced for the reproach she deserved. She expected the worst: a thorough dressing-down, recriminations, accusations, tears. Experience had taught her that with Dolly Holbrook, emotions ran high.

The woman remained eerily quiet for the span of several slamming heartbeats. Then she trotted across the hall and embraced Charity. "Have you quite forgiven me, then, dearest?"

Her jaw went slack. "Me forgive you? What on earth for?"

Dolly grasped her hands. "For all those awful things I said about . . ." Her voice dropped to a whisper. "Oh, dear me, I'm so ashamed. You know, Scottish people."

"Oh, Dolly—"

"I didn't mean any of it. Not a word. I was upset about Lucas. Why, I think Scottish people are perfectly lovely. Some of my dearest friends are Scots. Lady Glenfiddich and I go back decades and . . . oh, Helena did explain to you, didn't she?"

"Helena?"

"Yes. At your cottage." Dolly released her hands and glanced around the hall. "Where is she, by the way? And the boys as well."

"The boys?" Think, think. She certainly couldn't tell Dolly the truth. "They went to, ah . . . the village. Yes. I believe Helena needed a few items from the village and your sons accompanied her."

Dolly's eyebrows gathered. "How very odd. Then how did you arrive?"

"I, ah, walked, and . . ." She broke off at the approaching rustle of taffeta.

"Do allow the girl to come in and sit down." Lady Mary raised her quizzing glass and regarded them from the drawing room doorway. "Did I hear you correctly— you walked all the way back from the vicarage? You've been on your feet altogether too much for one day."

"Oh, I daresay Mama's right. Good heavens, what was I thinking?" Dolly took Charity's arm and all but hauled her into the drawing room. "Sit here in the wing chair. It's the most comfortable seat in the entire house. Would you like to put your feet up? Here's a footstool."

"Please don't bother." Charity's words went unheeded. Dolly dragged a petit point hassock beneath her feet, while Lady Mary shoved an embroidered silk pillow behind her back.

"There, now. Rest." The elderly woman tugged the tasseled bellpull. Within moments Esther curtsied on the threshold. "Tea, please, Esther. With mint if we have any. Mint has such restorative powers," she added as she took a seat in the matching chair beside Charity's.

Dolly settled on the settee opposite them. "Yes, and Esther, ask Cook to make up some of her delicious curried veal sandwiches." She looked sagely at Charity. "Meat, you know. Splendid for the constitution."

No, Charity didn't know. At least, she hadn't the faintest idea what fueled this inordinate fuss. Until . . .

"Earlier, you mentioned returning home. I assume you meant Scotland." Dolly tented her fingers beneath her chin. "My dear, do you think it wise to travel so far at this time?"

Charity's breath caught. Her eyes darted back and forth between the ladies, catching a fleeting wink, a brief nod.

Did they *know?* Had Luke revealed her pregnancy? Had they guessed? Or did "at this time" hold a completely different meaning? Perhaps the recent rains had washed a bridge out. Perhaps there'd been tales of brigands on the road. Or . . .

They knew.

Charity jumped up from her chair. "Excuse me. I need to speak with Esther."

"But she'll be back presently with the tea," Dolly called after her.

She bustled out of the drawing room, hoping neither woman followed. Her heart drummed beneath her bodice. Sweet mercy, she hadn't meant to scamper away so rudely but she'd panicked, pure and simple. With

Luke beside her, she might find the courage to discuss her pregnancy with his family. But alone? She hadn't the first notion of what to say, how much to explain. Did they believe the child illegitimate?

Dashing across the Grand Hall, she slipped into Luke's study and sagged against the wall. She needed to steady her pulse. She needed a plan. Only minutes ago she'd considered hiding out in this room. How long, she wondered, before the ladies came looking for her?

Footsteps in the hall decided the matter. Oh, she was far from ready to face them but she couldn't be so childish as to evade Dolly and Mary's concern for her welfare. Stepping to the doorway, she started.

"Oh! Mr. Dolan, it's you. Good morning."

He looked as startled as she. "Good morning, Miss Williams."

"Where are you off to?" She pointed to the portmanteau in his hand, the one he so obviously tried to whisk behind him when he saw her.

He regarded it as if surprised to find it there. "Yes, well, it's time I returned to London, isn't it?"

"I suppose." She glanced down at the valise again and noticed something else, something that prompted her to ask, "Have you seen Miss Livingston this morning?"

"I'm sorry, no. I've been packing and haven't left my room until now."

Her gaze dipped again. The solicitor bent his head to follow her line of sight. A kind of companionable silence fell as they contemplated an indisputable fact. Then Charity looked him in the eye and quietly said, "That's a lie, Mr. Dolan."

* * *

Lucas and Wesley slowed as they approached the small clearing that surrounded the mews. They muffled their footfalls with careful steps.

"Do you see anything?" Wesley whispered.

The trail skirted one side of the dilapidated structure, while a box hedge gone wild hemmed in the other. They saw no sign of movement, no heap of a muslin-clad figure strewn across the ground.

Lucas shook his head, watching as Skiff and Schooner halted at the edge of the trees. Their noses quivered with interest, but they remained silent and motionless.

"Perhaps your hunch was wrong," Lucas whispered back.

The dogs made a sudden dash toward the building. When they reached a ventilation opening in the brickwork, they pressed their noses to it and sniffed furiously.

"Or perhaps not." Lucas started forward.

Wesley grabbed his arm. "Wait."

"For what? She could be inside. As you said, she might have injured herself."

Wesley shot him a severe look. "And as you implied, she may have met with foul play."

Lucas studied the clearing, the nestled building. All lay quiet and still, except for the dogs.

Taking up positions behind two trees and a snarl of undergrowth, they watched Skiff and Schooner's progress along the side of the mews. Something inside clearly interested them, but Lucas wondered if it might be nothing more than a nest of field mice.

"This is ridiculous," he hissed. "Let's have a look."

Wesley shushed him. "You've all the finesse of a fat lady in taffeta."

"Do excuse my lack of military prowess."

"Speaking of which, I still say you should hand over that pistol."

Lucas opened his mouth to offer his opinion of that suggestion, then thought twice. He felt foolish crouching in the bushes waiting for—what? For Helena to jump out at them and yell *boo?* One of them should simply walk to the door and look inside. The other, however . . .

"Here." He thrust the pistol into his brother's hand, stifling a laugh at Wesley's look of surprise. "I'll explore while you stand guard."

"Lucas, wait—"

He strode into the clearing. Skiff and Schooner had trotted around the corner to the wide wooden doors. Snuffling urgently, they pawed at the gap at the bottom as if to dig beneath.

"Helena?" Lucas called, "are you here?"

He started as one of the doors inched open. A striped sleeve emerged first, followed by a worn black boot that prevented the Westies from vaulting inside. The sun flashed on sandy brown hair.

"Ah, Tom, it's you."

The tenant farmer slipped outside and closed the door behind him. If Tom Whitely remembered his initial encounters with Luke Martin, his face didn't betray the fact. His head tipped in a respectful nod that made Lucas want to grimace. "Mornin', your grace."

"Tom, have you seen Miss Livingston? You do know her, don't you?"

"A right pleasant lady she is, but I've not seen her about today, sir." His gaze crossed Lucas's briefly, then dipped to his feet. Murmuring noises issued from Skiff and Schooner's throats as they explored his trouser hems. A hammer dangled from Tom's right hand, tapping lightly against his thigh.

"So, then, why are you here?" Lucas asked him, his curiosity raised by a sudden wariness. Something felt wrong about the situation, very wrong.

"Repairs." He swung the hammer back and forth at his side. "Your grace's brother plans to use the place again. Mr. Mortimer wants to know how far gone the old building is."

As he spoke, the dogs continued their assault on his ankles. Tom backed up until he hit the doors behind him with a clunk.

"Skiff, Schooner, heel."

They paid Lucas not the slightest attention. Suddenly they scurried around Tom's feet. The gap between the doors and the ground consumed their attention.

Lucas watched them, eyes narrowing. "They certainly want to get inside."

"Not a good idea, that." Tom shook his head. "Too dangerous. All sorts of—"

Schooner let out a howl. Soon both dogs were barking loud enough to frighten nearby birds from their nests. Springing up on hind legs, they scratched frantically on the doors' splintered boards.

"Open the door, Tom," Lucas quietly ordered.

"Your grace don't want me to do that." The hammer rose several inches from Tom's side, menacing.

"Lucas, watch out."

Tom Whitely's hammer lashed toward his head. Lucas ducked in time to avoid the blow, but the other man lunged.

Together they toppled, Lucas taking the full weight of the farmer as they hit the ground. His side protested against sparks of pain. Fierce barking filled his ears as the cloud-like forms of Skiff and Schooner scuttled in circles around them.

As they struggled for possession of the hammer, it swung back and forth above their heads, a deadly pendulum. The dogs howled. Springing, one seized the back of Tom Whitely's shirt in his teeth. That gave Lucas the moment's leverage he needed. With a roar and a heave he rolled, wrenching Tom's arm to the ground and pinning it beneath his knee.

The Westy—he couldn't tell which—bolted away, yapping. Tom's free hand fisted; a blow to the ribs emptied Lucas's lungs of air.

Where the devil was Wesley?

A white muzzle came into view, and pointed teeth chomped Tom's sleeve. Lucas swung a fist into the farmer's jaw, but the robust laborer seemed little fazed. Tom shook free of the Westy. His knuckles struck Lucas's cheek. He blinked away stinging pain and focused all his energy on preventing the hammer leaving the ground and knocking a hole in his head.

He could certainly use Wesley's help right about now.

Curling, Tom Whitely shoved a knee into his gut. His insides heaved. As coughing overtook him, his hold on the farmer's wrist slackened. Tom slid away as Lucas hit the ground face first, sputtering. A metallic light sparked at the corner of his eye. He braced for the worst, knowing he'd not be able to deflect the hammer's blow.

The snarling dogs charged again. They latched onto Tom's clothing and gnashed their little heads from side to side. Tom kicked out a foot, but the Westies released and dived away unscathed.

Beneath Lucas's ear, the ground vibrated with advancing footsteps. Through the grit in his eyes he saw his brother grab a handful of Tom Whitely's hair. Words were shouted and Tom went still. Wesley bent over him, pistol pressed to the farmer's forehead.

"I haven't pulled a trigger in a rather long time," Wesley drawled. "I wouldn't mind a bit of practice."

The scrapper lay as though frozen, except for the trembling of his exhausted limbs. Lucas's own shook as though he'd wrestled a falling oak.

"Release the hammer," his brother commanded.

The tool-turned-weapon thudded to the ground, raising a puff of dirt.

"You still in one piece?" As he questioned Lucas, Wesley didn't take his eyes off Tom.

"Maybe." He sat up holding his side, wondering if he'd broken a rib. Or two. He made a vain attempt to gather his torn shirttails. "About bloody time you stepped in. What the devil were you waiting for?"

Even as he asked the question, the answer moved into his line of vision. "Helena. My dear, are you harmed?" He tried to negotiate his feet beneath him and stand, but his unsteady legs refused to cooperate.

She staggered out into the sunlight, fingers working the knots binding her wrists, already partially loosened by Wesley. A scarf hung guiltily about her neck, no doubt responsible for the red weals on either side of her mouth.

"I think so," she replied faintly. She ventured another wobbly step and sank to her knees, her frock ballooning around her. Skiff and Schooner tripped over each other in their eagerness to reach her lap. Her arms opened to them. Shaken and frightened though she was, her lovely face filled with outrage. "He's been trying to kill you, Lucas. He pushed the owl off the balcony. It's something do to with that girl you went searching after when you disappeared."

The sound of panting drew his attention back to his now subdued attacker. "Good God. You, Tom? You were behind Mavis's disappearance? Why?"

The man sucked his lips between his teeth and stared at the ground.

Wesley nudged him with the barrel of the pistol. "Answer the question. You'll probably hang for this, but you might make things easier for yourself if you cooperate."

"Hang?" Tom's chin snapped up, his eyes filled with fury. "Not alone, I won't."

"True," Helena broke in, "Mr. Dolan will swing beside you."

"What?" both brothers exclaimed as one.

Oh, God.

"He's the one who wanted you dead, Lucas," she said, speaking fast. "I heard them talking, and then that awful solicitor of yours left him"—an accusing finger shot out—"to do away with me. It turns out he hadn't the stomach for it, or I wouldn't be here now."

Dear God, no. Lucas was already on his feet, poised to bolt. "Where's Jacob Dolan now?"

Tom shrugged. Wesley prodded again with the gun barrel. The man scowled. "Look, I ain't never killed before, and I weren't about to start with a lady." His gaze, feral and frightened, rose to meet Lucas's. "Didn't want to kill your grace, neither, but your man, Dolan, he said you'd started remembering."

Though burning for answers, Lucas took off running. Over the pounding of his footsteps he heard Wesley demand, "Remember what?"

"The other one," Tom Whitely replied through clenched teeth. "The one what died. The Blackstone girl."

Mavis . . . and Jacob.

Oh, no. God, no.

Charity. Jacob knew who she was. He'd know just how to use her.

Charity held her breath and waited for Jacob Dolan to explain why fresh dirt and leaves clung to his shoes despite his claim of not having been out of his room.

"Well, Mr. Dolan?"

Voices drifted from the dining hall, punctuated by

the careful clinking of china being stacked and stored away. Footsteps advanced in their direction.

"Damn." The quiet fury in Jacob Dolan's voice turned Charity's insides to ice. Before she could react, his hand clamped her shoulder. As the danger of her situation hit her, Jacob forced her into the study. "All I wanted was to bloody leave."

He released her with a shove that sent her stumbling; she groped at the back of an armchair for support. The door clicked. As she swung around, Jacob dropped the key into his coat pocket.

"What do you think you're doing?" She tried to sound unafraid; tried to stand tall.

"Hold your tongue." He clenched his fists until they trembled. Rage burned in his eyes and distorted his features.

Her breath caught. A single thought formed and lodged in her heart: *my baby.*

"You should have bloody well minded your business. You and the rest of these simpletons."

Her hands went to her stomach, protective, ready to fight for the life inside. She linked her fingers to still their shaking. "What have you done with Miss Livingston?"

"If I were you, Miss Williams," her assumed last name dripped with sarcasm, "I'd worry far more about what I'm going to do with you."

With heavy strides he bore down on her. She flinched and tried to dodge him, but his hand shot out and tangled in her hair. She winced as he propelled her in a dizzying arc, landing her against Luke's desk, the beaded edge biting into the backs of her thighs. Jacob stood toe to toe with her, face inches away. His savage expression made her want to blot out his image by shutting her eyes, but she clenched her jaw, sucked air between her teeth and met his glare.

"If you've harmed one hair on Helena's head, Mr. Dolan, Luke will see that you pay dearly for it."

"You'd best be quiet, my dear lady duchess." He snickered, reaching into his coat pocket and withdrawing the sheen of polished oak and burnished steel.

She stared unbreathing into the black-holed barrel. "You wouldn't dare."

"I'd be doing the family a favor. Duchess of Wakefield? Duchess of Sheep Dung is more apt. I daresay no one would blink an eye. Except for Lucas perhaps, that lovesick fool. But in the end even he'd be relieved to have got rid of you, common baggage that you are."

He trained the pistol on her middle. All her muscles tensed. Gripping the edge of the desk behind her, she tried not to reveal the desperate vulnerability that pistol aroused, nor her cold terror for the child inside her.

"What to do now?" he murmured, and she knew he wasn't seeking her counsel. "How to get away?"

Gripping her upper arm, he hauled her around the desk to the window. As he looked out, she turned, her attention making a quick circuit of the room. A decanter sat on the sherry cart but a few feet away. She lifted her free arm . . .

Jacob jerked the other. Pain streaked through her shoulder, bringing tears to her eyes. She blinked them away.

"What do you think you're doing? Keep still." He waved his weapon in her face.

Fear made her knees wobble and sent an ocean roaring in her ears. A sense of inadequacy descended like a yoke over her heart that nothing more than her own fragile life stood between this madman and her precious child.

Oh, Luke, I'll do my best to keep our little one safe.

Jacob blew out a breath and took another glance outside. "These damned windows are too high off the ground. I'd break my legs, if not my neck, if I attempted to jump."

She bit back the suggestion that he try anyway.

"This is your own fault, you blasted busybody. You and your stupid questions." He strode to the center of the room, dragging her along. She trotted to prevent him tugging her sore shoulder.

"You don't really wish to hurt me, do you, Mr. Dolan?" she said, hoping to reason with him.

"Of course I don't." His glower lessened the reassurance the words might have held. "I never wished to hurt anyone, least of all that girl." He punctuated the last word by jabbing the pistol at the air, and Charity resisted the temptation to duck. "She should have cooperated, shouldn't have made such a fuss. I only wanted to quiet her, stop her infernal jabbering."

True panic threatened to strangle her, but she managed a choked whisper. "Do you mean . . . Helena?"

"No." He waved the gun in a dismissive gesture. "The local girl. Mavis something or other. Great crowing cockerels, what a mess. First her, then Lucas—and then Lucas again, damn his hide for not staying dead. Then that prissy Livingston girl stuck her nose in, and now, blast it all, I have you to contend with. Demons from hell, I can't win. But somehow, you're going to help me out of here."

He ran his gaze along the walls, murmuring under his breath. "Unless I'm mistaken . . ." Again she found herself forced across the room, this time to a bank of bookcases. He began running one hand across the edges of the shelves, his other still thoroughly occupied in putting bruises on her arm. "Isn't there a hidden door?"

Only briefly did Charity wonder what on earth he might be doing. Her mind worked furiously to bring order to chaos. That girl Jacob spoke of—had he killed her? Then what of Helena? And Luke—Jacob said he should have stayed dead. Then it was no mishap that landed her comely Englishman on the Scottish shore, no accident the owl plummeted to the terrace.

Luke. What had he and Wesley found in the woods? At this moment he could be on his way home. What would Jacob do if Luke burst through the study door? Desperation and not logic were deciding the solicitor's actions now. He continued probing the bookshelves like a wolf pawing at a snare, trapped and equally determined to escape.

"Every damned library has a bloody secret door buried somewhere in the blasted shelves," Jacob muttered.

Her fingers inched toward an alabaster bookend.

"Charity, dear, where are you?" came a muffled call.

Snatching back her hand, she jumped at the sound of Dolly's voice on the other side of the study door. Jacob whirled, scowling.

His cheek twitched. "Meddling old boot."

Charity chewed her bottom lip. What if Dolly tottered through that door right now—she might have a duplicate key. Would Jacob pull the trigger?

"Mr. Dolan, I'll have to answer her or she'll know something is terribly wrong. And after all, how long can we stay locked up in this room?"

His frown eased. "Perhaps you're right. She and the gargoyle have no idea what's going on."

"The gargoyle?"

"Mary." Jacob towed Charity across the carpet to the door just as Dolly called out again. "Cooperate, and they needn't know a thing. If you don't, the ladies will bear the brunt of it. Understood?"

"What would you have me do?"

"I'm going to put the pistol into my coat pocket, where it will be quite convenient to retrieve." He tucked the weapon out of sight. "You will precede me into the hall. We'll tell the duchess . . ." He trailed off, brows nearly meeting above his nose.

"I've already told her that Helena and her sons are in the village," Charity suggested, all too willing to aid in his deceit if it would keep Dolly and Mary from harm. "We'll say we've decided to join them."

"Very good." He released his grip on her arm, and it was all she could do to keep from massaging her throbbing flesh. She wouldn't give him the satisfaction. Jacob extracted the door key and carefully turned it in the lock. "Come along, Miss Williams." He picked up his valise in his left hand while his right disappeared into the pocket that held the gun.

When the door opened, she almost trod on Dolly who stood poised to knock.

"Why, there you are," the woman said and blinked. "Oh, and you, too, Mr. Dolan. Whatever are you doing in here?" She craned her neck to peek beyond Charity's shoulder into the room.

"I was just . . . helping Mr. Dolan locate a certain book."

"Oh? Which book? Perhaps I might be of assistance."

"You needn't trouble yourself, your grace," Jacob said quickly. "Just an account ledger actually, and now I think of it, his grace might have included it in the pile he handed me yesterday. I'll double check."

"Yes, well then, tea is ready. Won't you both join us inside?" She gestured toward the drawing room.

"Dolly," Charity began, then paused to clear a tremor from her throat. Steady now. This was her mother-in-law and her child's grandmother. The woman's life might very well depend upon Charity delivering a flawless performance. "If you and Lady Mary would excuse us, Mr. Dolan and I have decided to join the others in the village."

"Join the others?" Bewilderment creased Dolly's brow. "I thought we agreed you'd done enough walking for one day. It isn't advisable, my dear. Truly it isn't."

"Nonsense." Charity forced a laugh. "I'm not tired in the least and I'm quite used to walking several miles a day."

"Are you? Oh, but still . . ." Dolly's gaze flickered over Jacob, then settled back on Charity with a conspiratorial gleam. "I do think it advisable for you to sit down and have a bite to eat."

From right behind her, Jacob discreetly but pointedly nudged Charity with his portmanteau. "Ah, we'll be back for luncheon," she said. "And we'll bring the others."

With that they brushed past an astonished-looking Dolly.

"I could at least summon the coach for you," she called after them.

"No time," Jacob called back.

"How very odd," Charity heard the woman mutter as Jacob pressed her toward the front door.

It burst open before they reached it. Luke filled the doorway. He met Charity's gaze and went utterly still.

"What's going on here?" he murmured, taking in Charity, Jacob, the portmanteau, his mother hovering behind them. Panting, perspiring, his clothes in tatters, he looked as if he'd been dragged by his horse.

"Great heavens, Lucas," Dolly exclaimed. "You're deteriorating before our very eyes."

He made a fruitless attempt to smooth the soiled edges of his shirt.

"Luke. Where is . . ." Charity let the question go unfinished, for to ask after Helena's welfare might endanger Dolly.

She fought to keep her feet planted on the marble tiles when all she wanted was to run to him, seek the shelter of his arms. But to what result? Who would be struck by Jacob's readied bullet? "Are the others with you?" she asked, meaning *have you found Helena?* She widened her eyes in a signal she hoped Luke would comprehend.

"No. Not at the moment." Dismay, frustration and anger vied for dominance in his handsome features, yet beneath it all lay something more, chiseled in harsh relief. Anguish. Desperation. Charity realized he needed her in his arms as much as she needed to be there. "They'll be along shortly," he added with pointed emphasis on the last word.

Relief sent a haze swimming before her eyes. Even Jacob's abrupt intake of breath couldn't lessen her joy at the news. "They're still in the village, then?"

"The village," Luke repeated. His eyes registered understanding. "Yes, yes they are."

"Mr. Dolan and I were just coming to join you." For Dolly's sake, she forced a cheerful tone.

"We'll go together then."

Beside her, Jacob stiffened at the suggestion. His arm rose slowly until the butt of the pistol peeked out from his pocket, visible to Luke and Charity but not to Dolly behind them. Luke gripped the door frame, his knuckles white.

"But Lucas, you've just come all the way home." His mother's high heels pattered like gunfire in the stillness. Charity's stomach plummeted. *Don't come any closer. Go back to the drawing room.* "And now you're intending to walk all the way back? What *is* going on here?"

Luke looked at Charity. If he searched for some cue, she had none to give. She glanced sideways at a glowering Jacob. His coat pocket bulged and she knew his fingers had tightened around his pistol. A new fear gripped her. His weapon could discharge as a simple result of his mounting tension. The situation needed defusing and quickly.

"It's . . . a surprise." Turning around, she smiled at Dolly and prayed the flimsy lie would suffice. "One you'll simply adore. But if you insist on asking questions, why, you'll ruin all our plans."

"What's this about a surprise?" Lady Mary entered the hall and strode to her daughter's side. "Well? Come, come. There's nothing worse than tepid tea, you know."

Charity managed to bite back a groan, but only just. Dolly might easily be taken in, but Lady Mary? Charity would swear the woman saw straight into people's minds.

"It seems the youngsters are up to something, Mama."

"And we must be on our way." Charity started for the door, Jacob tight at her side.

Behind her, taffeta rustled. "Why are you taking that valise?"

"It's . . . for the surprise, to carry it home in."

Luke stepped aside as she and Jacob reached the front door.

"How very odd," Dolly uttered one last time before the three of them cleared the threshold.

Lucas stood at the edge of desperation, fighting for balance. He'd arrived too late. Again. God help him, this was not the first time.

In the moment of opening the front door and confronting the scene inside, a lifetime passed before his eyes. Not his own paltry existence but the cherished one he'd shared with Charity. Their labors, their tri-

umphs, their love. Their child. The stakes encompassed
the entirety of his world.

Another memory tumbled along with the others, one
that drained the blood to his feet. One other time, just
over a year ago, he'd arrived too late to avert disaster.

Mavis.

In a seedy room that stank of squalor and rat dung,
she'd died in his arms. It happened only moments after
he found her, and moments before her murderer stole
in behind him and knocked him unconscious.

Mavis whispered a caution now: *If Jacob leaves with
Charity, you'll never see her alive again.*

How could he have been so unthinking as to leave
his weapon with Wesley? He could have wrung his own
neck for his stupidity. There was nothing for it now but
to put his trust in luck and the grace of opportunity.

How inadequate.

They came to an abrupt halt on the top step. Uncertainty steeped them in silence. Impulse urged Lucas
to hurl himself at Jacob, to strike like an animal. But
Jacob stood too close to Charity; his gun, no longer concealed within his pocket, hovered closer still. Could
Lucas move faster than a bullet?

He doubted it.

"Well?" Charity broke the silence, eyebrows arched in
query. She sounded insanely normal, as if their dilemma
comprised no more than choosing the best place to pic-
nic. Belying her calm, her fingers splayed across her
belly in a clutch of protectiveness. "What now?"

"You should have gone into the house and stayed
there," the solicitor said, not to her, but over her head
to Lucas.

"Whatever you're going to do," he replied evenly,
"do it with me and not her."

"No, Luke—"

"Be quiet," he told her, eyes fixed on Jacob. God, one look at her now and reason would unravel. He needed a cool head. Damn it, he needed a plan. "For once, shut up and let me handle things."

From the corner of his eye he saw that, despite everything—the gun at her side, the lunatic holding it—she had the pluck to be indignant. Her lower lip jutted.

"You're both mistaken," Jacob said. "I'm in control here. The farmwife comes with me. If I took your grace, you'd only try something the moment you reckoned her safe. Keeping her at my side insures your continued cooperation."

"No deal."

"Deal?" Jacob sniggered. "What deal? The gun is in my hand, is it not?"

"An indisputable point, Luke."

Lucas responded by descending to the next step and blocking Jacob's path to the drive. "What can you possibly hope to accomplish? Your secret is out. Kidnapping, attempted murder—serious crimes, Jacob. You can't hope to return to the quiet life of a solicitor."

"Yes, but you see I don't need to." Jacob's cool smile and smooth voice raised the hairs on Lucas's nape. "I've funds enough for passage to the Continent, where I can live comfortably quite some time. All I ask of your grace is to stand aside. I'll release the girl soon enough. I've no desire to hurt her, though I certainly will if you force my hand."

Lucas held his ground. "Do you plan to walk all the way from Wakefield to the nearest sailing port?"

"My plans are none of your concern. But do rest assured they are most competent."

What did that mean? Did he have a coach or mount waiting, at Tom Whitely's perhaps? Or was his claim a bluff, for how could Jacob have known this day would unfold as it had, beginning with Helena stumbling upon his villainy?

"I could provide you with something even more valuable than money," Lucas blurted, grasping at hope. If he detained the other man long enough, Wesley might return from the mews. *Just don't let him leave with her*, Mavis warned with a chilling breath across his heart. "If you wait but a moment, I'll give you an affidavit, signed and sealed, stating that Mavis Blackstone's death was an accident. That she had been ill. That she went with you willingly. You'll be clear of all possible charges. All you need do is let my wife walk away right now."

Jacob appeared to consider, then grabbed the back of Charity's gown and raised the pistol. She gasped, glaring wide-eyed at Lucas. "Stand aside."

"All right." Lucas threw up his hands and sidestepped, frantic for an idea, a word, anything that might prevent Jacob from descending those steps with Charity.

They started down. Jacob forced her ahead of him, gun lodged between her shoulder blades.

Behind them, the door opened.

Startled, Jacob spun about. The barrel of his pistol skewed into empty space and Lucas saw his chance. Before he sprang, Mortimer poked his head out the door. "Ah, your grace, your brother has—"

The steward broke off as two shaggy bodies streamed around his feet and over the threshold. Skiff and Schooner clambered down the steps, heedless of the figure standing between them and their mistress. Jacob swung his valise to knock them away, but they dodged between his feet. He teetered. The valise slipped from his grip, thunking to the step below.

Lucas lunged and seized Jacob's arm. The solicitor's strength surprised him. They struggled, arms locked stiff and straight in the air, topped by the deadly pistol that tossed glints of sunlight into Lucas's eyes.

"Good heavens." Flinging the door wide, Mortimer hurried down the steps. "What is the meaning of this?"

He made a grab for the gun, just above his reach. A hop sent his weight falling against Lucas's side. Lucas pitched dangerously. Bracing his feet, he tried to shove his steward out of the way. Female voices shouted from the Grand Hall.

"Stay inside," Lucas yelled to them. "Shut the door." His arms burned with the strain of maintaining his grip on Jacob and the gun. The shouting grew louder; the dogs barked and yowled.

A sharp report pierced the uproar, stinging Lucas's eardrums.

Silence fell.

Gut in his throat, he swung his head round, searching wildly for Charity. She stood frozen just below him, tall and straight, her dress stained with nothing more ominous than grass and earth.

He hadn't been hit either. Before him, Jacob's face registered shock, but nothing to approximate the searing agony of a bullet. Mortimer had lurched away, his face a mask of astonishment. Lucas braved a glance upward, where he and Jacob continued to hold the pistol as if their arms were cast in bronze. No smoke, no heat, no powder burns.

At the top of the stairs, his brother slowly lowered his upraised arm. Lucas realized where the shot had originated.

Then from the corner of his eye he saw movement: pale muslin, a pair of slender if imperfect hands. Charity scooped the portmanteau into her arms, lifting it high above her head. From a throat half-clogged with terror, a voice, his own, bellowed for her to run to safety. She moved utterly in the wrong direction—toward Jacob—and brought his portmanteau crashing down on the back of his head.

Lucas felt the fight drain from Jacob's arms, the strength ebb from his body. As cognizance faded from his eyes, the pistol flipped from his hand and clanked to the step at his feet. An instant later, the man's knees buckled and he tumbled to the drive.

Chapter Nineteen

Before Charity had quite released the satchel, Luke's arms were around her. "My darling, are you all right? Are you hurt?"

She couldn't speak, too breathless and shaking, too frightened, perhaps more so now in the aftermath. But neither did he allow her the chance, for his mouth slid to capture hers. She leaned into him, letting her tremors dissipate into the strength of his chest, the heat of his kiss.

Finally, she managed a breath, then words. "No one threatens my family. Not my husband, not my child and not my dogs."

"My brave, sweet girl." He buried his nose in her hair, gathering her tighter. She felt the vibrations of laughter deep in his chest, rumbling guffaws of relief. It made her laugh, too, a joyous release. She felt dizzy with it, weak to the point of sinking to the steps and dragging him down beside her. Only the presence of the others kept her legs anchored beneath her.

They wouldn't have noticed. Within seconds of the

shot, pandemonium resumed. Helena, Dolly and Lady Mary spilled out the front door to surround Wesley on the steps. Whimpering now, the Westies pressed against Charity's ankles, half-hiding beneath her skirts. The acrid scent of gunpowder drifted on the air. Poised barrel-down in Wesley's hand, the culpable pistol emitted a final wisp of smoke.

Lucas aimed a nod at the firearm. "I owe you, brother," he said quietly.

If Wesley heard him, he gave no indication. He was too busy attempting to restore order. Dolly's and Lady Mary's exclamations of "What on earth?" and "Has every-one gone mad?" were punctuated by Mortimer's squawks of "Good heavens" and "My word" and Helena's high-pitched reassurances: "He had it coming. He's a rogue."

"Stand aside, everyone, I'm here to save you." Appear-ing suddenly on the threshold, Sir Joshua brandished his ebony cane. How he'd maneuvered there by himself Charity couldn't guess. Teetering and then achieving a miracle of balance, he raised his cane in one hand and gripped its ivory handle in the other. With a twist and a resounding scrape, he slid a rapier free and flourished it in the air. "Never fear, I've still got a steady arm."

"Father!" Helena scurried up the steps. Charity's hand flew to her mouth when the elderly man swayed, but his daughter reached him in time and thrust a steadying arm about his waist. "Come away from the steps, Father. You'll injure yourself."

"Never mind, daughter. When I hear the sounds of danger, I'm roused to action."

"But Father . . ."

"Thank goodness you were here, Joshua," Lady Mary said over Helena's protests.

"Yes, how very brave of you, Josh," Dolly agreed with a vigorous nod.

Wesley put two fingers in his mouth and produced a shrill whistle. "Quiet, all of you. Is everyone all right? Excepting him, of course." He pointed to the heap that was Jacob.

All heads angled toward the drive. Mouths closed and brows shot up. Face down, Jacob lay unmoving.

Awful, slithery chills swept Charity's back.

Mortimer was the first to move, venturing almost timidly down the steps and leaning over the solicitor. "Is he shot?"

"Of course not," Wesley retorted, "I fired into the air." He retrieved Jacob's fallen, unfired pistol and tucked his own into his coat pocket.

Schooner crawled out from the safety of Charity's hems. Skiff slinked after, both keeping low as if unsure whether to spring or bolt. Noses working, they clambered down to the bottom step, where scattered blotches gleamed like scarlet buttons. Charity suddenly felt quite paralyzed.

"Oh, dear," breathed Dolly.

A half dozen gazes converged on Charity. Rising horror clogged her throat as she stared down at Jacob Dolan, and at the stains on the step just above him.

Though Luke tried to hold her fast, she wrenched from his hold. The sound of her name tore like an oath from his lips as she broke free.

She lurched to a halt inches from Jacob Dolan's feet, one of which lay twisted at an awkward angle. Dread held her frozen. Surely the pain in that ankle should wake him. Surely he'd wish to straighten it and relieve the pressure. It could even be broken, but perhaps he didn't feel it because . . .

Because Jacob Dolan was dead.

"I didn't mean to, honestly I didn't. Oh, Luke, I've killed him."

He was beside her in an instant, arms seizing her in a fierce pledge of protection. "It's all right, my darling. I promise you it will be all right."

"Oh, how can it?" She might have answered her own question if only her throat permitted further speech. The reality of what she'd done closed around her, cutting off breath. A man lay dead—dead by her hand.

She gasped for air. Luke gripped her shoulders and shook her, pulling her close and whispering reassurances, words that made her love him more than ever. Words that broke her heart.

Because she knew nothing could ever be the same for them. No, not ever again. She had killed a man.

"Charity, my love, as God is my witness, this not your fault. You must listen to me, darling. He's gone mad. You may have just saved an innocent life." Luke held her at arm's length. Her lovely green eyes were storm-tossed and her breath came in frantic little bursts. He saw that she was not listening to him, not at all. Feeling helpless, he watched self-reproach wrest her further and further from him, sealing off her heart to reason or reassurance. He must do something.

Reluctantly dragging his hands away from her, he crouched, sucked in a breath and nudged Jacob's shoulder.

Nothing. Lucas felt a moment of true terror, true desolation. Never mind inquests and having to answer all the questions. Never mind that Charity's masquerade would only arouse further suspicion in the death of a respected London solicitor.

In the end, the magistrates would agree she'd acted in self-defense. Enough witnesses would testify to that. But Charity, his wild, radiant Charity, would never again be free, never laugh with unbridled joy, never love with single-minded delight. Not with the blood of another human life on her hands. The notion charred his heart until it resembled a burned forest, dead and smoking and churning with ash.

He murmured a quick prayer, one more fervent than he'd ever uttered in his life. For Charity's sake, for his own sake and for their child, he prayed Jacob Dolan lived.

She knelt beside him, her hand a tremulous weight on his shoulder. He drew hope from even that uncertain contact, strength from her nearness. Behind them, the others watched in silence. The world shrank to encompass only the two of them and the man sprawled before them. "Am I wrong?" she whispered. "Please tell me I'm wrong."

"I'm here," he said, unable to offer any other answer with honesty. Fear pressed his throat, his gut. He kissed her gently though his instinct was to consume her wholly. "I'm with you. Whatever happens, I am by your side."

He raised one hand to caress her cheek. Her eyes filled, magnifying them tenfold. Her lips parted with unspoken words, the ghosts of promises that might never be. She nodded. He forced himself to turn to the unconscious man.

Lucas nudged again, and again Jacob didn't stir. At his shoulder, Charity drew in a breath and held it. He realized he was holding his own. Even Skiff and Schooner stood quietly on either side of them, their only movement that of the tips of their fur, trembling in the breeze and their own excitement.

Then he remembered what Charity told him she had done to determine if the waterlogged stranger rescued from the North Sea lived or no. He pressed his fingertips to the side of Jacob's neck, searching for a pulse.

Relief surged in dizzying waves. Weak with it, he shoved the hair from his brow and let his head sag.

"What?" Charity whispered, more a gasp than a word.

"There's a pulse." He heard great whooshes of relief from the others on the stairs behind him.

"Are you certain?"

He nodded. A stinging in his eyes threatened to become something altogether embarrassing, especially considering that his brother was watching. "Feel for yourself."

"No." She clenched her hands in her lap. "I'll take your word for it."

He smoothed her hair, fingertips lingering at her nape. "Perhaps you'll take my word on another matter as well."

"Perhaps." Her lips formed a shaky smile; the brimming tears spilled over. By the time Lucas had her in his arms she was shuddering like a splintering mast.

"Lucas, he's waking!" Helena's sudden cry turned his attention back to Jacob.

Skiff and Schooner yapped and sprang away as the solicitor stirred. His fingers closed and opened against the gravel on the drive. A low moan streamed from his throat.

"Good heavens," Lucas's mother exclaimed. "Don't let him get away."

With one arm secure around Charity, Lucas motioned to his brother. "Bring me that pistol."

Wesley came down the steps, training the weapon on Jacob but making no move to pass it to Lucas.

"Hand it to me," Lucas ordered.

"Don't know if that's a good idea. You're angry . . ."

"I'm damned angry," Lucas snapped, "but I'm not about to blow his head off. I want answers."

"Wesley, give the blasted thing to Lucas," Grandmother called from the top of the stairs. "It's his right."

After a moment's hesitation, Wesley nodded and handed the pistol over.

Jacob's eyes opened. Letting out a grunt of pain, he rolled to his side to reveal a gash at his temple. Blood trickled to the corner of his eye and pooled in the creases. He raised a hand to his brow, and the dogs let out throaty growls. Jacob squinted at them, then up at Lucas. He groaned and squeezed his eyes shut.

"Quite a nasty lump you've got there," Lucas said mildly. He pushed to his feet then offered a hand to help Charity up. "Believe me, I should know. You're quite lucky to be alive. Come to think of it, we're a lucky pair of devils, aren't we? We've both had the good fortune to awaken from the dead."

Mute, Jacob glared up at him from where he lay.

Anger snapped like the stinging end of a whip. Releasing Charity's hand, Lucas crouched and prodded the pistol to Jacob's temple. "Mavis Blackstone was not so lucky, was she?"

The man's eyes sparked but he said nothing. Lucas launched a fist into his stomach. With a loud bellow, Jacob curled into a tight ball, sputtering into the gravel. The suddenness of his reaction sent the Westies darting forward, snapping at the air near the writhing man's head.

"What happened to Mavis Blackstone, eh, you murdering cur?" When the other man's silence continued, Lucas drew back his fist again. Behind him, Charity gasped.

"Lucas," Wesley muttered in warning.

Jacob thrust out a hand as if to ward off the blow. "We got her . . . all the way to Tyneside, but . . ."

"Go on. And this had better be the truth."

"She wouldn't cooperate. Kept trying to get away. She . . ."

"She what?"

"Made trouble. Had to beat her to make her stop . . ."

"Sweet mercy," Charity hissed.

"Then what?"

"It wasn't my fault." He dabbed his cuff at the blood now dribbling down his cheek. "I'm only supposed to deliver them. I shouldn't have had the responsibility of her once we reached Tyneside."

Lucas had had enough of guessing games. Heedless of Jacob's injuries, he gripped the man's shirtfront and hauled him upright. Ignoring his howl of pain, Lucas deposited him onto the bottom step, slamming his back against the stone baluster. This set off more growls and yips from the dogs. He heard a gasp from his mother, a soft cry from Helena. Charity called his name, a reminder to check his temper.

He regained control with a steadying breath but repositioned the pistol to make his meaning clear. "Don't tax my patience. Tell me exactly what you and Tom Whitely have been up to or I *will* blow a hole through that black heart of yours."

Jacob flicked his tongue across his bottom lip, seeming to weigh his options and coming to a quick conclusion. "Tom and I . . . we provide the girls to our . . . associates in various parts of the country. What they do with them is not our business."

"Not your business?" A black haze swarmed Lucas's brain. "Damn your miserable hide. They go to brothels, don't they?" He felt sick in his stomach. "Don't they?" he repeated with a shove.

Jacob grimaced. "Some. Others go to factories. Some to the houses of noblemen. Like yourself, my lord duke. God only knows what *they* do with them."

"You bloody bastard." Lucas fought the urge to let his trembling hands rip into his solicitor.

Something else besides common decency stopped him. His conscience pricked. What indeed happened to those girls? Free labor, free favors of the lewdest sort, and the girls powerless to do anything about it. Lucas had always known certain members of his class considered themselves above the law. He and most of his peers had always turned a blind eye.

What about his own, more direct, culpability? Shouldn't he, as master of Wakefield, have detected the crimes committed on his own lands and found a way to prevent them sooner?

Jacob's head lolled back against the pillar. Staring up at the sky, he pressed his coat sleeve to the cut on his brow. A bitter laugh burst from his lips. "Who'd have guessed a bumbling aristocrat like your grace would manage to trace the girl all the way to the coast?"

"I found her in a boardinghouse." It was a statement, not a question. Images that had haunted Lucas for weeks fell into place, nearly completing the puzzle of the past year.

Eyelids drifting closed, Jacob nodded.

"Beaten and dying." Lucas persisted despite the revulsion aroused by the memories.

The solicitor's eyes shot open. "That was *not* my fault. If only she'd stopped putting up such a fuss."

"A poor innocent girl. Dead." Lucas battled a suffocating sense of failure, of remorse. Still, there was one final detail to be learned. "How in the devil's name did I end up at sea?"

When Jacob didn't show any sign of answering, Lucas jabbed him with the pistol. The man winced and coughed.

"We . . . discovered you in the boardinghouse, in the room we'd locked her in. Apparently you'd kicked the door in." Jacob rolled his eyes, shook his head. "We decided we couldn't take chances . . . didn't know how much she told you before she died . . . or if you'd seen our faces. We had to get rid of you, make it look like an accident. Tom hit you . . . we dragged you down to the docks . . . and took you out in a small schooner. We shot the hull full of holes and paddled away in the dinghy."

"Gunpowder. That's what I've remembered smelling," Lucas murmured, no less horrified for having already guessed some of the details. "So you left me to drown."

Jacob's eyes narrowed. "Never counted on the storm. The waves must have torn the boat apart and tossed you clear before the craft sank. Of all the rotten luck. Should have simply shot you and dumped the body."

"Should have."

"You scoundrel, you villain, you . . ." Like a sudden and potent squall, Lucas's mother scrambled down the steps, fists clenched, outrage contorting her features. Wesley swung round and caught her just before she might have launched herself at Jacob. "Let me go, let me have at him," she shouted. Her arms flailed against Wesley's restraining hold before the fight drained out of her. She sagged against his shoulder.

Lucas held out his free arm. Wesley released their mother and, face in her hands, she staggered into Lucas's embrace. "It's all right, Mother. It's all over. He'll be punished for his crimes and no mistake about it. He won't hurt another living soul."

"All these years we've trusted him," she said sadly.

"Don't look at him anymore, Mother," Lucas told her. "Take Grandmother and Joshua and go inside. The rest of us will join you shortly."

"Yes." She gathered her skirts with a dignified air and started up to the door. "Yes, let's come away. Mama, Josh, I believe our tea has grown quite cold. We shall have to ring for more. Helena, Charity, will you come?"

Helena relinquished her place at her father's side to Dolly. "Not just yet, dear. We'll be along soon."

"Don't be long," Dolly said, and a moment later the door closed on the three elder people.

Helena lingered on the top step, lovely blue eyes glistening. Beyond that, she looked calm and composed and beautiful enough to make any man's chest ache.

And Lucas's did. Ached with a sinking and unavoidable dread. He would have to hurt her now. Dash her hopes. Destroy her dreams.

If only there were some way to let her down gently.

Opening his arms, he waited to catch her in his embrace as she gracefully raised her hems and flurried down the steps. He was left with arms akimbo when she skirted him and threw her arms around Charity.

"Dearest friend, were you harmed? I was so frightened I could scarce breathe." She buried her face in Charity's shoulder.

Charity's brows shot up in a show of astonishment. She gave a tiny shrug at Lucas as if to say, *I've no idea why the woman is being so kind to me.*

Helena raised her head and dabbed her tears with the back of her hand. "Those beastly men accosted me because I'd stumbled upon them and heard things I shouldn't have. I suppose it was my own foolish fault. But then he . . ." She pointed to Jacob and somehow managed to make an outraged scowl look pretty. "He told the other man to kill me. Can you imagine?"

"No, no I cannot." Charity's eyes filled anew, but she'd barely time to return Helena's embraces before Helena stepped away to regard Lucas.

He'd have given away his fortune to avoid what must happen next.

"Oh, Lucas. Dear Lucas." Her smile outshone even the brilliant summer sun.

If only the earth would do him the favor of swallowing him whole. Better that than harm this sweet lady. Especially when doing so would hurt Charity all over again as well.

Charity. Yes. She held his heart, his life and his courage within her lovely, capable hands. For her, the truth must be told.

Holding the pistol out to Wesley, he started toward Helena. She met him halfway, reaching for him, no doubt expecting him to sweep her into his arms and kiss her soundly. He was aware of Charity's gaze burning into him, beseeching him to act gently and carefully. He began slipping into an agony of uncertainty when Helena . . .

Cupped his cheeks, pulled his head down and deposited a kiss—a most sisterly kiss—on his forehead.

"Lucas, my darling," she said quite firmly, "I cannot marry you. I love you awfully much, but not as a wife should love her husband. I'm so terribly sorry about it. But I should think that in time, you'll see this as a fortunate thing."

His mouth dropped open. Not a word came out.

"Tell him the rest," Wesley urged. Skiff and Schooner, who had found some unfortunate creature to harass in the flower bed circling the fountain, barked their encouragement.

Lucas hadn't noticed when Mortimer slipped away, but just then the steward came loping round the corner of the house, a length of rope coiled in his hands.

"To tie him up with," he panted when he reached the steps.

"Good idea." Wesley rotated the pistol in Jacob's direction in an unspoken demand for the solicitor to turn and allow Mortimer to secure his hands behind his back. With a rasping oath Jacob complied, and Mortimer set to work.

Wesley descended to the drive and stood beside Helena. "She's in love with me, Lucas. And I'm in love with her. Despise us if you must, but that's the truth of it."

Helena tossed Wesley an exasperated, *let me handle this* look, then smiled apologetically at Lucas. "When you think about it, don't you perhaps agree that this is best for everyone? I must admit I've noticed how you so often gaze upon a certain person in a more than friendly manner, and I also happen to know how that certain person feels about you, for she confessed it only this morning."

"I . . . I . . ." If lightning had struck him where he stood, Lucas could not have been more astounded. "Why didn't you say something sooner?"

Helena's mouth pursed. "We didn't want to hurt you, of course, after all you'd been through."

"And we were supposed to have been in mourning," Wesley added with a sardonic twist of the mouth. "Imagine Mother berating me for not adequately mourning a brother who had never died in the first place."

Lucas didn't know what to say to that. He didn't know quite what to say about anything.

"As a matter of fact," his brother continued in a voice gone ever so slightly husky, "I did mourn you, Lucas. Long and hard. And contrary to what you may have been thinking, I never wanted Wakefield. It was only as I grew to love Helena that I learned to care about the rest." He paused to gaze at her with no small amount of adoration. "Couldn't help it. Can't change it. You may have your Wakefield back, but not this lovely lady. She's mine now. We're going to be married as soon as possible."

"We are?" Helena's beautiful azure eyes widened with astonished delight.

"Of course we are, my darling girl." Wesley's arms

went around her in a display of emotion Lucas had never before seen from his stoic, military-trained brother.

His heart did a little flip in his chest. It was all such an enormous relief.

Helena poked a reddened nose out from Wesley's shirtfront. "Can you find it within your heart to forgive us and wish us well?"

"I most certainly can," Lucas said, grinning.

"And do you think, perhaps . . ." Helena angled her chin at Charity and lowered her voice. "She loves you, Lucas. And I'm certain you've feelings for her, quite earnest feelings, or there wouldn't be a child on the way, now would there?"

"You know?" Lucas and Charity exclaimed as one. She stumbled to his side and he caught her around the waist as much to keep himself as her from falling.

Helena wrinkled her nose. "Well, of course, gooses."

"And you're not appalled?" Charity asked.

"Some things are meant to be," her friend replied. "Though I shall be irretrievably offended if I'm not chosen to be godmother."

"Why, there's no one else in the world." Charity threw her arms around her friend, a gesture returned with equal enthusiasm.

Then Helena turned quite serious. "Lucas, haven't you something to say to our dearest Charity? Something to ask her, perhaps?"

"Indeed I do."

Charity lifted a hopeful if tear-streaked face. He took her in his arms and kissed her. Then, stepping back, he grasped her hands and held them to his chest.

"My love, I cannot stop being the Duke of Wakefield. It is who I am, and I can't lie my way through life any more than you can."

"Aye, Luke." She spoke to their entwined fingers. "I

was wrong to demand that you give up your home and
family. I see now how very much you have to lose. But it
is no longer a matter of who has what to lose, is it? It is
what we have to gain by being together. The only home
for me is by your side, and I'd happily live in a castle or
a cave with you. If you ask me once more to stay, my
love," her voice hitched, "I promise I'll have a very different answer for you."

So willing to compromise, he thought. He studied her
tear-stained face. Never had he seen her so vulnerable,
so close to an emotional precipice. It was not where he
needed her to be, not with such a vital decision to be
made. No, he needed her strong. He needed her feisty.
He needed the fiery Scottish lass he'd fallen in love
with not once but twice.

"I'm not going to ask you again," he said.

Her tears trickled to a halt, leaving those sea-goddess
eyes frothing as shock thrashed with pure curiosity.
"What on earth do you mean by that?" she demanded,
and snatched her hands from his. "After all we've been
through? Why, just the past few hours alone—did none
of it mean a blessed thing to you? And we've a child on
the way. What was all that back at the hill fort about
being a family and sharing all you have with me and our
child? Do you mean to tell me, Luke Martin, that while
you're promising one thing, you're planning the exact
opposite?"

"Oh, dear," Helena began, but Wesley shushed her.

"We should leave them alone." He slipped an arm
round her waist and guided her to the steps.

"But—"

"But nothing." Wesley steered her toward Jacob. "Mortimer, let's each take an elbow and haul this baggage to
the nearest storeroom, where he'll find no more mis-

chief than a few sacks of flour and potatoes can afford him."

"What have you done with Tom Whitely?" Lucas asked.

"Root cellar. I think it best we keep them separated, at least until a magistrate can be sent for."

"Very good. Do you need help with this one?"

"No, thanks, we can manage. Here, my love, you keep him covered, should he be so stupid as to try to slither away." Wesley pressed the firearm into Helena's hand.

"The pistol? Helena?" Lucas wondered if Wesley had taken leave of his senses.

"Of course." Wesley hauled Jacob upright, supporting his weight when his sore ankle wouldn't hold him. "I taught her to shoot. Quite a markswoman, this one."

As if to prove his point, Helena wrapped both hands round the butt of the pistol, slipped a finger onto the trigger and locked her arms straight out. One eye squinted slightly as she established her aim.

Well. It had certainly been a day of revelations. With one more to deliver, Lucas thankfully watched his steward, brother and ex-fiancée impel the guilty man away.

He wanted to take Charity's hands again but she held them firmly anchored at her hips. He almost smiled at how quickly the familiar obstinacy had swooped into place, but he knew the merest twitch of his lips would be a dangerous thing for him.

He gathered his breath and did his best to sound authoritative. "You heard me. I'm not going to ask you to stay again."

She opened her mouth with an indignant huff.

"No," he said, holding up the flat of his palm. "It would be wrong. Like clipping a gull's wings. One of the things I most love about you is your spirit, your sense of freedom. You'd lose that living a noblewoman's life. We'd never be happy."

"Never be happy?" Her eyebrows arrowed inward. She seemed to have heard those words only. "Is your heart as fickle as all that? Do you believe you'll ever find happiness without me? I know you remember how it was, Luke. Our days together, our nights. And with the knowing of it inside you, do think you can ever be content with less? That's where never comes in. I know it. I know you."

Ah, here was the spirited lass who made his heart pound, his senses spring to the alert, his blood rush to strategic places. "Are you quite finished?"

"I am."

"May I continue?"

"You may."

"Thank you." Hand to chin, he began pacing back and forth, putting his parliamentary debate skills to use. "When my peers learn we are married, my dear, they'll be horrified. They'll sneer first, laugh second, and from there it will simply get uglier. They'll call you a fortune hunter, and me . . . well, once they hear I'm farming sheep in Scotland, I'll be forever known as the Dotty Duke. Or Witless Wakefield."

"Since when did I ever pay heed to wagging tongues?" The instant the words left her mouth, her bluster flickered and died. "Did you say farming sheep in Scotland?"

He halted in front of her. "Of course. I'm leaving Wakefield in Wesley's hands, in all but name that is. Hang it, I'd give him the title as well if I could. He seems to have made a far better duke than I ever did."

Charity's eyes filled with wonder and for the briefest moment he thought she'd jump into his arms. But the squaring of her shoulders revealed her effort to hold the emotions in check. Her gaze drifted across the front of the house. She nodded, a fond smile curling her lips. "The two of them will make a splendid job of it, I'm certain."

Her smile faded, and with it the last traces of defiance, vulnerability and tears. "What about Lucas Holbrook?" she asked, steady and even. "Can he return to the life of a simple farmer knowing what he truly is?"

"Since when was loving you ever simple?" He closed the small distance between them, catching her in his arms in the event she had any ideas of slipping away. "And who am I, really, other than the man who loves you to distraction? By the way, the name's not Lucas, it's Luke. Luke Holbrook."

His hands burrowed into the wild toss of ringlets spilling down her back. When her cheek pillowed against his shoulder, his heart thrummed; when her lips brushed his neck, his soul rejoiced.

"Luke, eh?" she whispered and chuckled. "Loony Luke is what they'll call you."

"Yes, and Harebrained Holbrook." He cupped her cheeks. "There'll be no end to it. Can you live with that?"

Her smile thrilled him. "We won't hear them much, will we, far away in Scotland?"

"No, we won't. Except for once or twice each year when I'm forced to make an appearance at court or sit a session of Parliament. Do you think, my love, that upon those occasions you might don your fancy gowns and your English accent and stop all those wagging tongues with the same charm that stole my family's hearts?"

She laughed and tightened her arms around his neck. He picked her up off her feet, kissing her, once, again, long and deep, kisses that left them gasping and laughing and just the faintest bit tearful. Then, like a stirring breeze, he heard her voice in his ear. "You're certain?"

"Aye, as certain as the coming tide. I've made my decision."

She stepped back, her hands traveling down his arms until they came to rest in his hands. "Then let's go home, where we both belong."

"Where the three of us belong," he corrected her with a pointed glance at her belly.

"Actually, the five of us." She grinned and pointed to Skiff and Schooner beside the fountain, pawing and making ferocious noises at whatever small animal continued to elude them.

"Come." He drew her to the bottom step and pulled her into his lap. "We have a wedding to plan, you and I."

"But we're already married."

"If you think my mother is going to let us leave Wakefield without allowing her the satisfaction of bawling over our nuptials, you are gravely mistaken, my darling. Besides, don't you think Helena would make a stunning bridesmaid?"

"And Wesley the most dashing of groomsmen, too."

"It will give them practice for their own wedding."

Charity relaxed her head against his shoulder. "I'm so happy for them, at the way things have turned out for all of us. Oh, I know." She startled him when she pulled up straight. "We have the most wonderful wedding present for them."

"And what would that be, my love?"

Her eyes twinkled as if he should already know. "The bower, of course! I just know they'd love it. You have to finish it before we leave. I'll help you."

"Hmm. You think?" He wrinkled his brow and tried to picture his elegant brother and dainty Helena traipsing through the woods, climbing the mound in the hot sun, fighting flies and burrs and clingy wet grass, all for the pleasure of sitting in a twisted jumble of branches and leaves. "You know, I believe you're right. You know what else?"

"No. What?"

"I love you."

"I've never doubted it."

"I'll never doubt it again."

"Not if you know what's good for you." She snuggled her cheek to his, sending ripples of sheer pleasure through him.

Their embrace became somewhat crowded when the Westies, grown tired of hunting, squeezed in between them. Lucas found he didn't quite mind, especially when Skiff raised a wet nose to Charity's face, making her laughter ring out across the drive. The sound filled him with contentment, calming the last of his jangled nerves as nothing else could have.

He lowered his head to kiss her again, only to have his lips met by Schooner's lolling tongue.

"Good God." Dragging his cuff across his mouth, he scooped the Westy up with one arm and hugged him to his chest. He mopped his free hand across a second shaggy head. "We are an odd scrap of family, aren't we?"

"But a family all the same." Holding out her hand, she giggled when both Westies began licking her fingertips.

"Aye, lass." Releasing the dogs, Lucas dipped her far back in his arms and leaned low to deliver that intercepted kiss, not to her lips but to her belly and the child within.

He could happily have sat on that step for hours, wrapped in the small circle of Charity and their child and two wayward but lovable pups. He knew if he ever felt lost or uncertain again, he need only look to the freckle-faced lass of the wild hair and wilder heart, who plucked him from the North Sea and showed him all a man's life could be.